Driving on the Rim

Driving on the Rim

Thomas McGuane

ALFRED A. KNOPF   NEW YORK   2010

THIS IS A BORZOI BOOK
PUBLISHED BY ALFRED A. KNOPF

www.aaknopf.com

Knopf, Borzoi Books, and the colophon are registered
trademarks of Random House, Inc.

A portion of this work previously appeared in *The New Yorker*.

Library of Congress Cataloging-in-Publication Data
McGuane, Thomas.
Driving on the rim : a novel / Thomas McGuane.—1st ed.
p. cm.
ISBN 978-1-4000-4155-8
1. Physicians—Fiction. 2. Interpersonal relations—Fiction. 3. Self-actualization
(Psychology)—Fiction. 4. Psychological fiction. I. Title.
PS3563.A3114D75 2010
813'.54—dc22   2010001255

Manufactured in the United States of America
First Edition

For Laurie, always

DISCLAIMER

The people and places of this book, inspired to some extent by forty years living in Montana, do not exist in reality or even entirely in familiarity. The staff of a medical clinic, here roundly calumniated, if based upon the fine institutions that have served my small needs might deny me their succor just when I most needed it. The appearance of familiar dogs and favorite hats is accidental. Ranchers and farmers are rarely this gloomy, Christians this delusional, or socialites this far from home. It serves no one to suggest that broken hearts are never repaired, especially if, like a blind pig looking for an acorn of truth, you made the whole thing up in the first place. As would be, this is a work of fiction, the last frontier. Take it with a grain of salt.

As for the double life, everyone lives one actually.
Why brag about it?

—Robert Walser

Driving on the Rim

1

My name is Berl Pickett, Dr. Berl Pickett. But I sign checks and documents "I. B. Pickett," and this requires some explanation. My very forceful mother, a patriot and evangelical Christian, named me after the author of "God Bless America"; so, I am Irving Berlin Pickett and well aware of the absurdity of my name. My father wanted Lefty Frizzell Pickett. That would have been worse. In any case, my very name illustrates the borrowed nature of my life, not easily denied. In fact, I've learned to enjoy my circumstances as I have moved among people trapped in their homes, jobs, and families—and their names! My esteemed colleague Alan Hirsch, mountaineer and cardiologist, calls me Irving, with a chuckle. When I first arrived at our clinic from the Indian Health Service, Dr. Hirsch told me that I couldn't call myself a physician until I had delivered babies to ambivalent parents or taught the old to accept their grotesque new faces. I don't know about that, but I do abide in the conviction that I've come a long way, and lately I've wondered how this all happened.

L. Raymond Hoxey bought an old mansion in Livingston, Montana, and converted the third floor into a delightful apartment with a view of the Absaroka Mountains. The second floor housed his print collection in archival conditions, with humidifiers and air-quality equipment. The first floor was divided into two smaller but still comfortable apartments, one of which was home to his assistant, Tessa Larionov, and the other, in summer, to a textile historian employed by the Metropolitan Museum in New York, who was also a trout fisherman.

The year the historian died, I was still in pre-med and painting houses to support myself; I moved into his vacated apartment. Acknowledging that there is a difference between being naive and being innocent, I will say that I was entirely naive. My parents lived a few miles away, but we weren't getting along and I needed some distance, despite the fact that my mother was sick and often ranted about God. There are many versions of God around the world, but my mother's was definitely a guy, and a mean one. Like many aspiring to study medicine, I planned to get rich but I wasn't rich yet; I was just a poor house painter—out of work and looking for whatever came along—and despite all other evidence, I feared that I would be one forever, packing a great wheel of color chips from one indifferent house to another. I don't mean to suggest mild insecurity here: by any reasonable standard, I was losing my mind.

Tessa Larionov was the daughter of a Russian engineer who had immigrated to the United States in 1953 and found his way to Montana, where he set up business building bridges for the railroad. His offices were in Choteau, where Tessa was born and grew up. Tessa's mother was not Russian; her father had met her in New Jersey, where he first landed. She may have been Italian. Tessa was a powerfully built but attractive woman, with black hair, black eyes, and the look of a Tartar, wry and a little dangerous. She was liked by everyone who knew her. Trained in library science, she had worked as an archivist at some very august places, including the Huntington, in Pasadena, where she'd met her future employer and our landlord, L. Raymond Hoxey, who had let Tessa talk him into retiring to Montana to run his rare-prints business with her help. Hoxey was eighty-one years old, and his arrangement with Tessa was a means of avoiding assisted living. She was very fond of him and had wanted to go home to Montana, and so it worked for both of them. Tessa was exactly thirty, still single, though she had enjoyed an active love life, leaving in her wake only grateful hearts, or so she said. "They're all still crazy about me," she told me. "That's why I left California." Settling down was of no interest; she'd grown absorbed with the prints, and she wanted to keep her eye on Hoxey. I was twenty, but she treated me as if I were even younger—a salute to my retarded behavior.

My father had worked briefly as a pipe fitter for the Northern Pacific Railroad. In the course of corporate takeovers, the railroad had actually changed its name several times, but Northern Pacific was the one that stuck in all our minds. It meant something. Burlington Northern meant nothing. Then he had a little stock farm he liked to call a ranch, whose main purpose was to let him keep horses. But he lost it to the bank and went to work for the post office. My mother was a hairdresser and, because of her big mouth and religious mania, had enemies all over southwestern Montana and very few customers. During my childhood, they had had a traveling rug-cleaning business, and the three of us saw most of the West as we towed the steamer behind our van, an old-fashioned Steam Jenny with an oil-filled crankcase and a picture of a Vargas-type girl in black nylons emblazoned on its side—wonderful years, really. As an only child, I was all but homeschooled, then run back and forth between our house and the less fashionable of the two grade schools, before going to the local high school, where I was anonymous, never having been allowed by my overprotective mother to learn a sport. My mother joined one Pentecostal church after another, followed by my father, whose skepticism had long ago evaporated in the heat of her enthusiasm; they stopped just short of snake handling. But I liked to fish; I'd fish wherever there was water, and I fished in a lot of ditches where there was no hope of success. I now understand that I was for my age a weirdly underdeveloped human being, ripe for the sort of encounter I had with Tessa Larionov. Even my mother noticed my immaturity; she was always telling me, "Stop staring at people!" But she had once given me a gift beyond price: looking down at me when I was a little boy, she said, "You're an old soul. You've been here before."

It was Hoxey whom I got to know first. The day I arranged to rent from him, he happened to have received several Reginald Marsh prints, of which he was very proud and which he wanted me to see. I acted like I'd heard of Reginald Marsh. I didn't know one painter from another, but I had a hunger for this sort of information; I felt it would be useful later, when I was rich. Hoxey was a pleasant old man who must have once been very fat, because he had loose flesh hanging from him every-where and as many as seven chins. I always tried to count them while he was speaking to me, but then something in his remarks would break my concentration. This physicality, which bespoke a lifetime of phlegmatic living, gave his discourse on prints the authority of a weathered desert rat holding forth on cactus. I remember him carefully unpacking one of the prints—a kind of crazy thing with blank-faced people swarming in and out of doorways, none of them reacting to anyone else. Hoxey said that it was the calmest Reginald Marsh he'd ever seen. "No 'Moonlight and Pretzels' in this one!" he cried. I could see both that he'd be an agreeable landlord and that many health issues lay before him. As someone aspiring to be a doctor, I could make a little game of guessing which one would kill him.

Tessa asked me over one night for drinks. She had done a beautiful job of making her apartment habitable, with comfortable old furniture that she'd bought cheap and upholstered. She also had a good many of Hoxey's prints on loan, though, as she explained, she was really just storing them, and her collection changed as things were sold from Hoxey's inventory. She made a little face when she told me that she couldn't afford to get attached to any of the prints, quite a trial for her, as she loved the art of all nations. Cocktails and art, I thought; maybe I'll get into her pants. I'm sure that at the time I had a big goober smile on my face as I contemplated such an outcome. Tessa said I reminded her of Li'l Abner.

"Because I work upstairs, I've had to become a walker just to get outside," she said, making our drinks in a blender. "You start getting curious about different neighborhoods—where the railroaders lived, where the ranchers retired, where the doctors and bankers lived. In the winter, when the wind is up, I have to tie a scarf over my face. Anybody you see in the street is ducking for a building, kind of like in the Blitz."

As I waited for my drink, I found myself leaning forward in my chair with my hands pressed between my knees. It was only when she stopped to look at me that I realized my posture was strange. I pretended that I was just stretching and leaned back in an apparently casual but quite uncomfortable position. As Tessa came toward me with a brightly colored drink, both she and it seemed to be expanding, and when she handed me the drink I wasn't sure I was strong enough to hold it. I felt suddenly that everything was bigger than me, that I was in over my head, trying to handle a situation which, when I was rich, I would take to like a duck to water. But things settled down quickly as soon as she returned to her seat, and I was then glad to have the drink because I was a bit cotton-mouthed. I had gone from my first impulse of getting into her pants to fearing that she'd try to get into mine.

I was not much of a drinker; water would have served as well. That summer I'd made an experimental foray into a local bar, feeling that I needed to learn to be more social. I struck up a conversation with a somber middle-aged fellow in a rumpled suit. He looked so gloomy that I regaled him with what I felt were uplifting accounts of my struggles at school. He stared at me for a while, until I sensed that all the timing was disappearing from my delivery. Finally he said, "Hey, boss, I got to go. You're creeping me out."

"Now," Tessa said, "let's start at the beginning: what do you think being a doctor will do for you?"

"I don't know." My answer came out so quickly it startled her. She leaned back into the sofa—she was at one end, I at the other—with her elbow propped on the back of it and her fingers parting the hair on the side of her head.

"You don't know?"

"I wish I did. Sorry." Involuntarily singing out this last word.

"No, that's all right. That's fine. If you don't want to talk about it, I'm okay with that."

I didn't share the image that I had of myself, still dark-haired but with a graying moustache, going up the gangplank of a yacht. I kept sipping my drink, looking into it as if it were a teleprompter and I were the president of the United States. The colorful liquid seemed like something I had found. I don't know why I made people so uncomfortable. As a kind of icebreaker, I thought to ask her a question.

"When people use the expression 'rest in peace' do you think they have some basis for saying it, or is it just wishful thinking?"

I can't imagine what made me believe that she'd have the answer to this doleful conundrum. But surely my mother's poor health was on my mind.

"You mean, about *the dead*?"

"Sure."

Tessa looked at me for a very long time before saying anything.

"You know, let's try this another time. Maybe it's you, maybe it's me, but at this point in time and space it's just not happening."

I backed out of there like a crab. I felt sorry for Tessa; she probably had trouble sleeping after this weird visit from the new neighbor. I just didn't know what to do about it—an apology would have made it seem even stranger.

Thereafter, we sometimes ran into each other in the hallway adjoining our apartments, and it did not get any less awkward. I made increasingly maladroit attempts to be cordial, these being received with growing skepticism, even revulsion, until upon seeing me Tessa would dart into her apartment and slam her door. What was strange was that if I lingered in the hallway after she'd gone inside, I would always, moments later, hear her phone ring.

Once she said to me, "I know you're tracking my movements." And another time, "Don't think you're fooling me." And another, a cry, "Please stop!"

"Stop *what*?"

A mirthless laugh followed and a slammed door.

I made every effort to avoid these encounters. Indeed, I did start tracking her movements, if only to avoid her. She headed upstairs to work for Hoxey at exactly nine, out for the mail at ten thirty, lunch with Hoxey in his apartment Monday, Wednesday, and Friday, catered by Mountain Foodstuff, out to lunch Tuesday and Thursday, but always back by one thirty, dispatching UPS and FedEx and other outbound packages at four o'clock, at which point her workday was over. I really didn't have a bead on her activities and so came and went from my apartment nervously. When she had men over, they seemed to linger around my door as if on the lookout for me. One strapping fellow with a shiny black goatee positioned himself as though to actually block my way. I gave him a big smile and pushed past. He smelled like motor oil. He said, "Hello, Doc." Tessa must have told him that I was in pre-med. I said hello. I was glad to get inside, and when I looked through the little spy hole in the door, I saw into his ear.

Concentrating on the Help Wanted ads calmed me down. I had discovered that I needed to look for work elsewhere, as people in town knew who I was and—this really is very funny—held my studies against me. "You can't paint my house," Mrs. Taliaferro said. "You're going to be a doctor!"

"Not necessarily!" I said in my warmest tones, while hers cooled markedly. I have no idea why I answered her that way. I was sure I was going to be a doctor, but when I was under pressure to make conversation, it was as if all my life's plans went up in smoke. I felt the need to persuade Mrs. Taliaferro that I would be a lifelong house painter.

I kept studying the paper. I recognized that real opportunities existed for those who would sell cars or apply siding, but given the trouble I was having with my communication skills, I thought those occupations might not be up my alley. Still, I really felt that once I got my timing back—and it was a timing issue—I'd be able to look into a different set of prospects. I was very much focused on the chance to be unexceptional; if I had the opportunity to keep my head down, I meant to take it.

I got a job working for a very nice guy, or so I thought, named Dan Lauderdale. He was an attorney in Billings who specialized in whiplash and owned a cute little turn-of-the-century cottage in Harlowton, which he used as a weekend place—or, rather, somewhere to vacation with his secretary, who did not enjoy the same legal standing as his wife. "Lawyers like me make doctors leave the profession every day!" he joked. "Stick to painting houses." But he was an amiable fellow with a big laugh that drew one's attention away from his shrewd, close-set eyes. His dark brown curls were so uniform and regular as to suggest the work of a beautician. When I asked him if they were natural, he told me to mind my own business with such vituperation that I actually flinched. The previous owner of his cottage had used stolen Forest Service paint for the trim and shutters, and Dan now wanted it to be all yellow, "like sunshine, get it?" I was basically rehearsing what I thought to be the style of my current position when I said, *"No problema,"* but he must have sensed something wrong with my delivery, for his eyes grew narrow and he just said, "Right." Many years later, Dan Lauderdale would become a well-known judge and part of my life.

I rented a pressure washer, masked everything, used a quality primer, and picked my weather for the final coat. It looked much better, but Lauderdale never responded to the bill I sent, nor the second or third. Live and learn. I wasn't much interested in exploring my remedies, and since other revenues were unassured, I sold my car and went on a grocery binge. Also, in celebration of two months in the apartment, I bought a bed, which I put out in the middle of the living room, where I could luxuriate in all that space and gaze east, west, and south, but not north, at fine window views that were better than any painting, in that they were full of those moving, changing parts known as "Life."

I heard a timid knock on my door and called, "Enter!" I was stretched out on my new bed in my shorts reading a newspaper I'd found in the doorway to the bank. My visitor was the chief of police. I was really pleased to see him, so pleased that I easily set aside any worries over the reason for his visit. I suppose I was lonely. In a decent society, the chief of police is the one stranger you should be able to welcome into your home without reservation. In this case the first thing he told me was that I'd better get dressed, as I was going to jail. He gazed at me with sad knowingness. He had a big, warm face; it shouldn't be misunderstood if I declare that he looked like Porky Pig, with all that guileless amiability, the same pink complexion.

"Tessa Larionov"—he gestured with his head in the direction of Tessa's abode—"has charged you with making obscene phone calls to her."

"Oh?" I said. "I don't have a phone." For one miraculous moment, there were people passing all three windows, and the chief remarked that I needed curtains. "How bad were they supposed to be?" I tried to picture myself as the twisted man placing these calls. In a weird way, it seemed plausible.

"They were not nice."

It comes as a great surprise to anyone jailed in a small town that it is a remarkably stress-free environment. If your reputation is of no concern, your troubles are behind you. The local jail was as good a place as any I've found to unravel all the causes for the state I was in. In a rare moment of lucidity, I suggested a wiretap. The chief didn't take my idea seriously, but tomorrow was a new day because Tessa informed him that the calls had continued while I was in custody. So the wiretap was tried after all, and it soon paid off.

Hoxey was making the calls. Tessa declined to press charges, and it all went down as a lovers' quarrel, once you swallowed the fifty-one-year difference in their ages. Tessa's routine continued unaltered, except that her phone no longer rang so much after her workday was done. I finally ran into her in the hallway just as she was coming down with the packages one afternoon. She stopped in her tracks, arms loaded, and regarded me quizzically. "Hello," she said. I waited before replying. I wanted her to think about what she had done to me. But she didn't seem troubled, and the longer I waited the less troubled she looked.

"Hello," I said.

"You look like you've been painting."

"Yes, I've been painting a house."

"Here in town?"

"Yes, a doctor's house on Third."

"How funny. Since you're going to be a doctor."

"Yes, I'm going to be a doctor." Riches danced before me like sugarplums.

"I don't suppose we'll ever get to the bottom of that."

"No, probably not."

"If you were sick, would you go to a doctor or treat yourself?"

"Oh, I'd go to a doctor. I'm not a doctor yet."

"I mean if you already were . . . Oh, never mind. Can you help me with these?"

We took the packages to the post office and I stood outside on the steps while she mailed them. I watched a grackle walk between parked cars, one of which had an American flag on its antenna. A strong young man was wheeling a cart of pies into the back of a restaurant. He looked too powerful to wheel pies. My mother drove past, blowing her horn, her colossal agitation visible through the windshield. People in town enjoyed such scenes.

Once the packages were sent, Tessa and I stood in front of the building and had a delightful conversation. She commended me for having taken the jailing episode with such good grace. I told her that I didn't know how I could have done otherwise, which she mistook for some form of chivalry. I used both speech and body language to indicate that I mostly understood and what I didn't, I forgave.

I had been raised to believe that time delivers our dreams and quietly carries our nightmares away, and that most of what lies ahead is welcoming and serene. It was part of the strange but cozy world of my home with God in the role of Mr. Goodwrench. Or at least that's how I saw it, peering out from the cocoon of my oddly sheltered Pentecostal house-hold, where there was nothing to worry about but the flames of eternal damnation, which didn't seem like all that much. I saw Satan as just another person who could be bought after my career took off. My mother was always telling me how deceitful the devil was, but that only made me think that I could handle him.

My parents lived on a small piece of ground north of town where there was no hiding from prevailing winds and the desolate ground-hugging plants offered no shade. My father soldiered on at jobs he dis-liked while my mother was busy with her evangelical splinter group. While my father's religious convictions were mostly an attempt to get along with her, both of them awaited the Rapture with a complacency that in my father's case was mostly the hope of getting out of the wind. They were aware of my impractical nature but proud that I had some-how got myself into a small college, even though they must have realized that my bizarre if loving upbringing had not fitted me well for life in the world. Schoolwork had been my anchor in all our wanderings, and hav-ing had an aunt who saw to my ardor and venery, I was able in my air-head way to satisfy the odd lonely girl during my school years. I called it "pollinating coeds" and thought I was funny.

Having heard of my godless ways in town, my parents moved me out to a friend's ranch, where I helped with chores until it was time to resume my studies. Gladys and Wiley were subsistence ranchers on an old place called White Bird. I had known them all my life. Wiley and Gladys liked my mother, whom my father had met at a USO facility in Arkansas, and they could tolerate her religious enthusiasm without sharing it. I don't think they believed my dad shared it either, and later, when he told me he believed in God but also believed that God was crazy, I began to realize that Gladys and Wiley might have been right. I have a thoroughly secular mind, and despite all the sessions I endured at churches in storefronts and old gymnasiums I never believed any of it. Still, I am content to have had this background, as it acquainted me with the fabulous range of hope entertained by humanity.

Wiley had fought in the Pacific, some very nasty places like Peleliu and New Guinea, hand-to-hand stuff. He had brought home a Japanese suicide sword, a *wakizashi,* which he used for all sorts of things around the ranch until it wore down and ended up in Gladys's kitchen drawer. After the war he had worked at many jobs trying to hang on to his land. He and Gladys spent three winters south of Billings feeding Cheyenne steers on beet tops and treating septicemia outdoors in winter conditions that included regular blizzards. Wiley was another VFW guy with my dad, along with a relatively new friend, Dr. Eldon Olsson, who had been a battlefield surgeon in Italy and North Africa. Dr. Olsson left a family practice in the Midwest, and then came to Montana to hunt partridges, practicing only enough to support his austere lifestyle. He confided in my parents that he had never married because his true love had married his best friend. He took up with my parents after he'd joined the VFW, and with Gladys and Wiley because they had nice creek fishing and a spring pond.

Dr. Olsson took me fishing quite often as he awaited the opening of bird season, and made me carry all his gear while he addressed himself to my future. At a time when I was universally regarded as an idiot, Dr. Olsson was sure I had great potential, though in need of a more substantial education that would involve getting out of my house. He was very fond of my parents but thought my mother was fanatical. I was flattered that he was so interested in me. We fished and hunted, he gave me books to read, he corrected my English. I still have a vivid picture of him looking as I thought a doctor should: medium height, thick white hair in a brush cut, a carefully trimmed military moustache. You would take advice from a man who looked like this, and I readily succumbed to his authority, though it led me on one of the strangest missions of my life.

I learned a great deal during my stays with Gladys and Wiley, and I was well fed. Wiley taught me to smoke cigarettes, something I no longer do but still miss and plan to resume late in life. And Gladys taught me over the many times I stayed on the ranch about the hard, wordless love of some country women who lead by example in these out-of-the-way places.

Gladys also liked cigarettes. Sometimes the three of us smoked instead of talking, in individual styles: Wiley rarely took the cigarette from his mouth and squinted one eye; Gladys held hers in an elevated manner between the first two fingers of her hand; I pinched mine between thumb and forefinger and sometimes sucked up the smoke that rose from the ash. Paper sticking to lips, irregular burning, the advent of filters, assaults by the surgeon general—all came under discussion. When we watched TV, I felt stylish lacing my hands behind my head, slouching in my chair, and allowing the cigarette to hang from the exact center of my mouth. We liked to fill that room with so much smoke you could barely see the screen. I enjoyed forcing one or the other to remind me that my ash was about to fall. The hiss when I dropped a burning butt into a beer can as Wiley fussed with the volume control was a memory that would recur long after Wiley was gone. Horses and farm equipment were dangerous and produced a fatalistic culture impervious to health warnings.

I irrigated, fixed fence, cut cedar posts, rewired the calving shed, repudiated the government, ate three squares a day, and borrowed Wiley's International truck to pay regular visits to Tessa, who treated me like something she might have acquired at a pet store. That was just fine with me, though. I only wanted to be around her.

Tessa soon took charge of my life. She would have given me money if she'd known I needed it. Instead, she decided that it would be good if we did something together, just for fun. "Mr. Hoxey feels terrible about all that has happened," she said. "He wants to treat us to a night on the town." That Friday, we signed up for tango lessons.

Tessa and I and six other couples entered the Elks Hall, with its terrible acoustics and all-consuming clamminess. We were conventionally dressed, I in a secondhand sport coat and wide tie, Tessa in a black sheath that struggled to encase her well-muscled shape. The others were more South American in style, hot-red lipstick on their small-town faces, tortoiseshell combs in swept-up hair. The men had gone with a pomaded look that spoke of their sense of mission. They seemed to smolder in anticipation of their future proficiency.

Our instructor was Juan Dulce, or just Dulce, a genuine Argentine who worked his way around the American West giving lessons. He had created a real interest in the tango in the most unlikely places—cow towns, oil towns, uranium towns, coal towns—where such a hint of another kind of life carried a special allure. He was perhaps sixty, thin as a herring in his striped pants, formal black coat, ruby cravat, and stacked heels. His hair, slicked to his skull, emphasized eyes that seemed to belong to some sort of marine creature. He was without humor in conveying the sacredness of his mission. I doubt that I shall forget the sight of him standing on a Pepsi crate and pouring out his introductory remarks in a deep and vibrant voice that seemed to make the room hum.

"When I am fifteen in Buenos Aires, I am longing for love and suffering and, above all, success—the hope of becoming a legend of our hot and drowsy tango. I underwent numberless deprivations, but success would reward the sensual designs that I displayed in many venues. Now the money I earn is exchanged for my fatigue, but I have no other way to go, and there are days I awaken upon wretchedness. Once I converted my dancing of three weeks' duration by a pocket ruler into three hundred seventy-two kilometers. Still, tango is all! Without tango, my face inspires doubt. Therefore, my advice is, press your tango to great advantage! And now we begin."

He turned on the big sound system, which had hitherto been employed to enlarge the voices of prairie politicians bent on higher office or nostalgic Scandinavian chorales with cow horns on their heads. The system had astounding capacity, and as the old tangos were broadcast by Dulce, the room was filled with the somber, inevitable cadences of this prelude to intercourse. At school, I had not only enjoyed several instances of copulation—albeit with Mr. Goodwrench staring down at me—but I had seen it explained on huge blackboards, so that there could never be any doubt about what was going on.

We began to learn the little steps, in the chest-to-chest Argentine style. We arranged ourselves counterclockwise and concentrated on maintaining our space between the other dancers. The great power of Tessa, at first exhilarating, gave way to apprehension, as though I were riding an unruly horse, and when I failed to comprehend the crossover steps as required by Dulce, Tessa, a determined expression on her face, used her might to drag me into position. To avoid humiliation, I attached myself by my wiry grasp to her flying carcass. Her cry of alarm brought Dulce to our side and the other dancers to a dead halt just as I was beginning to enjoy myself.

"*Señor!* Grappling has no place in our national dance!"

"I cannot follow her movements," I explained in an accent accommodatingly identical to Dulce's, which I found infectious.

"You are not to follow—you are to lead!"

"It's my fault," Tessa said. "I lost patience with him during the first *abrazo*. He just seemed lost. I'll try to do better."

"Perhaps, this is the time to work on our syncopation," Dulce said sternly to both of us, "with greater respect for the movements of each other."

"The music is unfamiliar," I explained. "You don't happen to have 'La Bamba'?" He held his head and moaned as though he'd been shot.

The other couples had deftly caught on to the oddly triangular chests-together, feet-apart position. An older pair of bottle blonds, obviously trained in other kinds of ballroom dance, made an effort to slide past us. The woman had a fixed and toothy Rockettes smile, and at close range she caught my eye and called out, "Piece of cake!"

I gave Dulce my word that I would syncopate respectfully, and I proceeded in earnest. At first, Tessa complimented me on my "good hustle," but she soon proved unequal to my speed and dexterity. Whatever had been going on in my life up to that point came out in my tango, and the exultation I began to experience was interrupted only when Tessa let out a real showstopper of a screech. Then Dulce came between us and made the mistake of laying hands on me. Insofar as I retained a modicum of male pride, this quickly devolved into a dusty floor battle, with the raucous music of Argentina and the angry sounds of interference from the other students. With their help, I was flung into the street. "Good night, Doctor!" I realized that Tessa had told the others that I was already out of medical school and that she was no cradle robber.

I recall feeling breathless and completely without direction as I allowed Tessa to take charge of our stroll home. She stopped momentarily, between two old commercial buildings, not far from the railroad yard, looked straight at me, and said, "Boo. Hiss." We went on. "I'm lucky you didn't request Mannheim Steamroller," she added. I was defeated. "Now don't be offended, and more importantly, don't walk in front of that car," she said. "I realize you aren't attracted to me, are you?"

"That's not the real story," I replied. "I just need a little encouragement." At these two sentences, uttered with such sincerity, Tessa responded with visible pleasure.

"Then let me tell you my own fears. Why? Because you're adorable. Of course you're a complete idiot, but within that, there is a certain appeal. But I have fears, too. Isn't that real friendship, to tell someone your fears? You could have been extremely disagreeable about those phone calls."

"What good would it have done?"

"None, but how many would recognize that? I sense that you have a good heart, a good heart trapped in a self that is a hop, skip, and jump from kiddie day care. Obscene phone calls from a stranger are intolerable. But when they come from someone you know, particularly a deluded old walrus like Hoxey, well, they don't arouse quite the same wrath. The right to revenge belonged to you, and you declined to take it. Mr. Hoxey and I are in your debt."

I had a clear glimpse here of the sensible side of Tessa, and a hunch that she would end up a friend, which rather worried me because she was the sort who might anchor me and teach me to accept reality, such as it was then emerging.

"How about you just walk me home?" she said finally. "That work for you?"

"Sure," I said, my voice rising.

We paused at the railroad tracks to watch a big northern express rip through. She peered intently, and I positioned myself behind her so that it looked like the train was pouring into one of her ears and out the other. I knew then that I would kiss her. I suppose it took ten minutes for us to get back to the house, during which time Tessa did her level best to spill out her hopes and dreams, which were honest and simple: ride old man Hoxey into the ground and clean out his estate. This wasn't how she put it, naturally. Her concern was expressed as a passion for aesthetic rarities. "No one knows the inventory as I do. No one cares as I do, and no one knows the importance of getting it into strong and caring hands as much as I do." I didn't say anything, and I suppose she took my silence as censorious. We entered her apartment. Before pushing the door shut behind her, she said, "At the end of the day, it is what it is." I wondered what that meant. Of course, it is what it is, and it didn't even have to be the end of the day to be what it was. I couldn't understand this sort of thing at all, and in a way kissing someone who said things like that was even more confusing.

When I did it, it was with the kind of apprehension one feels on placing a cocked mousetrap in a promising corner. She held me at arm's length, giving me what one of my professors had called the pre-copulatory gaze. Tessa seemed ominous. I thought of the Big Bang Theory, wherein a tiny speck of matter mysteriously expanded to fill the universe.

I said, "What do you think?" My heart pounded.

She said, "Let's give it a whirl."

We made love on the couch. I performed in a state of amazement at all that skin, Tessa egging me on with smutty cries. She asked, "My God, who taught you to do it like this?" and I said, "My aunt." And she said, "Oh God, no, please not your aunt. No details, thank you very much!" Skin everywhere! She said, "I wonder if you could change your expression. I can barely do this." When I reached that point to which all our nature aspires and where the future of the species is spasmodically assured, she gave a great sigh and remarked, "Never a dull moment."

2

I WAS NEARLY MIDDLE-AGED before I learned that my mother's hometown in Arkansas was not called, as my father had said, "Crackeropolis." It was Ayers. Ayers, Arkansas. When I figured this out, I then invested way too much time in analyzing my father's odd little satire. Was it contempt for my mother's origins? Probably he was just being funny; but I wasn't sure. I did a bit of research on Ayers and learned that it was the site of an annual slasher film festival held in a big old Art Deco movie theater that was in the registry of historic buildings. Otherwise, a quiet soybean town peopled by farmers in dashboard overalls.

Unwinding my mother's pointed remark to my father to the effect that the only good Indian was a dead Indian, I eventually grasped that it referred to his few droplets of Cree blood. My father always pretended to be of French Canadian stock, but I'd heard from other of his relatives that they were originally mixed-race folk who worked the lime kilns after the buffalo disappeared. All those people went back and forth between here and Canada looking for work and so got into the habit of saying they were French Canadians as a way to avoid being called half-breeds. The war and generations of marriage evaporated all that, turning that class of folk into garden-variety Americans with slightly exotic names like mine. My full name, Irving Berlin Pickett, will never find its way into common usage.

When I was in my teens I bought a set of drums: a snare, a bass with a foot pedal, and a broad, handsome Zildjian cymbal. I didn't go far, much past Gene Krupa's "Lyonnaise Potatoes and Some Pork Chops," which I got off a 78 rpm record called *Original Drum Battle: Gene Krupa & Buddy*

Rich and which I blasted for weeks out the window of my parents' house, exhibiting early and alarming antisocial tendencies aggravated by my rhythmless accompaniment. One day the drum set was gone.

"Where's the drums at?" I demanded of my parents with a fierceness neither I nor they had ever seen. I was just back from school and close to going off the deep end when they said—and I knew it was a lie—that they didn't know where the drums "was at." A neighborhood tipster, one Mrs. Kugel, a member of St. Andrew's Episcopal Church and so an enemy of my parents and their Holy Roller ways, confided that my drums were in the town dump. So they were: I stood on a cold winter day staring at them, crushed among the DeSoto parts, shattered lava lamps, and sundry garbage, paper, and dry-rot wood. I was alone with three crows.

Those drums had enabled me to dominate my household and substantial parts of the neighborhood without resort to ideas or speech. I was practicing, I explained, to join a big band like that of Harry James, he of the screeching trumpet. This last detail was entirely strategic, as Harry James was known to me only as a favorite of my parents, who, with their big black vinyls treasured in original sleeves, sometimes fell into music-induced reminiscence of the war years, even to the point of dancing by candlelight while I presumably slept. Their necking during "You Made Me Love You" grossed me out, as it would have any youngster observing his parents being happy in quite that way. I didn't want to join a swing band, whatever that was; I wanted to rule by noise, and in that I had entirely succeeded. Until the day the drums vanished.

Certainly my parents had made off with them, and I am in no doubt about the great courage required to cross their only child, but their lives had become unbearable: when I was not drumming, I was playing *Drum Battle* from my room and down the stairwell. My father read his newspaper in the backyard. I now see with shame that our home was really not habitable.

"I know you pinched 'em," said I. "The whole kit, to get even."

"Where's he come up with this stuff?" my father asked my mother, the fingers of his right hand checking his shirt pocket for his Old Golds. "Can someone please tell me?"

She swung her head, staring at the floor, as she said, "I don't know." Dad looked to her for a clue: he was a bit weak in situations like this and fished for a bailout.

I went to my room, returning with a pair of Vic Firth Number 3 maple drumsticks; I then removed a roasting pan from the cupboard over the stove and went at it. Heretofore no one had blinked, but this appalling racket soon brought them around and my father swung an open arm in my mother's direction, authorizing her to speak. I stopped and awaited her declaration, which can be condensed: they couldn't take it anymore. I considered this report with substantial silence before I spoke in phrases cribbed from God knows where. I said, "From this blow I foresee no recovery," and went upstairs to my room.

Ours was a cheaply constructed house, thin-walled, inadequately heated and insulated, with variously missing or inoperable doors to finish off what might have passed for privacy. Thus I was able to hear my mother and father repeat, with various intonations, my exit line, through their snorting and thinly muffled guffaws. Mrs. Kugel could be seen from my bedroom window, hovering on the sidewalk below.

I greatly profited by this lesson.

I didn't have an idyllic childhood, though it contained enough boyish pleasures, especially hunting and fishing, that in later times I tended to glamorize the Great Plains, especially when I was in medical school and during my internship when describing it to artificially elated mixed groups. We had a rather sardonic professor of neurology, Martin Chenowith, a bachelor who liked to be around younger people on party nights, hoping to meet women, obviously. I recall pouring out my love of the Great Plains to Dr. Chenowith—afterwards wondering where this enthusiasm had come from—and after several drinks challenging him to see past its grim, dusty, oddly featureless expanses, its rutted, exploited visage, to its hidden glory.

He interrupted me, his small face sharp under thin, carefully combed auburn hair, to say, "It sounds like the men's room at Grand Central." Appalling and inaccurate as this remark might have been, it put an end to my feckless nostalgia about my place of origin, a place I had endured in a van containing a malodorous steam machine for cleaning rugs, with my shaky, anxious parents staring hopelessly through the windshield for signs of the next town. While most houses in those towns had no rugs, those that did were a long way from professional cleaning services, or so my father's rueful, after-the-fact theory went. It proved just about the paltriest get-rich-quick scheme known to man, and we chased it for half a million miles, always discouraged and broke and mad at ourselves and unconsoled by my mother's conviction that "the Lord don't give us more than we can handle."

We usually rented well out in the country, where, as my mother put it, "our screams can't be heard." Those little towns were always in touch with one another and I think my parents wanted our arrival to be a surprise. I was never to find out what they were running from, but it couldn't have been much, bad checks too small to justify the gas needed to track us down. My father was a handsome man with a dimple in his chin like Kirk Douglas's, and I remember at the end of his life my mother asking him, "Where do you think that dimple will get you now, Kirk?" His handsomeness and wandering had long been a problem, and if there was a speech from her with a theme in my memory, it was "Keep it in your pants, Kirk." His real name was Bob; by calling him Kirk, Mother was invoking his rambling ways with lethal disapproval. In more understanding times, my mother said that the war had given him crazy ideas. They'd both run around when they were young; so, everything was canceled out except the language, which endured with a life of its own until the very end, when she repented and prepared herself for what she called the Great By-and-By. Forgiving my father for everything would only fortify her contentment.

When I was fourteen, we moved into my Aunt Silbie's large, clean, comfortable manufactured home (trailer) in Orofino, Idaho. Silbie, whose name derived from "Sylvia," was around forty and divorced, working as a paralegal for a water lawyer who stayed busy defending all the cases arising from the many dams in the Columbia headwaters. Silbie was a good-looking and very shy brunette with wonderful amethyst eyes; she was almost too shy to talk but very intelligent, and so indispensable to her boss that people said he would be ruined if she quit. The most notable thing about Silbie, belied by her meek exterior, was her tigerish sexual appetite. And yet my parents trusted me with her while they were out shampooing rugs. Big mistake.

At first she seemed to be interested only in my finding comfortable accommodation in her house. "I think this room will suit you just fine," she said, pulling up the blinds and checking the sill for dust with her forefinger. "You've got four nice empty drawers here for your things. Fill them in the order you dress. In other words, underwear here, socks here, and so forth. Are these your shorts? Oh my gosh, they're like little bathing suits. Let me see you, turn around—" I asked if there was a desk I could use. "A what? Oh. We'll find something. My goodness gracious, it seems five minutes ago you were a child and, and, now look—!"

"Aunt Silbie," I said, clamping my hand atop my old Samsonite suitcase before she could get at its contents anymore, "I can unpack myself."

"I want to help you," she cried. I didn't really feel I could say "please don't," and so I stood by helpless as she flung my clothes out on the bed, inspecting them, pinning things to my shoulders with her thumbs for appraisal. "Don't move. This is too important! This calls for celebration! You-are-the-first-to-occupy-this-room, my dear, my angel, my pet." She bustled out, and when she came back she had a bottle of wine in one hand. Her clothes she had left elsewhere. She always called it "disrobing," though I never saw a robe.

In my first six months in action Aunt Silbie taught me ninety-nine percent of everything I would ever know about sex. By the time I was in the tenth grade I could deliver to the willing, few as they were, a fairly adult performance. Girls my own age thought it sufficient to let me have my way with them, which left me daydreaming about Silbie's blazing needs, her hot vaginal grip, and the astonishing things she said. Indeed, Aunt Silbie had hung over my sex life until just a short time ago, assuming her ghost has departed me at all. I remember her saying that all the heat was explained by our genetic proximity. I believe that Silbie instilled in me a healthy attitude toward sex: she pumped and I squirted. It was completely lacking in a moral or religious dimension. Unfortunately, my parents caught us, and the fact that they were guests in Aunt Silbie's double-wide in no way prevented their attempting to chase her outside without her clothes. It is a truth universally acknowledged that a single woman in possession of a trailer has a gun, and Silbie pulled hers on Mom and Dad; just to make a clean sweep of it, she evicted all three of us. I can still see her with nothing on but a pistol as we left forever, a strange image indeed, as she was such a meek lady and the only member of our extended family who spoke reasonably correct English. Understandably, I was the one object toward which my parents could vent their wrath, and so I was abandoned to the streets of Orofino, Idaho. A possible version is that they were just looking for an excuse; I've had some counseling to address this version. I must admit that they only abandoned me for about three hours. Be that as it may, I didn't see Aunt Silbie again until I paid her a sentimental visit years later. Whether she had lost her attractiveness or not, I couldn't say, as she had not lost it for me, something she must have detected because her brief look of embarrassment, perhaps at having grown old, quickly gave way to the sly, timid, amethyst-eyed presence I profoundly recognized.

The home in which I was reared, after the rug-cleaning days, was quite normal once my folks had gotten the hang of conventional living and threats of eviction faded. My father got a job at the post office, and there he would remain for the rest of his days, his social life depending entirely on his war buddies. My mother, more solitary by nature, found her church fulfilling enough and required my father to attend once in a while, though he always returned baffled and dazed. In the end she took pity on him and excused him from going. He still went occasionally to please her. My mother and I usually cleared out when the men got together to tell war stories. In fact, "telling war stories" had been a euphemism for rambling, until we were much older or the men had died and we began to comprehend that these backyard chatterers had endured struggle and adventures far beyond anything we would see. My mother was an Arkansas hillbilly woman swept by war and marriage into a life she was slow to accept. She had all the virtues of subsistence living, needed very little—very little food, few material goods—and could make or grow nearly all of it. She medicated herself with things she gathered and cooked up, excepting only her Doan's Pills, and remained thin and tough until the night she didn't wake up. I have never known anyone as free of ambivalence as my own mother. What distinguished her from her Northern neighbors was the palpable sense that just on the edge of vision God and the devil were locked in mortal combat for her soul. She knew where she stood.

Gladys and Wiley, as my parents' best friends, often received us on their ranch, White Bird. My mother occasionally saw Wiley at her church, usually when he was trying to change some habit or another. Church had helped him battle drink but had been no help with the cigarettes, as most of the men at Rock Holy Ghost were contented smokers.

I worked at White Bird, though I was bereft of ranching skills. I flatter myself that Wiley and Gladys enjoyed my company, and I did everything I was asked, but I had little ability to find things to do on my own, as I really didn't understand ranch work. I think they were just trying to inject a few bucks into our hard-pressed family.

Wiley was an excellent horseman and to him I owe my love of horses. He showed me that patience and careful observation of a horse's ability to learn would be instructive in keeping me out of what he called train wrecks. I saw Wiley ride some cantankerous broncs when all else had failed, and the sight of him in the middle of an exploding outlaw, his treasured cigarette undisturbed, stays with me until this day, even though he told me that riding a bucking horse had as much to do with horsemanship as going over Niagara Falls in a barrel had to do with sea-manship. Wiley saved lots of little nuggets like this, but they were all about horses. His favorite was a big claybank gelding named Train, the only horse I ever saw that could jog over sliding shale without losing its footing. I rode Madelyn, a small chestnut mare with snapping black eyes and a clever trot. I suppose she's dead by now, but what fun we had together. Wiley was raised in the twilight of a world in which the horse was involved with everything. His father had dug the basement of the biggest hotel in Montana with horses. My father was in an army that used horses. I was only a generation away from a thousand years of horse-dependent farming, but horses were still very much on our minds. Cars just weren't the same. I say that, dedicated as I was in later years to my Oldsmobile 88, and I no longer had a horse but wistfully attended horse auctions in Billings and elsewhere. I was at a dispersal of the Bar J Hat Pin, a hundred-thousand-acre cattle operation near Cohagen that was sold to a man who had made a fortune selling vitamins on television. The cowboys, mostly older men, were all let go, and they brought their saddle horses to the sale. They pooled their mounts in a few thirty-foot gooseneck trailers and followed along in dusty sedans. I never saw such a bunch of heartbroken old men as many of their ponies were consigned to the killer pen because of their age, to be sold for meat. It all reminded me of Wiley, who by that time was long gone.

I admired Gladys and Wiley for the very realistic way they went about their lives. Theirs was a meager operation that sent a hundred calves to market each year; they were obliged to grow some winter feed, mostly non-irrigated wild hay that Wiley harvested with his 9N Ford gas tractor. I got a great lesson in precision by watching Wiley squint through cigarette smoke as he dressed and adjusted the teeth of the sickle bar on his mower when we prepared our annual siege of the meadows. His equipment was old and minimal, but it enabled him to swathe the most beautiful mix of orchard grass and clover, which we made into small sixty-pound square bales that he could ferry around in his truck and throw here and there "without breaking my goddamn back." His little herd of Hereford cattle always did well in those days before the Angus triumph, and he was expert at the treatment of sunburned udders, prolapses, and eye cancers that afflicted this pleasant breed in our part of the world. By contrast, my parents invested in a mail-order shoofly pie business that foundered in a matter of months, extinguishing my mother's pride in her baking and landing them in yet more financial turmoil, probably at least the twentieth episode since the days of steam-cleaning rugs. I once thought that my father was a willing accomplice to all these gyrations, but I eventually learned that the few years of war had crowded out the rest of his life, and thinking about them, re-imagining them, and finally relating them to some view of life took up much of his time. I expect most of his fellow veterans shared the belief that what they had experienced could never be conveyed but rather was owned as a private matter or, at best, shared with one another. I remember noticing when his war cronies were around a kind of contempt for that vast portion of the world that hadn't "been there." I heard one of them say that he had more respect for a German soldier than an American civilian and what a shame it was you could legally shoot only the former. That was the generation that raised me, and in general they were happy enough to watch us piss away our opportunities on cheap amusements because we were a mob of untested ninnies anyway and there was no sense spoiling our fun.

It must have been the last summer I worked on the White Bird that Wiley took me up to his summer pasture to clean moss and slime out of the stock tanks. One was on a sandstone ridge overlooking a shallow draw. Atop the ridge, a tall tree held a nest of prairie falcons, and the newly fledged young were gliding down the draw to another tree full of indignant magpies, lording it over birds that would prey on them by the end of summer. We had a packhorse carrying some war surplus panniers that opened from the bottom, and in those we carried several hundred pounds of salt, which we distributed to the salt troughs arrayed near the springs. We hobbled Train and Madelyn and took a break. Wiley shook a Camel from its pack and captured it with his lips. Striking a match with his thumbnail, he lit the cigarette and drew in the smoke with an air of grateful relief. "We ship in the fall. You need to get out there and be somebody," he said right out of the blue. I was finished with high school and had done well, though the poor ways of my family and our crackpot religion had made me something of a pariah possessing neither cowboy boots nor penny loafers. The story was always the same: someone would find a reason to be interested in me; then they would hit that little wall which consisted in their detecting my scrutiny of them. They weren't wrong, but I couldn't help myself. I perhaps made too much of my enthusiasm for animals, but they did provide me the feeling of being understood, something I badly craved. In my early years of medical practice and as a man about town, I would cultivate an entirely artificial hail-fellow-well-met personality fueled by alcohol, desperation, and my first taste of spending money.

I'd been going out to the ranch almost as Gladys and Wiley's only family by the time Dr. Olsson turned up asking if he could exercise his bird dog. He was new to the area, having bought himself a little cottage, but he hadn't yet made any friends, though he didn't seem to be in a hurry. Far more interested in finding a place to run the dog, he was pretty deft at fishing out information about the local landowners, the location of creeks, who had a grain field, etc. He was certainly not fooling anyone, but Gladys and Wiley liked him and became, for a while, his only friends. Then he met my parents and they hit it off too, because really Dr. Olsson was the kind of solid fellow you couldn't help but like. He had the look of a onetime football player, which he was, and despite plenty of sore joints he bounded around pretty well. Looking back, I think Dr. Olsson was no more than middle-aged. He first took a shine to me as a way of ingratiating himself with the grown-ups, I think, but maybe he actually liked me. He really seemed to give a damn about how I would turn out.

Gladys and Wiley understood me too, even enjoying my awful timing and geekish silences. They believed I was smart and knew how to work and that I would eventually find myself if I got out of town and away from my parents. While personally fond of my mother and father, they thought they lacked common sense in raising me and considered my mother's thermal relationship with Jesus to be beyond the pale. "Jesus is your friend," Gladys once told me, "but let's leave it at that." I later had a spell of poetry reading and in the poems of Saint Theresa found a new version of the Savior, who appeared as a sort of demon lover with all the tools of electrifying conquest. Saint Theresa can make Christ sound like a nine-battery Chinese vibrator. After that came Abelard and Heloise with their thrilling menu of mixed messages. I like to think it was otherwise with my poor mother, but God only knows what they taught her in Arkansas. She was certainly fixated and said of her own father, a crooked door-to-door shoe salesman, that he had "gone to hell with a broken back." I'm pretty well over all this, I say, but there was a day when the flames danced just beyond the next hill.

So Wiley said, "I had several chances to try something else, but the land claimed me and I was grown old before I realized the land didn't care about me."

"How about Gladys?"

"Neither one of us. We're like two ants crawling over it."

I suppose this made Wiley sound like a pessimist, which maybe he was, but his day-to-day demeanor was that of a cheerful, optimistic man. This seemed to be the case with people who knew the score, even if it was not encouraging, as though encouragement were just a matter of being pressed into the unknown.

Gladys and Wiley assumed correctly that I was headed for college and that our encounters hereafter would be social calls only. Their new friend Dr. Olsson was nudging me in the direction of education too. Therefore, they would need new help, and indeed that had long been the case, though they had made do with tramps and jailbirds and schoolboys like me. As it was well known that ranch work was hard and underpaid, the pickings were slim, and many of the men they interviewed were, if experienced, broken down or, if inexperienced, not able-bodied. The only exception was a lanky, gum-chewing wise guy in a hot-rod Ford named Dale Brewer. A lazy, scheming, no-account ladies' man, Dale would be the child Gladys and Wiley never had. They took him into their capacious hearts.

Once after school and during a late-spring snow, Dale and I were feeding cows from a wagon, tossing the bales out as we cut the binder twine. One bale had hit the ground still bound, and Dale got down to cut the twine. As he bent over to do this, an old swinging-bag cow butted him onto his face. Dale jumped up in a rage and screamed at the cow, "Someday I'll be rich and you'll be a thousand pounds of Sloppy Joes!"

It turned out to be true. Dale ended up with great wealth.

I was simply summer help, but Dale hoped to keep this job forever. I don't quite know why Wiley and Gladys took to him as they did; he was an absolute menace around machinery, the only thing that interested him on the ranch, and he broke more than he could fix. We had a low-boy trailer that was in constant use hauling farm equipment in to the John Deere dealership for repair, usually on account of Dale's neglect. The last summer I worked on White Bird, Dale had taken over the irrigation, resulting in terrible friction with the neighbors. Wiley declined to intervene or bank on his years of goodwill because he wanted Dale to learn for himself how the water was shared and apportioned; but Dale just argued with people, and eventually a ditch rider was assigned to us and everyone had to meet his expenses as he adjudicated every drop that came through the head gate. A ditch rider brings shame to the people of a watershed, a public announcement that the neighbors don't know how to get along with one another. Once Dale had his share of the water, he did almost nothing with it, and the small amount of alfalfa that ought to have been irrigated dried up on the meadows. Wiley and Gladys just let it happen as part of the education of Dale. Instead of attending to the appropriate chores of damming and spreading water, Dale focused all his attention on a badger living in the middle of the alfalfa field that had made a great, unsightly burrow, in the mouth of which his striped face could be seen. One day Dale handed me an old J.C. Higgins rifle with iron sights and told me to shoot the badger. "I'd do it, but I'm nearsighted."

Well, I tried and failed, both because of the wiliness of the badger, who after a few of my inaccurate shots, grew evasive, and because the old gun had probably never been sighted in; it seemed to me that the shots landed nowhere near where I aimed. It didn't help my accuracy that the several glimpses I'd got of the badger had induced sort of an attachment to it, giving me the sense of trying to kill something which wished only to live.

Dale was quite furious at my failures and professed to be fed up with this badger ruining the alfalfa, alfalfa that was going nowhere for lack of water. He put poison at the mouth of the burrow without effect. He tried running water from the ditch toward the hole but ended up eroding part of the meadow. This finally came to Wiley's attention, and he wordlessly shoveled the appropriate repair to the ditch bank, his silence betraying his dissatisfaction with Dale and maybe even with me. He walked off toward the house without speaking.

That night in the bunkhouse, Dale said that if we didn't do something about the badger we were going to get our asses kicked off the ranch. I was so young and credulous at this time that I thought Dale knew something about badgers I didn't, but now I still believe the problem was the lack of irrigation. Dale pulled a wooden box containing narrow, waxy red cylinders from under his bunk. He held up a stick of dynamite and said it had the badger's name on it. "Wiley ain't going to like this, but he'll like it after that badger goes to the next world."

Before breakfast the next day, we'd bundled several sticks around a blasting cap and led the fuse back across the meadow to a boulder we meant to get behind at the right moment. It was hot already and the sun was barely up, throwing white bands of light through the cottonwoods and willows along the ditch bank. We sat behind the boulder with a box of kitchen matches and took a last look around before lighting the fuse, which hissed and sparkled to our satisfaction before disappearing inside itself. It seemed to take such a long time getting to the dynamite that we stood up to see what went wrong just when the blast occurred, sending a wash of soil in every direction and throwing the badger nearly forty feet in the air, where it burst into flame and landed in the desiccated alfalfa, setting the meadow ablaze, a fire that quickly burned out of control. Despite the efforts of our extremely capable volunteer fire department, Gladys and Wiley lost much of their hay crop. In front of the firemen, and with an oddly contemplative expression on his face, Wiley knocked Dale senseless and allowed it was time for me to get ready for school.

3

I FOUND STRONG FEELINGS for my town to be always at hand. I loved its situation in the sweep of a great western river, even the steady, subdued clangor of its railroad yard, the faint but omnipresent background of our lives. And the violent weather kept everyone on their toes. My strongest impressions seem to have originated in summertime, when my life was out-of-doors and the towering clouds were like the castles in which I lived. When Gladys and Wiley didn't need my help, I spent my days mowing lawns and watching. I say "watching" because the peculiarity of my family and of my own personality gave me the vigilance of an outsider. Remember, we had only recently come in from the road as itinerant rug cleaners, and my education at the loins of Aunt Silbie had exempted me from the pubescent twittering of my classmates. When I finally had a girlfriend, she turned out to be the true Crow maiden Debbie Stands Ahead, who confined our ardor to kisses that, lasting an hour and expressing teen love, were more powerful than the somewhat abrupt gymnastics with my aunt. I always felt in the arms of Debbie a sort of peace of a kind I would be surprised to feel years later when one of my colleagues, Jinx Mayhall, inexplicably embraced me in my hospital bed after I had been stabbed. What on earth could Jinx have been thinking? I had hoped she was embarrassed; I know I was. Years ago when I learned that Debbie had married a dentist I fondly hoped she was denying him coitus: I was still jealous. As for Jinx, I just didn't know.

I mowed lawns all over town. I mowed Dr. Burchfield's, my precursor in the emergency room. That he spent the weekend in his bathrobe should have told me something. Mrs. Hetherington, whose brick house was built before Montana statehood, always made me iced tea and a sandwich. She was a lonely old widow who sat by herself at a white painted table in her backyard arranging flowers from her garden. She knew I was seeing Debbie Stands Ahead. "She's a fine young lady," said Mrs. Hetherington. "This all used to be theirs." After Debbie was gone I read the most god-awful books about the frontier, in which the Indian girls appeared as "dusky maidens." For some reason I embraced this ghastly phrase and was heartbroken that my own dusky maiden was gone (to college). Debbie, forsake your dentist and his half-breed progeny, and come back to me!

Earl Clancy's yard was almost too small for me to trifle with and he barely paid me. Earl, now retired, had been a supervisor at the waterworks, and I worked for him to hear his stories. Once a hobo, he esteemed those years as the best of his life. He had the same skinny frame and hangdog face he had probably acquired during his days riding the rails. He followed the seasons like a bird of passage and accepted adventures as they befell him. He had some skill as an orchardist and could bring his talents to McIntosh apples and Indian River oranges alike. In Florida, he was arrested for vagrancy and spent a month on a chain gang. When released, he wandered penniless down a dirt road, trying to think how to get back to Montana (it was hot). Passing a Holy Roller church, he heard the pandemonium within and a huge woman stepped out and called to him, "Come in and be saved!" Earl soon found himself rolling around on the floor, where he discovered a wallet with enough money to get him home. The stint on the chain gang had brought him to his senses, such as they were, and he went on to spend the rest of his working life at the waterworks. Because of his special understanding of the operations of the system, Earl was forgiven the very occasional summer binges that took him on sentimental journeys to pick cherries on the shores of Flathead Lake. He was the first of the innately talented, hardworking, somewhat visionary and out-of-control men I have known. I might have been one of them at heart. I hoped not, because all were bachelors and I was in search of the love of my life.

My summertime lawn mowing introduced me to the class system that burdens every community for the simple reason that east of Main Street, people mowed their own lawns. Mowing lawns in the humid summertime could be such grueling work that I began mentally aligning myself with that class of people who had others do it for them. There was a lingering contradiction here in that Dr. Olsson, who set me on my path, mowed his own lawn. But he was from out East, and that could have explained it. Still, here was another of my ambivalences: I seemed unwilling to rise to that class whose lawns were mowed by others. I wouldn't like being called "Doctor" if that became appropriate: it would embarrass me, though I expected to love the work. Maybe that was why I drove my troublesome old car. The last mechanic who worked on it said, "Doc, you need to shit-can this rust bucket before it shit-cans you." But I went on pouring money into it. I even lost my desire for money and developed some kind of sentimental attachment to the poverty of our early days.

I mowed lawns for nuns and priests. We had a priest from Ireland for a while, Father Noonan, a tall, somber man known to be an extremely bad-tempered golfer. The many Irish associated with the railroad in our town thought that Noonan gave them a bad name by being so humorless. They had a point. Noonan was never happy with my work and demanded that I use an edger, which he didn't own. When he presented me with one and pointed out the work it was meant to do, I quit. Father Noonan called me a bum and chased me off the rectory grounds as though I'd been fired. I got dirty looks from some Catholics, but that died down.

I wasn't the only lawn boy in town, and we all liked the Dairy Queen for lunch and ogling. We had the best tans, which drew some girls, including sophomore Edna Sedlicky, who made it clear she was available for whatever we might have in mind, which scared us to death, sending Edna elsewhere for fulfillment. School threw us together arbitrarily, but meeting at the DQ as boys of common labor seemed to produce more-enduring friendships. This was how I met Chong Wells and Second Hand Smoke. The three of us were fascinated by Louis Echeverria, a Basque-Cheyenne mixed-blood burglar who told us stories of his derring-do without quite tempting us, though the allure of creeping around where we had no business was attractive. Another Indian who worked at the Conoco station, Gary American Horse, known as "Walkman" because of his omnipresent audio device, told us that Louis was known on the reservation as "Louie Crooked-Fucker," and when we tried addressing him by this name, he fled, assuming his reputation pursued him. We never saw him again, though we learned that he moved to Billings to pimp and sell meth. At a football game in Great Falls, Chong saw him driving a new Eldorado with tinted windows. He was later arrested together with our mayor, Todd Bakesly, father of seven, for soliciting a prostitute. Louie went to jail, the possibility of which he once described to his admirers at the Dairy Queen as "the price you pay" and "the choice is yours." He had a philosophical streak.

One summer I traveled back and forth to Wild Horse Island on Flathead Lake, where T. Sam Vaughn, the owner of our town's bank, kept his big Chris-Craft with its cocktail bar and white Naugahyde interior. I had scraped and painted its bottom in the spring and twice touched up its varnish during the summer, after which Vaughn put me on a Greyhound for home with a check in my pocket and on my lap a nice lunch, made with his own hands. But by far my sharpest memory is of T. Sam, his wife elsewhere, a cocktail in one hand, the marine gas nozzle in the other while fumes arose around the cigarette dangling from his lips. I was sure we would go down as one of America's regular cabin cruiser explosions, but as you see it never happened. Once T. Sam allowed me to bring Debbie Stands Ahead as my guest; he chaperoned us in separate cabins and joined Debbie in preparing meals. At midday when my work was done and Debbie had tired of sunbathing on the deck, we would swim in water so cold that those who drowned in it were never seen again. Our banker was our lifeguard, watching vigilantly from the helm as we swam furiously to keep warm. Debbie and I always watched the sunrise over the Mission Range where Debbie had Kootenai-Salish relatives. When Debbie got out of the sun to study her schoolbooks, T. Sam would wink at me and nod: this is the girl for you. In middle age, I still found myself yearning, and Debbie's marriage to a dentist made me a lifelong connoisseur of anti-dentist commentary.

T. Sam and I were chums when I was on the boat, but if ever he brought a lady friend, I, by magic, made myself invisible once he made a locking sign with thumb and forefinger over slightly pursed lips. The two would then walk around me in the broad cockpit as though I were any other inanimate object. This proved a higher tier to lawn mowing in my study of the American class system, and the resulting aversion had much to do with my practicing medicine while pretending not to be a doctor. Perhaps, too, there was some nostalgia on my part for the days when I was presumed crazy. It always meant freedom, and none are freer than the crazy.

The day came when Mrs. Vaughn discovered the uses to which the cabin cruiser was being put, and she divorced him. "Miss Lillian" had been named after her. He renamed the boat "Miss Ruby" after a subsequent lady friend, then "Miss Alice," then "Miss Judy," and so on; the last time her transom was repainted, she was called "Queen for a Day."

I became Vaughn's physician, and as time went on, his mind would drift to the bygone days of the cabin cruiser, which proved to be less reminiscence than a prelude to dementia. I continued seeing him as he lived in contented oblivion at the Mountain Shadows Rest Home. I hope that Ruby, Alice, and Judy are with him, and even the younger Lillian. T. Sam was a good soul.

This wouldn't be a bad time to talk about how I came to be rescued from Christianity in time to become a doctor. I have previously described my days as a wanderer in a family of steam-cleaning Pentecostals, my carnal toils in the arms of my beloved aunt, my years as a ninny and scholar so oversexed that every time the cheerleaders of my school performed the pyramid at a ball game I came close to shooting off in my pants. Fear of this caused me to stoop even when such an event was a remote possibility and to develop a sort of meditation technique for classroom days to keep my mind, if not on the work at hand, at least off the flesh of females. In those days everything reminded me of girls, not excluding tomatoes, chickens, and parking meters—and even, at desperate times, my own shoes.

The day came when my beloved parents grew sardonic about their faith and entered a period they called Boozing for Christ. There was a curious synchronicity, if you shared quarters with them, between this and other forms in which they awaited the Rapture. Visiting my mother's family in Arkansas, they had been passengers on a powerful bass boat that sped through a crowded water baptism on the Ouachita River, scattering and injuring worshippers. Expecting divine retribution and not getting it seemed to undercut their faith. I think their particular kind of Christian longs for punishment, longs to be shriven, the only road to paradise they could picture. In any case, while awaiting trial for criminal endangerment, my mother and father began hitting the bars. Sometimes a Christian will deliberately go down a bad road just to produce eventual suffering. They're crazier than pet coons.

They were soon virtual derelicts in our town, my father hanging on to his connections among veterans of foreign wars and my mother seeing the very few friends that couldn't quite give up on her. Our home was a disaster and I was the subject of various rescue attempts, not just because I was the sort of obsequious ninny who appeals to rescuers but because my basic needs were not being met, and so I smelled bad, though I still did my schoolwork. Eldon Olsson became our family doctor; we were among his few patients. I believe he did this out of concern for me. I'm not sure how this happened except that through hunting on Gladys and Wiley's ranch he became their friend, and thence my parents' friend. They could see through their fog that monitoring my health was not a bad thing, and it might be preferable that I received the usual vaccinations. I had been born with a small abdominal hernia, and Dr. Olsson taped a silver dollar over it until it closed and left me with a conventional belly button. He removed my tonsils and bought me the ice cream that was the only reward for what in those days was a gruesome office procedure. Later on, we shared a love of hunting, which was once a boy's introduction to the natural world, leading often to science and conservation, curiosity and a love of earth. These activities put an end to my puling and whining and that part of my youth whose only promise consisted of fucking my aunt. He bought me a twenty-gauge Winchester shotgun with brass tacks in the stock like an Indian gun, and he kept it at his office. He bought me a white Shakespeare Wonderod and a Martin Blue Chip reel. He kept these at his office as well. I think he tried to maintain some sort of connection with his former professional life, writing articles on matters affecting doctors in law and insurance, all the while counting down to those golden hours when he donned his tattered sporting clothes, put Eskimo Pie, or "Pie," his setter-spaniel mix, into the converted hearse which was his hunting car and which sometimes sported a canoe on the roof or a johnboat on a rusty trailer bumper hitched below rear doors that divided at the center and opened to the sides to accommodate the coffin. Pie, named for her black and white colors, sat in the back and watched where we'd been; Dr. Olsson drove; I opened his beers and adjusted the radio.

Dr. Olsson, I now recognize, was a country boy, a short, strapping middle-aged Swede with a groove in his chin, jet-black eyebrows, and thick, unruly hair that tried to form bangs, which, since they wouldn't stay out of his way, were trimmed asymmetrically to accommodate his shooting eye. He too was the son of drunks and had worked his way through school on the green chain of a plywood mill, a terrible job. He still had the hands of a mill worker and occasionally drank wine with the air of someone either on a fabulously exotic mission or saluting the international community. His medical worldview, which I inherited, was that it is unreasonable to expect everyone to get better, much less survive, and great cruelty can be involved in unreasonably prolonging life. In his earliest days of practice, he had served in a Minnesota prison where—he once astonished me by saying—most of the murderers had killed someone who richly deserved it. Dr. Olsson wouldn't pass muster today, but I revere his memory. I'd give anything to ask him why I think Tessa's demise was my fault.

The great thing about hunting and fishing with the local doctor is that landowners don't dare to deny him admittance to their land. A doctor denied can hold his powder until the landowner's hour of need, and then it's all she wrote. People in ranching country know this, and so doctors flit around in social zero gravity, always ready with the silver bullet, always invoking a shamanic aura at the gate to the golden hills where we followed Pie to the coveys. I tagged along in this wake of such privilege and in time became a dead shot with my little Indian Winchester as we traversed the sundry Edens in search of game. My personal Virgil in these wild lands, in the high country beaver ponds where we filled our creels with trout, on the short-grass prairie where we found the grouse and partridges in bluestem and snowberry hideaways, and on the wind-blown prickly pear places where we stalked antelope, was always a step ahead of me, tireless countryman—he aroused in me a wish to become a doctor.

One day in late October on a vast juniper savannah north of Two Dot and next to a tiny spring where watercress grew and where Pie sipped and slept, we ate our lunch, following the hawks with our eyes and admiring the partridges we'd laid in front of us. The warmth of blue sky that had persisted all through September had given way to a steelier blue and the suggestion that the clouds sailing across us on prevailing westerlies would soon bring snow.

Dr. Olsson was watching me, and at first said nothing. Then, "We're going to get you out of your house before we lose you altogether." My rejected first impulse was to stage some defense of my household culture, which for all its deficiencies was mine and mine alone. But it was clear that Olsson would leave it at that and allow his remark to acquire its own weight.

One of the unusual things about Dr. Olsson was that he had never married. He had no children and was all in all a very proper fellow who neither drank to excess nor flirted, though he confessed to me that he once played strip poker with the nurses back in Ohio. My mother told me that he had been in love with a girl in school who married his best friend. His shamed grin at this confession was enormously appealing. I rarely saw him without a clean shirt, pressed pants, and often a tie. His great passion was hunting partridges with his black and white dog. Unless she was in trouble for running off or breaking point, she was just "Pie." Pie was a shrewd little mongrel, four years old, with a brisk, upright tail, a liver-colored spot on her right ribs shaped like Australia, one black ear, and a finely speckled muzzle. She hunted and pointed birds and would not retrieve the ones we shot, though she helped us find them. She handled nicely on Dr. Olsson's whistle, changing direction on one blast and returning on two. Dr. Olsson was inordinately proud of his whistle, which was of chromed brass and made in England, an "Acme Thunderer." It hardly thundered but had a nice sharp sound when compared to the spit-filled gurgle of a police whistle.

When Pie thought hunting was afoot, she would whirl in place, faster and faster, then tip over and bite her own leg, only to jump up with a cry and dash to the screen door, where she slid to a stop and awaited assistance. She was an outstanding and enthusiastic bird dog, found in a ditch alongside the Two Dot road where she had been tossed from a moving car. A Canadian tourist delivered her to the All Creatures veterinary service in Big Timber, where Dr. Olsson acquired her. He had her dewclaws removed, had her vaccinated and spayed, then brought her home and propped her beside him in bed where, night after night, he read the essays of Montaigne while feeding her treats with his free hand. Given the degree to which Dr. Olsson was besotted by his new prize, it was not unexpected that when she was half grown he trained her firmly in unstinting daily increments. By six months, Pie knew "here," "heel," "whoa," and "no," and she had them learned for life. After that, her days became less stressful as Dr. Olsson introduced her to game birds— partridges and grouse—freely allowing her to make mistakes as she determined her objectives and strategies in the mysteries of wind. Dr. Olsson told me, "A bird dog needs to be just that much wild" as he held thumb and forefinger an inch apart. I didn't think she could be very wild with her head on a pillow every night, but in the field Pie revealed not just energy and purpose but a thousand-yard stare. Dr. Olsson said, "They know things we don't know." Twice in the early days of Pie's training, she either left Dr. Olsson or got lost. Most would leave a personal garment on the ground, go home, and return in the morning hoping to find their dog. Dr. Olsson curled up on the prairie and slept until Pie found him. When he walked Pie around town, attentive at heel, people commented, "Here comes old Dr. Olsson and his wife." Pie was the wife and I was the child. He wore a sport coat when he was hunting, a worn old tweed from J. Press clothiers in New York. Sometimes he called a covey a "bevy," an old-fashioned term. He wore glasses except to shoot, and he trusted Pie so much that when she was pointing a covey he patiently removed his glasses, slipped them into his pocket, and then flushed the birds. He was an excellent shot. Dr. Olsson took me hunting as frequently as I was willing to go. He found me a timid shot at first and suggested, "Step forward, shoot a lot, and claim everything." I gradually rose to holding my own and even began to understand the management of a bird dog in the field. It required concentration on the dog. Shooting also required concentration. Understanding habitat and wild country took concentration. I had never tried concentration before, being such a random, disorganized young man when Dr. Olsson took me under his wing that he was lucky I didn't accidentally shoot him. He taught me to use the recoil to speed the slide for the second shot on the Winchester. It took me a long while to understand any of this, and I was predictably abashed as Pie led us to the birds I had missed while Dr. Olsson had harvested at extraordinary range.

I think some of my solitary ways derived from my early training under Dr. Olsson. He lived in rented rooms with Pie, drove an old car, and within two years of arriving in Montana knew the country better than the natives did. At sixty-five, he would not infrequently walk twenty miles in a day, wear me out when I was seventeen, and outshoot me. At times, I never raised my gun but only watched in awe as he squared up, focused, got his face down on the wood, and fired. When I visited him in his rooms and surveyed the sparse furniture, the half-filled closet, the worn shaving utensils carefully laid out by the sink, the wedding photograph of his parents, the small brown radio and single bed, I got an inchoate sense of why I would never outshoot him. In the single-car garage, he hung his birds next to his snow shovel and lawn mower. The garage contained a small workbench and vise as well as his reloading tools for the rows of shells lined up along the back.

We took Pie afield year-round, rain or shine, in or out of hunting season. In the off-season, we counted coveys and entered the information into Dr. Olsson's partridge log, which he sent to the department of fish and game without acknowledgment. I was very anxious to do away with the hawks that decimated our partridges during the winter, especially the northern harriers who hugged the ground and left many a feather pile behind. But Dr. Olsson gave me my first inklings of a holistic view via the old phrase "the balance of nature." He insisted that I learn to love the hawks. I didn't find that easy. When he learned that I had shot one from a tree out at Gladys and Wiley's, he stopped speaking to me for twenty-nine days, which I thought would kill me. I once poured my heart out about my love of hunting and nature to Wiley and my father, who squinted through their cigarette smoke as I talked. When I'd finished, Wiley asked my father if he thought I'd been drinking.

I think that Dr. Olsson was an atheist. When news of some fatality or another came to our attention, he always said the same thing: "Live it up." Over time this seemingly casual remark acquired a kind of resonance, and the subtext for "Live it up" came to seem, "That's all there is." It might have explained his friendship with Wiley, who often quoted the old-time trail cowboys to the effect that if you waited for Jesus to feed you, you'd starve to death.

It was widely felt that I was Dr. Olsson's surrogate child. When I overheard this, I was thrilled. This was the beginning of the hope of being a doctor myself, a wish so far-fetched that I shared it with no one and hardly took it seriously until Olsson urged me to think of making something of myself and medicine appeared as a duty that had befallen me. Running a modest practice with patients you knew inside and out, and from the downstairs of your home, was a model I must have gotten from Dr. Olsson. Olsson lived within his modest means, but surely something had propelled him from his place of origin.

Dr. Olsson had some money, or at least enough to do as he pleased. Now and then, he'd take a trip. He loved the Huntington Library in California, where Tessa had once worked. He went to Japan. Always it was something specific he wanted to see. He wanted to see Kyoto. He flew to Germany to have dinner with a Wehrmacht doctor under his charge in the war, a POW neurosurgeon. He flew to New York for the opera, the symphony, and the art museums. At such times, I took care of Pie and did a responsible job of it; I think he trusted me, though he called every day about her. One year he went back to Ohio to bury his sister; it was December. Partridge season was finished and he left me with Pie.

I decided to take her hunting.

I think too that Dr. Olsson helped me along on my somewhat indiscriminate love of nature. I became modestly knowledgeable about mountain wildflowers and birds, though my familiarity had to be renewed with regular resort to the guidebooks. After I was forbidden to shoot hawks, my predatory impulse was transmuted into a fascination with all hawks and especially falcons, including, on a medical junket in Texas, the exquisite aplomado coursing over the low salt marshes of the Aransas lagoons. I finally understood that my old enemy the northern harrier was a beautiful bird despite his stalking our partridges. I kept a great list of creatures I wished to see: the Stone sheep, Kemp's ridley turtle, the bird of paradise. And so on. I was particularly anxious to see a wild condor. "Who else lives here?" was a question I entertained as adolescent endorphins supercharged my imagination.

Dr. Olsson asked me to bring him my report cards, which I did, as I was not ashamed of my schoolwork, and because I thought compliance would assure me of his favor. He took me to the library to get my first and explosively important library card, soon confiscated by my mother.

She said, "Don't let me catch you there, you little nothing." Dr. Olsson quietly got me another, and I soon began to lead a covert life in the library, establishing the excitement that would attend the sight of books for the rest of my life. Still, I remember the fear I felt whenever my mother caught me reading. "He's got his nose in a book!" I would own thousands of books, but libraries were such a thrill that the hair on the back of my neck stood up upon entering one.

Given that Dr. Olsson's approval of me was so urgent, I don't know what impelled me to take Pie hunting out of season. I am tempted to pause over this conundrum, because episodes of the most incredibly opaque motivation have punctuated my life. There are viruses supposed to hibernate at the base of the spine—the various strains of the herpes virus, for example—which plague us and other mammals and which surge forth at arbitrary moments to assert their dominion over our health. This was the only phenomenon I could compare to the disruptive irregularities that cropped up in my life.

These were some of the things that inspired Farmer Lyles to forbid Pie and me from his acres on the grounds that I was "a disgrace" and moreover, "get out." Only later did I remember Backseat Melissa Brown, by sour luck, his niece. This was a bad omen, compounded by my being no longer secure in Dr. Olsson's converted hearse, for the driving of which I lacked permission; and my growing insecurity had made Pie restive, though she snuggled against my Winchester and her worries passed. It was necessary to find another place to hunt, and I was on a mission to prove to myself that all I had learned from Dr. Olsson about the hunting of partridges I was well able to perform without his oversight: the management of the hunting dog, the shooting, the preparation of the game (I already had a menu in mind), and a brief discourse on the rigors of the field.

I decided that I would not chance an encounter with another disagreeable farmer, and I crossed the Yellowstone River above Convict Grade, driving east until the country looked big and empty—then, as now, my favorite landscape. Pie could feel the rising excitement, and whirling in the backseat, she made little cries and licked the side window. "Cool it, Pie," I said sharply. Pie gasped and pretended to die by sinking onto her stomach and hiding her head between her paws. I had seen this before even under the firm hand of Dr. Olsson. I threw a piece of pig ear over my shoulder, but she ignored it. Soon, though, we found a small road headed north through hawthorn and chokecherry hills, about all that the hearse could handle, and when it ended after only a few hundred feet in a clearing under an old cottonwood, we stopped and I got out. On the ground before me was a small memorial, a slab of sandstone into which some bereft soul had scratched the word "Dad."

I carefully opened the rear door just enough to get my shotgun and held it crossways as I picked a direction of travel and went through a few surmises about the weather, which contained a delicate northerly breeze. A hint of moisture would help Pie with her job. I had just a few hours before sundown, and the unlikelihood of meeting the game warden was a great comfort.

Pie jumped from the car and stopped. She moved only her head, assessing the air, her tail at an indifferent angle while she bethought herself. As Pie was the more experienced of us, I deferred to her and stood by as she considered her options. Once she came to a decision she was off like a shot, straight up the thread of water from a distant spring, winding through the chokecherry at such a clip that I was pressed to keep up.

I struggled through the brush and slipped a single waxy red shell into the chamber and closed it, sliding the safety into position. When I looked up I felt a flash of fear to find Pie no longer visible, but soon she popped up on a hillside looking back at me and then resumed her hunt. I wished it wasn't so late in the day: I was climbing as fast as I could, Pie was casting back and forth but outpacing me by degrees, and the declining sun was on its own schedule. It was not easy to keep these three chronologies in the same plan, something I experienced as mild but creeping anxiety. I was pushing through a chokecherry thicket at the head of the spring, worrying that I had lost sight of Pie again, when five grouse erupted and flew like big brown bees straight back over my head and down the draw. In a few feet I found Pie on point, head cocked back to observe me. Undoubtedly, she wondered how I could have failed to get off a shot.

Once we emerged from the narrow draw, I was relieved to find us in ample grassland rising toward the Crazy Mountains to the northeast. I wished Pie would hunt closer so that I could see her always, but she reappeared often and I could keep track of her enough to allay my ascending fear, which was now based mostly on the decreasing angle of the sun and the spread of cold. To the west there was not a genuine horizon because the sun would fall behind the Bridger Range; as it declined toward the ice clouds above those hills its light seemed grayer. I hurried to keep up with Pie, who seemed in charge of things, and while I would have preferred a modest circle ending at Dr. Olsson's car, Pie wanted only to hunt straight into the wind with its scenting advantages, taking us away from what I viewed as safety and what little light we still had.

Again I found Pie on point and I was relieved, not because she had found game but because it gave me the opportunity to overtake her. I held the shotgun across my chest, thumb ready to slide the safety, and advanced. Several huge birds lumbered into the air: I fired and missed. These were sage hens and since they were scarce, Dr. Olsson had forbidden me to shoot them. Well, I hadn't shot one, though I had shot at one, and Dr. Olsson, had he been here, would have given me the cross look for which I had great respect and some fear. Perhaps I was triggerhappy. I'd have to be careful. Such thoughts were a kind of inattention and when I focused once more Pie was no longer in sight. I looked toward the sunset, then hurried in the direction I thought she had gone.

I never found her. I crossed the top of two broad coulees toward the Crazy Mountains, my last bearing before darkness fell. I'd thought there was time, but the sunset just snuffed out behind the Bridgers and I failed to resolve whether I was searching for Pie or trying to get myself to safety. I frantically reviewed the landmarks I had seen driving into the old road, but they were no longer of any use. I was lost.

Perhaps I'd never been lost before. I was startled by my state of accelerating dismay followed by panic. The broad field of references that I'd had in mind—that ridge of moraine, that tall spruce with the windslewed eastward branches, that rivulet, the two-track with its deceptively gradual change of direction, the yard light at the Swede's farm, the old windmill—were all arrayed as special markers reassuringly redundant, even cross-referenced. Yet something as slight as the bulb going out in the yard light, the perspective of the spruce that concealed the stunted limbs, the rising shadows which appeared to have the same mass as the landmarks before vanishing in twilight—all conspired to arouse the feeling that I no longer knew where I was, beset by the most ancient of enemies, darkness and cold. It was like the threat of being buried alive. I struck out in any direction, hoping that clarity would soon be at hand. It was not. I struck off elsewhere and felt a sort of eclipse. As each foray seemed to sag into confusion, the forays grew shorter and more rapid. Soon they were in circles, and I lost the capacity for traveling in a straight line. I felt confined and claustrophobic. I could not get out of this small and lightless room. Announcing itself, the darkness was cold, tangible as a black bird descending at stall speed.

A vertical slab of wet stone struck my face and I screamed, less from pain than from a rush of helplessness. I bumped into other things I couldn't identify. The river of stars overhead flared in a direction I could no longer grasp. My insignificance was so overwhelming that these impediments surrounded me with austere malevolence. My only hope was that by submitting myself to their awful power, I would be released. That was it! I would flatter the unknown and it would feel sorry for me! At last I caught on, saw the first fissure, and lay down in the densest brush I could find with my hands; I trained my humility on the hope of sunrise.

During the night and in those moments when I escaped my misery enough to think of how I had lost Pie, I was not entirely certain I wanted to survive. I imagined Dr. Olsson's spare room without her and my heart sank in agony. Even that agony was insufficient to preparing me for what I would feel when I finally was face-to-face with Dr. Olsson.

Sunrise revealed my hollow in the brush. When I stood up, it was easy to see the long slope of grassland to the south and, against its far edge, the winding county road I had driven. The light, the renewed orientation were insufficient consolation for the absence of Pie. By afternoon, I stood before Dr. Olsson. I had never seen him so sad. "You've let me down," he said. "I'm all through with you."

It was a long walk to my house, and the weather had turned worse. I had to navigate in the lee of the house and still I was soaked on arrival; I hardly noticed. The very abrupt loss of the approval of the only person who had ever believed in me was a blow of such magnitude as I had never experienced, to my stomach and mind at once. And apart from that, I feared that Pie was being eaten by coyotes or shot by a rancher finding her among his livestock.

The wind stopped shortly after midnight, and then the rain stopped as well. I slipped out from under the covers and dressed, tiptoeing downstairs through the sleeping household and out the kitchen door that led directly to the garage. It was difficult to raise the garage door without making noise, but I succeeded by raising it with agonizing slowness. In the light from the street, I could make out the contours of my father's black Ford, a six-cylinder coupe with its stick shift on the steering column. I opened the driver's door enough to slide in and shift the transmission into neutral, which allowed me to brace myself between the car and my father's workbench, put my shoulder against the grille and roll the car into the street, where its well-kept paint reflected the stars in the clearing sky. I drove several blocks before turning on the headlights, and soon I was tooling north toward the mountains and the last place I'd seen Pie. My feet were already blistered, but the pain was as nothing in the face of my mission, and I scarcely noticed.

I knew that I had little chance of finding her if she had disappeared into open country, but I was sure she had gotten lost, not abandoned me, and that she would seek out humanity somewhere. So I drove the county road along the base of the foothills and at each ranch I turned off the headlights, glided to a stop, walked to within sight of the buildings, and called as discreetly as I could, prolonging the call until I could be mistaken for a coyote. Several of the ranches had yard lights, and I was able to examine things quite closely while letting out my forlorn intonement of *"Pie,"* confident that if she ever heard me, she would respond. At a hardscrabble ranch-stead where Horsethief Creek came under the road I had to fight off the guard dog with a quickly acquired stick, long enough to make friends and send it whimpering back to the house. The dog had made so much noise confronting me that I called out Pie's name without discretion but drew no response.

I seemed to be leaving the territory where she might be. Certainly, I was close to a series of breaks, badlands almost, that Pie would have recognized as the end of her hopes for rescue. She had benefited from such good care that I had no doubt she would pin her last hopes on humanity.

I was excessively cautious approaching the next house, a dilapidated prefab with several cars parked in front and all its lights on. Drawing closer, I realized that some kind of party was still under way—strange in the middle of the week and so close to sunrise. I was frankly alarmed at the vehemence of the voices that emerged from the structure, a kind of mechanical hilarity and laughter that had become screams. I sat in the dark and stared at the shapes and sporadic shadows behind the drawn curtains. Overcoming hopelessness, I called out Pie's name firmly, confident that the people of the house would never notice above the din, and was answered by an inquisitive bark.

It was Pie.

She was tied with a piece of short, frayed rope to a steel tractor wheel, no food or water in sight. When she saw me, she leapt the length of the rope and somersaulted in midair. I untied it at the wheel and used it as a leash so that I could get Pie under cover of dark to my car and avoid the chance that her enthusiasm would give us away. Once in the car, we abandoned ourselves to emotion until I felt sufficiently collected to start the car, drive to a safe distance without lights, and then park again to go about removing the burs from Pie's coat and especially her ears, which were nearly rigid with encrustation. She was so unwilling to have them removed from the backs of her legs that I had to hold her mouth shut with one hand to keep from being nipped. I threw burs out the window by the handful, until finally I could run my fingers through her coat. The light was now sufficient for us to stop again at Horsethief Creek, where she drank greedily from its crystalline waters. Then we went to see Dr. Olsson, whom we found still in his bathrobe. He looked at me, then at Pie, a study in propriety and subdued emotion. Then he said, quite formally, I think, given the occasion, "Why don't you come in? I'll make tea. I think we have some planning to do."

4

I WAS HAVING A REMARKABLY SMOOTH SENIOR YEAR, my passion for the outdoors compensating for my lack of interest in team sports or, actually, my aversion to team sports. It disturbed me to even watch them, especially basketball, where fans huddled to watch two groups mob each other in their underwear. With football, I was attracted to the kick-off, but my interest waned thereafter. For two weeks that fall, I lived alone, looking after myself. My parents had gone to Idaho to care for Aunt Silbie, who was holed up dying of injuries sustained when a train hit her car, which she had parked on the tracks. She had once told me that she had kept her figure during her affairs with five different bosses while their wives grew fat. My mother was greatly consoled that the radio in Silbie's car was tuned to an inspirational religious station; and the wrecker, ambulance crew, and attending physician all attested that the car, nearly flattened, continued to broadcast uplifting messages even as it was towed away.

"The car just stalled on the tracks," asserted my mother with a glare.

I remembered the day I had been caught in flagrante by my parents and my mother called me an instrument of Lucifer and said that it would have been better that a millstone had been tied around my neck, etc., among other obloquies resulting in my isolation and unexpected grief at the death of my aunt, whose touch I would never forget. The harshness of my mother's brand of Christianity was forever impressed upon me.

I was going to college in Dr. Olsson's hometown and with his financial help. I would live in the home of his friends. Dr. Olsson did what he could to prepare me for my trip; I suppose he assumed some culture shock. "The Hansons are an old and important family in the town and as a resident of the Hanson home, under its protection, you will have nothing to fear from this new place. Karl Hanson is just the latest incarnation of a century of stability, as fine a man as I've ever known, and we've known each other all our lives." He hadn't said anything about Hanson's wife and so I asked. He paused, and then said, "I am older than Karl. Shirley was homecoming queen of Karl's class. She's a beautiful woman and Karl holds her in highest esteem." I could tell that Dr. Olsson had, for some reason, a low opinion of Shirley. This was enough for me: I couldn't wait to see Shirley!

I was soon on my way to Calabash College in northern Ohio, a tiny Congregationalist college that, once thriving, had nearly vanished during an imaginary Red scare when local farmers drove out the faculty with pitchforks. I was warmly greeted by my new host, Karl Hanson. He said, "Welcome" and then, after a pause, "welcome, welcome, welcome." I smiled all the way into the upper corners of the room. "And how is my honored friend Olsson?"

"Dr. Olsson is just fine. He sends his best."

"I wish we saw more of him. Y'know the bugger won't play golf. We could have had some winter trips to Camelback. Always out in the woods. Out in the prairie now, I suppose, chasing some dog. But what a guy, and a hell of a doc. He'd had enough. Dyed-in-the-wool bachelor gonna live his life, come hell or high water. He and *my* wife were sweethearts. She says he's still carrying a torch. You believe that? Me either. Female bull, is all. When Olsson tells me he's going to Montana, you could of knocked me over with a feather and, jeez, I've missed him ever since. We had the same Chinese tailor, came through once a year, shantung sport coats a tenth of what they ream you for here. I did try to get into the grouse-hunting thing, but first time he cut loose with his repeater I hit the ground. Not my game, not my game at all. Here, let me hang that up for you. I'll show you your room and then you can meet my ball and chain. Just kidding. Shirley's the queen of this castle! You could tell I was kidding, couldn't you? About Shirley?"

Calabash College had recovered in the intervening decades, somewhat, and served students who wished to attend college but could not find admission elsewhere. As a result, the student body was a heterogeneous group of idiots, local mediocrities, and brilliant misfits. Our backgrounds were so diverse that we acquired functional identities as the very first information about us emerged. As someone from the West, I found myself branded the campus cowboy. Wiley would have had a good laugh over that. An undernourished Portuguese boy from New Bedford was "a whaler." Girls who kissed with their tongues were whores. The kid with Hollywood mufflers on his jalopy was "Brick Track Jack" for the Indianapolis 500. The dorm room where we got free haircuts was Barber College, and so on. It was a loose atmosphere entirely, even from the standpoint of the administration. In my brief stint writing a sports column for the mimeographed campus weekly, I suggested that the chronically losing basketball team might look to ways to play better. The team beat me to a pulp, and even the president, a former tool-and-die executive, judged I had spoken out of turn. All of this was quite manageable, and in fact I did manage, with the expenses of my education borne mostly by Dr. Olsson and reduced by my living in a house owned and occupied by Karl Hanson and his wife. I'm sure Dr. Olsson had no way of knowing that in their subtle way the well-to-do and well-educated Hansons were every bit as strange as my own parents. They were only twice as old as me—that is, somewhere in their thirties, with Shirley sporting a sort of Jazz Age look that had lingered in these Midwestern pockets. The Hansons' house was somewhat disorderly, as their live-in black lady had gone back to Georgia. Each year a representative of Ton Yik Tailors of Hong Kong made the rounds of the Rust Belt, measuring local nabobs for custom-made suits, the equivalent of Hart, Shaffner and Marx at a third the cost; and each year Karl had a new one made, worsteds, wool, mohair, shantung sport jackets, and so on, all exploding from his closet on the second floor. Shirley's specialty was fox furs with the heads and black glass eyes that surmounted her fitted Chanel knockoffs and accented her excellent figure. I quickly noticed that excellent figure, and as soon as I could, I told her the men in my family were not long lived and that my greatest fear was dying a virgin. I just let this one soak while I went to class. I could tell by her expression that she couldn't decide quite what to do with me but that for the moment she would dismiss me as a hopeless goober.

I felt the futility of coming of age in the time of two iconic buffoons,

Ronald Reagan and John Wayne. And when I got to college I was still a very backward boy. I'll never forget the expressions on the Hansons' faces the first time they saw me licking my plate. But I'm a quick study, and it wasn't long before I was quite a conventional youth, managing at once to do my schoolwork well, get drunk, and manually inspect the occasional coed. I was well along in self-invention, representing myself to be the son of ranchers Gladys and Wiley. I'm ashamed to say that I was not proud of my own parents. I was at a ghastly stage in life, having raised faultfinding to a science. Some of this came from my Bible-crazed mother, who treated every phenomenon as a possible false sign or lying wonder.

At the beginning of my years at Calabash College, Karl Hanson and his wife, Shirley, were very kind to me. The Hansons had a strong social conscience, and this led them to hire a housekeeper, Audra Vasili-auskytė, a displaced person from somewhere in Eastern Europe, Lithuania, I think. Audra had come to America with her sister, and the two of them were gorgeous schemers. Audra's sister, Anya, had stolen a Great Lakes freighter captain away from his wife. Audra really stirred things up around the Hanson household, and in the end I was the beneficiary of her troublemaking. When Hanson would come in from work on cold winter evenings, Audra would help him off with his coat and even kneel before him to unbuckle his galoshes, a show enhanced by the omission of several blouse buttons. An excellent cook, she introduced Lithuanian dishes until once I heard Shirley cry out, "One more platter of kugelis and I'm outta here." Audra was extremely but coolly polite to Shirley. I was more age-appropriate to her enthusiasms, but she treated me with acidic contempt and took the fact of my social awkwardness as proof of homosexuality. She'd spit out, "You fairy!" when we passed in the upstairs corridor. Her mistake was assuming that I was not only gauche but also unobservant. Hence I was able to examine the cautious but steady gravitation of poor Karl into Audra's web.

In fact, I was more observant than even that: I took note of Shirley's vigilance as Audra went from helping with his heavy winter coat to meeting him at the door of his car, the better to touch his elbow as he clambered out. The biggest problem was that Audra at twenty-eight was, as Karl confided to me, "easy on the eyes." She was indeed: fresh-faced, cascading oak blond hair, and a tidy figure made poignant by the cheap Eastern European clothes she'd arrived with. She spoke an oddly correct schoolgirl English and radiated the sort of industry that predicted success in her new country. She was also a baseball nut, like Karl, and their amiable skirmishing over statistics drove Shirley to distraction. Audra feverishly studied baseball magazines in her room, as though she were trying to pass the bar exam. I several times sidled up to her, but she blew me off disdainfully, which I lamented as only a blue-balled late adolescent could. We each had our rooms on the north end of the second floor, at the end of a blind corridor, and shared a bathroom. That she sauntered around up there in her underwear, breasts spilling from an abbreviated bra, only emphasized how insignificant I was. Because of Audra, my energy was grossly depleted by jacking off, and had I not brought this vice under control, my grades surely would have fallen enough to keep me out of medical school. And what a way to fail a career in medicine!

At the point that Shirley looked likely to voice her indignation, I thought to reintroduce my manufactured fear of dying a virgin. From then on, it was merely a matter of waiting for Karl's next business trip to coincide with Audra's time off.

While Shirley drove Audra like a government mule, cooking, cleaning, polishing floors, washing windows from a ladder, cleaning eaves troughs, and ironing, Audra never lost her composure; only I knew how close to eruption her moods could be as she shoved me out of the way en route to the bathroom or pretended to spit in my face when I smiled at her. Karl only occasionally asked Audra to do something, and usually it was something quite small, like keeping an eye out for lost keys or glasses. If Shirley was present, Audra complied like a dutiful servant. If Shirley was not present, Audra let her joy at being of service to Karl shine in her eyes before purring, "Of course I find dose glasses. A lawyer must be able to see!" A pause before, a pause after. Then Karl, quietly, "Thank you, Audra."

Early college days were really a delight for me, my first chance at disappearing into a crowd. In so many places I had grown up, especially in the rug-shampoo years, when we were pretty much transients, ignorance was its own reward and standing out in school was a sure way to get beaten up. But I'd heard John Wayne say, "Life is tough. Life is tougher if you're stupid." And I took the Duke's words seriously, trying to be smart, haunting bookmobiles and the mildewed Carnegie libraries of the American West.

My clothing came principally from the Salvation Army store in town, no hardship implied: with a bit of imagination a person could dress well there and with great originality. I bought numerous Hawaiian shirts discarded by servicemen, bowling shirts and shoes, porkpie hats, and so on. This gave me a reputation on the tiny campus of a real sophisticate, a hipster even, my retro mishmash more mysterious than comprehensible. My great find at the Sally was a Chinese robe that had been dropped off by the family of a deceased Presbyterian missionary. It was a glorious blue silk garment with macramé buttons and a thin lining of down. Drawing upon my new reputation and the delightfully sordid memories of my late aunt out there in Idaho, I wore this on my first college date. It was a warm evening in early fall and I stood at the entrance to the girls' dormitory barefoot in nothing but the luxurious blue robe and a distinctive porkpie hat with a varnished pheasant feather in its band. The girl, Nancy Bellwood of Owosso, Michigan, was slow adjusting to my appearance and my anxiety-driven shower of non sequiturs, but as her friends gathered and approved enthusiastically of my festive getup, Nancy's zeal soon followed. It wasn't long before we found ourselves by the small and slow woodland river that bounded our campus; turtles adorned the low limbs of trees overhanging the water, dragonflies sparkled, birdsong poured from the forest. I rested against the trunk of a great beech whose canopy scattered the evening light. Nancy had all but vanished under the robe and, to prolong my enjoyment, I concentrated on the little fuzzy balls on the back of her tennis socks. "Caramba!" she cried through the robe, reminding me that she was a Spanish major. As soon as it was over, I began thinking again of my studies. I loved to study. It used to be that when people asked me what I was interested in I would say, "Electricity!" Now I told them, "Science!" Ooh, la la!

I admired the Hansons' home. So many houses in these small towns of the old Midwest were handsome. The towns themselves were beautiful and had been more so, said the locals, before the elms that once shaded them died of blight. Compared to the towns of the West they seemed remarkably wooded, sheltered really, and more contained than the sprawling towns I knew with only sagebrush to stop their spread. I saw photographs of this town before Dutch elm disease, and it looked like a huge green corsage set out in rolling farmland. The Hanson family had been in this house since 1841, and the attic held the Civil War uniforms of Hanson forebears, including the riddled one of a Hanson who died at Chickamauga, having served in a storied unit of Swedish immigrants. The spacious basement, now holding a stout coal-fired furnace, was said to have hidden escaped slaves. I particularly enjoyed the oak window seats with cushions fitted out into the bays that looked upon the small, well-tended backyard with its old roses and ancient black walnut tree. Here I sat with my schoolbooks, in my Chinese robe, entertaining unrealistic hopes for my future: my daydreaming, my fantasy life was still highly impractical.

The house was quite dark inside, enclosing, and had fireplaces in all the public rooms. A formal dining room opened onto an old utilitarian kitchen with a built-in gas range. The wood counters were worn to hollows, their edges held intact by steel bands and acorn-headed screws. It was a small space, and when I helped Shirley prepare meals there we rubbed against each other between stove and refrigerator with a steadily increasing frequency. The duration of these encounters was directly related to the complexity of the meals which were aimed at Karl Hanson's enthusiastic palate; therefore we avoided the simple preparations and natural-food approaches advocated by Gloria Swanson, Hollywood vegetarian, resorting instead to complex glazes and various potted things, an elaborate cassoulet, and so forth. By the time Hanson complained of gout and a defiant waistband, Shirley and I were regularly dry-humping next to the counter that held the big chrome Mixmaster and Pyrex coffee machine.

In my second year, I started studying Spanish, abandoned the Chinese costume, and affected serapes. By now my reputation as a sort of Western hipster had vanished and I was viewed simply as a damn fool, a fool with snow falling on his serape four months a year and with mariachi 78s on an old brown record player.

I'd better note that my relationship with Shirley, while steamy, was inconclusive and passed as ironic household play—that is, on Shirley's part. I seemed all too caught up in it, my experience having been confined to the pleasure my aunt Silbie dished out, and dished out directly. This was different. I resolved that some sort of legitimate barrier based in the marriage vows of the Hansons was going to require me to finish the work myself after one of Shirley's humpfests.

Between astronomy and civics, an unscheduled two hours found me either at the library or back at the Hansons' for an afternoon snack, usually prepared by Shirley. Since these were such obvious opportunities for hanky-panky, we made a point of avoiding it, and the result was that my snacks were often beautifully prepared little meals that sent me back to class content, and reconciled to my lost opportunities. Because I was so unassertive at these times, I blamed myself for awaiting Shirley's initiative and wondered what might have happened if I'd just had the nerve to reach out and touch her. The chance that she would scream, "Get your hands off me!" just as Hanson popped in filled me with terror.

Today she served me a lovely little wedge of homemade shepherd's pie and a green salad with walnuts and olives. She asked me, "Are you taking any history courses?" She had a beautiful smile on her pretty face, her auburn hair piled atop her head with a few strands tumbling over her forehead.

"I had American history last term."

"That's my favorite."

"American?"

"Mm. Especially the Civil War."

"That was good," I said.

"The Revolutionary War, well, you see those paintings, they don't really resemble us. But the Civil War, they had photos."

"It makes it so much closer to our own time," I said, fishing. I knew that I had sort of missed the point, so I added a few details about the incomprehensibility of the Revolutionary War period, Washington's wig, knee socks, wooden teeth, three-cornered hats, the whole nine yards. "Plus, they didn't free the slaves."

"We can't even imagine what *that* must have been like. Try to picture Michael Jordan or Bill Cosby as *slaves.*"

"I can't."

"Imagine how uppity they'd be?"

"I know, I know."

"So, let's confine our thoughts to the Civil War."

"Well, in American history," I said, "we touched on lots more than that. The Teapot Dome Scandal and so on."

"The difference is, the Civil War has such a hold on our imagination."

"Amen to that." I wasn't trying to be an asshole; I just didn't know how to follow this line of conversation. At the same time, I intuited a lot of passion behind Shirley's enthusiasm for that war. I felt so lost that I finally asked her why we kept talking about this particular subject; that was about as bold as I got in those days. She gave me a hard look and said, "I just lay the rail. I don't drive the train."

Shirley got the idea that Audra had the hots for me. This was no accident. Audra, who treated me with such savagery on the second floor, grew girlish in my proximity on the first floor. She seemed to have the capacity to emit light dew from her skin and add starlight to her eyes at will. By fluttering around me in the presence of both Hansons she produced a double effect: Hanson began to treat me with a new formality that verged on a surprising coolness; Shirley, doing housework for appearances upon Hanson's return, always straightened slightly when Audra entered the room, then turned with a wintry smile to greet the three of us without focusing on any one, a teacher welcoming a new class. In this atmosphere, Audra swam like a happy fish looking to Hanson's every need. Upstairs, she told me to quit acting like a member of the family: I was just a boarder. "And a fairy."

Hanson's law firm, three men, was small but it enjoyed a statewide reputation. That it had never departed this modest town in the generations following its founding by Hanson's great-grandfather gave it an old-fashioned dignity unshared by high-powered competition elsewhere. It was still a prestigious place to have one's legal work done, and this reputation was reflected in the decorum of the partners, who dressed with nostalgic severity and always paused before answering questions. I don't know how else to say this, but the longer Audra was in the house the more peculiar were Hanson's observations of his partners: one came to be described as "slow" and the other, now near retirement, was astonishingly referred to as a "prize boob." A far cry from the collegiality of old. These comments left Shirley wide-eyed, and their being offered in Audra's presence gave them an effect not experienced in this household before. Hanson had always seemed so somber, politely somber, though it's true he was jollier these days, despite the new sarcasm, and his clothes brighter. His partners now looked grimly drab in his company. When Ton Yik Tailors came through that fall, Hanson ordered some high-spirited and entirely ghastly plaid sport clothes. Families—in this case households—are always evolving; on balance, ours was now more pleasant, that is, livelier. A pretty young woman always has this effect on groups, and Audra was very pretty. Anyone could see that she was slowly turning Karl Hanson into an idiot.

I came in from class wet from a spring snow flurry, my books damp and my worn-out shoes letting water into my socks. I went straight upstairs to change into something dry and warm. Audra was waiting for me in the hallway. She was leaning against the wall, her hands behind her at the small of her back and palms pressed to the wall; her chin was on her chest and she was regarding me with patronizing amusement. The single low-wattage lightbulb that frugally illuminated the hallway gave the scene an old-time Hollywood quality. "I have a small word with you?"

"Sure," I said, simply hating my all-purpose enthusiasm.

"I'm thinking you show much fondness for Mrs. Hanson."

"Yes," I barked, "very fond. Very nice lady."

"Ooh no, is not what I mean. Is what I mean is *fond*."

"I don't know about *that*."

"Well, is not important. Is more important that Mrs. Hanson is *fond* of you."

"Well, that would be nice."

She snickered and I found it a bawdy snicker; curiously I noticed that I was morally indignant at this insinuation when I barely thought of anything besides sex with Mrs. Hanson, who exuded the ripe sensuality of early middle age. It proved another opportunity for Audra to one-up me: "I just hope the two of you don't upset that nice man!" she cried, turning abruptly into her room and slamming the door. It worked: Karl Hanson *was* a fine man and I felt guilty.

As part of my obligations to the Hansons, I seemed to be something of a yard boy, for Shirley was a passionate but careless gardener. Before I arrived at the Hanson house, she had made a terrific effort to renew the perennials around the place—and there were many little flower beds under windows, around airyways and trees, along the stone sidewalk and between the house and the garage, which had a trotting-horse weather vane. But she couldn't quite remember where she put things, and so in springtime she was consumed with mystery and anticipation as she awaited the appearance of flowers.

"I really don't like spring," she said to me as I followed her with an armful of tools—a forked implement for digging out weeds, pruning shears in three sizes, and an empty watering can. "Spring isn't about hope for the coming season. It's about being sick of winter."

"Can't it be both?"

"Shut up."

"Okay."

"See the dead ones? Can't you tell by the bark? Those are the ones you lop off. Right close to the trunk. I already showed you this once."

I had to keep one eye on her as I pruned because she changed her mind from task to task and I rarely had the chance to finish anything. My main job was keeping up as she strode around directing my efforts here and there while quite obviously drifting off in thought as I started each thing destined for incompletion. One bed I was supposed to spade up for annuals turned out to be full of crocus bulbs. She's the one who forgot she'd put them there, but she blew up: "Christ! Couldn't you stop digging when you saw the first one?"

"I didn't know what it was." I thought it was onions.

"What it was, was an annual bulb, for crying out loud!" But then she ran her hand over my buttocks while watching the street, so I felt I was forgiven. She said, "Baby, let's go to Florida."

5

THE HANSONS ALWAYS ENJOYED A COCKTAIL between Karl's return from work, his face often heavy with fatigue, and supper. One end of the living room served as a small private bar of a kind that flourished before the age of the exaggerated "wet bar." A leaded-glass cabinet held glasses, cocktail shakers with the patina of age, a cylindrical device into which CO_2 cartridges were inserted for the making of one's own carbonated water, a leather-bound ice bucket; then, on display, the "top brands" lined up with their somber labels to the fore. I would have a ginger ale on the rocks, while the Hansons tossed back highballs, invariably Crown Royal and soda. Audra, having long since made herself the bartender, lately cast melancholy glances at the three of us, once we had our drinks, before making an uncharacteristically mousy exit. This evening, when Karl came in trailing the smell of cold and snow, he joined us vigorously at the bar, clapping his hands together in a spirited effort at warming them, and directed Audra to make it a stiff one. I already had my ginger ale, resentfully proffered by Audra, Shirley her accustomed highball, and Audra now prepared Karl's, filling the whiskey to the usual level, then teasingly drizzling some a bit before adding soda. Karl watched every drop with enthusiasm, then suddenly said, "Audra, it's time you joined us for a drink." I saw Shirley cut her eyes at him, but if he noticed he didn't let on. Audra posed primly at the bar, indicating by the tiny space between her thumb and forefinger that a small amount of the libation was all that a little princess should want. To cover the silence, Shirley went on a bit about what a cold, snowy spring it was, and Karl, turning from the preparation of Audra's drink, raised his glass to one and all and said, "We need the moisture."

· · ·

Hanson asked me to help him in the yard. He did very little work around his property and was a fellow best seen in a suit and tie. In fact, on the weekends when he donned work clothes, usually worn-out elements of his office attire, he seemed almost a different person. As a fourth-generation lawyer in a small town, he supported a tradition that prided itself on its separation from people with work-hardened hands. He was not exactly prissy; delicate was more like it. He picked up any tool, even a leaf rake, suspiciously. But once he started, the lawyer came out and he became an authority—"You don't do it like that, let me show you," etc.—until the appearance of the first blister, which he regarded with an accusing and tragic air.

We raked leaves, but we didn't rake them very long before he stopped and, clutching the rake handle against his chest, leaned toward me and said, "I hope you will extend all the courtesies of a gentleman to Audra."

"I sure will," I said.

"I'm confident Audra will offer no provocation whatsoever. She is a brave wanderer in a very cold world. I don't want to say defenseless, but there it is. I know you'll respect that."

"Why even tell me this?"

A spark of irritation crossed his face. "Why? Because you're an aardvark and you never know what an aardvark will do."

I had no idea if this was a compliment or not. Later, I looked up "aardvark" without bringing any light to Hanson's remark. I didn't think of myself as a living fossil, nor did I eat ants and burrow at night. I was surprised, though, at Karl's concern for Audra.

Hanson volunteered to walk Audra through change of address requirements for her green card, but it meant going to his office and getting some help from his secretary. Shirley offered to make lunch for me, and so I came back between classes and found bacon-lettuce-and-tomato sandwiches on either side of the dining room table, as well as a mountain of material about Florida vacations. Shirley sat down heavily and stared at the pile as though this were the source of her fatigue. "I've been through all of this and as soon as you finish lunch, I'm throwing it out. The trouble is, we're stuck with the dates of your vacation and finding someplace in Florida that's not a spring break hellhole has been a problem. However, I have not failed us, Honey-Child. I've found a sedate little island where we can spend sunny days on the sand gazing out at the Gulf, a real change of pace. We'll eat fresh seafood, collect shells, feed pelicans, ride bicycles—"

"Hide the weenie?" I asked through a mouthful of BLT. I thought I was being funny but Shirley didn't take it well. She swept up the Florida material and left the room.

When she came back in, she said, "When people have time, and commitment, the full benefits of their God-given sexuality, they do not call it 'hide the weenie.' "

"I'm very sorry."

"Of course you are. You're not stupid. You're ignorant. That's worse."

In the evening, as the sunset watchers were leaving, the locals with their dogs and the vacationers, Shirley and I, with frozen drinks in to-go cups, followed the avenue of banyan trees to the Gulf. Then we swam, sometimes, shoulder to shoulder, as far out as we could go. We swam naked, out until our feet couldn't touch the bottom, and made love in a silence disturbed only by the lapping of salt water stirred by our movement. Another time, during the day, with other swimmers nearby, this antic lawyer's wife manipulated me underwater, surprising me when the sperm floated to the surface. Evidently I made a bit of noise, as the other swimmers stared and Shirley admonished me sharply to "get a grip," adding that there was no reason to behave like a trained seal. This all was new. I had had the straightforward initiation at the hands of my libidinous aunt, but she seemed to know exactly what she wanted and what I ought to have. With Shirley it was quite different; lots of elements imperfectly understood by me bore upon our activity.

Anthropologists say that every sexual act is a cultural collision, and I think this was true of my Shirley days. Shirley, I learned, was a hometown girl from the wrong side of the tracks, and her marriage to Karl was widely regarded as a rapprochement between elements that had not mingled since the nineteenth century. When Shirley told me one dinnertime quite proudly that both of their great-grandfathers had fought in the Civil War, Karl said, "Mine was an officer" and Shirley said, "Mine was born in America." If Shirley ran up too many charges at the local department store, Karl said she was trying to ruin him. I don't think Shirley understood any of this, and she had little contact with her own family or the people she'd grown up with, though they lived nearby. When Karl said, as he more than once did, that some social event was beneath him, Shirley said that everything is beneath you if you're on Mars. Karl found most things to be "too new," and he quaintly—I think this was him trying to be funny—viewed my home in the West as being on the frontier; he called it a "homestead" and asked if I, like Audra, wanted to apply for a green card. These days, Karl was full of merry jokes that left people uncomfortable. I did like Karl but noticed that he had no friends. To be fair, it's hard to have friends in an old small town if you are born to be dignified.

My sojourn in the Rust Belt certainly made me appreciate my home-place more than before I left. We had beautiful mountain ranges that kept their snow all summer, though very few of those of us who lived there ever went into them. We thought only out-of-towners went into the mountains, as most Westerners lived in town and were town people like anywhere else. My father used to say that the only thing that set us apart was cheap electricity. Some of that had changed of course, once we learned to keep outsiders from glomming our assets by appreciating them more than we had. It had been a long time since we proudly pointed out that you couldn't eat scenery. That sentiment belonged to an earlier generation, the ones with "Treasure State" license plates nailed to the garage. Tell someone today you can't eat scenery, and they'll put you in the old folks' home. Where I came from, the wind was the big issue, until you figured out that wind was the price of space.

Anyone might wonder how someone as inadequate as I was could get even as far as I got. Here is where I learned from the aardvark, which the encyclopedia informed me was known for its diligence. I was diligent. All the survival skills I had learned growing up in a family adrift I now focused on my studies. I went from ineducable waster to a driven explorer of my own ignorance; learning was a treasure hunt in a land of facts and ideas. I lit on the health of the human body because it was such a complicated system and would hold my interest. But for the time being, the only human body that held my interest belonged to Shirley, and it was certainly good enough to keep me going even when, resigned to her own indiscriminate carnality, she embraced me and called me a sap. I even had a twinge of jealousy for poor deceived Karl; "deceived" would turn out to be the wrong word, but I was jealous enough to ask Shirley if Karl made love to her often. "Yes," she said, "unfortunately."

Naively, I asked, "Then why do it?" She told me to think of it as customer golf. We settled in on the island, but I never really grew accustomed to the parade of sunburned fat people carrying ice-cream cones, or the noise. I had never been anywhere as noisy as Florida. Airplanes went back and forth overhead, people sped around on various motorized things, and horn honking was as popular as in New York. The leaf blowers roared from sunup to sundown. That many people with no good reason to be there filled the place with a kind of giddiness, not just everyday giddiness but the kind that precedes despair and catastrophe. It was nice to be warm, but the television was dominated by weather reports holding out expectation of more warmth or a rootless fear of cooling. The local weatherman, a black homosexual in a Palm Beach suit, could say, "Some chance of precip" with the air of a man headed to the gallows. Inability to control the weather fed disquiet, since, except for the weather, most would rather be anyplace but here.

Time was running out, and we needed to add a little something to our fling to raise its tone, so we made dinner reservations at a nice waterside restaurant and skipped lunch. I think we both knew that if we ended up at a quality restaurant with leisurely service and candles on the table, but had no appetite and little to say, we would be in for a very uncomfortable ride. I was pretty much over the sex and acted about like a pump jack in an Oklahoma oil field, prepared to perform day and night with my mind elsewhere. It made absolutely no difference to Shirley, adding to my disquiet at being something of a tool.

Looking over her menu, Shirley grabbed my forearm in hilarity. "I should order red snapper! Get it?"

"I'm afraid I don't." I did, but I didn't want to let on. But I asked her if she'd tried the planked pork.

"Ha ha ha." Then when I ordered a steak, she said, "Good God!" and ordered grouper, and another round. I was very pleased with the effect of the drinks. At first, sitting across the table, Shirley seemed aggressive and worried, her blond streaks symmetrical as the marks on a tiger, the way her nostrils flared when her mouth was closed, all worrisome. But the cocktails cast a spell, like the gauzy shots in the old tearjerkers, so that by the arrival of my sprawling T-bone I was in love. Even though I recognized that in this case love was a Russian import made from potatoes, it was enough to believe in for the time being. I reached under the table to put my hand in her pants as she grinned absently at the grouper. "I'm going to tell the waiter what you're doing." I withdrew and went at the steak with knife and fork like a drummer boy. The booze was rushing back and forth between my spine and my brain.

We couldn't wait to get back to the room. We had dined with such languor that the waiter was startled when we abruptly asked him for our bill and to "make it snappy." I don't know what chemical combination had us in such a rush, but nothing was happening fast enough for us. I had such trouble getting the key into the lock of our room I was afraid Shirley would fly off the handle. Looking left and right while I struggled, she had already begun unbuttoning her clothes. I wasn't handling the pressure and resorted to kneeling in front of the doorknob to sight in the key. Inside, the phone was ringing. Once the door opened, Shirley shot past me to grab the ringing telephone. Phone call no good. I remained on my knees as I listened to Shirley from the doorway. I smiled at several hotel guests as they passed. I heard her say, "I was just about to call you . . . I already thought of that. Is there a problem?" This question was the last thing Shirley said for quite a long time, then, "I don't think there's any need to speak to him . . . I don't understand why you're insisting, why you find it so important, except for your ongoing need to have everything your own way . . . Very well, Karl." She held the phone against herself, her face drained of all color, and said to me, "He knows. He and Audra have gotten together. He told me not to come home." I arose and crossed the room awkwardly, as my feet had gone to sleep.

"Hullo?" Then I was serenaded by Karl and Audra, "Love Is a Many-Splendored Thing," quite briefly, as they really didn't know the words beyond those of the title, which they repeated. Then Karl alone on the line, in a barely recognizable voice, flattened by hate, telling me I should never have tried this with a lawyer. Addressing me as "Loverboy," he asked me if I had "tried all the holes"; when I failed to answer he said, "How d'you like the smell?" Then, "I know you're still on the line." I confirmed that I was.

I said, "Karl, we wish you all the luck in the world. I hope you enjoy Audra. I know I did." I could feel this one fall as though into a dark well. I hung up.

Shirley demanded to know exactly what Karl had said to me; I thought mentioning the holes was out of the question and so I said, "He wanted to know how I felt about the smell."

"The smell! What smell?"

"I guess your smell."

"I hope you told that sonofabitch I don't have a smell."

"I thought it would be best if I just didn't say anything."

"Maybe so. Never wrestle with a pig. You both get covered with shit and the pig likes it. My smell! He's gonna pay for that one. When I get through kicking his ass, he'll never get up."

Shirley was gnawing the inside of her cheek, her eyes slewing around the room. Suddenly her face went calm. "You and Audra, eh? That could help." In the little time remaining, we tried to enjoy ourselves in bed; the effort held no appeal. Shirley asked if she was as good a lover as Audra, and when I reminded her that I made up the whole thing about Audra, she jumped out of bed and shouted, "Don't you dare say that!" We drifted off fairly early in our room overlooking a canal and a golf course. I awakened in the middle of the night to see Shirley standing, just her silhouette, in the dark window that gave onto the balcony. I then went back to sleep until outboard motors in the canal woke me up. Shirley was gone. I knew she was headed north.

Since she left me without enough money to get back to Ohio, I was obliged to stay in the room making frantic calls to anyone I thought could arrange transportation. In the end, good Dr. Eldon Olsson, way out in Montana, extended his credit card, and I was free to go. I had a lot of explaining to do, but Olsson said he'd seen through Shirley in the seventh grade when he had a crush on her, and if this was what it took to liberate his old friend Hanson, it was certainly cheap at the price. This did not incline me to help Shirley with a made-up story about Audra, but I was never asked and all my imaginary rehearsals for undermining her cause came to nothing. She didn't need my help; she made off with half of Karl's estate anyway, and five years later Audra got the rest.

I've lost track of Shirley, who lived in Florida for many years. I saw her later at Dr. Olsson's funeral, but by that time she was back in her hometown, residing in an assisted-living facility. Before addressing the issues having to do with finding new lodging and staying out of the witness box, I felt I had to absorb the full impact of this unsavory life episode, one that left me unnecessarily cautious in matters of ardor. This was too bad because I was an affectionate person who fell in love easily and might have brought greater enrichment to my life if I hadn't always smelled a rat at the pleasantest times. Karl seems to have made the most of things in his own buttoned-down, impervious way. The following I learned from Eldon Olsson: after Karl lost the fine old family house and was living in a downtown condominium, he befriended the representative of Ton Yik Tailors who came through annually measuring businessmen for suits. On successive visits, the friendship deepened and Karl went to Hong Kong, where he met the consortium of clothiers, which took him on as legal counsel for their growing U.S. activities. Karl married a Chinese girl and only came to the States on business. "He finally found happiness," said Dr. Olsson, adding, "I hope the same for you, Doctor."

6

I HAD BEEN BACK FOR ALMOST A YEAR, a practicing physician in my hometown, without making it clear to the community that I had entirely escaped my formerly anarchic ways. I don't think anyone doubted my skills or my commitment as a doctor, but I continued to demonstrate social deficiency and poor judgment. I guess I wasn't quite ready for rules-and-regulations just yet. Twice one week, I had gone out to the reserved parking lot to see an almost familiar figure standing there irresolutely, not looking my way, not occupied with anything, but somehow giving the impression that I was why she was there. I was startled by a voice at my window. "I wonder if I could trouble you for a ride. My sister left without me." I turned to face a young woman, attractive but for the anomaly of penciled-in eyebrows, unusual on someone this age. There was a familiarity about the way she grasped the window of my car. I would have known her if she'd worked at the clinic. Her pleasant smile playfully suggested that she saw right through me, promising preliminary banter, something I noticed once she was in the car and I could see her tanned, shapely arms. She wore bib-front overalls and a T-shirt that said, DO NOT RESUSCITATE. Her dark hair was cut short. She said, "Clarice."

"Hi, Clarice. Where can I drop you?"

"How 'bout taking me before you drop me?" she said with a wheezy laugh. "You allow ciggies in your world?"

"Sorry." I was too old for Clarice, but I fretted that disallowing the cigarette emphasized that fact. I wanted to start smoking again.

She pushed the cigarette back in its pack and the pack in the purse that seemed too small to be hung from shoulder straps: it was hardly bigger than a wallet. I looked away as I always did when women's purses were opened. I always felt they contained things it would be improper to see. The contents were so baffling as to be sometimes downright scary, as was the witchlike way their owners found things in the chaos.

"Head straight for the wrong side of the tracks."

I took her to mean the underpass to the north. It used to be the wrong side of the tracks, but that had changed. It had elevated its tone, though the cars at the curb that would never run again, the plastic toys of children who'd grown up and left ten years before, were still there. I noted a tiny ruby on Clarice's finger. At least I thought it was a ruby; there was some sort of stone they once put in mood rings, and on the chance this was the same mineral I wondered what dark red could mean. Whatever it was or meant, I no longer saw the things passing my windshield, not even the woman out in her yard, waving bemusedly and looking more at Clarice than at me. I guess I must have noticed her, though. Enough to feel uncomfortable.

A kind of stillness settled in the car; whatever passed beyond its windows had lost its sound track. The first indication I had that Clarice was aware of the change was when she ran the end of her finger around the top edge of her pants where it met her belly. She said, "It wouldn't take a rocket scientist to figure out what's on your mind."

I prided myself on the big sincere sigh I heaved. "Probably not."

She flashed a brilliant smile, full of heedless youth, followed quite abruptly by an indifferent gaze out the window on her side. She said, "Cross your fingers."

"I certainly will!"

What a fool.

She evidently took a rain check on putting me away for keeps and said, "But first you need to give me a hand. Turn here." We wound off toward a grade school, a railroad repair shop, a transmission rebuilder, and an electricians' warehouse. Two more turns and we parked next to a hot dog stand. We got out and walked over to it; a man and his daughter were being served by a girl Clarice's age, and when they had paid and gone, the girl, hands plunged into thick, silvery hair, began arguing with Clarice about Clarice showing up late. She shoved the cash box at Clarice, grabbed her purse, and said she was never coming back. Clarice flashed me a smile and said you couldn't get good help anymore. I saw the girl trying to overhear the remark, still spoiling for a fight. Clarice noticed and said, "I got it: never coming back. Bye."

Clarice had missed an appointment with her parole officer and was going to see him now. "He'll let me in. It's a formality." If I could just man the stand for an hour and a half, she assured me, one of my dreams would come true. To a person of my age, a physician, this should have been little more than a charming anomaly. At least common sense should have overruled my quite natural instinct, but it didn't. Clarice, tall and well shaped, was only too happy to let this sink in. I took in several ghostly images from my erotic future while running down my afternoon appointments: psoriasis, I could blow that off; the tenth visit about the same heart murmur as against Clarice splayed beneath me—the eagle has landed!—and so when I got to Jerome Bugue's tennis elbow, I knew it had no chance against Clarice's cervix, the gorgeously flushed perineum stretched taut by elevated thighs. God knows, I could sell a few hot dogs for that! I'm not a saint!

Next thing I knew she had my car and I had a customer. I forked up a glistening wiener from the steamer and placing it firmly in the bun I had wedged open in my left hand. I reached it to my customer, a mechanic in blue coveralls, name over the pocket, with no unease at taking his snack into an oil-blackened hand. I pointed to the condiments while he counted out exact change. As he walked off, I said, "I hope you enjoy that hot dog!" He stopped walking, back to me, and slowly turned.

"I intend to," he said.

A number of people seemed to be leaving their workplaces at three o'clock, and a significant number of those wanted hot dogs. I got a few tips. Only one, a teen with an anachronistic flattop, ran off without paying, and it seemed to me that all the planning—get-away-car and so forth was hardly justified by the savings. Generally, the hot dogs aroused enthusiasm, and finally they aroused mine. I hadn't eaten a real meat by-product junk hot dog in a decade, but this time I had two of them, oozing with sweet relish and mustard, some of which ended up on my clothes. My dentist, Ted Conroy, parked his Audi right in front of the stand, stuck his red head out the window, shut off the engine, and as he came to the stand I thought fast.

"What's this?"

"I'm helping out a friend."

"I didn't know you had such friends."

"You want a hot dog?"

"And tear up my Swiss electric toothbrush?"

"It was just a thought."

"You stay away from them too. They're nothing but lips, hoofs, and noses."

"I'll be careful."

"I don't know who your friends are, but this is not in the best interest of our community."

"Ted, give it a rest. They're hot dogs. They predate our community by a century." I was defensive about my little afternoon rebellion. As Conroy got back into the low-anthracite Audi, he said, "Distal erosion number twenty-seven crown. You're a year late."

After Ted, no one came and I was alone. I held absurdity at bay as I stood behind the open-air counter, a colonnade of old ash and burr oak trees ending at a distant Stop sign. A dog slept in the street. A yellow fish-and-wildlife-service helicopter passed overhead carrying fingerlings to high country lakes. The westerly breeze that had stirred leaves all day long was visible now only in the highest treetops.

I was still there at dark. I had eleven dollars and fifty-four cents in small change, which I'd put in my pants pocket for safekeeping, and then had trouble keeping my pants up from the weight of all that metal. And I had no car. An indeterminate countdown ensued while I held off facing the music. I began to tell the story to myself as I would have to tell it to the authorities. The raw facts—I cancel medical appointments to run a hot dog stand in hopes of being compensated by a dissolute young woman—were unpromising. Very often when one is out of line entirely, invoking the Good Samaritan is advantageous. Good Samaritans are associated with failed foresight, and it seems to belong to most people's embedded memory that anything beginning with "I was just trying to help" with its undertones of grievance is liable to lead to unintended consequences, of which ours is the golden age.

A streetlamp came on and shortly after the moths, the bats arrived. She needed a ride, then remembered missing an appointment and if I would just step temporarily out of my role as a misguided town physician and be a Good Samaritan I would understand she had no resources to offer save her humble thanks. "You want to spend time with me? Sell some hot dogs." I suppose I thought I'd heard what appeared to be an opportunity.

I started to walk, the leaden cluster of coins pressing against my leg.

To this day, I don't know why my car seemed, when I first found it, like a death ship. It was moving slowly with the lights out under a canopy of trees. In good light it was green, but in the late dusk it was black. It was an ordinary car, but watching its quiet passage aroused all my sorrows at once—the death of my mother, my father's amiable despair and vigil of mortality, and the suspicion that I was losing faith in my own work. I say "my work," but perhaps I mean myself. I understood it was only a car, but there was something unnatural to my impulse to just let it go that frightened me. I knew I couldn't do so without consequences, and they were more than was explained by the inappropriate desire the present driver had occasioned. Even this lacked candor as the scene flashed before me: my recriminations, the car reclaimed, remorse, the payoff as the minor fault was made flesh. Such inner conflict caused the hesitation during which the darkened vehicle drifted from view several blocks ahead. I began to stalk it. I began to stalk my own car!

There were times when I felt a sourceless smile forming on my lips, and these times could last for weeks. I mention this only because it is this faint, amiable smile that has always involuntarily formed when I was about to say or do something with a high element of risk. Why the fleeting glimpses of my own automobile in the dark should produce this rictus is no clearer to me than the elation I felt years ago during the tango fiasco. I suppose going over Niagara Falls in a barrel had some of this mysterious glory—the slap of river on the staves, the magnificent silence as the barrel falls through air, the prospect of catastrophe with its great plunging sound, the final gurgle inaudible to the many spectators, the honeyed ease beyond.

It crossed a few hundred yards away, and then crossed again. I waited several minutes, my eyes riveted on the empty intersection. Here it came: she was driving in circles or around a block, a block of interest, an air of waiting. The next time it went through, I hurried to the corner where she had passed and leaned against the trunk of a splendid amur maple, an ancient thing from the day of the horse; indeed, I rather formed my body to it until I felt myself becoming part of its deep shadow. I opened my mouth to soften the sound of my breathing and felt a zephyr in the branches scatter dark camouflage overhead. Just then I spotted a garbage can, still on the sidewalk from the last collection. I rushed out and rolled it into the intersection, then retreated to my maple.

As I waited, I thought of tomorrow's patients. What had happened to me today? I desperately wanted to see my patients. Harelipped Eleanor with repetitive stress injuries from her three decades of washing dishes at an interstate truck stop: I may have given her too many cortisone shots, but what relief they provided! Onetime jockey Dan Devlin, a near midget, had a tiny nursery that produced nice perennials—emphysema. A couple of pre-football physicals and then lunch. Couldn't remember the p.m. sched.

Here came my car. Proximity had not dispelled its lightless mystery, its frictionless deathship glide. I watched it slow down as if it were driving itself, approach the garbage can, and stop. I waited until I heard the creak of the driver's door, then moved quickly to the passenger's side and let myself in. The noise of rolling the can out of the way must have muffled my entrance because Clarice climbed behind the wheel and shut her door. It was a moment before she saw me in the shadows and screamed. Seeing who it was, she calmed down and told me I could keep all the hot dog money and wouldn't have to pay for any I'd eaten. I think that when I heard the indignation while turgidly explaining that I was capable of paying for my own hot dogs, I realized who I was for the first time—a feckless professional drawn from absurdity to absurdity by bad impulses. I thought of the small red tugboats that towed the great liners into port, the solitary tugboat skipper, the ship filled with a thousand voices.

Nevertheless—I love this—all had been set in motion. Clarice said, "I just needed a ride. I didn't know the other girl would quit. I was enjoying my freedom while you sold the hot dogs. You went for it! Do you think I'm a grifter? What do you do for a living?"

"I'm a private detective."

"Really! Well, I hope you don't charge people. You're not a private detective, are you? What are you? You look like a lawyer. Maybe you are. Or a senator."

I had a burst of near candor: "I'm a house painter." This reply swept me with happiness. The once dreaded color wheel appeared before me like a galaxy of cheerful stars.

She said, "You're not going to ask me to do anything, are you?"

"Hardly." I really surprised myself. Maybe I wasn't so bad after all.

I drove Clarice to her house. It saddened me to see so inventive a young woman walk into such a shack. I could only think of what I might have felt dropping her off had I managed to exploit her imagined debt. She didn't see the nobility. I could tell by the way she looked at me and shook her head that she thought I was a sucker. In a way, she was right. I do know that by the time I got home, there was something about myself, based on this extremely foolish episode, that I was sick of.

I would be embarrassed by my private detective charade when, three years later, Clarice appeared in my office as a patient. I remembered my lie immediately and took it as a benchmark of what I hoped I had left behind. Deluded again. Clarice had grown up, was out of trouble and holding a good job. I first hoped she wouldn't recognize me, but I realized as she studied me with surprise what folly that was: still, the discovery of my real identity seemed to humanize me in her eyes. She looked back on our episode of the hot dog stand with humor and affection, and I found myself caring for Clarice in the way I wished I cared for everybody. I was about to comment that she had finally grown up when she said more or less the same thing to me.

Clarice came to me only occasionally, for allergies at first. When she married, she began to see me more frequently, initially for chronic indigestion and then for various other stress-related ailments, hives and insomnia mostly. She moved around various county situations, and her husband had a dangerous job in a mine that paid quite well, so I didn't think financial issues were driving her problems. But she was a worried young woman and not candid with me about her marriage. We had become good acquaintances, which was not ideal for objectivity, necessarily, or candor. Worrying about her felt inappropriately parental.

I was told early in the days of my practice that the battered housewife was the bread and butter of the general practitioner. While this may have been an overstatement—sports physicals, pointless reassurances for things caused by viruses, and flock shooting generalized pain were more remunerative—it was disturbing how many women came to me with injuries that did not match the explanations. Clarice appeared the morning after our four-day rodeo with the customary facial contusions and a nosebleed that wouldn't stop. A nosebleed that won't stop is a serious problem, and a CBC indicated she had lost quite a bit of blood. This necessitated a very discomforting procedure after chemical cold packs and pressure had failed to stop the flow. The abrasions to Clarice's face made clear the sort of injuries that had led to the bleeding, which she ascribed to the dry mountain air. She was very uneasy about my moving her head around to get a better view of the nasal vestibule, as though flinching from the possibility of further blows. I was able to identify several bleeding sites with the speculum, one requiring cauterization. This, while not pleasant, obviated packing the nasal passages with cotton, which required twisting the material into place at the cost of considerable patient suffering.

I asked who abused her and got a remarkably philosophical reply made more dramatic by the condition of her face. She seemed ashamed of what had happened and may have explained her hostility to me whom she'd known for a long time. She said, "It's not abuse if you saw it coming."

"Are you saying you had it coming?"

"No, I said I saw it coming."

"And you didn't get out of the way."

"Right."

"And since you didn't get out of the way you share responsibility for what happened to you?"

"Right."

I said, "I don't get it."

She said, "You don't have to get it. It's not your life."

"Clarice! I don't believe this! I'm trying to help."

She began to cry. What was most painful was the thought that when I had first known her, when she had problems with the law and was just another reckless girl having not yet learned to conform and lead a regular life, she would have never put up with this. I had the fleeting idea that her problems arose from being domesticated and that she had been safe as a wild girl but was endangered as a wife.

Our dialogue would grow less formal on her ensuing visits. Some of it was even lighthearted: she reminded me that when she'd first met me I was actually excited to run her hot dog stand. But the comfort was short-lived. I had noticed that as battery went on, the injuries seemed to have migrated to less obvious places, which in my mind aggravated the anger with cruelty. On one visit, Clarice came in almost cheerily and sat down. She had put on weight, though a shadow of former girlishness could still be discerned. I at first mistook it for flirtation, but it was just a part of her self that still survived. In showing me the bruising around her midriff, her modesty seemed touchingly out of place. Once again I made my pitch for counseling, rescue services, restraining orders—and got nowhere. Nevertheless, she continued coming for her injuries, which she showed me with a rueful smile. It was driving me crazy in an abnormal, disorienting way, as though I were falling in love with her. I wished I understood this wild and emotional feeling, which was in some part the wish to protect her, and in another, the queer intimacy engendered by examining and treating this parade of lacerations. There came a point at which I understood that I was not handling this as well as I should, that my rising emotions were inappropriate to the caring detachment proper to a good physician; I had known her as a youngster and she had met me in the twilight of my foolishness. I was losing my objectivity and feeling far too strongly about Clarice's situation, into which, as she herself had pointed out, I had no business interfering; my job was to provide medical treatment, period. To the turbulence of my emotions, therefore, was added the indignity of rejected friendship. As to the possibility of these matters altering my life forever, the timing could not have been worse.

Clarice now worked at the county courthouse researching titles; she had been there since finishing her probation for something not major, shoplifting I think, making few friends among her coworkers, who found her girlishness unappealing. Clarice's husband was probably a drug user of some sort, a man who also consoled himself by drinking, consoled himself for enduring a lousy life in a platinum mine south of Columbus in exchange for high pay. I tried to offer Clarice advice and understanding, all of which was smiled away. I had at that time in my life and career an inadequate idea of what my responsibilities were, and I saw so many people doing things that were not good for them that I had grown quite detached—or at least detached once I had dropped my formulaic, avuncular comments and called it a day. I got rid of the little moustache. My colleagues seemed to know what was going on; in fact, Clarice had seen some of them when she thought I knew too much about her situation. I will say on my behalf that their angry wishes for the husband were unlawful. Clarice's worst physical problems were not visible as bruises would be but were the less apparent somewhat crippling effects of having limbs twisted. Physical therapy was out of the question because "he" wouldn't pay for it and besides "it's nothing I can't handle." My attempts to learn anything more just reinstated her sullenness and reminded me that I had gotten too close to her. I had adopted a pleading tone, which only made things worse. She ceased to seem like a friend or even a longtime patient. With a consummate lack of professionalism, I found that my feelings were hurt. I felt rejected.

"Do you have family in the area?"

"No."

"Where do they live?"

"Harlowton."

"That's forty miles."

"That's what I said. I don't have family in the area."

"Are your parents living?"

"I don't know."

That, such as it was, was our last conversation.

Cody and Clarice lived in an old railroader's house in a ravine crowded with such houses, a high-dollar muscle car in the driveway. I said, "Why the gun?" It was three o'clock in the morning. Cody was the one who had called me; he said there had been an unfortunate development. He sat on the edge of a well-worn brick-red sofa with protective plastic on its back and several cigarette burns on its arms. He wore acid-washed jeans, which were too small for him, and pushed a roll of fat up under his

T-shirt. He was holding a cookie, which he slowly consumed. The pistol he dangled from one hand was chromium plated with a concealed hammer. From time to time, he slid a latch and the cylinder tumbled from the frame, bringing the cartridges and their primers into view. He turned the cylinder slowly with a finger from the other hand and seemed to be counting the bullets. "I told myself she didn't make it I was going down the same road." I didn't say anything. He flipped the cylinder back into place and held the gun more firmly, against his thigh. "I don't need to live and I got the grit to see I don't." I didn't know why he needed to tell me this, and I took it that he was stalling. I wanted him to get on with it. "But," he sighed, "it's not easy. Deserving it don't make it easier." My silence seemed to make him indignant. Getting me to talk to him might have been his idea of a way back into the human race, but I meant to help as little as possible.

Cody rested the revolver in his lap and watched me try to save Clarice's life, a task I had no chance of accomplishing: she was already dead. The poor girl had been dragged up into a chair beneath a lamp, twisted away to keep it from illuminating her battered face, her one arm thrown back as if she had made a last attempt to fling herself clear. There were no signs of the battery that I had not seen during her office visits, but these had been the last, either through accumulation or some cunningly acute new manner of blow. Nothing more could be done for her. I told him she was gone and he pulled the cigarette from behind his ear and lit it. He said, "I told her nobody can live on Chicken McNuggets and popcorn. It's not like she wasn't warned."

"May I ask what you hit her with?"

"Thing over there. Whatever." He had the cylinder out and was checking the chambers again; then he closed it. This examination of the weapon, the cigarette, something told me he was not going to do away with himself. He didn't have the balls. What was odd, all this time later, was my ready access to a beautifully performed voice of compassion, one that I would have had a hard time calling up on Clarice's behalf when she came to me and described in her baby voice what her problems were. I told Cody that no one could tell him what led him to do what he had done and that he owed himself enough understanding to uncover what broken part in him had made him kill his wife. His eyes filled with tears; he moved the cigarette to the other side of his mouth. I gratefully noted the beginnings of a snivel.

I sat in a chair, a spare that had been pulled over next to the television set, under which was a rack filled with back issues of *TV Guide* and a large can of Glade Floral air freshener. I could not easily look to my right, where Clarice's corpse lay in its stupendous inertness. Her defeated excuses were too fresh in my mind to accept the impossibility of her ever stirring. I shook my head slightly and said to Cody once more that his wife was dead.

He said, "I told you what I'd do."

"I know," I said. "I guess I'm just waiting for you to do it."

"Are you in a hurry?"

"I've got all the time in the world."

"I mean, Doc, I know what I did. If I have to, I'll do the time."

"What time? You were going to kill yourself. Remember?"

"That's right, I was, but this is my deal and I'll do it when I'm good and ready."

"Probably the surest thing would be to put that gun in your mouth."

"Tha-ank you."

"And point up."

"I don't believe you have a lot of sympathy for me, do you, Doctor? It must be nice looking at this thing from the outside, a regular Monday-morning quarterback. I don't think you realize what made me do what I did."

"You mentioned Chicken McNuggets and popcorn. Clarice was my patient. My impression was that she wished to live."

Cody went on sniveling while giving me a hard stare. I was surprised at my own harsh voice: "Put it in your mouth, Cody. It's the right thing to do."

It wasn't long before he was angry. That was his drug; it was a great way to get lost and I could see what relief it gave him. I was a big shot, I'd had it easy, had no idea what guys like him had to put up with, wouldn't know a stacked deck if it bit me on the ass. He said all his life he'd given more than he'd gotten just to have sons of bitches like me look down their noses at him. He must have thought starting a fight with me might be an escape from the fate he'd called down on himself. I wasn't about to give an inch. He was trying to gnaw his way out of the trap he'd built. Perhaps, in some vastly dark place, some vengeful corner that I would have been happy to never visit again, I even enjoyed this. In short, I grew impatient for him to shoot himself.

With his meager question—"Isn't it time you called the police, Doctor?"—my contempt boiled over and I smiled at him pleasantly. This bolstered his conviction that he was misunderstood. "You think this is easy? *You think this is easy?*"

He looked down at the gun he was holding in his lap before lifting it up and pointing it at me. A laugh escaped his compressed lips. Now he used the sights as though to get me in just the right spot. He said, "You'll love this, Doc. Nine-millimeter hollow points get to twelve millimeters and never leave an exit wound. When eight hundred feet per second comes to a complete stop somebody's got to know about it."

"Fascinating."

He shook his head. "You think I'm getting nowhere."

I watched him closely for a long moment and said, "Pretty much."

"So, Doctor, what do you think I should do? You're the doctor."

"I think you should kill yourself."

I remembered his pensive look; or maybe it was a look of melancholy, as he put the gun barrel in his mouth. I gazed back at him and raised my hand, right thumb up. I said he was good to go. I at once remembered my father telling me how they lifted the right arms of German prisoners looking for SS tattoos. If they found them, they shot the prisoners on the spot.

A look of sudden innocence crossed his face, something I would forever live with, and he fired. Despite my glamorous view of my father as a deliverer of swift justice and my feeling that Cody had it coming, this was about to become the front parlor of hell. I wouldn't have felt any different if I had shot him myself. I wondered if I was still a doctor or even a human being.

I called the police and was sufficiently composed to describe the situation and suggest what equipment would be required. The telephone was in the same room as the bodies, a grisly tableau growing in my imagination as the associated personalities began to disappear. Any detachment my medical training had given me was gone, and I hurried from the house to the sidewalk, where I waited for the authorities. When they arrived, two older officers, I described the situation in such a way that they seemed more focused on my delivery than on what might await them in the house. I excused myself and set out on a walk that took me into the rest of that run-down neighborhood where I sought out signs of normalcy: papers fetched from porches, men with lunch pails, schoolchildren setting out with backpacks, a speckled dog sailing into the back of an old station wagon, a smiling senior pushing her walker down the sidewalk with a purse and a quart of milk in the basket, teenagers with their torsos under a car hood; I seized on everything, wishing I might always be able to seize on everything. In half an hour I found the railroad tracks and followed the cinder pathway toward the country, stopping only to admire the graffiti on a slow train, beautiful mammoth letters in spray-on colors. I walked out of town, the moving train giving me a pleasant illusion of greater speed. In an hour I was resting in the open prairie under a box elder, next to the tracks, the smell of steel and wild grasses, the air filled with the song of meadowlarks, as yet unwilling or unready to face my guilt. In the words of my late mother, I understood I would have to be shriven.

When they lowered Clarice into her grave I was swept by regret as much for humanity as for her. But when they buried Cody I thought, "It's Miller Time." It wouldn't last, though. I was lying to myself.

7

In the early days of my practice, I sustained an affair with an incredibly self-absorbed folksinger named Kay who left me for another man and a career in music that went nowhere. I remember an awful evening at her riverside condo, snow blowing against the double-paned picture window, when she auditioned for a New York impresario who held his head and moaned while she intoned, "I loves you, Porgy," over the big twelve-string. Tessa was still around town and I often heard that she was furious with me for dating Kay. If she thought I went out of my way to stay out of hers, she was right—not from a simple wish for avoidance so much as a recognition of the power acquired in my youth which she still held over me, and which, considering my standing, I now thought to be unseemly. I had grown to be an independent sort, a bachelor who thrived on connubial hopelessness and the outdoors. I kept bird dogs and horses, and I went on some sort of adventure at least once a year. I felt I was much too fancy even for acquaintance with Tessa. This was a form of whistling in the dark, because whenever I saw her she wielded exactly the same authority over me as she had when I was very young.

Over the years that followed, I'd occasionally see her going about the affairs of Hoxey. As he was now old, sick, and demented and Tessa was seen as exploiting him, she had acquired a questionable reputation around town. When Hoxey died, whatever worries I might have had for her were briefly allayed, as it seemed that she must have inherited the business. Then she made an appointment to see me at the clinic. I had forgotten her physical abundance and burning vitality. Her hair piled atop her head and held there by a bright-red plastic comb seemed to represent fulminating energy. She had a white streak in her hair, which she attributed to "trauma." She stared at me significantly.

"Henchmen of Hoxey have turned me out into the street," she told me, "with little more than the clothes on my back."

"Tessa, I find this very hard to picture."

"Perhaps a few prints, a negligible watercolor or two."

"Who exactly are these 'henchmen'?"

"Grown daughters. I never factored them in. They arrived on the scene like Valkyries hovering over the battlefield in search of corpses to eat."

"I'm terribly sorry."

"At a difficult time, Doctor, I offered you companionship and sexual healing."

"Is there anything I can do? Medication is my line, but I don't think that is what you have in mind."

"I'll have to start looking for work. I hope you'll recommend me."

I reached for a pen, poised to join the millions who've made their way out of a difficult situation by providing letters of recommendation. But Tessa said, "Not now. I'll let you know." That, more or less, was the end of our appointment. She seemed happy with my response, taking my hand in both of hers. I suppose she was just checking to see whether I was still on her side.

Tessa went downhill fast. Within two years, she endured spells of homelessness, punctuated by temporary jobs, none of which became permanent, because of her imperious nature, her contempt for owners and bosses. She never merely left a job, she stormed off. She took over the homes where she was briefly a guest. But even as her fortunes fell, Tessa didn't lose her rakish airs, though they began to seem almost detached from her, and just a bit automatic as she strode around town in worn-out clothes.

I was one of several who helped in small ways, but I rarely saw Tessa. I had established myself in a small-town practice that would not make me rich, though it might make me happy. Hoxey had since returned to California in powder form, leaving nothing behind him. In those years I seemed to have awakened from my own background and, without boasting, I can say that I had become somewhat less of a fool, though I was aware that my foolishness could recur at any time, like a dormant virus. I can't say that I saw Tessa as my responsibility, nor can I claim to have quite got her out of my system.

Bob Kavanagh took me to lunch on a Thursday. Bob was a hearty, shifty fellow who would do anything for a laugh. He owned a motel in Gardiner and the movie theater here in town. During that morning's digital prostate exam, he had deliberately farted into my examining glove, and taking me to lunch was by way of making up for his bad manners, which I had not thought funny. "How's your sandwich?" he asked. His incongruous smile suggested that the sandwich, too, was amusing. He must have been proud of his Panama hat because he wore it all through the meal.

"It's very good."

He smiled; he'd made it up to me. He said, "You know how people would find things in their food, cockroaches, fingers, stuff like that?"

I answered him warily. "Yes?"

"Last week guy come in here orders a chicken potpie and there was a cell phone in it. Just imagine if someone called that number and it rang in the pie."

"I can't."

The conversation rambled on until Kavanagh brought up the subject of Tessa, whom he described as a community eyesore. He wanted to get up a collection to ship her back to California. I said, "What if we ship you back to California?"

"I'm not from California. I'm from here."

"I'm sorry to hear that. I thought I was onto something."

I wanted to leave the restaurant, but I was spotted by Adrienne Wilmot and her husband, Raymond, dining alone by the bricked-up fireplace at the north end of the room. She was an attractive, actually wonderful woman, though it was mildly to her discredit that she seemed, in the absence of any other sufficient explanation, to have married for money or social standing. She'd had a couple of affairs in our town and left her lovers grateful. I say that from experience. There was really nothing wrong with Raymond, exactly; he sold high-end recreational properties to members of his far-flung society. He was known in the business as "Tightly Held" Wilmot because no matter what obscure neighborhood he was promoting, he always described it as "tightly held." She once admitted her moderate infidelity to me but added, "I never do it to get anywhere." Perhaps Raymond was the exception. In any event, Raymond Wilmot was making money hand over fist.

Wilmot's face and head, his small moustache, projected a sort of gloom. I thought he looked like Edgar Allan Poe. He told me that the lovely small towns of New England where he had once lived were now "stiff with fairies fixing up houses." He had a habit of throwing his head back, looking into space, and laughing; the effect was one of extreme condescension.

Adrienne said, "They don't call them that anymore. You're not keeping up, Raymond." And Wilmot said, "Oh, very well." To this he attached an elegant and contemptuous ennui. Wilmot knew of my family and often teased me about my breeding or sardonically complimented me on triumphing over my origins. I would always be displeased with myself for laughing at this, as I was actually quite offended.

Raymond got to his feet, pressed his napkin to his chest, and gave me a hearty welcome. He was the sort of person who smiled with blatant insincerity from one side of his mouth while addressing you as "Mr. So-and-So," sometimes preceding that with "Well, if it isn't old—" I think he was trying to be funny but I'm not sure. I hugged Adrienne as she stood, running the end of my forefinger up the small of her back to feel her shiver. Very responsive, that Adrienne, and she rewarded me with a twinkle. The three of us sat down together. They both beamed at me with the intense curiosity which we save for people we suspect might not be stable. I do think I was viewed as not quite under control, but some women liked that. Adrienne had once said of her husband, "I wanted him so badly, I can't believe I'm sick of him now." I thought she was either being provocative or just covering her tracks.

Quite inadvertently as my hand rested in my lap our fingers touched, and as she didn't withdraw hers, I let them intertwine. Raymond did notice this. "A little wine?" he asked sarcastically. "Some candles, perhaps?"

"Raymond, be a sport and let me at him." Expressed like this, we had to laugh. "Really, all of my antics are just for Raymond's entertainment."

Good one, that, and it took Raymond in, as his returning complacency attested.

"In English class," Raymond said, "we once had to write an essay on one of Dante's circles of hell, and we could pick whichever circle we wanted. I picked 'the Sea of Excrement' and it really has stayed with me."

When Adrienne and Raymond came with me one afternoon for a visit to my father, Raymond kept saying about his meager house, "It's all you need!" He seemed antic and uncomfortable. Afterward, my father remarked, "I wouldn't piss on him if he was on fire."

I knew Raymond didn't like me. My cherished friend Jinx said he hated me, but I thought that was a bit much. As a single woman, Jinx gets around more than I do, invited here and there: she had a very sharp ear and a sharper memory.

I had by now acknowledged my solipsism, my slow winding inward. I also noticed that Kavanagh left without a word. I supposed I had impolitely abandoned him, but after all, he had farted in my glove. Still, I'd been discomfited by the cold stare I had caught from Raymond Wilmot before he realized I'd seen him.

"You can make Adrienne very happy if you'll come for dinner."

"I'd love to," I intoned.

"And in the interest of appearances, I'll join you."

I told Raymond that that was entirely up to him. I knew how unsatisfactory that was, since he undoubtedly knew there had been more to Adrienne's and my flirtation than met the eye. I just didn't think he cared. I was wrong about that: he cared. It would later seem that it was all he cared about.

The December night that I was celebrating my fortieth birthday with a small cake in the emergency room, they brought Tessa in: into her abdomen she had plunged a serrated bread knife, an item she continued to clutch while on the gurney. I took it from her hand, and feeling the heat of her gaze, I quickly moved to dealing with her wound. I knew that if she were admitted to the clinic itself she would be subjected to what I viewed as diagnostic imprudence—laparotomy and various explorations, which experience had caused me to associate with increased morbidity. Though I would later have a chance to review these judgments, I honestly felt that they didn't alter the way things turned out. In effect, I was keeping Tessa to myself. I had hoped that this was a cry-for-help injury—the timing, during my shift, aroused my suspicions—but the knife, it turned out, had pierced the skin, the subcutaneous layer, the *linea alba,* and the peritoneum, and I could only hope that it had gone no farther, that is, into the viscera. Over the next four days, attending Tessa round the clock while she stared at me without speaking, I failed to contain the major leakage, the uncontrolled granulosis of the peritoneum, the necrosis, and an infection that laughed off antibiotics in a general cascade. She was looking right through me when she slipped away.

Aren't there things that your parents should tell you? After my mother's death, I had found her reading glasses. I'd sat down on our old sofa in front of the window, with its view of a stunted row of odorless rugosa roses, still knowing, after all those years, which part I could sit on without feeling the springs. I put my mother's glasses on. The earpieces were too short for me, and I had to press them down on my nose uncomfortably. It didn't matter: I could barely see through them.

I only felt that something quite terrible had happened to me. My first instinct was flight: I would just leave town, leave the area, try to leave myself; but that soon struck me as irrational and no more than a conversion of this terrible feeling into weakness that would open up into something worse. And something happened that was quite meaningless, however unsettling: driving home from the hospital, I saw children standing alongside the road holding tombstones; at closer range the tombstones turned out to be skateboards, but the first impression endured.

The death of Tessa gave rise to some misunderstandings in town, and at first the doctors stood by me. But we began having trouble with our board of directors, and the clinic went half speed as a kind of protest or strike. Raymond Wilmot was now chairman of the board.

But I wanted to work. I had to work. It was the only balm I had for the several kinds of mental pain that had beset me. I may have taken the whole thing too seriously. I had a classmate at medical school who was now marketing a homeopathic cure for jet lag; when I saw him at our reunion and asked if it actually worked, he said blandly, "There's no fucking way." He pointed out another classmate who had invented a universal stool softener. "He's making a fortune." It seemed that believing we were surrounded by people who enjoyed being fooled is what united all Americans. I had begun in the emergency room. Trauma was different: we knew exactly what to blame, and the literal qualities of the obvious thing that caused the injury was but a poor object to resent. The beauty of trauma lay in its peculiarly genuine qualities.

We kept having meetings, most among ourselves, and sometimes with the board, an altogether tiresome exercise, since the board really didn't understand what we did and seemed to regard doctors as a necessary evil. Wilmot preached fiscal responsibility and local control. He saluted himself for "giving back to the community" which had been so good to him by taking it in the shorts on every Wilmot transaction. He never failed to thwart us on equipment and facility enhancements and would blow up if challenged. Any doctor raising questions about the finances of the clinic was urged to stick to his knitting. We also had an obsequious clinic manager, Darryl Coutts, a native of Tennessee whose genial Southern ways masked his spineless inability to grasp the essentials of the job. We ignored him too.

It seemed that we had barely recovered from one of Wilmot's board meeting pep talks when it was time for another, with fresh rants about "emerging challenges" and "opportunities for greatness." It didn't help that Alan Hirsch made a cylinder with his right hand and raised and lowered it over his crotch while rolling his eyes. If the roof leaked, Wilmot assured us that a "capital infusion" was on the horizon and that our only obligation was to close ranks and provide better care for our patients. Hirsch whispered to me, "An absolute dribbling fuckwit." As Wilmot was looking my way, I nodded gravely, hoping to give the appearance of having just absorbed some insight supportive of his bottomless inanities. "He loves you," whispered Hirsch.

"So that you each may do the work you do best," said Wilmot, "we have chosen our trustees strictly from among the abundant reserve of community leaders. This will come as nothing new to you. But in this we differ from those boards substantially comprised of physicians." This was a sore subject, and we had no idea why he saw fit to revisit it now. "We are as empowered toward decision making as you each should be empowered toward healing." All of us could feel the generalizations rise toward a disorienting crescendo, and we were on our guard, sensing there was a fucking afoot. "I am in contact, thanks to the good efforts of Darryl Coutts, with Heritage Asset Strategies of Eldorado, Oklahoma, specialists in the management of acute care hospitals in small places like ours. They are owned by various affiliates of private equity firms and know from top to bottom what institutions like ours require. Heritage Asset Strategies boasts a combined experience of almost a thousand years and hence has a perspective few of their competitors can match. Because of the confidence of fellow trustees Bob Comstock of Big Sky Florists; Olan Berg, a car salesman; Joseph Pancrack, a rodeo clown; Genevieve Shanstrom, housewife; Oliver Perkins of Hair Today Gone Tomorrow; and Dr. Dave Manovich, dentist, I have been entrusted with their proxies to open negotiations with Heritage Asset Strategies as of start of business Monday."

Except for the emergency room and absolutely skeletal services in desperate cases, we shut the whole place down the next morning. Jinx made the somewhat sibylline remark, "I'm afraid we are always ruled by the collective disappointments of the community." I had several patients in the hospital wing—not gravely ill, I admit—but I went on seeing them. That's how I became a scab, persona non grata. Thus I visited Earline Campbell, recovering from an appendectomy, and arranged to have her television fixed; something in our food service was aggravating Roland Crowley's gout, so I brought him colchicine tablets and meals from his preferred restaurants; I continued to monitor ninety-five-year-old Donald Fairhurst, who thought he was dying and may well have been and who therefore, despite his great age, was frightened.

Three days into this I found Gary Haack, our orthopedic surgeon, and Laird McAllister, a family practice doctor, waiting for me at my car. They looked sad, reluctant to tell me what they had to tell me, that as I had not stood by them at this crisis they hoped that I would see what was best for one and all. Laird began, "We are very reluctant to say what we have to say but cannot do otherwise."

"Because I failed to stand by you during this crisis it would be better if I just left the clinic."

"I told Laird you'd be a sport," said Gary brightly. "You've made this easy." These weren't bad fellows, just committed to their situation, something that eluded me. However, I couldn't go along with them.

"My thought is," I said, "if you're a doctor you're a doctor. Who cares who they sell the business to? I had patients who needed me."

"Very naive," said Dr. Haack. "Bordering on infantile."

I was sensing the prospect of relief from something whose burden I had barely let myself recognize. As soon as the picture was clear, I said, "Just let me get through my inpatients and I'm sure we can work this out. I'll try to find a way to practice elsewhere."

That night as I lay in bed swaddled in unclean sheets and smelling the rail yards on the light north wind, I felt abashed that I had made such bitter innuendos to my colleagues. I admitted to myself—at last!—that there was something more to my distaste for hospital bureaucracy than just ordinary irritation with management. I had long felt that those who bent to their work, whatever it was, sooner or later landed in the hands of swindlers like Raymond Wilmot. We had an informal slogan in our town: "You can get used to anything."

I strolled over to the hospital in my new role to visit my handful of patients. Nurses were there seeing to the others and collaborating with the physicians by cell phone. There was little difference in the care the patients were receiving, and experience told me that my responsible colleagues were watching them closely while maintaining the front of negligent solidarity. On reflection, I felt they were on the right track and I, perhaps, was on the wrong one. If they kept the place from being sold to a consortium with its empty claims of local control, all except me would benefit. I was a scab. Even the nurses were distant, though I had to intervene when old Mrs. Kefler declined to "eat anything with a central nervous system" and had been put on cold cereal for several days. She complained of weakness, though she was overweight. I once read in an Icelandic book, "The world has never taken the tears of a plump woman seriously, and a fat martyr has always been considered contrary to the laws of reason."

When I went in to see ancient Donald Fairhurst, who ranched up the

Shields River for seventy years, I found him in good spirits and glad to be under the covers on a morning that was in his opinion "cold enough to freeze the nuts off a riding plow." He asked me who the president was this time. I told him and he wanted to know about the legislature; he said Americans had to get out of the habit of sending the village idiot to Congress. His ninety-five years did not seem to have blunted his wit. Donald once told me that he had been a hellhound in his youth before he started going to church. "Now I'm sanctified." He said he had no intention of dying until the time was ripe. He had attended the last public hanging in Montana as a boy and told me that in those days the young were encouraged to attend as a moral lesson. I asked him about the spectacle. "Wasn't nothing to it," he said. "It was like watching a turd fall from a tall cow."

I saw the nurses rush toward the room of a patient who was singing "Jambalaya" in a loud and despairing voice. An older nurse headed his way with a syringe on a tray.

Jinx Mayhall came into my office. We were very good friends with shared interests in cooking and the outdoors. An unpleasant stillness came upon us. Jinx stared at my face, her eyes a pair of gloomy orbs. "Whatever possessed you to do away with that poor girl?" she asked. My blood ran cold, I don't know why; though later I would wonder whether something like this had been in the air and I had registered it subconsciously.

"Do away with what poor girl?"

"Your old squeeze. The one who stabbed herself."

"Jinx, I tried everything I knew to—"

"—saying such terrible things about you—"

"—keep her alive. I didn't know that. I'd hardly seen in her in years."

"Never out of her mind. She made that clear to one and all. It's not that no one *understands,* a doomed soul surely."

"Jinx, stop. Now just stop this. I tried my best to save her."

"Did you."

We sat without a word for a long time. I had my hands in front of me on the desk, and I was staring between them while my mind whirled. Finally, I told Jinx that I thought it best she go. She stopped in the doorway in her big loden coat and without turning to me, said, "I thought you knew."

. . .

I looked at Bob Carmichael's chart and felt sad and unsurprised. Bob wouldn't be here much longer because of his age and diabetes, but he was so stouthearted he would doubtless have numerous amputations before the merciful failure of his heart. Retired from the railroad long ago, Bob was a ham radio operator and had a far-flung society of fellow "hams" he communicated with every day. He once picked up the distress messages of a crab boat sinking in the Gulf of Alaska, connected the crew to a Russian trawler, and from the comfort of his small house on H Street saved seven men from drowning in cold black water. Entering my office, he quickly sat to keep me from evaluating his mobility, which was greatly reduced. He wore a frayed flannel shirt, high-heeled logger boots, and suspenders. His white hair had the pinkish tinge of the redhead he formerly was. Bob and I were tired of sending him for blood tests and suggesting changes in his lifestyle. The unspoken thing between us was that it was in God's hands, sooner or later, though one of us might have called it luck. Bob did not feel he had been cheated by life, and after fifty years of marriage he and his wife still had each other's companionship. By checking in with me a few times a year, he felt he had done enough for his health. I agreed.

"Feeling okay?"

"Feeling okay."

That was it for medicine. Bob said, "About five this morning, there was a wolf on the baseball diamond."

"What was he doing there?"

"I don't know."

"Out by the fence?" I asked this because just past that is woods.

"Oh, hell no. He was in the infield licking the baselines. Might be there's salt or something he needed in them baselines."

"Did you see this?"

"The kids seen it."

"You sure you don't have anything to report healthwise?"

"Not really. I suppose something will jump out and bite me on the ass but not yet."

"Well, okay. See me this winter, unless something comes up."

Bob was my last patient for the day. I no longer knew what the rules were. I guessed I wasn't supposed to be here at all. I was quite disturbed by what Jinx had said, and it had the effect of widening my outlook on my life. Lately, I'd been dreaming about my mother. Sometimes she was in the dream; sometimes she was not but I got letters from her. In neither case did she do anything significant except that it must have been significant that she was in my dreams at all. She just walked around, did a few chores; or I went to the box and got the letters but I didn't open them. I was sometimes awakened by the longing for something to happen in these dreams, but they remained maddeningly innocuous. I suspected that this was the way we dreamt of our late parents; what we wished to have fulfilled was simply their presence. Psychologists focus on symbolism of events in dreams, which is part of their own wish fulfillment. The ones that meant the most were remarkably bland, like mine of my mother. Usually, she was in a room. That's it: she was in a room. It was unclear whether I was in the room as well. For some reason, it was heartbreaking. How it would have cleared the air if she could have shouted, "You destroyed me with your indifference!" or something along those lines. The dreams somehow told me that the significance lay in the disparity between someone who was there and someone who was not there. I wasn't alone in finding simplicity and plainness unbearable. I wished she'd speak up. Instead, she dusted the piano that no one ever played.

I awakened feeling confused. I remembered how I had met boyhood confusion with fishing, and I thought to try it one more time. The only other doctor still coming to work on a regular basis ("Hiding behind her gender," said Laird McAllister) was Jinx, and she said she'd fill in for me. I could tell she wished she hadn't said what she had and was trying to make it up to me. I knew just by the way people were looking at me that trouble was headed my way, and it was getting to me: this was my town!

8

Along the upper river the old forest was a corridor that led to the face of the glacier. Whether I was fishing or walking or just working around camp, it was hard to keep my eyes off it as it changed with the light and seemed to have a story that was going somewhere. Wherever that might be, I was never going to find out, but I watched the glacier anyway and wondered what was next. What was next was change, change of color and of shapes that arose and vanished with the advance of day. The glacier was always the last thing to sink into darkness.

I would be heading out in the morning. Not much was left of today. I didn't have a fish yet, and I was rather working at it. I'd had several unsuccessful days during the previous week, but it seemed unlucky to end the trip on a blank, especially since the point of the trip was to change my luck. The helicopter was to arrive at first light; with packing up to do I would miss the twilight bite, as I had to be able to see to pull my belongings together for the chopper guy, who demanded all gear be spic-and-span and arrayed in one or two bundles that could go in the pod. Moreover, I was counting on eating this fish I hadn't caught yet.

Fishing alone could be unproductive, as it turned into something ceremonial without the competition of other anglers. But I got lost in space as the long line opened over the water and settled. There was something ancient and fatalistic about it, like making the sign of the cross: I had done my part; the line tightened and swung through the world of the fish. It was not up to me. I just made the cast and awaited the results.

The double-handed rod felt light and purposeful. As it swung on the surface of the river the line had the pure curve of a bow. The river was pale green over white stones, darker green over the slots. On the far side, a tributary entered that was coming from the sunny face of the glacier. It was full of glacial milk and made a dense white streak against the bank. You couldn't fish there. A fish would never find your fly, if there was a fish there at all, which there probably was not. I couldn't imagine the suspended rock flour was good for their gills.

The cast that pumped down into the cork of the handle, the float and settle of the line, the taut curve of the swing, the progress down the run. The only reason anyone did this was to touch the eternal feeling, the circadian bigger-than-yourself feeling.

The arc of line flattened. A fish! It seemed to have come at the right time, and once I'd beached it, this fish so recently in the ocean, I could see through its fins to the gravel underneath. It was a hard cold bar of silver, gasping on the stones.

I used the rest of the light to pack everything but my sleeping bag. My fish was dripping grease over a small bed of coals. The glacier looked huddled in the incomplete dark of the wilderness, the stars growing closer. I didn't want to close the double-sided battered aluminum fly box Dr. Olsson had given me long ago just yet, not while I could still see the small colors inside, run my thumb over the clips that held them, feel the hook points. I ate in the dark. I ate all I could, my chin dripping, like a bear's. Tomorrow I'd want a napkin. This was certainly not my way of life, but it was surprising how quickly it came to seem so. In a day I'd be home, back in the loop, Dr. Pickett. I'd be the fish.

The sun was just up. I got into my down coat before I crawled entirely out of the sleeping bag, then rolled the bag and stuffed it in its sack. This I managed to get into the waterproof river duffel, and all was as orderly as the helicopter pilot could wish. I scoured face and teeth at the river, put the last items away, and using the duffel as a backrest, stretched out, hands inside my sleeves, to wait for my ride.

The helicopter never came.

I spent the day pacing up and down the riverbank, pausing hopefully at every sound, and in the end I unpacked my sleeping bag for the night. I had eaten of the fish three times, and now it was gone. I never looked at the glacier.

For the last ten days, I had lain in my sleeping bag and listened to the wolves as I fell asleep. Their songs assured me that this was no place like home, that no sensible wolf would sing with such majestic assurance without owning the place. Now I found them disquieting and eerie. I was sure they knew about me.

At last I faced the fact that no one was going to pick me up, that the arrangements I had made and paid for in advance were not to be followed. I tried blaming it on my declining the various added services the pilot offered. He may well have been disgruntled at my not electing side trips to see petroglyphs, totem poles, or grizzly bears, to fly to Mesachie Nose or Jump Across, requesting only a ride in and, at the appointed hour, a ride out. But he took the money. He should have picked me up.

More to the point, the food was nearly gone. I knew I had to walk out and take with me what I could wear. I had no backpack, and my attempt to adapt the wire grill I cooked on failed. I stuffed my pockets with snack bars, of which I had plenty, took my slicker, and left everything else, including my sleeping bag, behind. That was hard. Anyone who's spent time in wild places loves his sleeping bag beyond its actual utility. The mummy shape, the loft of the down, the neatly sewn gussets had their aesthetic attraction. My bag was twenty years old and yet I could still remember the exact moment I'd bought it in Seattle, the salesman's face, the weather, spreading it out on the floor of my hotel, looking at it as I brushed my teeth and as the expanding down inside it slowly pulled its fabric taut.

I left it behind. It was pale green and when I looked back to where it lay at the base of a huge cedar whose dew fell like rain, an odd feeling passed over me. I wasn't heading into the unknown, but I did have before me a two-day walk on river cobbles. The water was safe to drink, and the fruit bars that bulged in my coat were enough nutrition. Moderate alertness would keep me from unpleasantly surprising bears, and with the equinoctial storms a week or so away, one night sleeping in my clothes was nothing to worry about. It might be that a chopper picking up goat hunters or another angler would see me, but realistically I hadn't heard any aircraft in a couple of days. A walk it would be. There was a road-head and a native settlement, cars. I had credit cards and a bit of cash, among the things I took instead of the sleeping bag. For the first few miles, I thought of ways I could go back for it. I still pictured myself bent over and running under the blades of the helicopter.

What beautiful weather for a walk! Each time the river bent, the world before me changed completely, divided, rushed, shrugged off the old forest, spread before narrowing, always mindful of the sea. The few bears I saw departed at the sight of me, and at sundown I found myself in a canyon, a primeval wilderness crowned high above by a star-filled sky. I was tired enough that sleeping on the ground was not an issue, and my belief that I could smell salt water was part of what swept me to the next morning.

I walked into an Indian settlement in midafternoon under a beautiful blue North Pacific sky and could smell the ocean. I saw no one around but heard native radio blaring from one house, the theme song from *Welcome Back, Kotter,* then AC/DC "Dirty Deeds Done Dirt Cheap," my favorite song for waking up and getting going. I thought that was a good sign. When I knocked on the door, the music stopped; an old native man in overalls and a worn Irish tweed cap appeared and asked what he could do to help me. I told him I'd been dropped above the forks on the first of September and that my ride had never come back for me. I told him I'd left my stuff in the bush, maybe somebody would want it.

He said nothing was flying and when I seemed not to understand, he said nothing was flying anywhere, not here or anywhere in the world. I don't think he understood, at least at first, that I knew nothing of the attack in New York. I thought I was listening to some aborigine's mumbo jumbo about how nothing really flies, how we are earthbound, how flight was an illusion. I was well along this cul-de-sac when he patiently told me what had happened.

"The bus runs from Hagensborg to Vancouver," he said. "You'll be halfway to your house."

I got pretty well filled in by the passengers on the way down—forest, rivers, town, the smell of salmon everywhere, once in a while the northern ocean. Several passengers had watched the news on television and tried to describe the scene but gave up. They watched me gauge its effect, as though this had happened to us as Americans, of which I was the specimen. I would have thought it was a bit more general, but it hadn't happened to Canadians, it had happened to us. All very odd because whatever it was, I couldn't picture it. This was well before everyone fought to own it. To judge by the other passengers, half of whom were Indians, all agreed that things would never be the same.

In Vancouver I felt the strangeness of the flightless skies; and at the airport, where my futile hopes for a ride home led me, the sight of what looked like every airplane from round the Pacific Rim, a jumble of towering aluminum tails and cheery logos, finally persuaded me that all was indeed arrested. A van was hauling water to a queue of Chinese families winding out of the terminal to the parking lot. I was told they'd been there for four days. Old people slept on the tile.

I bought a twenty-year-old Oldsmobile Starfire 88 from a used-car salesman with a pencil-thin moustache. In my numerology, 88 is big: the tank traveling in front of my father's had been destroyed by a German self-propelled 88, a big gun on rails, operated by civilians—two men, two women, and a priest. My father's tank captured it, and in his crew were men from the Deep South who had a special view of war: they executed the gun crew. Others in my father's division, suffering from various kinds of battle trauma, were given pills called 88s and sent back into combat. The Oldsmobile 88 is a discontinued car.

When the car salesman in Canada learned I needed to get home, he marked it down two hundred dollars. That I was dirty and unshaven seemed not to matter. I gave him a check, and he said he didn't need the identification I offered. When the deal was done, he said, "I'm sorry." As I had not yet understood the situation, I could only shake my head ambivalently. I was still trying to absorb the event the bus passengers claimed to have seen on television. An old Indian woman used both her hands to represent the aircraft while she stared into my eyes. That didn't work either.

The car went on operating all the way across BC to the Washington border, when it first gave signs of giving up the ghost. I was taking in nothing, not the scenery, no time but the passage of miles toward home, where I meant to look for myself at all the pictures and listen to all the surmises of friends, family, and talking heads. For now all I could do was drive the car. When I hit rain south of Penticton I started singing "Maybellene," trying to imitate Chuck Berry's voice as I roared the lines, "The rain blowin' all under my hood, I know that I was doin' my motor good." I needed some luck getting into America, and the 88 felt like it was choking on its own fuel.

There wasn't much to entering the U.S., an extraordinary informality, more especially in that I had a jalopy with Canadian dealer tags. On the

American side, I made little attempt at explanation except to say that I'd been away when it all went down and assumed everyone just wanted to go home. The customs agent looked at me sadly, said, "No shit," and waved me on. I found a pay phone in the middle of a hundred square miles of rolling wheat and learned that a limited number of planes would be flying from Spokane. I booked a seat and pushed the choking Olds south, feathering the accelerator to keep the engine alive as I trained a worried eye on the temperature gauge. It grazed red-line as mountains began to show in the east.

I abandoned the car in short-term parking and we boarded on schedule. Every seat was filled and the plane was silent. An hour passed, and with it our departure time for Salt Lake City passed, yet there was no word from the cockpit. Indeed the door had never been open and there was no way for us to be sure that it contained pilots. There were no stewardesses, but hardly a murmur emerged from the crowd of faces.

I sat in the exit row and had room to almost sprawl. Not only was the legroom extended but the middle seat was occupied by an Igloo ice chest, strapped in as though it was a passenger, and at the window, I assumed, its owner. From time to time, he turned in my direction, but no expression crossed his face, a face that seemed not quite his own. The only way to let the air out of this thing was to strike up a conversation.

I rested my hand on the cooler. "Is this yours?"

"Don't touch it, please."

I withdrew my hand. He looked out the window. I looked past him to the field: there was no one out there. I could see the parking lot but not the 88. My seatmate wore a short-sleeved shirt in the kind of broad plaid you don't see anymore, a pattern to be found at Sears some years back but not even there now. His arms were very white and hairless, and he rested his hands in his lap, corresponding fingers of each touching at their tips. He sighed.

Perhaps I felt rebuffed at being asked not to touch the cooler and wanted to provoke him a little. In any case, when he returned his gaze to the back of the seat in front of us, I said, "What's in it?"

He turned and looked straight into my eyes. "It's a miracle on ice."

At that moment, the pilot made an announcement. It was quite startling to hear the intercom come alive, having had no prior assurance there was anyone in the cockpit. "The original cabin crew is not going to join us on today's flight. I'm sure all of you will understand. FAA regulations require us to have cabin crew before we fly. We're waiting now for new cabin crew. When further information is available, you will be informed. I'm sure you understand."

My seatmate, looking out the window, said, "Nice."

The passengers were extraordinarily docile. You would expect some sort of outcry, sarcastic remarks about skipping the peanuts and flying the plane, the perennial expressions of dissatisfaction, but today: silence. It made the passengers appear, when I looked back, like a sea of disembodied souls. I had not yet entered their world, but I knew that soon I would. I was afraid of it.

An hour passed.

"When you say the cooler contains a miracle on ice, what do you mean by that?"

"You couldn't stand it, could you?"

After a moment, I said, "The cooler has its own seat."

"Yes? Well, that's how we do it."

"That's how you do what?" I said sharply.

"That's how we transport a human heart." I had nothing to say and little to feel beyond a general sense of my impertinence. I must have communicated that because my seatmate softened immediately. I suppose he required some show of respect from me. "Let me correct myself"—yes, it was conciliatory—"This is how we *used* to do it before the cryonic shippers, the nitrogen drums, and so on. But things aren't like they *used* to be."

"I'm finding that out."

He looked at me oddly. "We have less time is what I'm trying to tell you. There's no pre-alert for the pickup in Salt Lake. I'm supposed to get this door-to-door. It wasn't a good day for the stewardesses to sleep in."

I suppressed an urge to say something.

"You harvest the heart, let the family decide if they want an open-casket funeral or not. You get through the elimination of blood, the rapid cooling, the packing, and the trip to the airport. It goes well, the heart's in a viable state. It's one hour to Salt Lake, the patient is on the table with his chest propped open, you've got a four-hour window from harvest to transplant, no ifs ands or buts, and the stewardesses slept in."

"I don't think it's that they slept—"

"I got it! Look, this thing has another hour left and it's getting to me."

"I understand."

I'm not sure I did, but that's what I said. The outburst from my seatmate was over and he fell silent again. So did I. Time now had a terrible weight. We heard nothing from the cockpit for an interminable period, then the door opened and the pilot appeared to tell us directly that we weren't going. He got off the plane. The copilot appeared and looked at the passengers with perplexity, unable to identify what species we belonged to, and he got off the plane. I turned and spoke to the back of my seatmate's head.

"What's going to happen now?" He seemed not to have heard me. I wondered if he would just ignore my question, and in fact he never looked back my way but continued to gaze at the empty runway.

He said, "What do you think happens when the heart dies?"

I drove toward the mountains. It didn't matter that the Oldsmobile barely ran. I was glad to be in it. It was an 88.

9

WHEN YOU IRRADIATED A PLACE as we did Nagasaki it didn't come back in quite the same way as a failed homestead, whose proprietors could move on to other hopes—unlike the pedestrians of that Asian city, who perhaps melted. I faced up to this being a different world and to the fact that we were ill equipped to absorb some of the newer differences. The New York catastrophe that greeted my return from fishing was one such alteration to our view of life. As a doctor, I had been kept aware of the changing threats to our health, which seemed to be macro adjustments to our environment—greenhouse gases, holes in the ozone layer—to which we made reasoned response—use sunblock, turn down the thermostat, etc. The destruction of the World Trade Center seemed akin to this; it was an environmental change of the kind that few understood but most could not stop talking about. Our exemption from the cyclone of world forces was over. As they said in Mexico, "We have seen the tips of the wolf's ears."

Awareness of larger themes was something we didn't much go in for where I lived. We tampered with ignorance to keep our lives miniaturized; the Internet made us feel like ants. We worried that we would no longer care about weather. I treasured my most rural and ignorant patients for the way other humans loomed for them. When someone died, they never said, *"Poof!"* It was always a good-sized tree that fell.

Jinx said that a special meeting of our board of directors had been convened in the wake of the attacks, and that our board chairman had made some remarkably inane remarks. "He told us it was a day that would live in infamy." Al Hirsch had said, "That rings a bell, Mr. Wilmot."

I asked her, "Is this like Pearl Harbor?" Jinx's hot water tank had failed and help from the plumber was several days off, so she was using my bathtub and if she couldn't get to it until late in the day, she stayed over in my downstairs guest room. It was probably not the best arrangement, as it fueled gossip, but more importantly it kept either of us from getting a good night's sleep because we talked late into the night. She sat at my kitchen table, a towel wound around her thick, damp hair, her face scrubbed clean of any makeup so that her green eyes seemed brighter.

"Pearl Harbor was the beginning of a war we knew was coming," she said. "We didn't know this was coming."

"I don't think we knew Pearl Harbor was coming."

"We knew war was coming. I think we knew that war would require a great effort but that it would be elsewhere."

"But is 'war' the right word? My father was in a war, but it wasn't consciously directed against civilians."

"I think in religious warfare differentiating between soldiers and noncombatants is considered a nicety, something superfluous. Look how the Christians went at it in the Thirty Years' War."

"The victims in New York were well outside the zone of conflict. It's hard for me to understand why anyone would do something like this. I hope you're not making excuses for these people."

"No, I'm just trying to picture the advantage they might see in waging war this way."

"Which is what?"

"It's cheap."

I was at once impressed by her objectivity and disturbed by her detachment, a perception that faded as we watched television and observed terrible scenes of suffering. We saw older, seasoned firefighters in a sheltered area shudder violently at the sounds of bodies falling on the pavement outside. Jinx covered her face, and when she uncovered it I saw that all her detachment had dissolved into terror. I didn't question it when she crawled into bed beside me that night, shaking, and I held her in my arms until morning, when we arose with averted eyes, dressed, made coffee, and went to work. She didn't come back, and though she must have had to make do with cold water at her place, I didn't ask. But when I saw her around the clinic I was aware of some slight new tension.

It wasn't much, but there it was, and quite mysterious too. It was everywhere.

Mortality is something people in medicine accept more readily than the general population, just through familiarity. I have, however, known doctors who have been diagnosed with fatal diseases and they didn't do much better than everyone else. Between every individual and the rest of the world is a stupendous firewall breached only by saints. For example, my mother's antic and superficial style, which I miss. When I say "superficial" I don't intend it in its usual belittling way; my mother's gift was to absorb the details and uproar of an ordinary day for what they were and no more—from boiling oatmeal to returning phone calls, from assaulting cobwebs with her broom to humoring my father, talking to her sisters with the phone tucked in her shoulder as she adjusted the curtains over the sink, telling my dad to jump-start her car because she'd left the key on, running out in summer, palms up, to greet a rain shower, doing her taxes, or feeding the cat who never hunted mice because of all the food she gave him—everything was exactly as it seemed, and nothing annoyed her more than the search for hidden meaning.

Her simple belief in God relieved her of a good deal of agitation, and I realized I'd missed an opportunity when I failed to quiz her about the nature of Him, Her, or It. My own conviction that life is somehow purposeful could have stood a little specificity, and my father's "God is crazy" was not what I had in mind. I've tried imagining it: a deity who fails to understand the consequence of His own actions and is unable to understand the difference between right and wrong. Unfortunately this smacks of a criminal defense. Or "crazy" like Patsy Cline, a concerned deity: "Worry. Why do I let myself worry?" There's a God I could understand. But my mother's God was a witch doctor; you could talk to Him only in tongues. And you crossed her God at your peril. Over a decade ago, my father renounced religion and promptly had a heart attack which looked like it might be fatal. Sitting next to him in his hospital room, my mother, worried but objective, said, "Soon you'll be with the devil." He recovered, though her failed prophecy did nothing to weaken her belief. And my father went obediently back to his imitation of faith.

The attack in New York felt more like a death in the family. A death in the family was something rarely experienced as an event. It was experienced as a change of seasons like the end of summer, or a spell of weather. A death in the family moved us closer to death ourselves. Religion had not made death less ominous: it remained a world we preferred not to enter. My mother's death not long after I began my career had the effect of removing a sort of white noise from my father's life and mine, a very pleasant white noise that I thought maybe only women could provide. It was the sound of life, unlike the logic of silence that appealed to men: women sought God while men sought Euclid. I wished they were the same.

I went over these things this way because I realized I'd been making myself out to be a solid citizen with the customary remorse and job weariness of anyone of my age and occupation. That was actually misleading. The temptation to claim common cause with the secret lives of everyone had its basis in fear.

My mailman, Spenser Hooper, had always taken an interest in me. Walking around and delivering mail in all weather had aged Spenser, who having been a couple of grades behind me in school had watched my transformation from nincompoop to physician with kindly fascination. He was very much aware of my troubles at the clinic and, standing in my doorway with a wad of mostly junk mail, he brought it up. "Well, Berl, this is awful, isn't it? You can't work, can you? How will you survive? You didn't actually do that to the lady, did you?" Never mind the assault of Al Qaeda on America.

"Why, that's the question, isn't it?" I said. Spenser found this as unsatisfactory as everyone else did, but he merely raised one eyebrow in exaggerated skepticism and handed me the letters. The bafflement of my mailman and onetime schoolmate sharpened my solitude. I saw it as something of a hardened position, neither willfulness nor indifference; and it combined a profound need to learn how I was judged with a disinclination to glorify the proceedings against me. I'm not sure why I was uncomfortable confusing my mailman.

I could tell that Spenser was out of ideas as to how he might continue with me when he said, "I'll still bring your mail" when he left, "unless your address changes."

I found this bland remark to be curiously ominous. It reminded me of my earliest school days when teachers would order me to "pay attention" and I would gaze all around the room looking for a suitable object for attention, which the teachers mistook for insolence.

I have always believed that it was my great good fortune to spend the first part of my life as a nitwit, and to have stayed in my hometown, where my limitations and peculiarities would always be in the air. The feeling you got by such persistence, of enlargement and occupying space, greatly outweighed the disadvantages of whatever you were known for. I could tell when I ran into my old teachers that they still viewed me as a dunce. Though I had become a good student by the end of my high school years, you never get a second chance to make first impressions.

Jinx was clearly more grounded than I. I didn't mind this discrepancy because I seemed comfortable at my own particular altitude believing as I did that a certain lack of attachment to the world yielded its own benefits. For example, sometimes Jinx and I cooked for each other: I got out a cookbook and followed the dotted line; Jinx looked into her refrigerator and winged it. She didn't know why I made a federal case out of cooking a meal; I didn't know why she set out on a course prone to failure, or at least lacking the authority of a cookbook. In short, Jinx was a real cook and I was not. Also, human beings were less mysterious to Jinx. When she found one of them up to no good, she simply took note without surprise. Injecting drama into the everyday was not her thing. As my mother's son, I felt that we are always swept by a mighty wind.

We were taking our lunch in the city park. Jinx ate a sandwich with one hand, holding her binoculars in the other to watch some hawks that in turn were studying the pigeons collected around the waterworks. I sat at the base of a tree, carefully prying open my sandwich to study its contents. It bothered me that I couldn't remember what I had put in there that very morning. It turned out to be some kind of processed ham and Swiss cheese, also processed, with Miracle Whip and a piece of iceberg lettuce.

She said that this internal investigation of possible malpractice had been instigated by the board of directors.

"Wilmot?" I asked.

"What's his problem with you?" Jinx asked.

"I wish I knew."

"Wasn't he your patient?"

"Yes. He still is. He was married to a wonderful girl, Adrienne."

"Is that it?"

"Well, sure."

"I get it," said Jinx. "He's embarrassed."

"You think?"

"I do. He's extremely vain. With your usual shirker's style, you rarely come to the board meetings. Wilmot is really onstage. One time he had a pince-nez and a hankie in his sleeve. The other board members are somewhat afraid of him: he's quite vindictive. Wilmot has little to do, and what little there is he finds beneath him. Perhaps you are his project."

Wilmot knew of Adrienne's indiscretion with me. It was hardly an accident and came out of strong feeling on both our parts. I really wish it hadn't happened, but it occured at a time when their marriage seemed to be ending. I was besotted with Adrienne for good reason, and if they had divorced at the moment it looked likely they would, our relationship, which was based at the very least on tremendous affection, might have ripened into something quite significant. But they patched things up, and even though Wilmot knew what had occurred between us, he didn't appear to mind; in fact it seemed to point toward a friendship. But two years later when they did divorce, our very brief affair became public knowledge, and from then on, Raymond Wilmot had it in for me. He took a very traditional view of his situation and by all reports threw himself into a cuckold's rage. After the divorce, when I'd see him, I knew what was on his mind, but the way he kept his distance and theatrically projected a burning gaze, made me think of of Rudolph Valentino in eye makeup.

"And now Niles Throckmorton is calling me up and telling me I need to be ready for trial."

"What? I think Niles is well ahead of himself. No one goes to trial out of someone's ill will unless it's the Khmer Rouge. I hope you're not taking this seriously."

There was no point in telling Jinx that I had done enough in my life to acquire all the culpability I'd ever need and that, at least in low moments, it didn't really matter what I was accused of as long as I was accused. She wouldn't have gotten that: she wouldn't have tried to get it.

I knew most of our local law enforcement, some of whom I had gone to school with. People ending up in law enforcement were not likely to take a warm view of anyone as weird as I was when I was young. Curtis Seaver and I had an especially awkward relationship because his family went to the same church as my parents and he knew that I told anyone who would listen that they were all crazy. In school, Curtis was the scourge of immorality and reported anyone he suspected of wrong-doing, whether it was shoplifting candy, smoking dope, or engaging in heavy petting. He was known to make citizen's arrests in traffic matters. The police department at that time and the local judge considered him at best tiresome and at worst a pain in the ass. Curtis Seaver was over six feet tall by the time he got to high school and never weighed less than two hundred pounds. Always prepared to enforce his judgments, he stalked the corridors solemnly, the archetypal frowning Christian. Twenty years had changed him little, though the uniform, the straps and badges, made him seem only more intractable. Unfortunately, Curtis also had a Realtor's license and was a shirttail associate of Wilmot's. Surely that was behind his paying me a visit and questioning me with surprising aggression.

"When did you first meet Miss Larionov?"

"Miss Larionov? What does she have to do with it?"

"Answer the question, please."

"I don't know, twenty years ago."

"And you've known her all this time?"

"I *did* know her. She's dead."

"But you knew her all that time?"

"No. We'd lost touch."

"Are you aware that Miss Larionov kept a diary?"

"No. I don't think she kept one when I knew her."

"I'm afraid you're not correct about that."

"Okay, she kept a diary when I knew her. Who gives a shit?"

"It may be important."

"I wouldn't know."

"It may be you will know in the future."

"Thank you, Officer Seaver. And, as a courtesy, can you tell me what this is all about?"

"In due course. Shall we continue?"

"Go for it."

"When you were with Miss Larionov, were there relations?"

"I believe she had an aunt and uncle in Great Falls."

"I don't think this is any time to be clever, if you understand your situation. Our records indicate you made obscene phone calls to Miss Larionov."

"Are you serious? I was cleared of that a long time ago."

"Really? It's right here in the records. I've never known them to lie, but let's just let that pass for a moment. Now once more, did you have relations with Miss Larionov?"

"None of your business, cocksucker. And give Wilmot my fondest regards."

"You clearly have no idea what effect such replies may have on your future."

"A fair wind to your ass, Curtis. By the way, which hole do you shit out of?"

He just smiled.

I went on working. I treated a farm wife for gonorrhea. She was a plain young woman carrying a leather purse with rodeo scenes carved into it. She sat before me in utter defeat once she'd had the diagnosis but seemed to cling to the hope that if this wasn't the same thing they called the clap she could live with it. I didn't tell her it was the same thing they called the clap. Initially, she had presented asymptomatic pelvic pain only, no bleeding, no discharge. I had her in twice because it took a couple of days to culture the cervical smear, and looking for bacteria on a stained slide was inconclusive, as it usually is. I told her I should see her husband as well, since he had every chance of contracting it. This threw her into further panic. "He'll kill me!" "Well, we don't want that," said I in the tones of the medical detachment that had contributed to my going nuts. As I wrote out a prescription for one of the third-generation antibiotics, telling her that I expected good results from them, I questioned her a bit to find out how she had managed to come down with this disorder. Her husband, she told me, was a fanatic about controlling weeds on the farm. Outbreaks of spurge, spotted knapweed, star thistle, and water hemlock had defeated his efforts to control them, and the only hope lay in buying expensive herbicides, which they couldn't afford. Therefore, he enlisted her in a Billings escort service, and by the end of the first year the weeds were gone but his wife was fighting several sexually transmitted diseases. She did seem to fear violence from him but thought that so long as it wasn't "the clap" she might have a bit of leeway. Rather than level with her—I'm not proud of this—I told her how she could secretly add antibiotics to his everyday food and drink, thereby preventing him from getting this "ailment"—she couldn't remember the word "gonorrhea"—and things could go on as before. "Thank God," she said. "After all, there's no good reason to upset our happy marriage."

"All the same, I think you should give up your other occupation in the interest of your health."

"I told you the weeds were under control. You weren't listening."

I did not let this sort of thing make me cynical because then I would have been the casualty of these disorders that I treated, and I had strong survival instincts. Many of the people any doctor sees do not have strong survival instincts; in fact, when I look at their smoking, drinking, obesity, and trauma-prone ways I'm inclined to think they scarcely cling to life. And when I poke around for positive things I could emphasize for them, I often find that they have good reason for submitting to gradual painless suicide. At first glance, there's nothing really terrifying about a half a million doughnuts or cigarettes, and the exhilaration of driving fast on black ice is anesthesia enough for the casualty waiting in the wings. What I may be cynical about is my wonderment at how all of us are dealt such different hands. This is, of course, religious cynicism, and though for thousands of years mankind has tried to unwind it, it remains as obdurate a conundrum as it was in the beginning. Being a doctor keeps one closer to it than some other jobs do. When I worked in the emergency room it was rare to hear stories beyond the immediate circumstances of the injury. "I missed a turn and hit a tree," not "My husband made me turn tricks to buy weed spray."

At the end of the day, I saw Alan Hirsch in the parking lot, scrutinizing my car. "Is this an 88?"

"Good for you. Yes, it is. Bought it in Canada."

"The Hitler car."

"The what?"

"88. HH in the alphabet. Stands for Heil Hitler."

"Oh, my God."

After resuming conventional duties at the clinic, I made a bit of a sortie. One of the nurses. I suppose that wasn't smart. Her name was Scarlett and things went well, but not at first.

"So you go to work and then you go home."

"Yeah, that's about it. I look after my dad."

"Well, that's not so different from my M.O. I go to the movies . . ."

"I don't go to the movies."

"You don't like movies?"

"No, I don't go to the movies."

"I go to the movies, by myself, with friends. I like movies."

"I like the good ones. You have to go through too many to get to the good ones."

"You probably think it's a lot of germs."

"Not really . . ."

"A public place. It's like an airplane, people mushed in. Here come the germs!"

"Well, I'm in germs all day. I spend the day with sick people."

"I guess it's the same case with me, all around me. But it's rare I get anything."

"You just draw blood all day. Half those people are in for a lipid profile, they're not sick."

"Sure, I suppose."

"Mine, half of them cough in my face, sneeze all over my shirt. But I don't get sick. It isn't germs we need to fear. It's something going haywire."

"Well, maybe if we went to a movie, or for a meal. Maybe this is a little abrupt, don't you imagine?"

"Maybe."

"I'm not suggesting performance issues or anything; I'm just saying 'sudden.' "

"I'm with you there."

"So, what now? Shall I put my clothes back on?"

"I think so, don't you?"

"I do, I do. I just feel a bit odd I got into this situation."

"Of course you do, but there you have it."

The deaths of my parents were the stepping-stones by which I'd crossed the latest river. They spoke in tongues, righteous Holy Rollers to the end. At least my mother was; my father acted his part and may have occasionally believed it. He once told me he actually enjoyed speaking in tongues. Because of what they had been promised, they couldn't wait to be dead and soon they were. My mother had no last-minute adjustments to make from this life to the next, and though she saw death coming, she crossed over peacefully. I was present, and my mixing grief with the apprehension that a loved one was getting her way has baffled me ever since. My father, on the other hand, had several things in mind, and I'm pleased I got to hear about them. I owed to them my occasionally sporadic social skills, as was often the case in Holy Roller families, and this despite never believing a speck of their doctrine from the very beginning. I was just a natural-born, but not stupid, oaf. I grew out of most of it.

I treated my father in the last days of his life, all geriatric stuff, nothing special. I was sure he missed my mother, but widowhood was easier than marriage and he was generally lighthearted. He came in readily, but the real mission was unpacking the parts of his life that were most on his mind. You would have thought this had happened long ago, but the setting made all the difference: sitting in my examining room with me in my white coat gave things just the formality he required.

He wanted to talk about war. He was close to the end of his life and had quit going to church. "Everything all right?" I asked him, not quite out of the blue. He didn't look so hot.

"About half the time."

He began to muse again about his experience in the Ardennes, the

Battle of the Bulge. He seemed to feel fortunate to have been part of it, even though he saw many of his comrades killed or wounded. His reasons were interesting: it was the biggest war of all time; it starred the most evil regime of all time; the desperate German breakout, "Watch on the Rhine," was the one Nazi offensive conceived entirely by Adolf Hitler, the most evil man of all time, etc., etc. The Panzers, Tigers, and King Tigers, were the best tanks with the most tactically sophisticated tank crews and with air cover by the Luftwaffe, which had sixty jets in the hunt. In some ways, the experience seemed to justify a life otherwise uneventful and even less accomplished. My father led a platoon of infantry right into the first onslaught south of the Losheim Gap; and at Manderfeld and Krewinkel, using the skills he had learned in the woods of America and imparted to his men, my father and his comrades killed twenty-one Volksgrenadiers, experienced soldiers from the Eastern Front in snow camouflage. "In the year 1944, our world offered no greater thrill than shooting Germans." His group crept up close enough to German transport to shower with lead an armored personnel carrier bearing SS Panzer Commander Jochen Peiper, "a blond fellow handsome even in the binoculars, guilty of many atrocities in Russia, especially Kursk, retired to France after the war, a pleasant life until the village communists burned him alive in his own house. After the fire was out they found Peiper, winner of Hitler's Knight's Cross. He weighed three pounds." Thumbs-up to this, still happy about the roasting of Peiper. He hated Germans. When they dispersed after firing on Peiper, four of his men were killed; one lingered badly wounded and, after a long night of listening to his groans, a trooper from New Jersey tried to go to his aid, whereupon both GIs went up in the same bomb: the Germans had booby-trapped the wounded man's body.

"Right after the surrender at Schnee Eifel, we ran into a splinter of the Fuhrer Escort Brigade, who drove us into a farmhouse and then overran it. Then while we fought from the back of the cellar, the Germans got overrun by our infantry and we sat in the dark listening to the firefight all night long. When it was over, we climbed to the first floor and saw the dead Germans piled halfway up the walls. Don't get me wrong, I loved killing Germans, but when I saw all these bodies, they didn't seem to be Germans particularly. Some of them were too young to be in this at all. It wasn't like you could ask for someone's driver's license before you shot them. I guess the whole logic that kept us all there became less and less clear to me. I watched our men cutting off fingers with wedding rings and I knew I was going to leave the war. I headed downstream as the battles were subsiding and as the Germans retreated to slow the Russians to the east. I crossed the Meuse and kept going west, staying in the countryside because of the snipers still hiding in the rubble. I don't remember the towns, I remember the bodies. There were seventy-five thousand of them and no route could keep you out of them for long. But guess what? I got to Paris. And in Paris, absent without leave, I began to live again!"

I hadn't heard this before. And I didn't understand it. His own father had deserted in the First World War, and that story, told over and over, had functioned as an original stain, even one which in fraught moments my mother would disinter. I was getting the feeling that it was merely tangential to what I was hearing now, as having long been given to understand that my father's valor had at its heart my grandfather's desertion and the need to redeem our blood, ordinary as it was.

"I ran into another AWOL, Donald Boyes from Garden City, Kansas, and we found a taxicab with an English-speaking driver. We wanted to hit the nightclubs and told the driver where to go, but it became obvious he was taking us to the MPs. When the driver took a shortcut to where we knew perfectly well the MPs were headquartered, up between tall dark walls just wide enough for the cab, Don Boyes shot him with a Walther he was very proud of. It had SS proof marks and a real clear swastika, a great souvenir. From then on, we were on the run and soon fell in with a group of men also AWOL. Some of them were even Germans who were living in rat holes all over Paris, stealing gasoline and selling it on the black market, hijacking vehicles, counterfeiting three-day passes, and so on. Do you want to hear this?"

"You bet I do." I wondered if patients were piling up at my door.

"I'm not taking anything with me. I want to be light as a feather." After a very long silence, he said, "Your mother forbade me to tell you any of this while she was alive." He looked at his hands in thought. "My group were all from out west, some of them crooked, some of them shell-shocked, some of them defected from Patton after he lost men trying to rescue his son-in-law. We turned into gasoline pirates and I was their king. When the Krauts surrendered, we just drifted back into our units and said we escaped from POW camps. We had a couple of months in occupied Germany." The Fräuleins were available. Though the men were undeterred by army rules against fraternization, they had a motto: "Copulation without conversation is not fraternization." They whistled "Lili Marlene" just like the Boche and were disappointed when they could no longer listen to jazz on Axis Sally's radio show. Don Boyes and my dad demobbed like all the others and went home. "After the war, I joined Boyes in Kansas. We had a lot of money and we spent it all on big, well-fed strong American whores and whiskey. When it was gone, I thought I better go into the hospital, but Donald took me to a Pentecostal church. He was anxious to repent, and that's where I met your mother. I don't know whether she cured me or God did, but I was in a bad way. It took me over two years to stop shaking and get a job."

Whenever my old man went to the VFW he indulged his sole dandyism by wearing the parachute-silk scarf he'd worn all through the war. It was German silk.

I hardly knew what to do with my father after the death of my mother. A big plank bridge built on the skeleton of a railroad car, right where the cattle ford was a hundred years ago, spanned the racing green creek. On hot days, we took lawn chairs there and the breeze from the creek kept us cool. And birds—there were always so many birds there, goldfinches and juncos, warblers and magpies. In a dry landscape, this small, persistent water gave life to an eternally busy community of creatures. I could see some water hemlock and an ancient cottonwood that had abruptly died that spring, already colonized by sapsuckers in its metropolis of leafless branches. He was still baffled by religion and felt there must be something or other he could go by. Instead I could tell by the way he gazed upon this lively scene that it would at least do until something better came along. A Socrates man myself, I never felt that human spiritual development prior to the birth of Christ was canceled by his arrival. Still, I was very anxious for my father to have whatever consolation was available, despite my usual harkening to Harry Truman's remark "When I hear them praying in the amen corner, I head home and lock the chicken house."

A raucous kingfisher dove from the willows, heedlessly hunting tiny trout in the rushing surface of the stream. From my vantage at some elevation in my lawn chair there was something boyish about my father dangling his legs from the bridge. "Very strange thing about living," he mused. "You start out by yourself but head for the crowds. The infantry, that was a fine crowd. But then the crowd dispersed and kept on getting smaller, and in the end, I've wound up almost by myself again. I think it's pretty normal."

"Sure."

"Your mother and I, we got old. No surprises. I'm still hanging around. That's about it. Hey, relax! I like it. What I'm headed for, it's a mystery. Mysteries are good. Let me at 'em."

We just lay low the next several days. My dad had checked out a best seller from the lending library; I couldn't believe he'd ever get through it, eight hundred pages about a straying but remorseful husband, set in the Hamptons during the Civil War. And we rented a movie: Bruce Willis dynamites the sewers of Chicago to rescue an autistic Navajo boy. I had to get him away from this sort of thing. We built a fire. I read him some poetry, Saint-John Perse, *Seamarks,* John Donne, *The Eve of St. Agnes,* and an epic that had been appearing serially in our local paper, *Love Slaves of the Upper Yellowstone.* He fell asleep and I had to wake him and lead him, groggy, to his bed. I tucked him in, opened his window a crack, and set a glass of water on the side table. I laced my fingers over the top of one of the bedposts and just kind of hung there watching him sleep, unable to tell why my heart ached. I'd gotten into the habit of sailing through moments like this and I thought if I could get it right, I wouldn't do that anymore; I'd stay right there with it until it was clear.

10

SOMETIMES AFTER LUNCH, I climbed the sandstone bluff behind the clinic, which, after the first ascent, opened onto vast rolling grassland that seemed to extend forever. I did this for my health, of course, but the great vista, which changed continuously with the light and the seasons, was something I found heartening. Shadowed in places, lifted here and there by breeze, the grassland that afternoon looked silken; about halfway across were small circular shapes, of several colors, bobbing and drifting in the summer air like ectoplasms. I stopped to stare: I couldn't account for them. I'd been up here often but this was new. It was a long walk until I could confront the mystery: five colored balloons, JUST MARRIED on their sides, bobbing on zephyrs.

On these walks, I always expected to have some small experience of the sacred, something to help me become not so much a doctor as a shaman who sets out on his flight through home skies. I walked toward the wedding balloons with that hope. I had observed my mother speaking in tongues, but her attempts to indoctrinate me went in one ear and out the other. Still the longing remained.

Seneca said, "Each of us is sufficient audience for the other." I tried to live up to this, but I was well aware of my frequent failures as the recitations of others embedded in their sufferings only reminded me of my own. I did plan to rise above this but hadn't arrived at that station, and so I went on grinding at my own story without much satisfaction.

One of my patients, an old Harvard man, had come west with a private income when very young, bringing his bride. For the last thirty years the two had tried most of the barstools of our town, first out of fascination with the ways of a region not familiar to them, then out of a fascination with alcohol and the inability to go home together until obliged to do so, for they were famous battlers whose shouts could be heard all over town. Roger was known as "Old Yeller" for his share of the bellowing; Diana, the wife, died of cirrhosis of the liver and Roger was not far behind. But he went on seeing me and in fact all the doctors, and inevitably I served as listener to his various salutations to the late Diana, intoned in his remarkable diction. A small and finely wrinkled man with a high forehead showing thin blue veins, he began to speak as though others besides me awaited his remarks. "Nothing ever quite picked Diana up like a libation presented at an unexpected hour. She had such marvelous blood." I was working on my listening, but the visuals that ran through my mind over Roger's sound track of their falling in and out of low bars made the story harder to follow than plausible conversation might have been. He had told me over and over that he and Diana had met at dance class: "She caught my eye while I attended a pair of lissome suffragettes." Roger's hands were shaking, and as he rambled on I gradually fought off my daydreaming to note that he was headed somewhere, and indeed he was: Roger wanted me to help him die. "I've read everything under the sun on the subject, and the bottom line is I won't feel a thing."

"Roger, it would be highly inappropriate. You're the picture of health." That was a lie, but I was trying to encourage him. At least he wasn't fat. "In this state, assisted suicide is murder. Roger, I wouldn't murder you under any circumstances." That wasn't true. I don't think there was a doctor in our clinic who hadn't dispatched someone to the happy hunting ground. Roger was weeping.

"Send me to Diana."

"I can't, Roger, and I won't."

"What about that woman you took care of? You seem to be able to help your old girlfriends, don't you? Well, Doctor, I'm afraid I'm not one of those." Roger got to his feet and, plucking a tissue from the box beside my examining table, turned to me with a transformed face, an expression of lofty annoyance. "You tin-pot sawbones. I'll find someone who will do as I ask."

"I'm terribly sorry . . ."

"Oh, no, you're not. Let's not part on that note."

As he left, I heard him addressing people out in the hall. He would no longer support the clinic, he would put in a call to Washington, he would yield to the pressure of his lawyers, and so on. He was furious and probably knew that his wish for assisted suicide was wholly focused on the potions I might use to bring it about. He had really ruined his little wife, who was not a bad sort. She had a gesture of slinging her shoulders to get her hair off her face, something preserved from girlhood no doubt, since her hair had grown light as air. She arrived in our town, according to my father, full of gentle cultivation, only to be transformed into a dazed barfly by her husband, whom my father called "a vicious nonentity." For good reason, Roger was friendless. "When he dies," said my father, "they'll have to screw him into the ground."

Many of the problems I treated were related to overeating. Almost everyone these days was wholly focused on his or her stomach, what Dante called "that miserable sack that makes shit of what we eat." I also got a good many women complaining of stress, and the stress often turned out to be the thug they'd married. Some of the women put up a good fight, but the effort took it out of them. The wife of a big-game hunter who came home from a bear hunt in Canada two months late, bringing by way of propitiation a Canadian souvenir, was told by this spunky woman to "take the little Mounty and shove it where the monkey hid the peanut." This precipitated a battle wherein the bear hunter offered to cut off her head and defecate down her neck. After reciting each of these tales, she smiled, upper teeth resting on lower lip as if the smile had to lean on something to stay upright. She withstood these barrages, but in a matter of days she came in to see me, asking me for tranquilizers. I prescribed an SSRI instead and, as they are slow to work, gave her a pile of Xanax samples and advised her to stay half gaga until the SSRIs elevated her serotonin level. "I don't suppose you'd consider dumping Big Boy, which would be best, so we'll just medicate you so you can go on until the next catastrophe." She said it was a beautiful bear and they were having it mounted.

On days like that, I saw this as a town spoiled by God's displeasure.

But that never lasted and I came to love the sight of ordinary activity once again, the thing that had sustained me most of my life. When I had the Oldsmobile serviced, I spent time with the mechanics. I began to frequent the breakfast cafés again, even the clubby ones where the farmers and ranchers huddled like conspirators. In the happy years between the steam-cleaning service and the post office—that is, before my father lost his dream ground to foreclosure—we would make the short drive into town on our winding road through walls of chokecherry and hawthorn past bounding deer and the occasional bear to arrive just as the bicycles were wheeled out in front of their shop and awnings were cranked out, or the aged were taking their constitutionals and the flags were being raised and groggy children were heading out to their schools and the train could be heard down in the valley. Nowadays, experiences came at me like bugs hitting the windshield. I wasn't sure I could keep up. Of all the mysteries of life, nothing was more mysterious than the return of happiness. I was willing to wait.

I drove a little over a mile outside town to the place my parents had lost. It may have been absorbed into larger property around it, but in any case the house was long abandoned. I pulled into the yard and got out of the car. Then I walked across the footbridge that replaced the creek ford of a century ago, carrying my drink and making a desultory effort to recognize the birds around me. I followed the trail through a small forest of aspens, the dense canopy only here and there revealing the bright clouds and blue sky just then taking on the scrim of evening. I finished my drink and left the glass beside the trail.

The creek turned sharply toward the north as I left the aspens and they followed its bank. This created a tiny meadow protected from all normal winds, and in this meadow stood the oldest cottonwood I knew of. I'd been visiting this tree all my life. I didn't think it was unusual for children to hit upon a favorite tree, and I believed that this early affinity came from a memory of a time when trees could be sacred; I felt no need to shake off this conception. Perhaps it sheltered Crow people. There was something too about this tree as an aerial being held from beneath the ground by the grand starburst of roots, life and death, with the earth as the threshold between worlds. I've courted this state at times all my life—comparing bones to the stones around the tree, breath to the wind, eyes to sunlight, head to the moon, and so on. I'm not sure what I got out of it, but I have always found in nature something of a cosmic liturgy.

The old tree stood alone, but to the east a few strides away its seed-bearing flowers dispersed by insects and wind had created a forest of smaller trees. I sat at the base of the cottonwood, my back against its deeply furrowed gray bark, and looked up into the world of its branches toward its top, which might have been a hundred fifty feet away. The clouds of leaves and catkins blocked my view not far above my head; I knew that by midsummer fledgling birds would venture to the ends of its branches to begin their first attempts at flight, a skill that would take some to the sea, some to the pampas. Then all the leaves would float to earth and against a darker sky the somber outline of the great cottonwood would emerge and brace itself for the long winter; a willful crookedness of its limbs, defiant and imploring, suggested the long fight ahead. Here and there on our old place, one of these giants lay on its side, several tons of earth reared up around the tangled root ball, a few branches half a story high trying to live on. I used to hear them go down in windstorms all the way from the house and the abrupt subsidence, a welter of sounds, spoke certainly of the surrender of a great soul. It had been a long time since any of this was ours. I guess we couldn't afford it.

The dispute with the board was finally resolved when Wilmot suddenly found other interests, something about a ski resort he'd invested in, and without his egging them on, the rest of the board slipped back into their customary status as airheads and boobs. Still, I found myself in bad odor with some of my colleagues for having continued to go to work as though there was no problem. That there turned out to be in fact no problem seemed to have little bearing on my situation, and so my discomfort was not alleviated. There was to be a staff meeting in the morning, and I think it was my dread of it that encouraged me to hook up with some old school chums and go on a bit of a bender at Pine Creek Lake. It was wonderfully just like high school. We had girls and a campfire, s'mores and an old M1 rifle to fire tracer shells into the night. One of my friends, a chiropractor from Miles City, was rolling blunts of high-octane BC bud, and I ended up sleeping in my Oldsmobile. Sad to say, I had to go straight to the dreaded staff meeting at the clinic, still half asleep, though not sleepy enough to relieve my apprehension at the sight of the reserve parking entirely occupied by the cars of doctors. My hair was filled with excelsior or some other packing material from a box of

Christmas lights that had been in the backseat of the Olds for a couple of years, and it was clear that a number of the fastenings to my clothing had not made the trip back to town. I was late but I was also a doctor.

Before entering the building, I took a long look around the outdoors—the blue sky, the lenticular clouds, the treetops encircling the pretty houses. What reluctance I felt, and what disinclination to enter. I was the last to arrive and far from reassured to see those assembled. Gary Haack, the orthopedic surgeon, was the first to remark on my arrival. Gary is a compact, youthfully muscular man, a tennis player and bachelor who takes his vacations in places such as East Timor. He sprawls in his chair like a highly paid linebacker bored at a team meeting, flipping the lid of his cell phone. He cried, "What happened to you?" I turned to the other jackals, who gazed at me with elevated eyebrows.

"Changing a tire on a dirt road. Ever try it?"

"After you changed the tire," Gary asked, "did you spend the night under the car?" I ignored him.

"What's the state of play here? Are we getting anything done? I see I'm late."

Laird McAllister, the cold-blooded old family-practice guy, tented his hands and said, "Little to report, Berl. Lots of administration, not much medicine." Laird had once famously remarked to a woman patient, "Cosmetic surgery being what it is today, there's no reason in the world for you to go on living with a nose like that." Jinx Mayhall looked like she was asleep, though she covertly watched me with a worried gaze. Alan Hirsch seemed pained by Haack's aggressive tone.

Then Haack said, "I just wish I could walk in and know what my day would be like without the detective work." I think he was addressing me, but he didn't seem to want to look my way.

"I'm not sure I know what you mean."

"It's not that complicated: appointments, billing, patient history, easy retrieval of diagnostic data." He seemed to be lecturing me.

"Buy the software."

"Hell, no, I'm not buying the software."

"Who did you have in mind to buy you the software?"

"Berl, you need sleep."

Jinx Mayhall said, "I have no trouble keeping track of my patients' history, but I don't have hobbies and it pleases me to have the well-being of my patients fully in mind at all times. We have a clinic manager and he sees to the billing. I hope it's fair and appropriate, but I don't worry about it much. I'm comfortable in my house and my car runs. I don't change my own tires, I have Triple A. I like my figure, but I avoid being seen in a bathing suit. I look after children, period, full stop."

Unseen by Jinx Mayhall, Dr. Gary Haack rolled his eyes for the benefit of Dr. McAllister, as they were in cahoots, two well-bred, cut-to-the-chase doctors. Unheard from until now, Dr. Elvis Wong, our eagle-eyed radiologist, asked, "Who sets the information parameters and where is the database? Is it here?" Wong was always the most up-to-date of all of us, and he turned out to be right about the needs of the clinic more often than anybody else because his individualism and ego were under control. I was having a terrible time caring, but that might have been my state. I mean, of course it was my state.

I didn't want to get politicized in our claustrophobic group, but I did say, "As I understand it, we'd set the parameters according to specializations, exams, blood groups—all that stuff. The database is elsewhere. I'm not recommending this. We may be too small. I'm just responding to Gary wanting this from elsewhere."

"That's right, blame me," said Dr. Haack.

"No," I said, patiently, "but my caseload is too diverse for this sort of thing. You're just looking at bones."

Haack said, "How about a shower?"

"In due time."

This was all fairly good-natured, but I was tired. We had a clinic manager and he seemed to be doing all right, despite being a Wilmot appointee. Once in a while we'd get annoyed and fire the manager, but this wasn't one of those times. And we used to have better control of our board. We often excluded the manager from our meetings in case the impulse to fire him overtook us unexpectedly, and with Wilmot elsewhere surveying lift sites, we'd leap to do so just because the opportunity was there. Things were moving along. Mostly, I noticed the air of contentment among these doctors, hardworking men and women all. This was their life. I alone seemed to have missed this accommodation, though I'd had it once until several blows uprooted my certainty. I wondered whether I might be over-crediting my particular subjectivity, whether, in fact, all the other doctors were likewise seething with doubt, though they didn't look it. They looked bored and anxious to go back to work they enjoyed. I think they believed themselves to be necessary. I wasn't sure I did. Not today anyway. I was just beginning to feel if not ashamed about the binge at least baffled at my own behavior. But I was mistaken: they were not anxious to get back to work; only I rose to leave. A conspicuous pause ensued and I knew it was about me.

"Yes?"

"I wonder if you'd stay for a minute," said Laird McAllister. He was the only one looking up; the others seemed to have found something in their laps to be interested in. I was most worried by the look of compassion on McAllister's lined old face. I knew he was just acting.

I said, "Of course." This brought the heads up, newly adorned with concern, anger, and inquiry. By this point, however, Laird McAllister was swept by awkwardness and inauthentic embarrassment. It was terribly quiet and I thought for a moment of getting them out of this, but I refrained. At length Jinx addressed me.

"Berl," she said, "is everything all right?"

I said that it was. I should have reflected on the somber state of things. Instead, I reacted to Jinx's earnest concern by staring at her lips. Nice lips. I didn't dare subject Jinx to my primitive wooing under so many prying eyes, but I did want to give her at least a little smile. I caught her trying not to return it.

Laird McAllister, animated once again, suddenly threw his head back and bayed, "Nothing whatsoever has been normal about your behavior, Berl, for a very long time." Laird, from New Hampshire, our sole Yale man, had a declamatory style that defied contradiction: lofty and blunt. I had known this was coming even during his theatrical run-up.

"All in the eye of the beholder, Laird. I've never found you normal. But it's a great country and we accept one another."

It was true that I was a little indisposed as I appeared before them; it had been a long day and night. I saw no advantage in this roadshow assassination of Saint Stephen and so I went to my nurse for the day's schedule, which was promptly obliterated by an emergency which looked to be entirely open-ended. McAllister's accusation rang in my ears. I thought that my nurse was a bit cavalier as she informed me, and I concluded that my deteriorated standing was showing up everywhere. Now she stood before me with a gift box of Dole pineapples acquired on her vacation in Hawaii and I couldn't remember her fucking name, which caused me to enthusiastically celebrate the pineapples.

Gladys was now a very old widow living out in the tall uncut practically by herself—she had a hired man, Dale, equally if prematurely decrepit, a hundred cows, eleven bulls, and three swaybacked horses. Dale, my sort-of-moronic playmate when I had worked for Gladys and Wiley, was the one who had called the clinic to say that he thought she might be dying. She had spent eighty-three years under the south-facing rimrock that formed the edge of her grazing land, a great plateau of native grass where ravens built nests in low trees. She was a clever old woman whom I was always ready to serve, on house calls and otherwise; she was canny about what would become of her ranch after she was gone, but all alone and, from the drift of today's report, dying. Gladys had seemed to be quite old the whole time I'd known her; I think she was older than my mother and father, whom she outlived. But now she was genuinely very old.

I was standing in the corridor trying to puzzle out my day, gauging just how much caffeine it would take to get through it, when Alan Hirsch sidled up and accorded me a long gaze in which I thought I saw some affection. "I hope the detachment you exhibited at this morning's meeting was simulated."

"It comes and goes."

"Because if it wasn't, your problems are even bigger than I feared."

I was having a hard time following this. We had, between how I was perceived by my colleagues and the ways in which I saw myself, true cognitive dissonance. That was enough to piss anybody off. Of course I understood what he meant, but I had to occupy some middle ground as a strategic matter. Groups that are of one mind, like the gathering this morning, are really only content with weeping confessions. It was time to throw Alan off the trail, and so I told him about a crow that had turned up on my flagpole several times this past month and addressed me in various combinations of caw-caw-caw in a way that made me understand it was an invitation for me to become a crow too. "Obviously I'd love to turn into a crow. Wouldn't you, Alan?"

"No, Berl, I feel no need to become a crow. Cardiologist seems to work at the moment." Alan had in fairness always been on my side, but I was unwilling to take on one more disturbing bit of self-knowledge.

Gladys was unable to come to the hospital. We'd been through this before—it was clear that she understood death was near, and her ranch was the place she intended to meet it. We'd had a couple of years of close calls, but each year's calf crop reinvigorated her. Nevertheless, I'd had to make several diving catches to keep her on the planet a bit longer. Her neighbors, me included, branded for her, and as she looked out on the massed pairs in the drifting smoke, the horsemen moving slowly among them with the loops of rope pinned under their elbows, she always seemed to find enough life for another season. But today when I talked to Dale, I got the impression that this was it. "I doubt you'll get here in time, Doc." I started to put together a kit, but in the end just brought the electronic stethoscope. It was amplified and I could hear a pin drop anywhere in the body. I really trusted it to hunt down the faintest murmur, and auscultation was my personal juju: heart, lungs, intestines—just let me listen! Those turds at this morning's meeting couldn't hear a diesel backfire through their stethoscopes. I seemed to know that I was bringing it along for the moment when I heard nothing. You name it, Gladys had it. As to the clinical information, the on-site stuff I had just gotten from Dale: Gladys was a goner. In the long run, and without unwarranted credulity, you need an eyewitness. Dale had been studying Gladys for a quarter century and Dale thought she was about out of here.

Gary Haack caught me just as I left the building. I had farmed out all my afternoon patients and was ready to go. I was tired of his hyper little performance already, but it looked like I was in for more as he bounced around in his high-tops. "What's this you've left me with? A twenty-five-year-old anorexic potter?" Sherry was not an easy case. I was glad he stopped me.

"Talk to her, Gary. I don't know what to do with her. She needs counseling, really inpatient would be best. She thinks she has a tapeworm."

"And you want me to talk to her about her tapeworm?"

"Yeah, talk her out of it. Get her some help. You'd be a new voice."

"Here's the only thing I know to do for tapeworms: You bring a candy apple every day for three days and shove it up the patient's backside. On the fourth day you bring a hammer and no candy apple. When the tapeworm comes out of the patient's behind and hollers, 'Where's my candy apple!' you hit him over the head with the hammer. That's the only cure I'm aware of." I stared at him.

"Gary, the tapeworm is imaginary. If you start believing in the tapeworm, we can't help this girl."

I departed before Haack could object, leaving him, I hoped, with the impression that I thought he was as deluded as the patient. In any case, he'd have plenty on his hands: Sherry claimed to know all she needed to know about her body. When I told her she should get a little counseling about the tapeworm, to which I thereby lent inescapable credence, she snarled that she wasn't about to walk into *that* trap. She placed one hand on her throat and the other on her buttocks to indicate the home of the parasite, and said, "He's there. It has to be dealt with." Since Sherry was an utterly beautiful young woman, I was sure plenty of people had bought into the worm.

Anyway, off to see dying Gladys at last, I took the road northeast over Tin Can Hill, off toward all those coarse and evocative features, "Dead Man," "Hangman," "Lone Indian," "Sourdough," gulches, draws, benches, coulees in a rangeland that on first look seemed tortured and on second, vigorous, confronting sky and grass and threadbare human occupation. Here, Gladys Bokma, child of settlers who cooked over buffalo dung, stood it all off in the little kingdom she called White Bird, which she herself had named in childhood, generating a persistent mystery to everyone, including her late husband, Wiley, who with a nicotine-stained hand always waved away the White Bird question and said it was something "she don't share." But inside the ranch gate, a hanging sign said "White Bird," and I of all people who wished to be a crow had no intention of asking her about it.

The road to the house followed a dashing creek, and the sun shone down through the streamside brush, igniting parts of the running water and small pools where clouds of gnats danced in the shadows. Just shy of the ranch yard, the stream had hollowed a sandstone face into a tall, deep shell, its roof layered with the nests of cliff swallows.

Dale waited for me in the stand of windblown hollyhocks that surrounded the doorway. A straw hat shaded his gaunt face and concealed his ever shifty eyes. I could note that he still wore Wiley's shirts, as they were a good deal too big for him. A sprinkler made its weak attempt to keep twenty square feet of lawn green, but it was in a bad fight with the west wind. Dale had started here so long ago, an incongruous figure in a ducktail haircut, Lucky Strikes rolled in the sleeve of his T-shirt and a hot-rod Ford coupe. He wasn't worth a shit then and he'd gone downhill ever since, but Gladys liked him. He had grown children in town with various mothers from the hot-rod Ford days. Right up there with White Bird as a mystery was the fact that Gladys and Wiley had never run Dale off. They acknowledged that he didn't do much but answered all queries with, "Where would he go?" He'd try at the brandings, all right, but he always got knocked down and Gladys would have to make him a poultice of some hallowed if useless sort. When I thought about Dale post-Gladys, I foresaw my ending up with him in some way. I kind of hated that.

Dale had a resonant baritone that over the years had more than once forestalled discovery of his shiftless nature. No one hearing that deep timbre say, "We've got a day's work ahead of us!" would ever suspect that Dale had no intention of doing much of it. My mother was taken with his voice too and made him sing in the choir at her crazy church. She had him all dressed up and booming out of the loft before Wiley demanded he give it up. It broke Dale's heart to be back on the manure spreader Sunday mornings. Strangely enough, his deep voice and sauntering gait encouraged Wiley to believe that Dale's problem was that people undervalued him; so Wiley stole him away from a neighboring rancher named Grey Gaitskill. Many's the time I saw Gaitskill beat the dust out of the back of Wiley coat, shouting, "He's yours, Wiley! Not 'til death do you part!"

"I'll just go in and see her," I said to Dale.

"I'll go in with you."

I declined his offer mildly enough, but Dale appeared to have received a gallon of ice water in the face. I just couldn't take the time to explain why I thought it best to quietly enter without introduction or surprise and assess Gladys's state without introductory remarks by Dale. So I left him where he stood, seemingly staggered by rejection. His arms hung at his sides, and in his face indignation and grievance were at war. Out of the sun his unfortunate eyes were visible.

I knew my way around the house well enough that, having left my pathologist's hat behind, so to speak, I was able to stride straight to the bedroom—there was only one—and open the door slightly but enough to look in: a dresser, a bed, a photograph of Wiley at the Big Timber rodeo—I recognized the grandstand—and making a small mound under her comforter, Gladys, at the extent of her life span as one of earth's longest-living mammals. She seemed asleep—a tremendously different appearance than the airless gray look of the dead—and a pitcher of water on the stand at her bedside still had a few ice cubes floating. Good on Dale. I entered and sat at the foot of the bed.

Gladys opened her eyes and said, "It's the end of me."

"I don't know if it is or it isn't," I said, "but you've lived a long time."

It was a while before she answered. She said, "I suppose." I think she must have drifted off. She seemed peaceful and even comfortable. This was looking like a fairly jolly segué considering the options of which as a physician I was aware, especially the brutal fights to live I had seen waged by accident and shooting victims during my ER days. Mortality and the sense of unfairness were poor bed companions.

Gladys dying made a modest bump. Nothing there to claim admiration for the thousands of miles she'd ridden through her herds, the horses, dogs, and husband she'd outlived, the thousand pies baked, the cattle cars she'd helped crowd, and the hours she'd listened to the radio wondering about the world. The Stetson hats it took a decade to rot out, the britches that went first in the seat, the war-surplus sunglasses she wore, the Ford tractor that after a quarter century could take no more of her abuse and died. The little flower bed in her front yard never got better; in fact, after Wiley died, it got worse.

She didn't regain consciousness right away, and I could see that her respiration had declined markedly since she'd spoken her few words. I reached over and found her pulse at the carotid and, without trying very hard to count, got the impression it was down around forty. Gladys had every right to fade away and I had every intention of permitting it. If her throat muscles began to fail and the dreaded rattle began, there would be no intubation, which I felt violated the old. If she failed to wake up, we wouldn't haul her to town and introduce isotopes to her system to determine whether or not there was blood flow to her brain, though that was just what a couple of the turkeys back at my clinic would do, especially if they were trying out some new machine. By keeping her right here on home ground, I would see to it that no one turned to hopeless ventilation out of some bogus respect for life, or moved her around strange places, for fear she would awaken at the end and not know where she was.

I was tired and struggled against objectless inertia, relieved only by lending my car to the still moping Dale and sending him to town for a pizza.

"Plain pizza," he said, barely moving his lips.

"Surely not. With everything."

"Even pineapple?"

"Yes, which reminds me: go by the Dairy Queen and pick up a Tropical Freeze. What d'you want?"

"Beer." Then he cried out for emphasis, *"Beer!"*

"Get that too, but go to DQ last so the Tropical Freeze doesn't melt." I could see Dale bridle at this bit of micromanagement, but he said nothing before heading for my car, wavering off like a windblown rag.

When Dale was gone, I was free to sit on the porch, on an old church pew, and look out at the land. The base of ledge rock was deep in shadow, but the crown of grass was luminous gold in the late-evening sun. I'd had old ranchers tell me that the day always came when they realized the land didn't care about them; I think it was a moment of despair. I don't think Gladys had ever had such a moment: this was White Bird. The wild grass no more needed to care about anybody than the doorway to the house needed to remember Gladys and Wiley's honeymoon. They were an unlikely couple: Gladys part horse and Wiley part cigarette.

I went back inside and gazed at her. I believed I saw great fading, but distrusted myself and got out my stethoscope. Her bowels were silent, her lungs were torpid, and her heart was lagging its own meter. I'd be lucky to finish my pizza before Gladys went through the pearly gates. While I insulated myself with such whimsy, I knew all along that when the moment arrived it would be impossible to remain unmoved. While the changes might be microscopic, the difference between life and death always communicated itself with terrible solemnity. A dead person looked nothing whatsoever like a living one. In anatomy class, we greeted our first corpse with unholy terror until the absence of its original owner sank in and we went to work on "it." We had a well-muscled old six-footer and felt frightened only when someone put an R. G. Dun commemorative cigar in his lips: *"It's a boy!"*

Dale arrived with the pizza and we sat out at the picnic table under the spreading ash with the great complicated disk before us to be eaten by hand. I tested my Tropical Freeze for firmness and concluded I could eat the pizza first. Dale ostentatiously picked the pineapple off his side of the pie, and then separated a wedge to eat, indenting it skillfully in the middle with his forefinger so that the mozzarella wouldn't run off. Dale had good pizza technique and I was not above copying it as we fell to. When he talked, he gobbled with his mouth full and, suddenly touched by the precariousness of his future, I was inclined to talk with my mouth full too.

"She's all done, ain't she?"

"All done."

"Comfortable?"

"Out like a light."

"When someone had a great life and don't suffer, do you think it's sad, Doc, when they go?"

"It will be when it happens. I don't know why."

"Big difference between here and gone?"

"Huge."

Our pizza eating came to a stop. Deep thoughts. Everyone was implicated by every departure. As I looked at Dale, and heard his inappropriately profound voice, I realized that after Gladys was gone, he would face what to him would be a terrible emptiness.

"So what happens to the place?" There was something wild in his eyes when he asked.

"The lawyer will tell us or the State of Montana will tell us. I've been through this before and they never let the bodies cool."

"She asked to be buried right here. Have the service sometime later."

"Where's 'right here'?"

"In them trees. Right opposite Wiley. You were here."

"I was?"

"Wait till you see how hard that ground is."

I'd have to have a nap first, let all these pizza proteins restore my vitality. I didn't even want to think about reorganizing my patient schedule. I was somewhat impatient this last time checking Gladys's vital signs before returning to the Tropical Freeze, which Dale stared at after eating two-thirds of the pizza. "I'm not sharing," I told him firmly.

Talking to Dale about Gladys's long decline, I was pleased to notice how closely he had observed her. I did think that things at present were going about as they should: his account suggested a blood deficit to the brain, with the usual neurological decline, a cruel scenario without hope of revision. There had been no big events, but the increasing recurrence of transient ischemia episodes was chipping away at her humanity and, as she had already beaten the odds, I was content with the present situation. If I dreaded anything, it was her revival. My stethoscope had already told me that the renewal of blood was hardly coursing, and all things considered, the end was at hand, as Gladys had herself seemed to know. I gathered from Dale that organized thought for Gladys was already slipping away. She'd been sputtering along until something happened that occasioned Dale's summoning me; I supposed it had been a stroke, infarction of brain tissue, the oxygen cycle winding down toward the waiting stillness. Basically, it ends in a riddle. Meanwhile, Dale and I had not only pizza but sunshine and oxygen, those delicious metabolic elements of the ongoing. I suddenly felt joyous, with no doubts about intervening in Gladys's situation. This above all things branded me a country doctor, and I fancied myself part of the countryside, a sort of pizza and Dairy Queen shaman.

"Doc, I don't feel so good myself."

"You've eaten too much."

"I'm low-spirited."

"You'll have to work on that."

This didn't satisfy Dale, and it was time to check on Gladys, who was awake again, but barely. I leaned very close to her face so that she could see me. I thought she looked quite serene; she muttered something unintelligible about going to White Bird and closed her eyes. Something told me that they wouldn't open again and she wouldn't again speak. Dale slept in the bunkhouse and I slept on the sofa in the front room. I got up, washed my face at the kitchen sink with cold water, went into Gladys's room and confirmed her death. She hadn't moved since I'd seen her last, but whatever it was, was gone.

She left Dale the ranch, and in time Dale saw to converting it into real estate.

11

I READ A COMIC BOOK VERSION of *Don Quixote* when I was a boy, and then an abridged one as a young man, and finally I read it entirely in later years, and more than once. It was now part of my general memory, and some of its ideas emerged unexpectedly, especially when I was oppressed by the feeling that I was living my life under an evil star and that everything in life was circular—the seasons and so on—except human life, which hastened in a straight line to the end and, moreover, without hope of renewal. The death of Gladys, which I had attended with such sangfroid, had produced a delayed reaction that, as best I can tell, had to do with my final severance from the world of my childhood. I thought I had dealt with this long ago, but I must not have because I was very downcast and regarded my life, or anyone else's, as an adventure dubious in the extreme. The part of Cervantes's disquisition which had once given me hope I had memorized: "Many who have lacked the light of faith, being guided solely by the illumination that nature affords them, have yet attained to a comprehension of the swiftness and instability of this present existence and the eternal duration of the one we hope for." As to this, Sancho Panza, who his master said feared lizards more than God, had the last word. To Sancho, death was a lady with no flesh on her bones; she was powerful but not squeamish and devoured every single thing that came her way. She on no account took a siesta and was "as hungry as a dog that never has its fill." I did feel a truth in the idea that just beneath our follies and day-to-day distractions a terrible grinding mechanism was at work and had a full tank of gas. This was not necessarily a bad thing and gave gravity to our madness and ignorance, our persiflage, our deviousness and clamor for renown. In the news today, placentas were being found in urban sewage. I don't know if the Trade Center bombing just pushed this sort of thing to the surface, but since then we seemed to have lost a layer of skin. And such things as fate, which I had long since viewed as discredited, seemed to have come to life all over again.

Also, I'd say things lacked a certain sparkle. It was Lewis and Clark this and Lewis and Clark that; traveling dinosaur shows and children's theater staged by aging potheads; ranchers scheming for a buyout and watching the inbound flights from either coast; and the political races for the state legislature in Helena: one notch above a greased-pig contest. Furthermore, I was losing my capacity to go along and get along with my more obstreperous patients. One fellow, a tousle-headed middle-aged wheat farmer from a small valley to the north, suffered, it seemed to me, from unreasonable pride in his origins, which he viewed with outlandish romanticism. While I took his blood pressure and felt his thyroid, which seemed a bit enlarged, he proudly went on about how suspicious the people in his valley were of anyone they hadn't known for three generations. I agreed that people were very backward in his parts. With much animation, he explained that they had accustomed themselves to subsisting on what little the land and weather yielded. I explained that ignorance and shiftlessness seldom provided reasonable comforts. When he disclosed that his great-grandparents were all born in that same valley, I offered my most heartfelt sympathy. Of course, he went away mad and I doubt I'll see him again. A doctor who views his patients as clay pigeons has seen better days. I'd by now had many come to me needing a kick in the ass more than any other treatment. You can't urge them to change their habits or exercise; they just want to take something. Well, anyone could see where that was headed.

Some of my sickest patients have been those indifferent to mortal health issues. One woman thought she would go to outer space when she died and rarely followed my advice, and that reluctantly, because she feared landing on some strange planet only to be called "earthling" by the locals and never really being accepted. One old fellow told me, "It's been a wonderful life. I wish I understood it." Another had all sorts of intestinal problems from drinking rainwater out of a barrel. At my urging he drilled a well but complained he "didn't get enough water to run a washing machine." I lost a twenty-five-year-old girl to suicide when all my pharmaceutical remedies had failed; her husband had "moved to Nashville to write cheatin' songs." Some of the problems in a region where energy development and resource extraction are king came from the battered values of small towns sitting in country desecrated in the search for platinum or gas or coal, whatever you can dig out, dam up, chop down, or sell: the wild world of philistine commercialism had its price even in places like mine. I didn't always think in these terms, but stretched out on my office couch, listening to NPR and languidly guessing at a piano puzzler, I was inclined to be gloomy. If I bothered changing stations, it was On-Air Bliss for the Demented. It beat flailing. I put on a Pablo Casals suite for unaccompanied cello and felt way better. I promised myself to leave well enough alone with the single nurses, even acknowledging that one's reputation as an accomplished wencher was at stake. Success in these matters resulted in the circulation of pheromones, which took the guesswork out of venery. I was just trying to give a sense of my daydreams, all of which were unrealistic, fanciful, or ironic.

I've said all I can stand about the rug-shampoo years. The lesson I came away with was both to strive and to rebel against the grim and meager standards that had made my home a pleasant place for average people. First, I became a philandering doctor on an Indian reservation—the latter serving a thin social conscience obviated by my many flutters with Indian women: I skipped the sweat lodge but ate the peyote and wandered around the sagebrush having visions. An enduring effect of those days is that women still don't look quite right to me if they're not Indians. I'm trying to get over that, as every town contains a few pleasant whites.

The Indian Health Service proved to be accelerated training in emergency medical care. We dealt with the results of so many car wrecks that we began to think of ourselves as a branch of the automotive industry. At any rate, we rebuilt numerous motorists, returning them to the road, and some we lost. I tried to advise the tribal council on the prospects for a safer life on the reservation, but in reality I was just one more witness to the desolation of Indian existence. Years later, when shopping for a laptop computer in Portland, Oregon, I met an Argentine trauma surgeon who told me that the torturers in the basement of his hospital in Buenos Aires would send their victims up the elevator to the surgery interns on the fourth floor. I guess he'd had more practice than I and he was pretty aggressive about his deluxe training. He lived in Portland, supported azaleas in city planning, drove a Porsche, and was passionate about his Mac. Portland is a real outdoors town, and since he focused on sports medicine, it had all worked out for him. I wonder if he felt better about those dark hours in Buenos Aires each time he got another skier back on the hill.

When I left the Res and came here to begin my actual practice, I was still an odd combination of competence and imbecility. There had been enough things from early on in my life to teach me that being an imbecile is a tremendously effective way of getting along in America; if it had been more satisfying, I would have stuck to it. Wanting to cure people of illness robbed me of all that happy conformity. Sometimes I worried that my ambivalence about a career in medicine was best understood as a wish to be stupid again. I might have done better to stay longer on the reservation, where hard times and hard lives had begun to anneal my foolishness and make a man of me.

Wilmot's latest wife, Jane, was a gruesome woman with big red hands and an overbite. She had a very strong personality, terrifying really, and held opinions on everything, far right politics of the bomb-them-all-and-let-God-sort-them-out school. Once more, Wilmot was my regular patient. He seemed to have forgotten all about tormenting us from his post on our board. "I used to be a leg man," he confessed to me. "The ankle, the knee, the thigh, all infinitely important. Those days are gone. Now I'm into hereditary landowners. I've had a good life. I'm a great guy, but I'm careful. I have never had relations with any woman who was not required to sign a release. I call it the 'Wilmot Proviso.' Only you can tell me how much runway I have left. I do hope to defy the actuarial tables, old friend."

"You have as good a chance as anyone."

"I noted a dwarf in the waiting room. Is that your patient?"

"Yes, she is."

"I had a word with her. She said she was a staunch Republican. We take them all sizes. Have you ever had a dwarf?"

"No."

Wilmot had either mellowed or was slipping into dementia. And why, when he chaired our board of directors, did he so frivolously torment us? I thought he was cruel. There was still a challenge to his bouncing gait and the air of the world at his feet, perplexing and grotesque. I was fascinated that he was so successful financially. That was always a mystery; the relationship of people to money was a much more closely held secret than their love lives, far more covert. We all love stories of the shabby recluse who raided a corporation, lived in a cellar, and hid his fortune in Switzerland. As for my patients, they would rather have to admit they ate ten pounds of mothballs than let me glimpse their bank accounts.

Wilmot would fire me, from time to time, but then he rehired me, and he often had some little ailment he wanted me to look into. He also had some larger problems, most especially a failed kidney requiring dialysis: of such things he never complained. I realized, based on my experience, that Wilmot was one who would face the largest, even terminal illness with equanimity without failing to complain about smaller issues—his hemorrhoids, eczema, dry eyes—because those were signs of ongoing life.

Before the Adrienne affair, I'd bought a rental house on his advice and later sold it, averaging nearly twenty-five percent profit a year for five years. And Wilmot found the renter, a skilled handyman who paid on time and improved the property. In business, he was most helpful; it was what really interested him and briefly suspended his many neuroses. At such times, he even looked normal, the tension gone from his face, his mouth less ready with an unpleasant remark. The other directors on our board had never dealt with a tyrant before and just gave in to him. Wilmot was a high-end idiot savant with Neanderthal social views and the air of continuing crisis. I don't think he had friends, not real friends, but he did have social connections that were wonderfully enabling whenever he wanted to get something done. Where were those social connections? All over the world. They came with his birth certificate. I think he kept in touch with me in the hope that my peculiarities would see me fail. It all went back to Adrienne. Even when he was laughing at my conciliatory jokes I could see the hatred in his eyes.

Guy McCracken was another of my regular patients, but one of whom I knew remarkably little considering that I had seen him, advised him, and treated him from the beginning of my career. He had previously been cared for by Al Christiensen, a general practitioner who retired to Hawaii. Guy was an unmarried man in his forties, remarkably private, of a cultivated demeanor and very fit. There was never anything wrong with McCracken, but he was punctilious about his annual physical and following up on any health concern, usually dermatological, as he worked outside and had unusual exposure to the sun. Guy was a handyman, in great demand because he could do absolutely anything— plumbing, electrical, carpentry, automotive—and he made a very comfortable living at it. In town he had the standing of a specialist in the several crafts he practiced, and his advice was sought by homeowners. His home was a Craftsman cottage he had restored to perfection, and it was considered an exemplar of its type on the annual home tour. Guy never struck me as being happy; his reserve seemed more a bulwark than anything else. It may have only been that the local habits of forced jollity were not his style.

Right after the Fourth of July, Guy came to see me, still in his work clothes—well-washed jeans, a clean flannel shirt neatly repaired here and there, and work boots. His tanned face was almost unlined, though the flecks of gray in his short, neat brown hair correctly asserted his age. He nodded formally and showed me an infected thumb. It must have been painful, as the swelling had emerged around the base of the nail in an angry red mound. "We'll give you a shot of antibiotic and may have you back for another." Guy nodded without expression.

I had my nurse, Chelsea, come in to give the shot. Chelsea is no longer with me because, as entertaining as she often was, Chelsea was a consummate airhead who misfiled records, abandoned patients in examining rooms, incorrectly recorded weights and blood pressure, and so on. She was sweet, comical, and madly insecure, and ended up the affluent wife of a real estate developer, a big fat lout who thought she was a scream. They've had several babies, round little tubs that Chelsea brought in for the staff to admire. Extravagantly adorned, she herded them around for the other nurses, though after she left, they said terrible things about her.

Chelsea blew the injection, the needle skimming through a pinch of Guy's skin and into the palm of Chelsea's hand. I gave Guy another shot while Chelsea moped in the corner, and this should have been the end of it. Unfortunately, the event triggered the AIDS protocol series of questions and answers, shrouded in political correctness and colored, I'm embarrassed to admit, by my own suspicions. Guy disliked these questions as I read them from a sheet, and his glances at Chelsea encouraged her to leave the room. Finally, I put the paper down and said, "Well, what these questions are meant to determine . . ."

"Whether I'm gay? Of course I'm gay. What else is there to do in this town?"

I didn't have a good answer for that. I flicked the sheet of paper onto my desk with affected weariness and said, "If that doesn't do it, follow up with these." And I wrote a script for antibiotics, bearing down on my prescription pad with warranted concentration. Guy smiled at my efforts, stood up, took the prescription from my hand as I sat at the desk, gave my shoulder a friendly shake, and, with a small chuckle, left my office.

I lived in an annoying house. I'd bought it in the spirit of nostalgia and the hope that its looks would confer some of the old-time virtues, especially the one we all long for, the one we call "simplicity," which—it doesn't matter—may never have existed. The doctors, the fellows nearly retired when I first started, gave me a sense of the old-time simplicity, and it wasn't that pretty at all. Some of that simplicity spat out corpses like a Gorgon. As to the house, there was nothing simple about it; the wiring, the plumbing, the heating all required expensive attention. Sensible people had moved away some time ago, into homes that were more easily used, and many of the places around me had been divided into apartments. Across the street from my house, a second-floor apartment housed a battling couple whom I'd never seen, but I heard their often hair-raising shouts.

The first story was old bloodred brick, the second white clapboard, and it had a gruesome mansard roof whose reward was a bulging mildewed attic. Its pinched kitchen, inquisitional living room, vertiginous staircase, and mean second-floor sleeping cells all conspired to capture and retain odors. There were things no one would dare cook in such a house. Cabbage was out of the question. Even a fresh filet of some pleasant whitefish, a chicken breast, or a dainty filet mignon could turn Floor B into an abattoir. Often when amorous pursuits had taken me to one of the upstairs bedrooms, my partner would demand another room until we'd exhausted them all and resorted to the first-floor sofa, barely below the observation of pedestrians whose suspicions must have been aroused by the puffs of dust rising rhythmically beyond the venetian blinds. One acquaintance who had passed my window during one of these episodes sent me hurtling back to childhood memories when he asked if I had been steam-cleaning my rug. He seemed baffled when I remarked, "You can say that again!"

Every Wednesday evening, Jinx Mayhall and I had dinner, a meal we prepared together and which she had usually conceived before I had a chance, turning me into nothing more than a *sous chef* compliant to her *chef de cuisine.* Dr. Mayhall, who styled herself my executive and made reference to the brigade system, forced us to envision various line cooks, patissiers, station cooks, and other cannon fodder of an imaginary French kitchen. Obviously there was drinking before, during, and after the meal; and Jinx was a splendid inebriant—upright, controlled yet as otherworldly as a religious visionary. She had a very Anglo-Saxon style, russet hair straight to her neck, long shinbones, reassuring directness, and plain purpose. It was easy to become entangled in the peculiarities of Jinx's character and fail to notice that she was quite beautiful. I was capable of this mistake myself. Without meaning to, she made you feel, when you disagreed with her, that you were wrong. Perhaps as a result I had never been so drunk in Jinx's presence as to bend the proprieties. I found her attractive, erotic even, but I justly feared blemishing our delightful friendship with some gesture that might be misunderstood. Still, it was difficult not to touch Jinx. Sometimes she widened those green eyes in such a provocative way that it was easy for me to feel terrified. Jinx was a real woman and probably too much for me.

The French atmosphere was just submerged farce because we really only cooked American dishes. Tonight we were having a sort of nostalgic meal, one that I had made for our first dinner but that this time Jinx cooked as a kind of salute to that pleasant day, a chicken dish that James Beard called "a remarkable old San Joaquin Valley recipe"—using onion, garlic, cornmeal, nutmeg, cumin, coriander, almonds, olives, sesame seeds, red wine, chili powder, and one whole, large chicken, preferably one that had disported itself under Montana skies. I liked watching Jinx cook—the straight back, the hand on hip, the absence of false moves. The period when we covered the dish to let it simmer—often almost an hour—was when we did the most drinking, and by the time the meal was on the table we were pretty mellow. We'd have two bottles, tonight's being a nice wine from Cassayre-Forni Cellars in Rutherford, California. Probably that was one too many, but it never became a problem except that I'd have to give Jinx one of the terrible little bedrooms, more than probably starting new rumors. Sometimes I tucked her in and that was just fine. I would pull the covers up around her lovely face and we would smile.

"This was a five-pound chicken, and I believe we'll eat it all," said Jinx. I spooned some sauce onto the bird, olives glistening among the almonds and infusion of spices, wine, and oil.

"We're not fat. It's okay."

We filled our plates and sat across from each other, lit by candles and the last of the evening light coming from the dining-room window, which faced into the side yard and imbued the light with a delicate quality of chlorophyll. When the cottonwood seeds were blowing, the sense of snow in early summer was so persuasive that I had been startled, fearing that I'd forgotten a season and our long winter was upon us again. There was something of the atmosphere of romance—that is, all the best parts of romance: the sense of occasion, of ceremony, of friendship—we'd had these meals for a few years—everything, really, except sex. It was not easy to imagine Jinx having sex; she wore her independence so militantly. It would take some assertion, some conviction, but it might be great! The smart ones were the best, but they were a lot of trouble too. I supposed she would be a spinster someday. I certainly never made a move, but I must say that after a couple of pops she seemed to hold it against me. Of the many complications to our friendship, this was the most conspicuous—this, and her inclination to read me the riot act from time to time, which always hurt my feelings.

Jinx reminded me of a girl from the forties—the thick russet hair, the smart but unprovocative clothes. I thought she looked like Gene Tierney. She had never had a steady male friend, leading to several inferences: that she was gay, that her longing for children led to her career in children's medicine. Neither was true. She had flings on adventure cruise ships to Antarctica or Cape Horn—"To get it out of my system"— and was unsentimental about children to the point of indifference. Her interest in them—indeed, her passion—was entirely clinical. Only the children recognized this: they were not drawn to her. Her renown was based altogether on her success in treating them. She was such a good friend of mine that when others viewed her sexually, it annoyed me— which should have been a sign. We had a little spell in which we turned into a couple of drunks. That was fun. It just amazes me now: we'd sit around my house and talk, half fried, and never lay a hand on each other.

A year or two ago, in the spring, I went up to the headwaters of a mountain creek and brought back a dozen small, gorgeous brook trout, which encrusted with *panko* lay before us on a platter, surrounded by broad homegrown tomatoes, new potatoes, sliced Spanish onions, and Manchego cheese. I bought the cheese next to the railroad station that morning under the scrutiny of a hulking man with a black moustache, massive under his nose. He stared at me with such intensity that I awaited his coming outburst with grim patience. At last it came. *"My God, I love Manchego."* Jinx had taken on the lassitude one associates with old historians or bookshop operators who hate their customers, a possible effect of the cold bottle of Riesling we'd shared. "That was a goodish white, didn't you think? What else is there to drink with these minnows? I feel drawn toward inebriation." We had another bottle, some stony-tasting thing, after which Dr. J began eating the little trout with her hands. Watching her languid moves as she ate, I felt my heart race. Then she was merry and laughed to herself. She plucked a brochure for Airstream trailers from her purse, held it in front of me, and said, "This is how Americans must live." I remembered when, years ago, the Wally Byam Caravan came to our town and filled the IGA parking lot with their silver Airstreams. A group of hippies parked in the midst of them, wrapping their old vans in aluminum foil from the IGA, and smoked marijuana in broad daylight while making sardonic forays into socializing with the Airstream people. Anyway, Jinx bought the Airstream but never took it anywhere. Finally, it became a kind of office, and from it she published papers in pediatrics. When we had finished the brook trout and the rest of the wine, Jinx gave me her lowering, authoritarian look and advised me to take a real inventory of my life. "Any life," she said, "consists of myriad elements, two-thirds of which are superfluous. The gift of living lies in enlarging the discard pile as we move to our true gestalt."

"Our who?"

"Purpose."

"Of course that's what you said."

I found myself examining the figures in my napkin, some old linen my mother had prized. Jinx had risen from the table and was standing at a mirror over the sideboard; then she stuck her tongue out at her own image and returned to the table.

She said, "I wish we'd get a phone call."

"I know what you mean."

"There are automated messages, weather and so forth."

"I think we can do better than that, Jinx."

"There's always work."

"There's always work."

"And we are useful, which is quite different from indispensable." Jinx stared into space and said, "A couple of sad caregivers."

This seemed unimaginably despairing, and I put the sounds of the humpback whale on my modest sound system. This had a terrific effect on us as the room filled with their oceanic howls. We arose and circled the table with an undulant gait, imitating the movement of the great marine mammals. It seemed as we came up for breath, our spirits rose too. When the recording was stopped, she plopped back into her chair. "Nothing like the sea," she said. I noted in an utterly abstract way the light falling on the side of her face, candlelight.

"More are cured by salt air than all our ministrations combined," I groggily proposed. "The people who live near the sea have more plausible ideas about mortality than mountain people, who from birth tend to be a bubble and a half off plumb—not to mention the empty schemers of the prairie, who covet everything between themselves and the farthest point they can see. They drive enormous automobiles and race them at the horizon hoping to expand the objects of their greed. As new things rise up toward them they are seized by a sort of mania, and this goes on until they run out of gas."

"How right you are," Jinx murmured, face resting on her palm. "I'm a prairie person and it's so easy for me to see those folks parked at the end of the world. Life was never easy for them, but there comes a day when it's time to leap into the void, leave that Cadillac behind."

Another bottle, a lovely Pedro Domecq, seemed quite harmles, and we went at it with respectful restraint, talking about the "busy bees" at the clinic, the "clueless" we billed. "We're cloaked in ignorance," said Jinx, "and yet they come to us with open hearts."

"A good thing too," I twanged. I tapped the neck of the Domecq with the ball of my forefinger. "This don't go for the same as soda pop." I was just trying to be funny—but my ER days had given me, as it had given others, a certain detachment. No good came of lamentation over the mangled we had to put right. They seemed pleased enough, coming and going on gurneys as was their wont.

I had a houseguest named Clancy Boyer, who had been a classmate of mine at medical school before he dropped out and went into commercial real estate, at which he prospered. Clancy still lived in Ohio, but he came out each year to hunt and stayed with me. He was a dark-complected, wonderfully fit, lanky sportsman who hiked alone in the mountains with a lightweight .270 Winchester over his shoulder, an old-fashioned big-game hunter who did it the hard way and lived on wild meat despite the riches of commercial real estate. He packed out quarters of mule deer or elk from the far reaches of the local mountains, sometimes making two or three trips on foot. I thought Clancy would be just perfect for Jinx, and so I fixed them up. I don't know where they went or what they did, but Clancy didn't get back to my house until three in the morning.

I blew up.

"Do you have any idea what time it is?" I demanded. Jinx had given me pajamas for Christmas and I had put them on, thinking that coming down the stairs in only my shorts and the heat of indignation wouldn't do. I failed to notice until it was too late that the pajamas' depiction of French Pierrot-type clowns throwing colored hoops in the air could have made me look ridiculous at a time when I meant to be taken seriously.

"What business is it of yours?"

" 'What business is it of mine'? Is it necessary to point out to you that this is my house?"

Clancy looked at me in astonishment, walked out the door jingling his car keys between thumb and forefinger, and was gone. I have not seen Clancy since. The next day Jinx said that she thought Clancy was a goon. "I know a goon when I see one," she said, but the whole thing was for my benefit and I saw right through it. We were painfully uncomfortable.

12

NILES THROCKMORTON HAD BEEN CALLING frantically, and I guessed someone had advised him—before advising me!—that I was about to have a problem. Up until then, I'd thought Jinx was off her rocker. I didn't even try to understand it. I felt that would just be complicity. Nor did I expect to see Officer Seaver again, and I told him so. He smiled in a way that let me understand he saw right through me. Meanwhile, Throckmorton just couldn't seem to get enough of my problem. The first thing he said to me was, "I called and left a message on your chickenshit answering machine. Turn that thing in to the county museum. Fucking sprocket noise is off the charts."

In fact, I was disconcerted by his enthusiasm for a couple of reasons: I had known Niles most of my life, and while he certainly respected my modest rise from abject stupidity, I remained a somewhat indelible dunce to everyone who had known me since my boyhood; furthermore, Throckmorton was considered by some to be more or less crazy.

Everything changed. What once seemed absorbing society for such a small place was replaced by a queer sense of thinness. I felt isolated. I reviewed all the responses from my colleagues after the death of Tessa, asking myself if I now saw in their condolences something else, and of course I began to think that indeed I did see something else, less accusatory than slyly knowing. That was worse, doubly so because I wasn't sure I had seen it at all.

Looking back as I now could, I noticed first my inexplicable concern with the pressure of my tires. As I drove along on perfectly good pavement, I would sense imbalances in all four wheels. I sometimes pulled over to have a look, but could find nothing amiss. So I bought a tire gauge and checked the respective pressures, sometimes more than once a day, and if I found them uneven, sometimes by only a pound or two, I headed for a gas station immediately.

Also, if the moon was more than half full and the tree shadows around the house too sharp, I had to sleep with a mask over my eyes but woke up at every coyote or owl. At one particularly low point I awakened to imagine that coyotes and owls were in cahoots, calling across my darkened yard and laying plans for me which I might not have enjoyed. It didn't help when one of the horned devils fluttered to rest on the outside windowsill.

My first inkling of the general view in town that Tessa had died of foul play and that she had died in my hands and on my watch and that there was a connect which, for the nonce, would not be formally made, arrived at the coin-operated car wash where I lovingly bathed my Oldsmobile; in the next bay a blue Lexus pulled out as I deposited my quarters and parked by the vacuum cleaner, and from it emerged the vice president of our local agricultural lender, Enid Lawlor. She was tall, a former basketball player, and groomed in the style of an old Hollywood pinup, with blatantly bleached blond hair in a long pageboy and a slightly mannish blue suit with pants that flared over spike heels. She kept her fingernails long, bloodred and perfect. She stood her purse on the roof of the car as she vacuumed the inside and didn't notice me until she saw me through the rear window of her own car while she vacuumed the backseat. She stopped everything. I kept my wand moving the spray over my Oldsmobile and wondered what Enid had in store for me. Her swinging gait in those high-heeled shoes seemed to convey a lively menace.

"You've been making yourself scarce!" she cried. I said that I didn't think I had, but I had been working hard and at the expense of some objectivity about my patients so that their lives were becoming entirely too much a part of mine.

"Enid, I don't even see you at the clinic. You still use us, don't you?"

"I'm never sick."

"Well, good. I hope it stays that way."

I happened to know something about Enid's bawdy sense of humor, which I saluted without having been its beneficiary. Jerry Kagy, one of our general practitioners, had taken a crash course in sigmoidoscopy, which he abandoned because his rough and unpracticed technique was producing complaints for the whole clinic; we had to ask him to stop. Enid was one of his earliest attempts as part of her annual physical; I gather that she was essentially naked on some sort of examining table while Jerry, like a student driver, awkwardly manipulated the flexible sigmoidoscope in her rectum, intermittently inflating the lower bowel to better examine its lining. Lacking much experience, Jerry, a heavyset, redheaded, and rather monstrous-looking man, repeatedly overinflated the bowel, causing Enid to loudly break wind. In response to her gruesome situation, Enid looked over her shoulder at the sweating Jerry Kagy and said, "Doctor, have I ever told you that I love you?" Kagy, entirely lacking a sense of humor, abruptly ended the exam and left Enid to dress in the empty room. Kagy told us the story himself, and we marveled that he had no idea Enid was trying to be funny. He thought she was in love with him. Well aware of the shortcomings of his technique, we found her heroic.

"It's so sad," Enid said to me, "that poor Tessa is gone, don't you think? Don't you think she had a place here?"

"She must not have thought so."

"Oh?"

"Why else would she have done away with herself?"

"Is that what she did?" Enid asked carefully, looking at me the while. I saw where this was headed. It was headed for an old issue that had nothing to do with Tessa, but if it arrived there, I felt, the consequences would be bad. I immediately attempted to quell its progress.

"That's what she did."

Enid gazed at me for a moment, then, without a word, she got in her car and left.

At the clinic, I was routinely cheerful, a mad if mechanical greeter by name of all I saw, but since the rumors, I looked on myself doing this—the same as I had always done—as though I were watching a busker at some street fair addressing the monkeys. While I knew what had happened to Tessa and felt sufficiently guilty in a maddeningly nonspecific way, it seemed I was even guiltier because others thought that I had done away with her. That it was not true seemed to make little difference. If I failed to find my way out of this mess I was very liable to become a murderer in my own eyes, because when I went over Tessa's last hours to reassure myself, Cody would suddenly appear. I recognized an emergency: something which could ruin me in my own eyes, despite the fact that "ruin" was a word that came with a faint romantic whiff. The sensation of being trailed by false rumor was its own lure, a costume drama, just behind which lurked something far worse. At my lowest point, not many days after my latest dinner with Jinx, I admitted cultivating an enigmatic smile, even, for instance, while checking my tire pressure. Anyone electing to be touched by my plight will recognize that I was merely holding the wolf at bay with what feeble means were at hand, though I had nightmares in which my struggle to save Tessa in all its visceral detail was converted into something ghoulish and horrible, the face of a dying Tessa replaced by Cody's innocent gaze. It was not hard to see that something awaited me from which no good could come.

I crossed the bridge behind the clinic and sat over the rapid seam of river that curved in there, making a small back eddy for ducks and other swimmers. Here I could view the clinic, all the bustle, and the occasional faces of daydreaming staff gazing at the water. Often there was a single contemplative raven working along the current edge, sometimes finding something with a gay pounce, but I didn't know what. Something to eat, I supposed, though I knew that corvids are no slaves to their stomachs or to anything less than schemes for the future of the world.

I had begun grieving unreasonably over the death of Tessa, imagining her young and old, big and bigger, loud and louder, crookeder and crookeder still—all pictured in loving detail just as a man mourns a dog that had bitten three paperboys. I stared at the poor raven as though he could answer my disquiet. I wondered why I had neglected Tessa.

When I returned to my house, I had a message, a returned call, from Vicky Speiser, a very beautiful girl who has cleaned my teeth numerous times. We had a rather awkward conversation when I tried to get her off dental things and invite her out to dinner. I succeeded and we found ourselves across a candlelit table at nine that night. I basked in the observation that Vicky seemed unaware of my problems.

"This is the sixteenth anniversary of Nike's Air Jordan tennis shoe," she told me, luscious red lips forming each word lovingly. "Nike says, 'It's the last year for that shoe.' Michael Jordan says, 'Let's wait and see.' Who d'you think will win?"

"Nike."

"How unromantic! Michael Jordan's going to win! He's Superman. *He's from Krypton!*"

Escapism caused me to think about Superman and how he was described as leaping "tall buildings in a single bound." Wasn't it enough to simply say that he leapt tall buildings? "In a single bound" really gilded the lily, and gave the whole thing a corny, retro feel, as well as suggesting that Superman was a sort of ape.

I think that by the time our meals came, I had already asked myself, "Where is this going?" And the answer was, "Nowhere." That was when I started to enjoy myself. It was barely raining outside, about like a cow pissing on a flat rock; this was a good time to stay indoors, eat, talk. I thought I had only to strike something up and the rest would take care of itself; but Vicky was making eyes at the county attorney, a dilettante politician with great landholdings along the Big Horn River; and the county attorney was responding by taking in the ghastly artwork around the walls, eyes swooping unpredictably to meet Vicky's. I sensed that some sort of delectable situation was at hand, during which I could turn my attention to the handsome cutlet adorning my plate while the eye play went on without any effort from me. As I dined and made perfunctory conversation, watching the lovebirds exchange glances, I began to notice that the county attorney's wife, who would have been a beauty but for the prominent bags under her eyes, was aware of the situation existing between her husband and my date, the very beautiful Vicky. When I had the chance, I gave her a co-conspirator's wink, to which she nodded grimly. I realized that it was the food that interested her, too. At the end of the meal, I made a cordial stop at their table. "Why, Earl," I said, for that was his name, "you've hardly eaten a thing."

Earl said, "New cook." I introduced Vicky and said that she too had eaten like a bird. Earl's wife, Edna, bragged that she had cleaned her plate while I claimed that not enough was left of my cutlet to attract an ant. When Vicky returned to the table, I had a sort of out-of-body experience in which I raved on about the dessert cart and aperitifs. This dyspeptic display went nowhere: Vicky said she'd had enough, and I took her home in a remorseful mood despite my real attempt to be charming and funny. She was stone-faced all the way to her door.

Well, I couldn't really say how I felt, nor why I went to the clinic after hours, let myself in, and walked along the examination room doorways, glancing in at the scales and wall-mounted blood pressure cuffs as though they could tell me something. Seeing from the clock at the end of the corridor that it was almost midnight did no wonders for my mental orientation either. I went into my own room and stretched out on the paper-covered exam table, fingers laced behind my head, with the intention of thinking—but I fell asleep. However, I quickly awakened, the idea of being found snoozing on my own table feeding worries of seeming even stranger than I already did in the eyes of my colleagues. So I got up and, looking into a few case folders, came up with "you're born and you die," with the rest an avalanche of minor footnotes—no attitude for a doctor.

I left my office and went down the hall to the waiting room, which in a medical facility is an inherently unhappy place. At the check-in desk, there is usually a staff of lady cannibals inured to the suffering and anxieties of the patients registering their stories, their fears, and their Social Security numbers. No matter what happens to them, their stories will be digitalized, and no previous human fear of inconsequentiality can compare to the reduction of mankind by such frontline operators as those of us in medicine. Heading our group was the traditional explosive fat nurse, who raised hell with the fretful while applying order to the huddled masses assembled at her desk.

I sat among these ghosts in the waiting room. A television hung on a wall bracket in one corner of the room. I remember voting for this item as a way of softening the effect of the inevitably delayed appointments, but a squabble broke out once too often between patients and the nurses who controlled the channel changer, and it became necessary to turn the thing off. I went behind the appointment desk, found the remote embedded in a box of Kleenex, and turned the television set on: great moments from the NFL including Vince Lombardi with those terrible teeth carried from the field by the men he had tortured. A Bette Davis movie. She wore a kind of ruffled collar in this one, and she just pitched her head back and went to throwing spit. I was on the edge of my seat. When that was over, I found an extraordinarily peaceful story of migrating penguins, even more peaceful with the sound muted, so that I could watch the ballet of these little persons in arctic seas. This is when I fell asleep, and where I was found by the staff.

I spoke to no one but headed to my office, locked the door, and resumed sleeping on the examining table. I slept much of the day, tormented by dreams that vanished as soon as I awakened, as though from amnesia. And it was quite an unnatural sleep too, based on need not for rest but for escape from the consequences of my strange behavior.

Eventually, I stirred. I went to the washbasin and tidied up, drying myself with tissues, then grimacing by way of an examination of my teeth. Perhaps I was noisier than I realized—when I stepped into the hallway, it was filled with gazing doctors and their gazing patients. Head high, I walked through them, through the lobby where I had first dozed off and which was now bright with sunlight and disordered magazines, noting only the resumption of murmuring as I made my way through the front door.

There was a steady turnover of nurses in our practice, a bit above the general turnover of residents, which was plenty. Some nurses had been in the clinic long enough to know much of what we doctors knew, but there was an unspoken agreement that they wouldn't use the knowledge, as though their hard-won comprehension could infringe on our relationship with the patients. I did once see Laird McAllister blister his poor nurse in front of a lot of people for telling a patient his resting pulse rate, just after she'd taken it. "*I* tell them that. That's what *I* tell them." Some of the older nurses serving older doctors began to resemble priests' housekeepers. We had good doctors and mediocre doctors and only one like me: well trained, with exceptional medical instincts in an emergency, but lacking conviction. It may have been that some of my mother's evangelism had persuaded me that life on earth was trivial.

I thought the best thing would be to meet with my friend Dr. Jinx, knowing full well the jokes headed my way for seeking counsel from a baby doctor. As it was, when I asked to speak to her—she was standing by her desk in her office and straightened slightly when she heard my voice behind her—she replied, "Gladly, but not where we can be seen."

We sat on a bench by the old waterworks, the damp, weathered bricks giving pungency to the balsamic air arising from the shrubs around the duck pond. The very high white clouds over the Absaroka Mountains seemed to demand attention. We could hear children playing over by the soccer field. In my present mood I reflected that decade after decade you heard the same quality of noise from that direction, as though the group of children never changed, always seeming to be the same group. This thought merely deepened my disconsolate inner weather suggesting that of all the people on earth, only I stood still, serenaded by the zombie children beyond the duck pond. Were they calling me? At that time I'd have believed anything. I'd have believed the children were calling me to oblivion.

Jinx said, "Give me the headlines and please don't set it to music."

"I guess it was extreme reluctance to enter the salt mine."

"If you think it's a salt mine."

"Evidently I do. It comes as a surprise."

Jinx looked at me for such a long time that I felt scrutinized, almost as though I was meant to cough something up. At first, I worried that I was expected to admit to something about Tessa, as though I had anything to admit, just acknowledging that the question was in the air. And I was not willing to do that, but she read my mind. She said, "I have no interest and no suspicions about that poor woman, but you seem to have dropped a stitch right in the middle of your life and it is time for you to *do something else.*" I was well aware of the owlish look on my face as I failed to comment, knowing it was no use when Jinx was in launch mode. "Perhaps," she said, "you find it difficult living in a morally bankrupt and hate-filled nation, and it's not for me to say. But you go around like a cat ruining a blanket trying to find a place to lie down."

Jinx had long harbored somewhat radical notions, ignored by her colleagues as the frustrations of an unmarried woman. They found them cute. I sometimes considered her views more eccentric than convincing. In the context of what seemed about to turn into a lecture, however, they had the sting of authority. As my rage grew over the next few days, I finally had to accept that I was its only object. Something would have to be done: I was burning up. "What about my skills, such as they are, my experience?"

Jinx told me they no longer applied. "Do you mean my life?" I asked.

"You tell me. You're going nowhere."

By the end of the week, that was no longer true. What had come to an absolute head in the aftermath of Tessa's death was not my acceptance of responsibility for it but my beginning to understand my guilt for her neglect, and that one day I would have to work out what we had owed each other with greater clarity than I had so far. This was at considerable odds with the planktonic drift that had marked my days to date, punctuated by the gruesome pop-up figure of the late Cody Worrell.

13

IT WAS IN THE MIDDLE of the long northern evening; the dust devils had died in the fallow fields and off to the west a small island range of mountains floated in shadow. I had a tall bourbon and water with lots of ice tinkling in a handy holder between the seats, and as I passed the empty old country schools, grain elevators on abandoned spurs and glimpses of creeks running through brush that slowly reclaimed home-steads, I thought I could feel the lives of the missing population like so many sad, if amiable, ghosts. As usual when faced with troubling things I seemed unable to understand, I resorted to fishing. I had a favorite fly rod with me, a nice, leisurely old glass Winston, and Dr. Olsson's English aluminum case that had gone on so many trips. My plan was work-ing: I was in a very good mood.

I took a two-track road used by irrigators and crossed a cattle guard, culverts, and a wire gap before getting into the field I intended, at the far edge of which was a slow mountain creek that held lots of cutthroat trout, vigorous spotted beauties with orange slash marks at their throats. A crop duster was flying in the distance, just at the ledge of mountain where yellow panels of grain extended toward the valley bottom. As it pulled up at the end of each run, clouds streaming behind it, the chang-ing pitch of its engine carried all the way down to where I could clearly hear its whine. I parked under a power line that angled off toward the town of Wilsall and heard the dense murmur of summertime insects as I got out of the car. I saw clouds in the hood of the Olds in the late light, the crop duster rising and falling in the distance. The plane was treating wheat fields right at the edge where the foothills broke elevation, revers-ing direction by a dangerous maneuver called a hammerhead stall, sending the plane straight up at the end of each field right in the face of the hills for a falling turn down the next row. Suddenly one wingtip caught a juniper ridge and the plane tumbled.

I wasn't absorbing the scene quite as I should. What seemed implausible was the complete lack of movement from this so recently dashing machine, which at the slightest contact with the earth had turned into junk. I got back into my car and drove recklessly until I was close to the accident. I got out and ran the rest of the way to the wreck. I smelled fuel and heard a voice—"Get away before this thing catches fire!"—a woman's voice. With the smell of gasoline and the word "fire," I admit that I nearly bolted. Instead, I approached the cockpit—the propeller was wrapped back around the nose and fuel was running onto the ground—and discerned the torso of the pilot somewhat pinned under the plane. I began to pull her out, expecting screams, but I was met with only a weird silence, made even more inexplicable when I finally had her clear and saw that one foot was pointing in the exact opposite direction from the other. *"Keep moving. Get farther from the plane."* There was such urgency in this command that overcoming my aversion to moving her at all I kept pulling until we were both many yards from the wreck. The plane went up in flames and a rush of air. She said, "Was that the plane?"

The burning airplane spewed a column of ugly smoke into the clear, windless air. Whatever chemicals that were aboard in addition to its fuel combined with the wiring plastics and other petrochemical elements in the craft to lend the smoke a greasy industrial quality that soon towered against the foothills.

The pilot lay faceup on the grass in front of me. She wore the sort of crash helmet you'd associate with motorcycles, and since one foot was still headed the wrong way, I declined to move her any more than I'd had to in order to get her clear of the coming fire, now a small throbbing inferno that made an X-ray of the airframe. With great delicacy I removed the crash helmet. A surprising mass of auburn hair spilled out. Physical anguish had transformed her features, and so I had no idea what she looked like. I knew she mustn't be moved. I had seen results of accidents like this before, and I was well aware that the internal injuries could be anywhere and anything. There was always a list of things you hoped not to find, and the sometimes mad process of elimination during a race against the clock of declining vital signs was life's most awful rush.

A ranch hand on an ATV arrived first, turned straight around and headed back downhill for a telephone. I wedged my coat and sweater on either side of her head to immobilize it; the worst things I knew were when the victim was vomiting or choking on blood and it was impossible to move the head without knowing if the neck or spine had been injured; you could only lift the jaw forward and with your fingers try to clear the airway. But no signs of head injury presented; the woman was not losing consciousness nor had she lost control of her bowels or limbs, the familiar signs. If she expressed anything, it was exasperation, but her discomfort prevented much of that. In a spell shortened by my obsessively checking vitals with squeamish glances directed at the upside-down foot, a compact four-wheel-drive ambulance from the small med center nearby arrived, and the pilot was lashed in place and rolled inside it. This whole while, though clearly conscious, she made no sound. I watched the ambulance ease its way down the two-track, before hitting the pavement, when its emergency light popped on and it was gone, heading west.

Thus my fishing, the vaunted evening rise, went right out the window.

Not a week after I saw Enid at the car wash I saw her again. I had paid a visit to one of my elders—mature folks in my first practice who had grown old—up the Shields River valley, and I'd stayed late, deciding to stop off at the Wilsall Bar for a drink before boarding the Oldsmobile for home. The only other customer was Enid, who this time saw me before I saw her. She motioned me over to the table, and I called my drink out to the bartender to save him the trip. Enid must have had a few drinks already, for she wore a mellow look I'd never seen on her face before, and it was quite becoming; one drink and one drink only was what I had in mind, but Enid's demeanor suggested we were both headed for last call.

"Doctor, how nice to see you. I don't like drinking alone but that's what I've been doing. It certainly beats not drinking at all."

"I was looking in on some of my old patients."

"God's little waiting rooms, all over the county."

"I suppose so."

"I've been doing much the same thing, and now I'm treating the pain.

I always thought agricultural banking suited me. Times have changed. Now they call me the Grim Reaper."

"It must hurt."

"What about your old car? Did you ever get it clean?"

"I did. How are your ranchers? Some of them doing okay?"

"Very few. The ones that stayed away from machinery on credit. On the other hand, their backs are gone."

"What'll they do?" I had some of these people on my customer list too.

"In some cases they'll face the fact that ranching doesn't pay, take someone's ten million for the spread, and move to Scottsdale. The rest just dry up and blow away."

This was where her posture changed and she started sizing me up. "But for the moment anyway, we're not so different from everyone else who's got no place better to be."

We ended up using her car because it had four-wheel drive and I could take it out into a CRP field no one ever visited. There were wires running all over the ground for a methane exploration project and I tried not to drive over them until I found the creek bed I knew from my hunting, followed it into a grove of junipers, and turned off the engine. I'm still surprised at how tenderly we made love. This sort of car-borne episode is associated in everyone's minds with something feral, but it was as if we had met in ideal circumstances and this was the result of substantial courtship. Partly, it was the warm air and the smell of prairie flowers and the remnants of grain farming really sort of caressing us, and the odd light coming from the dashboard instruments was quite becoming to her flesh. It struck me as grown-up, knowledgeable sex—you might say respectful sex, unsentimental, detached from any larger context. I wished all need could be addressed so directly. We didn't stare at each other with theatrical grimaces at the familiar crescendos but struggled around in a grateful knot, welcoming all the fluids as we went. When we were finished, Enid sat straight up, thrust her hands into her hair, and stared through the windshield in thought. Then she turned to me with a mischievous wordless look. We gathered our clothes and dressed under the stars as though at public baths, as though merely acquaintances, which of course we were. It had been such a big success that there was not the smallest chance we'd try it again.

.   .   .

I was not always comfortable seeing patients at the office, and so I'd find excuses to see them in their homes or to run into them in the street. One old patient, Frank Kelly, entertained me with tales of his youth while I examined him. We sat on his enclosed porch with its view of the west side of the Crazy Mountains while his wife puttered around behind us in the living room. He grew up near the Missouri Breaks, the son of a renowned cowboy and an Indian woman, in the years when the small ranches, theirs among them, were condemned to make way for the Fort Peck Reservoir, a federal project of the New Deal years. Some ranchers resisted, but accusations in local papers that they were unpatriotic soon had them moving off the land, barely recompensed. Frank always had stories of his family's years adrift, usually a new one on each of my visits to keep me coming back. It worked. Today's had to do with his father's job riding cattle in a huge circle on one of the big ranches south of the dam near the town of Jordan, still vast and now empty. Frank was a very young boy when his father would take him out and leave him at an abandoned sod house, ride all day, then come back for him at nightfall. Frank described these as extremely boring, lonely days of rock throwing and daydreaming. One day while he was playing atop the old sod house, the roof collapsed and he descended into its interior in an avalanche of dry dirt. "When I landed inside, on my feet, I had an old buffalo rifle in my arms that had been hidden in the ceiling. I went into the navy in '42 and the neighbors stole it."

Since various and sundry had given me to think that I had some hand in poor Tessa's departure, I began to brood about my instance of actual guilt, that of avenging the beaten wife who was my patient. Was I gloomy? Hardly. Perhaps I was simply entertaining this recollection as an exercise in irony. Of course that was not true. I had attended the funerals of this poor couple, and I remembered thinking that it was tragic for her life to end as it had but that my helping Junior make his way to the next world had given the family closure—as we now say—that they might not have otherwise had if he had been punished more conventionally. In this, too, I was delusional. There were, I suppose, even then, signs that the situation could get out of hand; the first sign was my desire, not felt in decades, to revisit the scene of the "crime" or crime. I listened to a retrospective of a favorite band as I drove along, getting into an admittedly inappropriate merry frame of mind. Listening to "Plastic Seat Sweat" and "Girl Fight" really got me bouncing in my seat, and when I arrived at the murder locale with "Too Much Pork for Just One Fork" on at the loudest setting, I found myself dancing beside the open car door as I tried to evoke guilt for the demise of that wicked husband. I was really on a tear, and it was only a matter of time before things went sideways. Actually, I did feel a little guilty, and I was sorry that it dampened my inclination to boogie in broad daylight. It quickly came back, though, as I remembered happy hours with the great Tessa and was overwhelmed by my own adrenaline. With "Too Much Pork for Just One Fork" booming from my car door, I began to do my own version of break dancing, spinning on the lawn with one hand while attempting to shout out a rhyme on "pork." Presently the homeowner emerged from his front door, and it was as though his gaze slowly extracted Tessa from my arms. I felt a storm cloud arise in my chest. The owner was a small man somewhat older than me, wearing a cardigan sweater over a white T-shirt and laceless shoes serving as slippers. He turned a pitying gaze on me. "It can't be that bad," he said, and I could see Tessa—obnoxious, deluded, life-filled Tessa—receding into nothingness as she was replaced by Cody Worrell. I needed to explain myself.

"There was a double suicide here some years ago."

"I'd heard."

"I was the first on the scene. I hope the place has seen better days since."

"It has. It's been a happy house. I wouldn't give it up for the world. We raised a boy and a girl here. They moved away, but they're doing fine. They always call."

"Oh, very nice."

"On Sundays."

"Ah, good, catch everyone in."

"At exactly one o'clock."

"Mm."

My growing impatience with this levelheaded old man was instructive, and I drove home in silence, as nothing could have been more annoying at that moment than music. I wondered whether that family had emptied that house of any bad spirits; it seemed they had. I certainly never entertained the idea of myself as a murderer, at least not until recently when the idea was put into my head by people unfamiliar with the facts. If I had done wrong, would my instinct have been to dance on the lawn, to exult at the music pouring from the door of my Oldsmobile? I didn't think so. Not if Tessa was who they had in mind.

John O. Danowicz, an old railroader, came to see me this morning at my office. I gave him several goings-over each year under the terms of his pension. He was almost eighty years old and showing a bit of dementia, that awkward stage at which one is uncomfortably aware of these troubling changes. I suppose we could have tested him for Alzheimer's, but I didn't think it necessary as he was so well adjusted and living at home with his old wife. He was a thin, immaculate man with the big hands of a machinist, tidy and organized, and very interested in the operations of his body. He knew what his weight, blood pressure, heart rate, and lipids should be, having made his health his hobby. He played checkers with his wife and did crosswords, the latter having provided signs that his memory was failing. He felt that he had lived a very long time and looked forward to stealing as many days from mortality as possible. His philosophy had always interested me, as he saw himself the reification of an infinite number of chance events, starting with his parents' meeting on a steamer in Puget Sound. His recurrent line—"I just want to see how far I can get"—intrigued me as proper to an adventurous spirit like John O. Danowicz. He would have made an encouraging centenarian, and I took his well-being most seriously.

After John left, I had a cancellation, so I idled in the hallway and made small talk with the nurses, and the occasional colleague, none of whom seemed anxious to speak to me. Perhaps I began to smell a rat. I don't remember. We at the clinic, like everyone else around here, were spending most of our time reacting to the sudden growth of our world as retired people and amenity migrants of all sorts began to settle around us. They'd fetishized our terrible weather and made us locals feel like sissies for ever having complained about the wind and cold. They were a virtual LL Bean–Patagonia road show, and what we complained about I suppose had never gotten to them except in a bracing secondhand way. Our town now had so many people who did not seem to exactly need anything we offered—employment, supplies, fellowship. I suppose it might have been a good thing to have had a significant cohort of people who did not feel threatened, since most of us had always felt under siege, if only in our minds, and probably as a consequence of the root-hog-or-die ethos of the region. What had happened to the Indian was happening to us. My father told me that we ruined the American Indian. "We won the Indian Wars. We should have made every Indian an American citizen and then let them tough it out with the micks, the wops, the kikes, the Japs, the krauts, and the spics. They would have done just fine." Well, okay. But what of us broken-down old conquerors?

So many times, my father told me that we get along by going along. This prescription seemed somewhat at odds with his real nature, especially that of the old warrior whose proud past surfaced now and again, but my mother had talked him into her blustering God, an array of obsequious saints, an earthly existence in which the roof was ever ready to fall in until time came to an end. In ten years he had gone from an M1 Garand to a steam cleaner and from the bleak agnosticism of an infantryman in winter to a thrice-dunked primitive Christian twisting like a rag and speaking in tongues in churches that rented space in failed strip malls. I think he was just doing his best, getting along by going along with my mother, whose piety and evangelical fever had preoccupied her family since the last century. She knew no other world—God the Tyrant and a supplicant humanity crawling on its belly to be forgiven for sins they never knew they'd committed. "It's no sense defying the Lord," she told me. "He's got all the coons up one tree."

There was some reason I remembered all this and it had to do with my somewhat intense focus on the pilot. It might have been the way she, like Audra, like Tessa, flew into our lives—Tessa in the aftermath of California, Jocelyn in the aftermath of an accident. I began wondering if she would live. I supposed they had taken her to the medical facility in White Sulphur Springs, a little thirty-seven bed facility whose staff I knew cycled between the hospital and clinic, the nursing home, home health care, and so on. It was in technical parlance a "frontier" facility. I would go there. I was drawn to White Sulphur Springs as though by some winch fastened to the town and attached to my Oldsmobile, and I found myself at the counter asking to be directed to the patient's room, a request that only met with hesitation from the young girl at the desk with the severely plucked eyebrows and the tribal tattoo on her neck—until I explained that I was a physician.

The pilot was in the first room down a very short corridor. Her arms were bandaged, her face badly bruised; someone had secured her hair atop her head with an elastic, and under one slate gray eye hung a swollen blue-green bruise. "You're the guy at the crash?" I said I was. I was skimming her chart: her name was Jocelyn Boyce and she was forty years old. She was from Two Dot, Montana, and listed as next of kin was her father. The ER summary indicated blowout fracture of the left eye socket, broken ribs, probably torn rotator cuff. She seemed fairly pert in view of these pain producers. The crow's-feet I had already found attractive as suggesting someone not going to give in easily to hurt, but I didn't know what sort of medication she had on board.

She did not seem dispirited by her condition. She said, "I thought I had the rookie errors out of my system."

"I can't comment," I said. "I don't know anything about flying."

"It'll be a long time before I live it down."

Her physician came in about ten minutes after I got there. We knew each other vaguely, and he returned my greeting with reserve. He must have thought I'd been called in until I told him that I was at the accident. At that point, he cheered up and went into bonhomie so abruptly that I was startled and caught the glimpse of an ironic half smile from Jocelyn Boyce. He was Dr. Aldridge and had practiced here and there as he dodged the effects of his drinking, which he had finally controlled, though he was now trailed by his obsolete reputation. He was a good physician and looked the part with his neatly trimmed gray moustache and clear gray eyes. He said, "You can see Miss Boyce has quite a shiner." He turned an infatuated gaze on his patient.

"I do see that."

"She has a blowout fracture of the eye socket." I knew that, but I thought it best for him to tell me. As Jocelyn Boyce and I kept glancing at each other, something odd was going on between us.

"The whole thing?" I asked.

"Just the floor, I think. She doesn't have double vision and I've ruled out surgical repair. And no one wants us going in for that, do they, Miss Boyce?"

"It sounds creepy," she said. "I'll give you that."

"There's really no sign of muscle entrapment. If Miss Boyce gets bored with us she can roll her eyes whenever she wishes." In fact, she did so, either at the banality of Dr. Aldridge's remark or merely as a demonstration.

"You see?" said Dr. Aldridge. "No sign of spinal injury, thank the Lord, but the jury is still out on head trauma for as long as that eye tells us something about the blow she received."

"Is that the worst of it?"

"The worst of it might be the knee. We've got it secured, but it was near disarticulation when she arrived."

"It's a long way from my heart," said Jocelyn.

"You'll be in the hands of a smart orthopod for that. We're just the nuts-and-bolts guys, aren't we, Dr. Pickett?" I smiled at this. "So, this is me going home to feed the cat—" His eyes glanced off mine; I knew his wife had left him during the bad years. "Miss Boyce, I'll be looking in. I don't live far and if you need me before my next visit, just call. I've left my cell number here—" He pointed to the papers on the bedside table. He was more than interested in Miss Boyce; it was almost embarrassing.

After Aldridge left, it was quiet in the room. Finally, I said, "It looks like you'll get better."

"So they say. "

"It's time for you to rest. I'll be on my way."

"I wonder if you might think of stopping again."

I looked down suddenly. "Yes," I said, "I'd like to."

At least once a week, my travels took me past the old strip mall where my parents' Pentecostal church formerly met. It was now a Radio Shack outlet, and the electronics buffs and various tech weenies going in and out the door obviously felt no residual vibrations from its Holy Roller days. But *I* did: I painfully remembered when my mother began taking her raptures to the street, accosting pedestrians in tongues. My mother was a small woman, unthreatening in physical presence or demeanor, so she was no more than a curiosity at these passionate displays, with my father, abashed and meek, trailing at a safe distance. I, too, was influenced by my mother's activity at this time: I started to look for signs of craziness in myself, and I found plenty. People with a crazy parent will be unsure of their own mental health all their lives. My grade school classmate Roscoe Tate often remarked when my mother made a public nuisance of herself that "the apple doesn't fall far from the tree." Facing such things definitely budged me out of a childhood in many ways pleasantly prolonged by my mother's peculiarities. It also occasioned the deepening of my friendship with our family doctor, Eldon Olsson.

We met in his chaotic office, bird dog sleeping on an old and overstuffed armchair, a well-worn sixteen-gauge pump gun standing in the corner. Dr. Olsson leaned back in his chair and lit a cigarette. I thought that it must have seemed unlucky to Dr. Olsson to have stumbled on Wiley and Gladys in his partridge-hunting forays and ending up with my family as his patients. I suppose he realized we didn't have the money for a more regular arrangement.

"Your mother needs some help."

"What kind of help?"

"Inpatient psychiatric help."

"Because of her religion?"

"I don't know because of what. I only know that Health and Human Services won't allow her to do what she does much longer without stepping in."

I was growing up fast. "What can we do?"

"We can head it off through a voluntary commitment, which would allow us to specify the date of release. That way we hold the cards. But you're going to have to sell it. She's got your father under her thumb, and he may be a nut too." This hurt, but I withheld reaction. "Your task is to make your mother see the light on this one. Good luck."

I sold it, and on a winter day we drove my mother to the Warm Springs State Mental Hospital, old buildings under bare trees by the Clark Fork River. She hardly seemed defeated by her situation, and dressed in her wool coat with the rabbit fur collar and unbuckled galoshes, she strode into her room, looked around, and pronounced it wonderful to see that Jesus was there too. I could hear the cold river through the window. It was clear that in her odd kindheartedness she was doing this to make my father and me feel better.

My mother's spirits helped me a bit with the guilt I felt at talking her into this arrangement. As we drove home my father found much to marvel at in the winter landscape, especially the colossal statue of Our Lady of the Rockies outside Butte, a ninety-footer sitting atop the Continental Divide; the vast mine diggings around the city which I found such an assault on nature, he saw as a tribute to the determination of men. "That Berkeley Pit filled a lot of lunch pails. Crying shame it got so big they had to tear down the Columbia Gardens, but people got to eat." As we passed the great wheat farms west of Three Forks, he averred that Americans fed the world. I may have been a bit offended on my mother's behalf at his very high spirits. I was brooding over the fact, which I recalled from publicity at the time it was raised, that Our Lady of the Rockies was dedicated to all the mothers in the world. The Army National Guard supplied a sky crane to install the Virgin's head. I don't know what I had supplied on behalf of motherhood. Not much.

We followed a snowplow into Bozeman Pass, spewing a great falling wing of snow on the roadside. My father turned to me to give me another boost out of my youth. "There's something I'd like to tell you," he said. I glanced quickly his way, fearful of taking my eyes off the slippery road. "I became an atheist the first time I saw a German tank and I've been one ever since. So never think I'm not devoted to your mother."

In arranging my mother's voluntary commitment, the hospital required us to accept that she could be held for five days after the requested release. On the occasion of her emptying a tub of Tuna Surprise on the dietician's head, the facility exercised this option and used the time to request that the court convert her deal to an involuntary commitment. Thanks to what I would long view as my betrayal, my mother was often institutionalized until she died. Since going somewhat AWOL from the clinic, I have been trying to forgive myself for this sin, and several others. That's right, sins. What else could I have called them? On one long drunken night in February I found myself at 8,500 feet gazing up at the illuminated Our Lady of the Rockies towering over the forlorn town of Butte, waiting for something that would lift the weight of my mother's life from my shoulders.

14

I HEARD THAT IN YEARS PAST, pigs were drawn into the slaughterhouse of the Chicago Stockyards by hooks attached to their noses. A pig is a smart animal, but this placed the decision elsewhere. It was in this spirit that I headed once more to White Sulphur Springs to pay a call on Jocelyn Boyce. Wasn't I in a sense a first responder at the scene of the accident? Naturally I had an interest in the outcome. But it was as if a tiny animal living in the corner of my mind, smaller than a mouse, smaller than an ant, and unobtrusive even considering its size, was saying, "Bullshit." Anyway, it was a nice drive and the 88 seemed to like it as we coursed along a well-kept highway not too wide for its passage across sandstone bluffs, juniper savannahs, and dashing spate streams. A pickup passed me heading south, a dead elk in the bed and small American flags attached to each elevated leg. The sun was just over my left shoulder, warming my neck, and every few miles I glimpsed a herd of antelope in the distance, its movement syncopated with its shadow's. The dashboard, with its discolored plastics and deep layer of dust, radiated the pleasant warmth it had absorbed from the sun. A small cloudburst darkened the road ahead of me, then vanished. This daydreaming interlude was soon succeeded by anxiety about the visit. What business was this of mine? Was her asking me to come back a pleasantry which acted upon would arouse annoyed surprise? What if she said, "Can't you see I don't feel well? I thought you were a doctor!" And was that the risk? Back to the corridor for a squirming session, fuel up, drive home? If so, I decided to accept the risk. Unfortunately, I went off the rails imagining how I might describe myself to someone like Miss Boyce should they wish to know me as I am: irritable, hypercritical, obsessively orderly, claustrophobic, impatient, antisocial, and agoraphobic, filled with objectless dread, pessimistic, and faultfinding. This led to more general reflections of my current state: my dreams at night were populated by strangers ordering me to pay up and threatening to "discard my application," and the recurrent "Why can't you remember your password?" A phantom gate agent haunted my dreams as well. He holds my boarding pass to his eyes and says: "Someone has folded this, or has begun to fold it and has had a change of heart. I'm afraid you've run out of luck." In one genuinely appalling dream, which also recurred, I am at a dinner and have selected the wrong condiment, causing my tongue to swell; it overfills my mouth until I can see it, red and horrible, at the edge of my vision. Breathing mulishly through my nose, I begin to smother. This was poor preparation for my visit, and the thoughts fell upon my mood like a ton of bricks. Once at a fund-raiser for our clinic and hospital I had been charged with babysitting a major donor and had somehow thought it wise to have a candid conversation about where I believed the country was headed; we lost the donation. I recall the donor all too well and how I'd misjudged him for an open-minded soul: an old man dressed in a mixture of styles—tight hip-huggers, a blue Oriental silk shirt, and a corncob pipe. He had long hinted, as his own medical needs increased, that he was contemplating coughing up part of his cheese ball, but in the end it was given to the Elks, B.P.O.E. He was hard of hearing and had the TV turned up so loud I couldn't understand him when he talked. When I quietly reached to lower the volume, he barked, "Don't fool with that TV!" Somehow I went off on the state of the nation, based on earlier fund-raising experiences that a rising cloud of amiable generalizations was great preparation for the kill. It was an improvement over Jinx's sardonic suggestion that I begin by saying, "Stand by for the ram." I think I said something about the military-industrial complex, or something equally well-worn from the lips of Eisenhower, when I first heard the words I feared again now: "Get out." For him the military-industrial complex was the last hope of mankind. How was I to know? I can still see him, teeth bared around the stem of his pipe, eyes blazing as I backed out of the room with its roaring TV.

She was standing next to the bed folding a blanket, arms outstretched, its middle held between her chin and her chest. She said, "Grab the end." I helped fold the blanket, which she threw across the foot of the bed before climbing back under the sheet. "Too hot." She was wearing white pajamas with blue piping, her knee taped and wrapped. A radio next to the bed played at a murmur: a minor ayatollah was explaining to the world that God had not made America; he had made all the other countries but he had not made America.

"I came to see how you were getting along."

"Did you." She smiled at me. "Good then, they're turning me loose."

"Well, you said stop back."

"That's right, I did. And you did. Very nice to have a visitor. And I need a lift to my car, if you're up for that." I nodded.

"The eye's better?"

"Yup. Can you see if you can get the Venetian blind to work?" I got up and sorted out the tangled runners.

"Are you rested?"

"Evidently, I am!"

I found Jocelyn comely but a bit unnerving; she seemed to be one jump ahead of me in conversation. "You can't watch the news anymore unless you're a fan of ethnic cleansing. I love the sports channel, but they just had someone named Stone Cold Steve Austin beating someone up. I'm a baseball fan. I love the radio. In fact, when I get to my car the first thing I'll do is turn on that radio."

"I love baseball too." I hated baseball, but I wasn't ready to close that door. I noticed that the blacks were leaving the sport. Only whitey could stand around all day like that. I don't have any idea why I said I liked it: I don't know dick about baseball.

"Was I in a fog when you were last here? Dr. Aldridge told me you were a doctor. I didn't realize that." She was gathering her belongings, tossing them into a day pack and a purse.

"I'm a general practitioner at a hospital south of here. I might have been more help where you crashed, but I was afraid to move you by myself."

"There's nothing left of the airplane. Nice airplane, too. Beautiful old Piper Pawnee. It's no excuse, but flying right on the deck in this damn country to avoid chemical drift, well, you're just going to hit stuff."

"When you say 'this country'—I thought you were from around here."

"I'm based out of Snyder, Texas, or I was. No airplane. Did you hear what the Cubs did yesterday?"

"I didn't, but why would you be way up here from Snyder, Texas?"

"Well, it's a job where you have to travel according to the season if you want to make a living at it. Still pays peanuts. My first love was horses. When I was a girl, I went around with two canes pretending I had four legs so I could be more like my horse. Don't let me forget the radio. A doctor. Has that been a nice life?"

"I had a kind of foster father who was a doctor. I might have been trying to please him. It was a decision I made when I was very immature, but its effects have been long-lasting." We were really sailing along now! I would have done well to realize that unchecked impulses were not far behind me. Filling in the biographies, it was so good and there was definite excitement in the air. "I gather this is not the easiest country to be a . . ."

"Ag pilot. That's what we call ourselves, ag pilots. Well, mostly I've sprayed in flatter country. I sprayed peas in Michigan, not too bad if you don't hit a tree. Cotton in Texas, citrus in Florida and California, rice in Texas, sprayed cotton big time around Snyder. That's where cotton went to get away from the boll weevil. Then the boll weevil followed it there. But yeah, it's not the safest job in the world."

"The risk of crashes . . ."

"The chemicals. You mix a lot of chemicals. The chemicals get in the cockpit, too. I mean, we're not really part of the environmental movement, if you know what I mean. That bothers me. I've done other kinds of flying. I could go back to that if I got another airplane. You're lucky. It's all in your head . . ."

"I guess. What little there is."

"The trouble is, most flying jobs are boring. For a long time I towed banners, and that was just awful. South Florida. Flying almost at stall speed pulling a big long one that says BEST BUY or FIND IT IN THE YELLOW PAGES or FLAT LINE SPORTS BAR, that sort of thing. Ten hours sitting an arm's length from the exhaust pipes relieving yourself in adult diapers. And I've pulled some doozies. The worst one was HOT CHICKEN WINGS AT HOOTERS EVERY WEDNESDAY. We had to do it as a combination billboard and letter banner because they wanted to include a girl with large breasts on the billboard portion. When we stacked it on the ATV to launch it, the pile was so big I never believed we'd get the whole thing airborne. Seriously, my choice is to be down in the trees and power poles, jumping hedges, landing and taking off on dirt roads. You could say that's where the romance is." I didn't know what she was supposed to be doing. Now she wanted to go get her car.

Everything about her had a dangerous iridescence, doubtless for me alone; for Jocelyn, a simple question, as for all women, could be sorcery. Thoughts went through my mind like "fumbling for the keys" and "lost highway." I said, "I'll wait for you in the lobby."

"Take this." She handed me the day pack. "I'll wind her up here. I've already logged out with the staff, but I've got to get a move on. I'm meant to be at the Billings Airport by one." I didn't get the chance to ask her where she was flying. I supposed back to Texas. I almost got the feeling she was flying the coop, and I wished I'd had a chance to consult first with Dr. Aldridge, who had gazed upon her with inappropriately hungry eyes.

There were two decrepit old fellows waiting for their appointment; no nurse was at the desk and I sat down to wait, and listened. They were having some kind of a disagreement, in high-pitched, annoyed voices.

"I honestly did the best I could to make a happy home."

"You did like hell. You boozed your way right into the spin dry, you did. Lost your family, you fuckin' idiot."

"Now, now, that's just your slant."

If one of these men was the older of the two it was the one in the ragged but voluminous coat, from which he extended a hand, like the last days of Pope John Paul, in a gesture of peace. The other took it, and after a pause their conversation resumed about the five-dollar box of Cheerios they'd both seen that morning at IGA. "It was big, I'll give you that. But still."

Jocelyn came into the lobby, carrying a battered purse, wearing a baseball cap and gold earrings, jeans and a thin, tailored white blouse that emphasized her pretty figure. She was on a cane and used it with athletic dispatch. "We roll."

She directed me to the small airfield southwest of town on a road that was almost too much for my Oldsmobile, whose oil pan felt like an extension of my own viscera. Looking around the car, Jocelyn said, "I thought medicine paid better than this."

"It's a ride."

"I guess. Go over that cattle guard and just follow the two-track into the pucker brush and you'll see it, little flat mesa hangs out over the creek bottom."

I glanced over and found her eyes, in no hurry to glance away. I reached for her hand, which she put in my lap like something I'd misplaced. "Oh, Doctor." There were several ways to look at this remark, the first being that I had misjudged the situation. Jocelyn smiled at me, but there was a bit of amusement in it. She raised her cane and gave it a little shake in my direction.

A grass airfield ended at the mesa edge, where a bedraggled windsock hung from an unpainted steel pole. A coyote dug for gophers in the middle of the field and trotted off at our arrival. All that remained was an anonymous rental car glinting in the sun. In other words we had arrived and something would have to change.

Jocelyn asked, "How much time should I allow to get to the Billings airport?"

"Hour and a half, to be safe." I pulled up next to the sedan.

"Then I'd better keep moving along."

"Where are you going?"

"Where am I going? I'm going to the Billings airport."

"I mean where are you flying to?"

"I'm not. I'm picking up my mechanic. He's going to help me drive to Texas. This is his car." I had the disquieting sense that she was making this up: she was talking too fast.

"Oh," I said, as though landing on the heart of the matter. "I thought it was a *rental* car."

"No, no, it's his car. I flew the ag plane up and he was supposed to meet me when I was done. I got done sooner than I thought."

"I'll be darned, I thought it was just a rental car." I couldn't have been more of a fool. She smiled compassionately at my confusion and slung her pack out of the car. She came around my side and kissed me on the cheek just as I was coming to my senses.

"I'll call you if my whole life changes," she said. "Maybe we can have dinner."

"Please do. I'm crazy about you." My face was red.

She laughed out loud and got into her car. "Who knows? You in the book?"

"I am."

I watched her pull away. I offered a wave, but looking at her receding rearview window, I saw no hand raised in my own direction. A sort of twist went through me of something akin to embarrassment, though there was no one there to be embarrassed in front of. I did wonder if several days of unspecified eagerness had contributed to my outbreak of foolhardiness, or if I'd wished for something I really needed. It was no mystery to me, who had seen the various results, some soon after, some decades after, of the unexpected electricity between people. One of my patients was an infantryman who had fought in the Second World War and returned to Seattle to a job cooking in a café. In 1946 the cashier, a young woman from eastern Washington who had come to Seattle during the war, dropped a roll of nickels, which burst on the tile floor. The infantryman and the cashier knelt to gather them up, and fifty years later the old couple were my patients. Surely something of lesser magnitude had happened to me, but there had been some sort of event at the crash site, and I think it was no more than seeing a small curve of forehead between the edge of her helmet and the slight rise of flesh where her ear disappeared inside the gear. In my embarrassment, I tried to come up with something more substantial and barely resurrected the shape of one nostril! I was like a picnic ant on two square inches of anonymous flesh. Fool!

I got called in to stitch up Jasper Carroll, a fireman, for the fourth time in nine years, each due to being stabbed by his wife. I don't think she intended to kill him and he always offered the same explanation: "We was having a discussion and she come with the blade." You might say that I had lost all respect for Jasper's injuries. He always brought his dog, a little Chihuahua named Manolete, for fear his wife would take it out on the dog. He lay on his stomach on the operating table with very little anesthetic, the nice wide but fairly shallow gash extending from just below his left shoulder in a downward angle to his spine. Jasper was an old hippie, and his gray ponytail hung below his black Chevron gimme cap almost far enough to be in the way. I listened to ZZ Top singing "Mexican Blackbird" as I worked and Billy Gibbons's loping guitar created a nice rhythm for the stitches—poking, yanking, snipping.

And Manolete's occasional howls punctuated the soft-shoe boogie I performed next to the table. Alan Hirsch peeked in to watch me work and said, "Get down with your bad self." I kept the *Chrome, Smoke & BBQ* boxed set in the emergency room to lift my spirits when the hours got long. I suppose it hurt my reputation with the rest of the staff. They had had a word with me about what they considered to be an excessively festive atmosphere. I think it just places me on the side of life, where a doctor should be.

The next time Jinx and I had lunch she tried to bring up the subject of my general unseemliness. We had taken pita wraps and beer to the park on an unseasonably warm day. Jinx wore a thick gray-green sweater with a shawl collar and the oddest pillbox hat I'd ever seen. I quite admired her indifference to her appearance and the impatience that caused her to speak through her hand when she was eating. Canada geese were standing at the edge of the park pond, which was so dark and still that their reflections were indistinguishable from themselves, and on a nearby bench an adoring young father rocked and gazed at his baby boy with shining eyes—a kind of Pietà but for the big ears and long black beard. I had spent the morning counseling a meth-head roofer from Walnut Creek, California, who had hit bottom here in town and wanted to talk about it. Surprisingly, he hoped to find a medical approach to maintaining his addiction and seemed strangely unaware that he was on a short straight road to hell. I got him in touch with our addiction counselor from my office phone, and I could tell by the upbeat dialogue he affected that he was not going to do anything for the time being. I told him I could see he wouldn't even keep his appointment. He was a handsome young fellow of moderate height in jeans, Hush Puppies, and a worn blue suede jacket. He had jet-black hair that stuck out and clear blue eyes. I could see how bright he was, his imperfectly concealed suffering showing just under the surface of his bonhomie.

"No, Doc, honest, I'll see him today."

"No, you won't."

"You don't think so?"

"No, but I wish I was wrong. I think you're young and tough enough to picture that great feeling. I realize it's like falling in love, but it's a lie.

Wait till you start rotting, it'll seem like expensive love." He didn't like this and his face soured.

"You get this from Nancy Reagan?"

"Uh-huh."

The young man backed to the door.

He said, "I'm Chad, by the way."

"See you, Chad."

Our most pleasant lunch in the park led up to the oddest question from Jinx: "What are you doing here? Have you no pride?" That's really all I remember. No, not so. I remember the food, or the taste of it, but it disturbs me that I can't remember who brought the food or why I kept looking at Jinx as though I were seeing her in a book of old photographs. For the moment, I was lost in her heedless sort of antique beauty. It always moved me. The fullness I felt in my heart I mistook for general high spirits.

After lunch with Jinx, I saw numerous patients, but while I may have given them appropriate treatment and advice I believed I did so from afar. Something was stirring, as though someone were standing in an adjoining room, the shadow on the floor the only sign of his existence. To give good medical care you must really see the patient and if possible lay hands upon him or her where convention permits. You must not stand behind the counter as though selling tickets at a shooting gallery. Every patient measured this distance subconsciously and weighed your suggestions against the measurement, and either results were achieved or they were not achieved.

On returning home at about midnight, having sat in a somewhat dumbfounded state on a barstool for several hours, I went to the windowsill on the north side of my bedroom and contemplated the alarm clock. I had owned this clock for several years without fully understanding it. You held one button to set the time, another to set the alarm, one to set the hours, another to set the minutes. AM and PM came and went like the days of my life and I often failed to set them properly. Sometime, hours after midnight, some woman came into my bedroom and asked me to not come to her house ever again. And she handed me a bill for the beer. She must have picked up my bar tab. I remember that it was almost undrinkable Grain Belt and I asked her if she carried any top brands. She slapped me and left. Whatever was disturbing me, it was not this, because I went straight back to sleep and had not a single dream until the alarm went off. I gazed around at the gray early light, arose, turned off the alarm, and went back to bed. I remained there for two days in a state of non-specific, writhing anguish. As it was rising in intensity with no end in sight, I arose and dressed from the pile of clothes at the foot of the bed and fled the house into frightful, fast-growing morning sunlight. I began passing people, some of whom must have recognized me. To allay my desperation, I pictured myself and attempted to arouse a sense of absurdity. The result was a hissing giggle emitted from between flattened lips. Though I was going nowhere, I was making phenomenal progress and passed through one neighborhood after another. When I recall the many automobile horns honking at me I feel very fortunate that I was not harmed. My mother loomed up taller than the ninety-foot Virgin Mary statue in Butte.

It was Sunday.

I stood in front of the old creamery, a concrete-and-stucco edifice with no windows and a remarkably small entrance, a commercial area that had been bypassed by the frontage road to the north where today's activities centered. During my teenage years and later, this had been my mother's church, one of several buildings around town where the ministry congregated. When I was a kid, a snake handler from Alabama brought his own rattlers and cottonmouths and offered to join but was turned away. He was told, "We don't do that anymore." Seeing it immersed me in pain: I had never gone inside. Why? Because I was embarrassed by my mother. Nothing gives you greater shame. I knew its reputation as a Holy Roller church, and it was infamous around town as a crackpot hotbed. As I stood there trying to connect its shape to my own history, I tried to keep up my well-practiced detachment, but it seemed to have little power in the face of my shame and guilt, all of which had been frozen in time by my mother's death canceling all possibility of reconciliation. Wait a minute. What reconciliation? My mother and I got along well enough and knew each other's limitations, but maybe this was different, my being ashamed of her beliefs or ashamed of the widespread view that she was crazy. Was she behind my remorse over Tessa? Behind my guilt over Cody? Anyone would see that I was headed inside.

I didn't know if I was just late for services or if they were nearing their end, but at first sight it was bedlam, a large, earsplitting crowd pressed between the walls of the old creamery. Most of the men wore cowboy hats. Some of the women did too, but they were attired as though they were at home, some in unpretentious wash dresses and some of the younger women in jeans and halter tops. All had a faraway look and my ability to wander across their lines of sight without being seen was unexpectedly reassuring. Opposite the doorway, shipping pallets and planks had been used to create a stage where a drum machine blasted out a relentless pulse. Only one musician was on the stage, a bass guitar player, an amplifier at his feet, who throbbed along to the drum machine. A fraught woman stepped from the crowd and asked me where my shoes were. Next to the bass player an old man with a white beard and huge belly swayed and threw his arms from one side to the other. There was nothing menacing about this mob, and the further I penetrated it the less anxious I felt, the better I felt. Given that I had left my bed in a state of unbearable anxiety, it was a relief to be in a group so exalted that the eyes of half of them rolled out of sight. Several were clearly in the ecstasy of holy laughter. My mother had done some holy laughing around the house, and now, my seeing so many others at it seemed to absolve her in a way I found cleansing. Leading this pandemonium was the pastor, Rawl Pennington—one of my patients!—who stood a few feet from the bass player with his own amplifier and microphone, a very long cord necessary to his feverish movement. He was an older man, astoundingly active. As he exhorted us, he moonwalked from one end of the platform to the other, or raised one leg repeatedly to the height of his chest, a kind of goose step, as he shouted about the Rapture, the need to meet the Holy Ghost, to read the Book of Acts—I mean, this was beyond shouting—and as he invoked a mighty wind of what he called apostolic witnessing to the end-times, the crowd seemed to rise with him, the youngest skittering off with chattering teeth and faces in a peculiar mask like the last stages of diphtheria. There was much weeping, though it was weeping that expressed relief rather than grieving. I must have been drawn in, because my eyes filled with tears. Groups tottered with raised arms while others ran through the crowd in a low crouch. I joined the latter and was transported in a state of fascination at being able to run blindly without hitting anyone. Shoes and cowboy hats flew. When I leapt straight up, an old woman cried out, "He's under a special sign!" The pastor stalled out on the shouted word "Unto!" He kept crying, "Unto, unto, unto!" before resuming about false signs and lying wonders and the need to cast out the devil and be anointed *now*. I very distinctly remember the sense of a pulse, a throbbing, possibly the music, if you could call it that, the exhortations of the pastor or the collective cries and moans as the whole crowd seemed to lose the beat and individuals, jerking in spastic movement, began to fall out. The pastor was down among us then, and to be perfectly clear I stopped racing around in my crouch, and I fell out too. Wonderful! The pastor was standing over me in a state, burning eyes, trembling jowls, hair tumbling over his ears from his bald crown. I was acutely aware of everything and could hear his legs slapping around inside his suit trousers, see the glint off his microphone, the triumph and rapture in his face as he called out to his flock, "He wants his mama! The doctor is calling out to his mama!" A grand affirmative noise filled the room.

They knew who I was. I didn't care. I was riding along on my interior tumult as on a big wave whose force I hoped would take me far up the beach. It was only at the door to my own house that I noticed the shoes on my sore feet, and the mismatched socks; they were square-toed brogans, quite comfortable, but they weren't mine.

15

I HAD A NORMAL REST OF THE WEEK at work. I ignored Jinx with a smile when she said, "Go." I had a cancellation Friday afternoon and it was taken by Pastor Rawl Pennington—he who had fed the pandemonium!—who had a sore throat and the beginnings of an infection. My sense was he had grabbed a cancellation to take my temperature on matters of the spirit. As I somewhat rigidly greeted him, my first thought was that he would try to initiate some sort of revival meeting in my office, shredding what little remained of my reputation. Rawl operated a mobile welding service subcontracted to the Burlington Northern Railroad and lived at the south end of H Street near the rodeo grounds. I swabbed the white spots in his throat to have them cultured and wrote him a prescription for antibiotics. I don't think church would ever have come into this had I not tried to relate all the shouting on Sunday to the poor condition of his throat. He agreed with me. "Should have been toughened up by this time, don't you think?" This was the first acknowledgment, if a bit off the wall, of my attendance at his services.

"Well, I don't know how much of that you do."

"Ever' week. Say, did you get anything out of it?"

"I don't know, I might have. I have to be honest, it wasn't exactly a religious experience."

"Did you feel any better?"

"I felt way better."

"Good enough. Maybe you just need to see folks more." At the door, I shook his powerful hand and thanked him for the advice. "Don't worry if you can't make it again," he said. "It's not for everybody."

Before I left for home that day, I prayed at my desk. It was hardly the first time I've prayed, because my mother embedded that in my habits from the beginning. But I just kind of launch these petitions into the unknown, as I am hardly a person of faith. You could say I believe in that vast entirety that is not me and I find it a suitable destination for prayer. I also pray to those manifestations of the natural world that catch my eye. I have prayed to clouds, canyons, springs, at least one landslide, birds, Swimming Woman Creek, the town of Martinsdale, the Jefferson River, and so on. I've prayed to my old 88. After a rain, I prayed to a mud puddle. Today a pair of teal flew past the window of my office, and I directed a really heartfelt prayer to them for the people of my mother's church. This has given me great consolation. I will go on praying. However, when McAllister's nurse came in with a stack of Medicare forms, she wanted to know why I was kneeling by the window. I felt there was no reason to back away from my new understanding and I told her simply that I was praying to ducks. She dropped the papers on my desk and left without saying anything.

As far as patients, I was just taking what came through the door. Something was afoot with me, and no pattern of regulars had emerged recently, old regulars being notably absent. I had ranchers reluctant to come to town because they considered all towns parasites on the ranching community. I had railroaders anxious to acquire workmen's compensation looking for someone to verify their claims of disability. It was the age of hard-to-specify complaints of the spine and neck. At least once a week, someone came to me hoping for prescription opiates, sometimes the spine-and-neck folk hunting early retirement and sometimes unemployed night owls. Every one of these small western towns had a nocturnal population, people you never saw during daylight. Generally, they were up to no good. A prairie town usually had a dense grove of trees somewhere, often a cemetery, to which the night people resorted. And most were no strangers to the legal system. One of the biggest problems was the indiscriminate making of babies, and I handed out birth control pills with the feeling of pounding sand down a rat hole. I even tried arousing a sense of responsibility in the young fathers. Of course they all professed to want nothing more than the coming child, but these young men were easily bored and the poor girls who took them at their word were soon left holding the bag. I recall one young man, a baby-faced cowboy with a baritone voice and vaguely arrogant air, who was the father of three of my patients' babies. I may have been less diplomatic with him than was my custom, but his reply has stayed with me to this day: "I only screws them what needs screwin'." I was so entirely flummoxed by this remark, delivered as it was with obstinacy and challenge, that I could only tell him to keep up the good work, and I saw him to the door. I failed to understand how innocent he was of irony, for he walked away in triumph, determined, I now admit, to do as I directed, and now with my blessing.

Being a doctor in a small town was a strange experience indeed because "doctor" implied affluence, though it had come to seem nothing exceptional now that the easiest money came to those who didn't work. Still, the title retained some of its old value, and you often heard that such and such ranch was closed to hunting because it was rented to "a bunch of doctors," even though no doctors were actually involved. Napoleon said that if it weren't for religion the poor would kill the rich. This may be all you needed to know about any human community. The churches were the real police stations, the real keepers of law and order.

Todd Clancy visited me at home on Thursday night, bringing a couple of beers which he managed to dangle between the fingers of one large hand. He had a cigarette between his lips, his suit coat flared over his substantial belly, and his tie pulled loose from an unbuttoned shirt collar. Todd had the broad, substantial, and florid face that I somewhat unfairly associated with the name Clancy. "May I come in?" His high voice was as incongruous as Mike Tyson's.

"You may."

Todd followed me into my kitchen, where he unceremoniously deposited the beer.

"Mind if I sit?"

"Nope. Is this an occasion?"

"Uh-huh."

That made me nervous. Moreover, whatever was on Todd's mind, he didn't seem in any hurry to speak. He appeared to think I could guess what was on his mind. I could not. It came to his attention. He said, "Do you have any idea why I'm here?"

"You needed company?"

"You really don't know?"

"I really don't know."

"That makes my job tougher."

"Todd. Rise above it."

Todd gripped his beer, and then embedded the tip of his forefinger in the opening. He was the county prosecutor and a pretty tough guy, used to all sorts of unpleasantness, but he had a very painful time telling me that it was possible I'd be charged for negligence in the death of Tessa Larionov. I really had no reply to make but stupidly asked anyway, "Why would I do that?"

He went into his prosecutor's number. "Why does anyone commit a crime? I only know that my job has to do with whether or not they did it, not why they did it." I found this irritating.

He settled down a bit. "I've been given a job to do."

"I have to say, I'm having trouble getting my mind around this one. I did everything I could to keep Tessa alive. Who has suggested otherwise?"

"Are you going to drink that one?"

"No, I don't want it."

Clancy took the other beer and immediately drank from it. "I would say that your board of directors aren't your friends. It's none of my business, but coming in I noticed that you've let all your bird feeders get empty."

"Oh."

"I don't buy mine from the bird store. Just go to the elevator. Get millet, sunflower, whatever you want, at ag prices."

"You say my colleagues at the clinic supported this?"

"Let me put it this way: they were unwilling to go up against the board. And they said you didn't support them when they had the slowdown. They're not too happy with you. Except that Dr. Mayhall, but I understand she's a loose cannon."

"That hurts."

"Sure it does. No matter what you may have done, you're still a human being. You have your hopes and dreams no matter what."

"Todd, do stop."

"You need a lawyer."

"I have a lawyer. Niles Throckmorton."

"Oh, for Christ's sake. Good luck."

Todd's expression changed and he seemed cold as charity. It was really then that I began to take this whole thing seriously. "It's almost eight. You want to grab something to eat? I started the day drawing up charges for the owner of the Trails End Hotel. Had a window give way and this salesman fell seven stories to the sidewalk. I don't know why it's supposed to be on my desk. The only applicable statute was the law of gravity, which is no respecter of persons."

"I'm not hungry."

"Nothing tempting? A nice chop?"

"No."

"So, then, guess I dine alone. I have only myself to blame, bringing this news. See you in court."

And, of course, back to work! I got very odd looks from my colleagues, however, and my remark, "No one to murder, I shall turn to healing," produced hardly a smile. I'm accustomed to making people smile and have a complacent faith in my wit; therefore, this failure to gain a response produced a shift in my mood.

The news had yet to spread, and things were altogether normal until early afternoon. I did a couple of physicals, ordered X-rays for an ankle injury that turned out to be a sprain. The young electrician was very disappointed it wasn't broken, and I tried to console him. I should never have told him he could go back to work immediately, as it caused him to leave in a somber mood without a word to me. I was for a moment reasonably happy, handing out SSRIs and birth control pills with abandon. I ate lunch from the coin machines in the lobby while reading *Field & Stream*. Things started going downhill in the middle of the afternoon with unannounced cancellations, all my appointments, really. I sat alone in my office and watched clouds in my window. As the day heated up, the clouds moved a little faster, but that was about it for celestial change—i.e., no revelations except that I began to wonder whether I was actually guilty in some way and if, after a very long time rising from my unpromising origins, I was finally ruined.

I was, of course, guilty of the crime, but the victim wasn't Tessa. Was this a technicality? Would honesty compel me to plead no contest? I had ethical standards to guide me from time to time, but they tended to flit in and out on the winds of that day's mood. The great difficulty lay in my feeling no guilt for what I was being accused of. The actual source of my discomfort eventually came to me. We are most of us romantic enough to imagine that the perfect partner exists for us somewhere in the world. We know this is not true, the idea that only one other human being could suffice. But it doesn't bother us that it is untrue, and that's the essence of romance: indifference to truth. I felt that only one person could have been my life companion and that I had failed to recognize her through obstinate want of self-knowledge. It was Tessa. Who cared if she was an utter fright? She alone had understood me, and I had failed her. But did that constitute murder? Of course, she would have driven me completely crazy and that would have seemed sufficient motivation. When I thought of a lifetime with Tessa, a crime of passion seemed not out of the question.

I believed my colleague Gary Haack was someone who might have something heartening to tell me. He was a reasonable man, a secular man, free of all social juju, levelheaded in practice and in staff meetings, a man who made few bones about the fact that work was no more than a means to an end, no matter what kind of work it was. He once told me that if he spent a decade ministering to the victims of the atomic bomb, it still would be a means to more skiing and hot-air ballooning. I don't know why we believed this thoughtlessness gave Dr. Haack some kind of authenticity, but I expect that the Hallmark card view of medicine had come to seem cloying: the kindly old shit in pince-nez and dangling stethoscope bending over the rosy-cheeked tomboy, a worried spaniel occupying a nearby rag rug. I also thought that the fact that Haack had never particularly liked me increased the chance of his being objective. I didn't like him either, the asshole.

He was faced away from me, toward the window and its view of restricted parking. I announced myself, and he straightened slightly at the sound of my voice. He said, "Do please leave me out of this."

I was taken aback. Walking the corridors, I found not a single face turned in my direction—plenty of backs, though. After the first moments of paralysis and dismay, I sank into unexpected and unfamiliar rage. It came as a spiraling, helpless anguish and an abstract revulsion at my plight. But what was my plight? I was new to this pariah status and could have more readily accepted it if only a few of my patients had shown up. It also seemed to me now that self-pity was fuel for this fire and a powerful fuel it was. I don't know if you can beat the anger and self-pity cocktail for real mayhem potential.

When I was in school I worked part-time as a telemarketer. It was surprising how many people, on hearing my message, told me to eat shit and die. Telemarketing was a distressing glimpse of human nature which I ought to have forgotten but hadn't. It's no damn use finding deficiencies in human nature, because sooner or later you spot them in yourself. My job was to sell candles over the phone: car candles, soy candles, church candles, scented candles, pillar candles, colored river rocks to go with your floating candles, votive candles, wedding and anniversary candles, citronella candles to keep bugs away, birthday candles. Always the same result—"Fuck you. Eat shit. Et cetera." I'd tell them, "I know where you live, I'm gonna get you." Then when I was an intern, I heard about people shoving candles up their rectums. I've had a lot of trouble with candles and they've *given* me a lot of trouble. You won't find them in my house. I don't know who thought them up in the first place. Poor light source anyway, and a fire hazard.

For several days, the nicest thing I heard about myself was that I was not a flight risk. On reflection, I found this offensive. After a rocky beginning, this town had tidied me up. No flight risk. No flight, period. I certainly didn't want to go to prison.

The very thought slowly turned a leaf of dread inside. I have watched patients stare into the parking lot knowing that they were not to leave for the time being or, in other cases, ever. I found that more dreadful than violence. I've seen the anguish in a patient's face when someone they were watching got in a car below their window and drove away.

You can't leave.

I avoided my office for nearly a week. Our receptionist had organized a small pile of message slips under an old souvenir letter opener from

Butchart Gardens in Victoria, British Columbia, where I had gone with a girl I thought I'd marry—two girls I thought I'd marry. There were several notes trying to explain cancellations "in view of the circumstances," several solicitations, and one very short note. Some had left in the most extraordinary circumlocutionary style messages plump with exit strategies, in case I was acquitted. But back to the shortest of them all.

"Please call as soon as you can." This from the crop duster. The delectable pilot. Jocelyn Boyce. I felt instinctively that it could change everything. Take this job and shove it, etc.

I stuck with my decision to use Niles Throckmorton as my lawyer. To begin with, he was so passionate about my case. Hadn't he called when I had not even been charged with anything? Too many lawyers are inclined to gloat at the misfortune of doctors, but Niles was an old friend. Still, I was surprised at his enthusiasm. I guessed that would be a good thing, but though I am misfortunate, it is not my mission to help others gloat.

The death of my mother was a very confusing occasion. I can't say we were close, that wasn't it. Her periods of "rest" at various institutions increased her distance from us. At the end, adult-onset asthma, which had for a long time predisposed her to bacterial infections, resulted in one that we ultimately couldn't control. I say "we" because for obvious reasons I didn't want to be alone on that one, and because I sensed that she couldn't wait to get out of here (earth) and be on her way to a better place (heaven) and was making very little effort to stay. I could see why the death of persons with those views persuades others of their truth; Mama's peace and delight at dying gave the three attending doctors, including me, the inspirational feeling that here was a person who had just left behind a burdensome vessel, her body. Perhaps we could see how the body was an ongoing annoyance, and she seemed so glad to go. The three of us definitely felt exalted and disturbed. But my father's ill-concealed relief gave rise to secondary confusion, though time helped me understand that the oppression of her religious views had lifted at last. After decades of faithfully attending those noisy services—which I now read as simple devotion to my mother—he never went again; and when that muscle-bound whack job of a pastor made his third importuning visit to the house, my father slammed the door in his face so vehemently that we went to the window to see if the pastor was still on his feet. Flying coattails disappearing into a four-door sedan were our reward. My father ostentatiously dusted off his hands, and that was that.

My situation, under the law, was so fraught with ambiguity that I wondered why I found it comfortable. My earnings were at an end, though I was in no peril economically, having reasonable savings and even a few investments. Stranger still was my indifference to all things my income might have provided. My eating had long been confined to basic needs, I used only one light in the house, and I had all but quit driving my car. As I walked I felt the aura of my disgrace shine out before me like the beams of headlights. Seeing familiar faces turn away fascinated me. Human entanglement was so tiresome that if we were of sound ego, we would find it exhilarating to arouse disgust in others. Besides being guilty of the death of Cody Worrell and knowing guilt was guilt, I could well accept the fact that the people of my town considered me guilty of the death of Tessa.

My mother's Southern—that is, Ozarkian—origins afforded her several distinctions compared to neighbors, and among them was a taste for what she called without bigotry "race music," a kind of postwar rhythm and blues that she played on our home Victrola. God knows where she got the records. And she had a source for moonshine: both my parents drank it, but not with the feral abandon associated with that substance. They treated it as a superior liqueur and sipped it on special occasions. My father said, "It's just bourbon, but it's handmade." I do remember them once having more than a taste and dancing on the exhausted linoleum of our kitchen floor in modest abandon to Ike Turner's "Rocket 88," after which my father said plainly that he never wanted to hear that song again. My mother danced with a lot of soul and seemed faintly amused at my father's rhythmless hopping around.

I had some success in going on about my business as though things were normal, and in an odd way they *were*. I even popped in at the clinic on one pretext or another, getting this and that from my office or merely amiably greeting my former colleagues. I did so often enough that at first they grew somewhat accustomed to seeing me; then they seemed to have forgotten the charges against me, and finally a bit of compassion emerged from one or two of them.

Some nights I was terrified.

I lay sweating on sheets overdue for changing and racked my brain for happier days. Often I went back to my hours as a house painter but could never quite put my finger on what I had liked about that besides its inconsequentiality. I did remember the pleasure of making something change color.

Whenever Jinx wished to see me, she always just came to my office or any other empty room I was purported to be in, as there was a certain informality about working spaces at the clinic. This time, she had our receptionist call and ask me to "stop by at my convenience." I didn't like the sound of that at all. But I went. I found Jinx in the consultation room she had staked out as her own, much the most commodious, and originally meant as a sort of conference room, her intense, intelligent, battle-ready face already fixed in the ominous pause that would precede her remarks and her graceful body propped against the broad, paper-stacked desk that also held the odd assortment of hats she cycled through during the week. She tried hard to avoid being beautiful, but it wasn't working. I didn't have to say anything. I merely raised my eyebrows inquiringly.

"Close the door." I did. "Well, sport, it's coming your way."

16

IN RETROSPECT, I realized that the tone of my working world had changed with Wilmot's installation on our small board of directors. At first it was hard for me to see how this could have happened. Wilmot had money in ample supply, which often proved a cipher for personal capacity. It mattered little if you found it under a rock: it was yours and it spoke volumes about your merit. Moreover, he'd quickly risen among his fellow directors to the chairmanship. That was when he'd begun to call in efficiency experts and to insist on more-stringent board oversight, down to the appointment of nurses. We doctors also saw to the small rest home, which relied on minimally qualified but mostly competent care-givers. Wilmot got his mitts on this too, and we had a lot of devastating resignations as he called on various employees, including impoverished older women, to supply professional bona fides. For a short time, the old folks were virtually abandoned to the whims of family members and doctors like me who found time to enter their exceedingly gloomy world and provide what minimal help we could while the draconian fallout that showered down from Wilmot settled. I think that seeing our cardiologist, Alan Hirsch, operate a waffle iron at daybreak in that shadow world made us realize how far off course things had drifted.

A special meeting was called and it stopped just short of acrimony. We doctors politely informed the board that a certain flexibility was required in a small town where the employment pool contained not just the niche-ready, trained personnel but ordinary citizens willing to adapt to things that were as new to them as they might be to us. Wilmot seemed to listen politely from where he sat at the end of the board table in blazer and perky spotted bow tie embedded in his ruddy neck. Only his eyebrows, oddly antic, gave any indication that he heard us at all. The board members—salesman, dentist, and housewife— especially seemed uneasily deferential to Wilmot, who had not spoken; even the usually argumentative rodeo clown, a middle-aged cowboy in tight jeans, large belt buckle, and snap-button shirt who had been a scourge for our lackadaisical bill collecting, kept his trap shut today. Doctors are reliable guardians of their own cheese balls, but the divaga-tions of human nature led them to occasionally notice the straitened cir-cumstances of some fellow humans. I later assumed that this reticence of the board had been a prearranged stage setting for what followed: a blis-tering call for the members of the clinic to raise our standards of effi-ciency and expertise. It was an astonishing performance, since Wilmot to all appearances hardly knew what he was talking about, a fact that had little effect on his rant. Gripping one wing of his bow tie between thumb and forefinger while he shook the forefinger of the other hand at us, he demanded that we act . . . like grown-ups!

I had to hand it to my colleagues: we all learned to look forward to these meetings, which we viewed with barely suppressed hilarity. Over time, Wilmot delivered sermons based on a loose group he called "the founding fathers," whose nature became more Nietzschean with every meeting. Our clinic did have problems, mostly financial, and these drove the looniness of our board with unfailing regularity. The rodeo clown blamed everything on falling cattle prices, out-of-staters, and ethanol. The car salesman saw the Japanese titrating unhappiness into the Amer-ican economy. In this context, the housewife seemed quite sensible, see-ing men behind everything. The dentist played his cards close to the chest and cringed when we congratulated him on avoiding weekend emergencies. In reply, he pantomimed his golf swing.

Dr. McAllister said, "Thank God they're clueless."

I retrieved with wan hope the sheaf of bills in my mailbox and met my old nurse Scarlett as she walked home with a rake she had just pur-chased jauntily balanced over her shoulder. I did not feel whimsical or ironic but meant to speed her into my home. I said, "Put down that rake."

"My goodness," said Scarlett, switching the rake from one shoulder to the other, "you're leading an exciting life." She wore a tattered, man's crewneck sweater, cranberry red, with her wristwatch over one sleeve, and open-back clogs that revealed her pretty ankles. I don't think I'd ever seen her out of her nurse's uniform. She looked far better this way.

"Yuh," said I dully, "I am."

"Is all this true?"

"No," I said, but the ambivalence came spearing back.

"Are they letting you work?"

"Er, not really."

"Bummer. So what do you do?"

"Well, I've been catching up on my thinking. Can you come in?"

"Ho, ho, ho. The answer is 'no.' "

As though this reply was of the greatest indifference to me, I said, "Well, then, let me just stroll along with you, if that's all right."

"You know, it's not all right. I realize you're innocent until proven guilty, but I don't need a lot of people watching me socialize with you."

"I understand."

"Probably you don't, but that's just how it is." She went on her way, the rake over her shoulder. Without looking back, she said, "Call me if you're acquitted."

I doubt that Jinx was being formal with me so much as practical. I must not have been ready for practicality. I asked her, "Do you have a minute to talk about this?"

"Talk about what?"

"Oh, come on. I'm in trouble."

"Sure, I'll talk about it. What do you want to talk about?"

"I want to know if you had a hand in it."

"Why would I have had a hand in it?"

"You tell me."

"I think it's more important that you think about what you have done and what should be done to you as a consequence. I'm not asking you to tell me: that's between you and your god."

"Excellent. We spend a lot of time together. We'll work it out."

"When you do, get some advice about operating on a somewhat different plane. Neither I nor anyone else in town can figure out where the hell you're coming from." I found this tone of Jinx's alarming: she had never talked to me like this.

I think that medical school, where I found myself by way of a painless knack for academics and some democratic scheme by which poor boys from hick towns received modest preference, was where I first felt the gust of fear that if I didn't straighten out and fly right I might well end up a flop and an idiot. Therefore, I got my head down and my butt up, and bent to the work at hand. As a consequence, I had few personal memories of medical school, which had all the charm of a Soviet assembly line. If we drank, it was in pursuit of oblivion; if we fornicated, it was to relieve discomfort. At length, we found without jubilation that we were doctors. I lurched home to celebrate and did my best to enjoy the gruesome party my parents had arranged in my honor.

There was much alcohol. My father had set up a huge barbecue pit in the backyard, and some animal was turning on a spit. A few of the fancier folk in town were back there quietly disputing what sort of beast it might be. A sober and extraordinarily energetic knot of Pentecostal boors organized square dancing for themselves—no one else seemed to feel welcome to participate—and an authoritarian lout in blue coveralls called out the moves to the blank-faced revelers. They had brought their own tape deck and speakers, and it was only when Mayor Kavanagh with his 1890s moustache told them to "turn that goddamn thing off" before jerking the cord out himself that we were able to resume speaking in normal tones. Thereafter, the fundamentalists kept to themselves and watched the party warily. My mother, for all the strangeness of her thinking, was a lively and sociable person; I don't know how she had tolerated these people for so many years. I guess it just goes to the genuineness of her convictions.

My father stood on a chair and tapped his glass with a spoon. I realized with dread that he was about to make a speech. The gist was that he was a nobody, my mother was a nobody, and I was a great man, a doctor. It went over like a lead balloon. My mother was furious. People stared at my father in dismay. He began to sob. I took him by the elbow and helped him down from the chair. To ease the crisis, I said a few formulaic words about how I stood humbly in the shadow of their sacrifices.

The guests absorbed this with varying degrees of relief, all except Tessa, who covered her mouth in helpless laughter. At any rate, the moment had come and gone. We went to the dead animal turning on the spit.

Fate headed me to Tessa. She uncovered her mouth and said, "I couldn't help it." I knew it was funny but thought indignation fitted the situation better. Her hand went back over her mouth. I told her, "Those are my parents." She snorted through her nose and said she was sorry.

I may have only on the occasion of that barbecue really noticed what a dump my folks' place was. I had never been there before in a coat and tie. All those people standing around with beers and other drinks to welcome me home, including the usual suspects—Mrs. Voorheis who owned the secondhand store on the frontage road; an alcoholic horseshoer named Hooty Cox who was there for the drinks; Don Funk who ran a pawn operation out of his house; Elvin Bird in Ground who was a Crow Indian diesel mechanic; Sister Calista from the Catholic grade school who never missed a party with spicy food; cabinetmaker Cal Schreiner and wife; Conoco station owner Bus Clancy, a widower, and his two grown daughters; big-game outfitter Riley Cash in full cowboy regalia and trailing moustache; our two most popular backhoe operators, Jack and Jerry; renowned snowmobile mechanic Tim Varian, soon to be punched by Hooty Cox, himself to be swiftly subdued by Don Funk while Elvin Bird in Ground rudely ogled Bus Clancy's two large daughters—as well as the medical staff of the clinic to which I would be attached, the small group of doctors who stood to one side and smiled . . . faintly. My mother and father wore themselves out in solicitous darting between the two groups. I thought the senior internist, Dr. Laird McAllister, was a little abrupt in declining the plate of food my mother brought him, raising the palm of his hand in her direction and saying, "No way!" Under the single shade tree stood the two old brothers Eggs and Bugs Ackley, wheat farmers from the Cottonwood Bench, in matching red-white-and-blue suspenders. Their real names were Elvin and Darwin Farquahar. Long ago, because of their enthusiastic manner of affirmation—"Exactly!" and "But exactly" oddly pronounced—they came to be know as Eggs and Bugs Ackley. I drifted into my accustomed out-of-body state, absentmindedly popping the unfamiliar necktie between thumb and forefinger and musing that the life ahead might prove complicated. The mild malaise I experienced I trained upon the rusty Ford Fairlane on blocks that defined the backyard and which I employed as an object of meditation while I allowed the various waves of my story to wash over me.

Dr. McAllister stepped over to welcome me. I guess it was a welcome. Coming from such a tall, patrician Anglo-Saxon, it was not easy to tell, and his speaking style—launching the words without seeming to care whether they landed—contributed to the abstract atmosphere. Dr. McAllister wore a beautiful gray and brown houndstooth sport jacket, broad soft lapels meeting at the top of two buttons. The red silk tie seemed to disappear at just the right point. He had a highball in hand, and he delicately bobbed an ice cube with the tip of his finger.

"I led the review committee, Doctor, that looked over your qualifications, and it wouldn't be wrong to suggest that I led the effort to see you land in our clinic. You're a very well-prepared physician, and we especially liked that you're a general practitioner."

"Oh, good." I smiled.

"General practitioners have become the redheaded stepchildren of our profession, and we're thrilled that the role claimed your ambition. Welcome!"

"Thank you."

He tipped his highball toward my beer: clink.

Slowly surveying the guests in my parents backyard, he said, "I hope you're prepared for the changes coming to your social life." This I liked less.

I said, "I don't think it will be a problem. I've always lived here. Where are you from?"

He didn't say a word. He only gave me a wintry smile and returned to his companions.

I got a turn in the emergency room right early on, and one of the first patients I saw was a gas station robber shot by the police; I saw that he would survive the .38 Special hollow-point round that went right through his thorax and out the back without expanding. As time went by, I chatted less with the people who came through the door on gurneys and otherwise, but this fellow looked like a recent college graduate in his slacks and blue Windbreaker, his Seattle Seahawks cap, his loafers. When I asked what'd inspired him to stick up a gas station, he told me with peculiar sincerity, "You're only young once." I guess I had to accept that, but it became an enduring enigma.

I was not an excitement-oriented person. I liked what they call on TV "a slow news day." I may not have been as interested or informed about the big wide world as I should have been, and what news I got of war, disease, and famine did not inspire in me a cascade of solutions. I wished it were otherwise, but this was hardly my worst inadequacy.

When I was in high school, my father kept some horses on a patch of stock farm he owned for the few years he could afford it. Among them were my saddle horse and a government mule he'd acquired from the park service, which, when he tried to shoe it, put him in the hospital. This big wary mule with its suspicious ears and sloped muscular build was the only animal with smooth enough gaits for my father's old bones. So he put up with him—named him John Lee. I don't remember why. I helped Dad shoe John Lee by giving him a generous injection of sedative, then laying him on his side so we could shoe him horizontally while the comatose brute snored and blew bubbles out his nose. I nailed on the big, iron, strangely narrow keg shoes, and Dad, crouched and wheezing, clinched behind me. When we'd finished, we leaned up against the old cottonwood that shaded the pole pen in the middle of the rented ground and waited for John Lee to wake up. Dad seemed to think John Lee had died, but wake up he did. My father was so pleased to see him restored to life on earth that he promptly saddled him and rode off.

After my problems began, I found myself riding more often too. My horse, Errol, not only was easy to catch but actually seemed eager to be ridden. Errol began life as a mustang. I bought him at a BLM auction at the Red Desert corrals in Wyoming. Like others in the band, he was bigger than a pure mustang, having acquired some genetic advantages from the draft horses turned onto the desert during the Boer War.

Now that my medical career was suspended, I rediscovered Errol. I felt guilty about having paid so little attention to him while I worked at building my earthly cheese ball. In some abstract way, I hoped to make it up to him. I remembered when I'd acquired him, a stout yearling that we roped and loaded into my trailer, a pretty grulla colt, frightened and sweating with anguish over his lost freedom. He grew into a big, happy horse, and when he was three I rather timidly tried to break him to ride. It was my first year in practice, and I imagined I had a responsibility to my career at odds with risking my bones on a horse. The fact is, I was a bit scared of Errol, who now weighed over a thousand pounds and was not entirely predictable. I led him around on a halter rope, backed him up, shoved him all over the place—and he accepted it. I longed him with a saddle on his back, stirrups slapping his flanks, and he never objected. His complacent acceptance of all I threw at him encouraged me and beat back my fears until the day came to mount him. I even felt that Errol was telling me the same thing, that the time had come. And so I mounted Errol confidently.

I never had a chance. Errol bucked with four feet off the ground, lit on his front end, fired out behind, then bucked me straight over his head into the dirt like a lawn dart. There I could observe his leisurely grazing on the scanty orchard grass at the edge of the corral. I watched as he wandered over to my father's house and looked in the front window.

I was not hurt and walked over to Errol. He looked at me as though wondering what my problem was. I unsaddled him and called a man in Clyde Park who broke horses. I explained that as a busy doctor I just didn't have time to break him myself. I got him back a few months later, ready to be used. The cowboy said he "tried to tear me up" and asked if Errol was by any chance a mustang. I said, "Absolutely not."

So, I had time on my hands. I wanted to continue to live under the questions that had befallen me and resist the rising sensation that here lay opportunity. Treating the disentanglement from my career as an opportunity would be the way to some badly needed enlightenment. But I failed that test: I started to be happy contemplating my guilt like some obscure marine creature recently dredged from lightless seas.

I began to wander around town, watching people, visiting construction projects, school recesses, and so on. One day I found a small parade celebrating something or other and was impressed by the look of joyless fatalism in the faces of the marchers. I speculated that they had been ordered to this event by their superiors but later learned it was some sort of sweethearts' club with the mission of rekindling first love. On a cool afternoon with arrested white clouds hanging over the town, I loaded the push mower into the trunk of the 88 and drove to the cemetery, where I did, I must say, a fine job of clearing my parents' graves, virtually primping them, feeling not sadness but remarking the peculiarity of our funerary habits as though I were a visitor from another planet. The word I have most often associated with death—*"Poof!"*—appeared nowhere in this humble memorial park. A good many folks strolled the cemetery while I tidied things up—the young visibly anxious to get it over with; the old mindful and gloomy, thinking perhaps of what my mother called the Great By-and-By.

The real reason for my coming to the cemetery dawned on me but slowly. It was only when I had finished the job and should have been loading the hand mower into the trunk of my car that it began to surface. I pushed it back and forth while I thought, enjoying the whir of its oiled blades and the subtle knock of its ball bearings. In the end, I left it right where it was, while I sought the grave of the man I had urged to oblivion. I might have remembered where it was since I had attended his funeral, but there had been a surprising number of mourners and I remembered only the outpouring of grief for someone I saw as not worth mourning. I must have simply been drawn to the gathering without reference to where it was taking place. Of course, my unique role in the proceedings, known only to me, must have focused my thoughts in such a way as to obscure awareness of my physical surroundings. This was a working cemetery, hardly one of the antique jobs so old they spared the onlooker any of humanity's burdens. I had to go from grave to grave until something rang a bell. I keenly looked forward to being inspired on such a beautiful fall day. I left my father's well-cared-for lawn mower right where it was and set out.

In taking exceedingly good care of my parents' graves, I had begun to expand my territory. I don't think I realized what I was up to as I made my way from burial site to burial site. Everyone, myself included, looked for headstones with a relationship to some war. They were so plentiful! I found a little nest of them for WWI members of the Balloon Corps. What exactly were the "Woodmen of the World"? Civil War veterans who had served in Michigan or Ohio companies, landed here. Even some Confederate soldiers. I noticed that the urge to place flowers is not terribly long-lasting and that the preponderance of stone and grass with no further commentary in the form of posies, messages, or whiskey bottles suggested that the facts were eventually faced. The immigrant names like Stefan, Wolfgang, Ulrica, Sven, and so forth faded with the newer interments. Even Esther and Gladys weren't quite making it anymore. On the other hand, it was a fine place to be a tree. I should have recognized what I or my subconscious was up to when I came upon Tessa's headstone, which I seemed to know a lot about, i.e., Georgia Gray granite polished on one side—no urn, vase, cross, wing, book, diamond, or favorite pet—just name and date. But a weird shape. I should have known all this because I bought the fucking thing! Good God, I must have suffered some sort of blackout. The salesman talked me into an ogee. I was feeling like a cheapskate after fending off Botticelli's Venus, the Greek Winged Victory, Christ the Redeemer, an unbelievably ghastly Pietà, and various other high-dollar giant knickknacks; so I succumbed to the ogee. I didn't want an ogee; I wanted a rectangle, but I was weak from the whole experience and ended up with an ogee. For a moment I was furious, seeing that ogee. Of course I was, egged on by sadness, remorse, guilt, and the recurrent surprise that you can't turn back the clock.

It was a sunny day with a light breeze from the southwest, beautiful clouds, a rustle of leaves, the smell of newly mown grass and even of the flowers surrounding a grave or two. I liked seeing people walk so slowly. It seemed to have a balletic quality, just a few people moving quietly through the trees like deer. I found that I enjoyed coming here, and having more than the graves of my own dead to visit seemed to enrich the experience. With my garden shears, I was able to nip away some of the stray weeds around the base of Tessa's stone, tidy it up a bit.

At St.-Lô, Hagenau, and the fights at the Saar Bridge, I gathered, my father had staved off battle fatigue with alcohol. Drinking water was not always in reliable supply, and so various forms of "stupor juice" and "Kickapoo joy juice" were kept on hand by tankers from captured stores, but eventually all went back on water, the liquid courage draining from their systems, and there were breakdowns. My father was among those whom medics tried to restore with Blue 88s, high-dose amobarbital tablets; the idea was the pills would return you to combat, but when he came to, he walked out of the war. He told me that with large armies of young men all rushing to the same massacre, it was surprising how quiet the countryside was after you'd traveled a couple of days. He remembered when he started seeing the clouds again as an extraordinary epiphany. Once he was gone I sometimes felt I was seeing clouds again through my father's eyes.

Jocelyn had fallen out of the sky into my life, literally. Fortunately, I'd made enough visits to her bedside, sparking sufficient electricity that when she returned to home base in Snyder, Texas, to learn that nothing awaited her at the spray plane base and reluctant to return south and fly sun lotion banners over bathing beaches, she called me on the phone, and I her.

"Do you remember me?" she asked.

"I do. How's the eye? The knee?"

"They're fine. I thought I'd hear from you by now."

"You did?"

"I sure did."

I had certainly had Jocelyn on my mind, but reason had kept me from pursuing it. I thought that our encounter was too insubstantial for me to pursue anything beyond state lines. Certainly, I remembered feeling something when in Jocelyn's hospital room, even imagining that it was reciprocated—all dismissed. By me but not, evidently, by Jocelyn. How exciting!

I told her I was pleased to have her call me, and we arranged to meet for dinner. I was distracted during my few appointments by my anticipation of the evening. Enough so that I spent some time wondering what I could possibly be expecting and even feeling some alarm at my own enthusiasm as some new form of instability. I suppose I had a glimpse of the advantages of my complacency and feared anything I couldn't predict. As soon as I had made a dinner reservation, I found myself daydreaming about exotic travel—that is, escape. It was pathetic. How about the honeymoon, you damn fool? All this while palpating a half-naked fat man on my table, trying to find his liver behind two feet of blubber. I must have gotten a bit avid in my exam, imagining myself flying into the Seychelles with Jocelyn, because Tubby let out a cry, "Go easy, for Christ's sake." I should have been more careful, as the corpulent figure I was examining was Throckmorton, my lawyer. Throckmorton had been my patient for a long time and had frequently shown up for sometimes frivolous examinations. Each of them an ongoing search for an enlarged liver.

There were several reasons the community or its minions thought me guilty of negligence or even manslaughter. The first proposed was that I was reckless, which I gather faded in the face of tepid protest from my colleagues to the effect that I was a good and circumspect physician. A couple of things had come out in the paper exciting the credulous that it was murder; but after that, calmer heads prevailed, supported by the hearsay of several homeless people who attested to Tessa's wish to end her life. Nonetheless, I was charged with assisting in her suicide and planting the knife to avert prosecution. What I was offered was the chance to reduce deliberate homicide to negligent homicide, unless we could dismiss the case.

Overnight I became a hero of the local Hemlock Society and its right-to-die sympathizers. One old woman called and said that if I beat the rap, she'd like to have me euthanize her. There were demonstrations of support around town, increasing my joyless ambivalence, yet another out-of-body spell as I felt that by my silence I was misleading these well-meaning people, some of whom already faced terminal illnesses. Maybe this was where I first thought up my nolo contendere posture, which my lawyer translated as throwing myself under the bus.

"Over my dead body you're pleading no contest," said Attorney Throckmorton in a most inapposite turn of phrase. Throckmorton beyond being a victim of chronic obesity also suffered from a belligerent crew cut and the loudest sport jackets since the death of Liberace. He was a controversial lawyer who traveled his bailiwick in a garnet-red Audi A8 über-sedan with fitted leather seats holding coolers of fancy food. Some of our conferences took place in this car, and I accepted these arrangements because he had taken my case "out of the goodness of my heart." Nevertheless, as we tooled down the interstate at or around 100 mph, his eye on the state-of-the-art radar detector, a hunk of cheddar and a stout length of boudin sausage carelessly wrapped in pita bread and clamped in one hand, I felt it might be better to pay Throck-morton for his hours rather than endure these death-defying sagas in a fog of food smells on the American highway. As this went on over days, I found myself—while for example parked in front of his burly mistress's condo listening to the radio in the big German car—poking through the delicacies and finding various items that appealed to a finicky appetite now allied with the real need for escape: smoked oysters, emperor figs, potted meats, pâtés, duck liver in oil, and commoner things: Pop-Tarts, Hostess Twinkies, and so on. It was always the same fight: my refusal to plead not guilty. But Throckmorton didn't really know the whole story, and he never would. Nor would he realize the profound feeling of one's relationship to one's community that can be learned by declining to claim innocence. I'm not a masochist, but from the earliest days of grow-ing up in a crazy family I have wanted to throw myself upon this town to see what they would do with me.

When Throckmorton lumbered off the examining table, he said, "If changing my habits would add a decade to my life, I wouldn't consider it. I don't think people like you, looking from on high, quite realize how much I enjoy my life. Every time I pass inspection as I have done today I feel the gods have approved my habit of living. Tonight, when you put your head on the pillow or on some fair maiden's bosom, say this to yourself: *'Not guilty.'* "

17

My recent conscientiousness about tending my parents' graves had proven to be a consolation, as though I were tucking them in. When I saw others at the cemetery I began to theorize that this was a universal feeling—those people with pruning shears and watering cans had become serenely familiar. From time to time, one or another of us would simply sit down next to a headstone and weep with cleansing ordinariness, before getting briskly back to work, tidying up, trimming, tending. I did so a couple of times, until it finally became part of my no-contest attitude: *The Floater*, coming to a theater near you. I became increasingly aware of the landscape of a small-town cemetery with its trees and weather and purposeful visitors. As I had seen others do, the time came for me to move out of the vicinity of my own graves and see what was what. Hands plunged in pockets, an amiable and bemused expression on my face, the well-executed passing nods—all plausibly put the lie to the mission I was so slow to admit: I was looking for the grave of Cody Worrell.

At the time of the funeral I was so comfortable with my part in things that I'd attended as a kind of tourist, just curious. I did remember that it was a nice day and I enjoyed that. I had always been remarkably sensitive to and moved by weather. I remembered the zephyrs that fluttered the cottonwood leaves so attractively and the little cavalcade of ill-dressed people with their prematurely old faces. That carelessness, my almost aerial contentment, things having turned out as I supposed they should, I now saw as one of the lagging indicators of my prolonged adolescence. Whatever comfort I'd enjoyed, whatever pleasure I'd taken in the day, was now gone. I began to feel tormented by my part in Cody's death almost immediately after the funeral. And the thought remained: something was wrong with me. My indignation about the abuse of his young wife, my irresistible incentive, seemed to fade; I tried to revive it, but it returned as simple sadness, insufficient incentive for what I had done. I even caught myself angry at her for having been so hapless. I thought I had better put an end to this line of thinking before I started blaming her to get myself off the hook. No matter how I went at it, the issue would remain twisted inside me until I did something about it. That last moment of innocence in Cody's face . . . unbearable.

I found his grave quite easily and, I suppose, from memory—on the expanding edge of the cemetery where the trees were smaller and the direct sun starker. From here, too, the houses of the living were more eminent and unaccountably intrusive. I sensed the distinct peacefulness of the old cemetery lost in this funereal sprawl. In any case, there they were, another surprise: the two graves. I had not recalled that the young couple had been buried side by side forever. Perhaps it was because I came to their funeral only out of morbid interest as to whether or not anyone missed him, and the peculiar pleasure of attending incognito when I was the reason all the rest of them were there. But here they were, the young couple, side by side. It wouldn't be long before their brutal history would be subsumed in forgetfulness. She might reappear as the shy bride or he on his first bicycle. I would have to go on wondering what had impelled her repeated availing of herself to his rages. Then or now, I didn't care what had inflamed him. His abuse was sufficiently prolonged to accord him opportunity for change, but he never missed a step.

For my part, this review of the facts was just whistling in the dark. I had, as was said, taken the law into my own hands. My father, when describing the pleasure he took in shooting Germans, said that we came from a long line of people who shot first and asked questions later. But I knew perfectly well that he had arrived at this only when seeing friends fall had made his accustomed humanity vanish in anger. I recall him admitting his surprise at how easily charity could slip away. He had thought it was a bit more enduring. Apparently that surprised all those soldiers, especially infantrymen. They had initially admired the Wehrmacht for its efficiency, but as their friends were mowed down their hatred grew in detail. My father recalled the first time he tipped up the head of a dead German soldier for the purpose of guessing his age. He remembered thinking "somewhere around fourteen," which disturbed him anew, undermined his anger. At the time of that recollection, I was helping him repair our unreliable furnace, and he held the big red pipe wrench in his hand as his eyes drifted off: it was all quite present to him, the burning figment of the boy in the Wehrmacht helmet, my father's boot under his chin.

I may have been enduring the same fear, the eventual acknowledgment that in suspending the rules of humanity for the convenience of emotion we gave way to wickedness; at a bare minimum, we were in error. The matching headstones with their chiseled hearts encouraged my view that everything real was eventually reduced to human contrivance. As I walked back through the old cemetery to my car, every inscription seemed lurid with deceit.

I supposed that I was guilty.

I noticed that Jocelyn was limping. Otherwise she had changed little since I'd seen her in the White Sulphur Springs hospital—the same nice crow's-feet that seemed to intensify her gaze, the same slightly weathered quality of some good-looking women entering middle age. Her expression was, I guess, amusement at our turning up like this. However, she caught my glance. We had stopped at a steak joint, the Trail Head, just off the interstate. "Yes," she said, "it's permanent." We went inside and were given a table.

Jocelyn shrugged off her Windbreaker. Underneath she wore a snap-button shirt that seemed somewhat incongruous with her cotton skirt, but her vitality made it work and would probably have made anything work. If I'd taken her to one of our clinic get-togethers, I would have been afraid the wives would have found her a little tough even as they noticed their husbands' interest with irritation.

I said, "I'm happy to see you again. But I'm surprised."

She smiled and didn't say anything right away. "I expected to be well received. Weren't you flirting with me at the hospital?"

"Was I?"

She burst out laughing. "Oh, never mind!"

Anyway, our drinks arrived, whatever they were. It didn't matter what was in them: I was slipping into a trance. But not an entirely guileless trance. I was already trying to imagine how I might avoid telling Jocelyn about my problems. A doctor hoping to have charges reduced to manslaughter didn't seem like much of a catch. There was hardly anyone in the restaurant on this off night, and the sparseness seemed to isolate us. I felt something happening to me and would have appreciated some background noise.

"I'm not in Texas anymore. I'm back in Two Dot. My father died."

"I'm sorry, I didn't know that."

"Well, he was ninety. I think he had long since figured there's worse things than dying. He wouldn't leave the place, kept mortgaging it to pay nurses. It was a mess. I couldn't fly anymore, not ag flying, because I was no longer insurable. So now it's my place, for better or worse."

"Well, I'm sorry. It's always tough."

"Not in this case. He was a mean old man."

Our food came, a couple of little steaks and salad. Jocelyn said, "You're watching me eat!"

"Was I?"

"Yes! You were looking at my mouth! Okay, you try it. I'll watch your mouth while you try to eat that steak. You'll never get it down. It'll just get bigger the longer you chew it."

We talked about our situations: I suggested that I was on some sort of leave of absence, which went unquestioned; she was struggling with what to do with her dad's old place. The restaurant began to fill up, and I knew most of the people who came in, though nobody stopped at our table. Several stared at Jocelyn. You could just feel the atmosphere going downhill.

Jocelyn said, "Let's get out of here. Your neighbors don't look friendly." She started toward the front door. I left a few bills on the table as we arose and noticed that the room had nearly filled with other diners and they were staring. The waitress had been somewhat formal, I thought. Several men were observing Jocelyn walk. She had a somewhat grand manner that made the limp somehow fabulous. At least I thought so.

It was still light outside. Main Street with its rows of angle-parked automobiles and old storefronts seemed to frame the snowcapped peaks to the north. A few diners stood in front of the restaurant, hunched up against the cool air, nervously getting cigarettes out of the way so that they could go back inside and eat. Jocelyn's truck was parked in front of the bank; it was a small Japanese vehicle with Texas plates, mud right up to the windows.

"Did you forget what you did with your car?" she asked.

"No, no, it's just over there."

"Well, hop in it and go home. I'll see you when I see you."

I felt myself to be under suspicion at the clinic. My former bravado was gone, and I quickly realized how much I wanted to work, having no other source of income—though I lived cheaply. The savings of course would suffice, but I'd always thought I was saving for some as-yet-undetermined scheme. Still, I had tried for a short time to maintain my practice, and I had been genuinely touched by the patients who persisted in seeing me, because they thought I was either innocent or had good reason to murder Tessa. The latter had its disquieting side, as Tessa had come to seem something of a town pest. I was not reassured when Adelaide Compton, whose dermatitis had forced her to discontinue giving piano lessons, said of Tessa, and in a congratulatory tone, "Good riddance." I could only smile weakly while writing a prescription for cortisone cream.

In the end, it was out of my hands. The clinic partners were called to a special meeting where Dr. McAllister spoke, ostensibly to the whole group but really to me. He began with a peroration on compliance, expectations, work environment, and duty to the community, which could have applied equally to the space program and the whaling industry, before giving it up and speaking directly to me. Holding one wing of his bow tie between thumb and forefinger, he let it be known that all the clinic partners assumed that I was innocent but that for the good of all it would be best if I awaited the outcome of my trial or hearing before resuming work; and that in the meantime it would be no great matter if the "team"—had we ever used this term before?—took up my patient load.

I guess in my exasperation I had given some flippant advice to my more trying patients and they had gone to the board. A hypochondriac who kept demanding an explanation for all his imaginary ailments I diagnosed with Saint Vitus' Dance. A cowboy whose wife had complained of his crude erotic approach I urged to give mounting the same respect it is given in horsemanship. A water bed was no cure for undulant fever. And so forth and so on. I should have kept my mouth shut.

I think my first impulse was to hang on like a bulldog in a thunderstorm, but the folly of that was soon clear and I consented with a show of magnanimity that produced great relief in the room, including not a few audible sighs. Voluble noise filled the room, and everyone gathered around me with our old amiable muddle. When Dr. Haack joshingly punched me in the shoulder and asked, "Well, did you do it or not?" the room fell abruptly still as all eyes turned toward me.

I just smiled.

I got plenty of cold shoulders, but Jinx continued to see me. I don't think she was explicitly lonely, but she was so opinionated that not everyone considered her good company. We went pretty far back together, back to when my astonishingly callow behavior attracted few allies, let alone social contacts. She had me over for one of her expert suppers, a beautiful *entrecôte de veau* with braised garden vegetables and a bottle of Côte-Rôtie that I don't think she could have readily afforded. Her small house felt like the most cosmopolitan apartment filled with books, none, so far as I could tell, medical or scientific. The books were in cases except where they were stacked near a worn armchair, places marked with bits of paper. There was just one room where one could sit apart from the dining room, and its floor was nearly covered by a worn but beautiful Samarkand rug. Two rows of old novels were divided by a brown radio.

At table, we clinked glasses and let the unspoken be unspoken, though Jinx signified a little with a prolonged glance. I let it go right by me, not eager to thicken the atmosphere. I was quite resigned to my current fatalism. I had spent too much of my existence at manipulation and had at long last turned myself over to the world, savoring a sort of peace I had never before experienced. This was zeal in its most serene and contradictory form. I was self-sufficient and a good doctor, but this was my greatest achievement. Once I'd accepted that I was guilty and a criminal, the skies cleared.

"Are you making good use of your sabbatical?" Jinx asked while directing a faultfinding gaze at the food she had placed on the table. "I could use one myself. Later we can discuss whatever saga you are generating at the moment. Tell me what you think of this wine?"

"Didn't I say anything already?"

"You only peered into it and sniffed."

"Well, it's fantastic. I suppose you sent away for it."

Just then, her world seemed sad and orderly. Jinx could have used some of the disarray that currently lay over my days. Being useful to the end seemed insufficient. Whether this was a proclivity or an excuse I couldn't have said, so consumingly focused was I on the food and wine. I hoped there would be plenty of the latter, as I planned to get drunk. Very often that gave me the feeling of falling in love with Jinx and at the same time feeling I mustn't. I wondered why. Already I was feeling something very much like love for her. Sometimes it didn't wear off, either. I must have been crazy.

Out of work, I took an extreme interest in the newspaper. I spent extraordinary time in one surmise after another based on the minutes of the commissioners' meetings or the most opaque remarks of the mayor or, best of all, the "courthouse blotter," where all things human from burglary to skunk removal to missing cats could be found on any given day. And with almost fatal gravity I was drawn as I had not been in many years to the classified ads and finally to that grim, black river of type labeled "Employment Opportunities." Here was where I discovered Mr. and Mrs. Haines, who wished to have their house painted but, as I learned, had a limited budget to do so. Here also was where I imagined plunging into my own past, since the future was currently impaired.

As I looked the house over while awaiting an answer to the doorbell, I estimated it had not been painted since it was built, and it was a very old house. Mrs. Haines came to the door, opening it just wide enough to see out, then invited me in upon learning my business. She was a tiny white-haired woman, in her seventies I guessed, and quite excited to have a guest. I soon met her husband, a more phlegmatic type, who sat next to his ashtray in the breakfast nook that looked into the small backyard, which contained several well-tended raised flower beds. The house seemed to have had all the care that money couldn't buy—clean, worn, and orderly—a small sequestered homebody's niche.

Mrs. Haines did all the talking. Mr. Haines occasionally lifted a hand to add something but seemed to forget or change his mind, and the hand dropped to the table. Luckily, neither of the Haineses seemed to know who I was. I summarized what painting experience I could remember from long ago days and applied myself to winning their confidence. Within an hour, I was back with paint chips and insincerely applauded the good taste of the Haineses as they selected Chantilly Pearl with Spicy Chrysanthemum for the trim. I declined a deposit. Mrs. Haines was clear about what they were willing to pay. I accepted immediately because, euphoric about the prospect of scraping and painting their house, I was fretful that something beyond my control, like the weather, would delay me.

About a week later, Jocelyn called and asked if I wanted to see her place. I said that I did. It turned out she was already in town, and so she picked me up in her truck. I'm not sure why she wanted me to see it, although I began to suspect that it was to give her some advice about selling it. More than once she said, "You're from around here." We went through Big Timber, where the wind was blowing hard and the pedestrians were not only holding on to their hats but clutching themselves with a free hand to keep their coats from blowing open. Some students from the university were working in a vacant lot, what had been the Chinatown in the days of building the railroad. "I love this road to Harlowton," Jocelyn said as we headed north. "Everything so open. Once you get used to seeing a long way it's hard to accept anything less." There was little activity on the ranches—wheel line sprinklers idled in cropped meadows, cows alone, bulls sequestered in corrals now that breeding season was over. I knew the calves were in the Midwest bloating on corn and antibiotics, quite offensive to a doctor accustomed to watching the corn lobby's assault on American health.

We turned west up the Musselshell Valley toward Martinsdale and Two Dot. It was more tucked-away country, and Jocelyn drove slowly, seeming to examine every hill, every watercourse. She sighed and looked troubled. She reached over and held my hand. I can hardly say how I felt: I stared straight through the windshield and the empty sagebrush hills and sensed my breath was leaving me. She released my hand and returned hers to the wheel. I asked what she was thinking about and she said, "Riding the school bus."

The road into the ranch left the pavement between two small hills, marked by a rusty mailbox with a cattle brand painted on its side. Once leaving the highway, it descended toward the river bottom, and a sprawl of buildings and worn-out farm machinery was visible around a grove of cottonwoods. An old railroad flatcar served as a bridge across the small river, and beyond was seemingly endless rangeland. She pulled up in front of the house. "I grew up here."

It was a poor excuse for a single-story house, once white and now something else. On its small and uncovered porch sat an old TV with a kicked-in screen. A large farm thermometer with the profile of a cow gave anyone using the front door the bad news. Several sagging wires led to the house from nearby poles.

As soon as we had parked, the door opened and a lanky male in his thirties stepped out next to the TV and proclaimed that there wasn't a damn thing to eat in the house except half a jar of peanut butter and one egg and that he hoped Jocelyn had brought groceries "or either" he'd like the car keys now. He wore Wrangler jeans, scuffed boots, and a black T-shirt, and his straight hair hung down to his collarbone. Despite oddly flat lips, he was a distinctive-looking character with a riveting set of crooked teeth.

Jocelyn said in a low voice, "That'd be your average Womack. If I'd taken better care of Womack, he might not be so whiney, but that's water under the bridge now. And of course he's got a point: you can't do much with peanut butter and an egg." Now Womack was among us.

Womack said to me, not altogether warmly, "You must be the doctor."

"I must be."

He extended a limp but calloused hand and said, "I hadn't had the pleasure."

Jocelyn said, "There's groceries in the back, Crybaby. You want to get them?"

I followed Jocelyn into the house. I believe this was the first house I'd ever seen with standing ashtrays like those of an old-time hotel lobby. On the floor was a large parti-colored hide rug, which Jocelyn explained was Rags, her father's boyhood horse. Newspapers and magazines were stacked nearly to the sill of the window that looked into the yard and through which I could see Womack coming in with the groceries.

Jocelyn bade me follow her into a room whose door was shut. She held it for me and I went into a small space with a pipe-frame bed, walls covered with children's drawings of flowers, horses, deer, dogs, and cats—in a kind of evolution that included posters for Kiss, Guns N' Roses and the big red lips of the Rolling Stones. I said, "This was your room?"

Jocelyn pulled open the closet door, and on its inside was a collection of aircraft pictures. I thought of the picture my father kept of him standing next to a captured ME-109 just inside the Westwall. You could see the Dragon's Teeth of the Siegfried Line in the background. My father often got it out to look at, which caused him to drift off and sort of glaze over. Jocelyn's pictures were all domestic aircraft, including several like the spray plane she had crashed.

Womack was looking me over from the doorway; I never heard him arrive.

From the window of Jocelyn's bedroom, as I learned of other rooms in the house, the view was entirely given to abandoned machinery and deer hides of various vintage. The wind was a continuous background sound, never steady but punctuated by the slap of rope against the iron flagpole in the front yard. I had noticed that nothing was designated as a place to park; rather, you kept driving until you got as close to the front door as possible, maybe in deference to weather, but it was surprising to see the front grille of the truck so close to the glass of the living-room window.

When Jocelyn went into the kitchen to put the groceries away, Womack stayed close to me. With one finger, he moved his hair behind an ear and said, "Where you from?"

I said, "Around here."

"I guess you got room to roam. I could do without the winter myself."

"You get used to it."

"I'll take your word for it."

"How about you, Womack?"

"Hobbs, New Mexico, but south of the border is my main deal. Only place I know where you can do what the hell you want."

"What business are you in exactly?"

"Import export."

Womack's tone was annoying me, and I asked him rather sharply. "Importing and exporting what?"

"Anything needs importing and anything needs exporting."

Jocelyn came back into the room—our conversation was going no-where anyway except to begin to disclose a mutual dislike. She was taking Womack to the airport and would come straight back—which assertion produced a faint smile on Womack's archetypally Anglo-Saxon face, his first expression of the day, at least that I had seen: he could have been grinning like a monkey before I met him. I was calculating the time in my head for the round-trip to the airport, and it looked like I was stuck for a couple of hours. I found myself at the front of the truck shaking Wom-ack's horny hand all over again and reciting formulaic wishes for safe travel. He waited until I'd finished and said, "Pleasure," like a poker player saying "Fold." Jocelyn was already at the wheel, and I walked to her side of the truck in the hapless manner I couldn't seem to shake. She smiled and said, "Womack's going to Denver to get me an airplane. Don't you agree that's thoughtful?" Staring through the windshield, Womack seemed to hear none of this. The several hours that lay before me seemed a very long time. Who were these people? I had the disquieting sense that my being left here was no accident.

I watched them drive off, even giving them an irresolute wave, before turning to my surroundings. I was stuck and forced to make do with mild curiosity about the property and its accumulated detritus. Occu-pancy of the place was long-standing, I concluded, because a horse-drawn harrow was among the discarded machinery and bundles of rusty barbed wire, broken posts, feed sacks, as well as a small brown plastic TV and an early washing machine. I suspected that the wind blowing over this mess probably never stopped, and I thought about the rural people I had seen in my practice who wanted something to help them with the wind of the Great Plains, a superb marketplace for sedatives.

I couldn't fathom being left here. It had happened with such routine that its inconvenience dawned on me only after it was too late to do any-thing about it. I had a house half painted back in town that I wanted to finish. At the moment, I was surprised at how urgently I wanted to paint that house and even paint many more houses. In this isolation, I day-dreamed about all the pleasant colors of the houses I could possibly paint. I had tried to get my father to agree to paint our house, but he didn't think it made any difference whether his house was painted or not. War had greatly reduced the number of things he cared about and home improvement didn't make the cut. I remembered feeling that my wish to paint the house only revealed how trivial were the values of those of us who hadn't been to war. I may have been ashamed of wanting to paint our house. I recalled revisiting the colors it could possibly have been and assigning inappropriate attributes to them: cowardly gray, immoral yellow, and so on. Almost all of my father's stories were war stories, and it wasn't until I emerged into a wider world—later than most—that war occupied a more usual place in the array of human experiences. Nothing absorbed him so much as unrolling the old silk invasion map of Europe and tracing the roads where he and other infantrymen had followed the tanks east. I did notice during the Vietnam days that returning veterans had a separate society, but not quite like my father's because they felt unwelcome. I saw some in my practice who seemed almost unreachably forlorn. My father and I were close, and he told me about his life sort of in secret since my mother was sick of the whole thing and generally focused on her spiritual education, which consisted mostly of fires, floods, perdition, and inestimable glory.

The only room that had a clean bed was Jocelyn's childhood room. The old man's bed was stripped of its clothes and mice had nested right in the middle of it. It appeared that Jocelyn and Womack had stayed in her old room. I thought that after a walk I might nap there and think about that. I wasn't in so deep I couldn't be objective.

I took a walk up the coulee that led south from the ranch and kept me out of the west wind sweeping the prairie and the juniper savannah. At a muddy spring surrounded by willows I surprised a brood of wild turkeys, camouflaged young pullets, which left the spring in no great hurry and even continued feeding as they ascended. A grove of choke-cherries made a nice protected place to rest and so I stretched out and watched the clouds. Today was a day of high-traveling altocumulus: they were crossing the earth, and watching their departure to the east pleased me. I understood that meeting different ground conditions might cause them to halt their travels and simply disappear—they were not like trains leaving the station. My mother believed that heaven was overhead, and imperfectly understood even by the faithful. When I was a child I stared into the blue sky trying to see it, believing—since it provided so many rewards to the saved—that it must have a few nice facilities, but I could never quite see them. My mother hadn't conveyed enough of her cosmology to make me see that the Rapture was a state that didn't require furnishing. At some remote place I was a man of faith. "Creation" was as good a word for what mattered as any other.

I returned to the house and immediately looked for something to eat. The refrigerator contained a discouraging collection of energy drinks and snack foods, none of which appealed to me. This must have been the crap brought in by Womack. Next to a well-worn armchair a stack of magazines rose several feet from the floor, *Drovers' Journal, American Rifleman,* and an ancient copy of the *Playboy* with centerfold of Bettie Page, the pinup girl with the geometric black bangs. The *American Rifleman* profiled one Elmer Keith, a sourpuss in a ten-gallon hat and a meerschaum pipe who tested his guns on horses. I flopped them all back on the pile, went into Jocelyn's room, stretched out, and fell asleep. I didn't mean to fall asleep, but I started replaying some of the better clouds—I realized I was still ranking them—and drifted off. Probably I dreamed. I don't know.

I woke up very briefly disoriented because Jocelyn was sitting on the edge of the bed smiling at me. My first feeling, that this was a bit awkward, left me perplexed, as though sleep had transported me to someplace unfamiliar. I resorted to a banality: "You just get back?"

"Womack's plane was late. I didn't want to leave until I was sure he was on his way. You were in a deep sleep. Have any dreams?"

"One. Painting a house."

"That's not much of a dream."

"No?"

"No. A dream should be about hope."

"Well, I hope to paint this house." I immediately regretted saying this, since I had no interest in explaining why I was painting a house or my enthusiasm for the task, which I inadequately comprehended anyway. In fact, with Jocelyn sitting so close, the idea of spending the day rolling enamel on clapboard had lost much of its romance. "I suppose I ought to get up."

"You in a hurry to get someplace?" I said I was in no hurry to get someplace. "Good, then stay where you are."

I thought it had become obvious what was going to happen. With the slightest tug on the edge of her blouse, I encouraged her to recline next to me. With my face in her hair I found I was not wrong about the smell. Probably it was nothing but shampoo but I was swept away by this cosmetic product. I ruefully considered that I could have gone into a grocery store, opened a bottle of the stuff, and saved myself a lot of trouble. Jocelyn wiggled amiably, sighed, and said this was nice; but before we got off on some sibling nap, I slid my hand over the gentle curve of her belly, then held one of her breasts, firm as a chalice. Jocelyn turned around sharply and stared straight into my eyes.

"What's going on here?"

She didn't say anything. We were very still for a long period of thought, at the end of which she abruptly got up and announced she was taking me home. I sat on the edge of the bed, running both hands through my hair, trying to revive the thrill of house painting. But as we retraced the road back through Harlowton and turned south toward the Absaroka Mountains, she talked about her life growing up, the early departure of her mother, her dislike of her father, and finally of the place itself. I found hope: maybe the house was the problem! But in this too I was mistaken. She dropped me at my door and said, "You've got my number. Put on a clean shirt and take me someplace nice."

I resumed work on the nice old folks' house. I bought a few things—a couple of scrapers in different sizes, some paper dust masks, a pair of coveralls—but everything else, starting with the ladder, I had to rent. I was more than a little aware of the escapism of my house painting endeavor: I didn't need the money, I didn't need the job. But what was wrong with escapism? I was in a situation that made escape in every form entirely attractive.

The ladder, an aluminum extension type, I raised to its full length and rested between the two upper windows on the sunlit clapboard of a cool, sunny morning. Ascending the first two rungs revealed the old couple gazing into my face; I freed one hand and gave them a friendly wave before climbing past their window. With each rung I had a new view of the sun making its way through the lawns and alleys of the town. Higher and higher I climbed, until an intimation of eternity infused my survey of rooftops. The chimneys were wonderfully individualized: some straight and tall, some listing to one side, some brick and wrapped in silvery flashing. A pair of schoolchildren stopped at the base of the ladder and gazed rung by rung until they found me and gave uncertain waves before moving on, occasionally punching each other or trying to grab each other's hat. As the sun rose, I could smell the wood warming before my face, a pleasant smell that intensified as I scraped the curled old paint away until it showered and fluttered to the ground.

By the end of the day I had prepared the front of the house and started on the north side, which was less forgiving: the wood was damp from shade and the paint clung to it, requiring more diligent scraping that sometimes sent the tool astray and gouging into the soft material underneath. When it started to cool and I felt too tired to continue, I descended the ladder and made a neat array of my tools, masks, and gloves, which I covered with a plastic sheet weighted down with rocks.

Then, still in my rumpled white coveralls, I walked to the cemetery, pruning shears in my pocket and wearing a paper hat I had picked up at the paint store from a bin of promotional paper hats. I chose one with a Rottweiler on the front (I liked dogs) without realizing that it advertised a condom popular with the hip-hop culture and urged the viewer, "Don't be slippin' in yo pimpin' " on one side and "Get yo freak on" on the other. In fact, I was oblivious until I noticed the excitement it created among young people along my way to the cemetery. I went on wearing it out of defiance despite the great urge to throw it away. I wished I had picked the "Do yo thang" hat I'd first spotted, but it lacked the dog picture.

The summer annuals at my parents' graves were still managing better than any of the others I saw, and I reflected on the proprietary smugness I had acquired since first looking after this small place. In fact, it had attained something of the quality of home ground through my care, and it was hard to avoid thinking of how it might be improved. I was sure that anyone visiting family burial places looked back on their own lives as set against the time when the now dead were living. Surely that was what such visits did. At the edge of this cemetery was a small stream where I'd once fished, almost militantly, when I was expected to be doing something else.

I'd had an aquarium which I stocked by investing my savings in tropical fish that I carried home from the pet shop in Billings on the Greyhound bus in plastic bags. It was a thrill to hold those bags to the flashing light of the highway and watch the aquatic denizens within, the tetras, guppies, swordtails, gouramis, and the little catfish that was guaranteed to keep the sides of the aquarium clean. Eventually I just wanted to go fishing, to see the native fish of my world, and since this fervor coincided with my rapidly declining interest in religion, my mother concluded that unseen and possibly malign principles were at play. One Sunday as I headed out the door with my fishing rod, she confronted me about going to church. Addressing her in the elevated diction I affected at the time, I said, "An hour with those fanatics would seem like a lifetime." She gazed at me, tears in her eyes and, calling me her angel, asked if I was able to remember that she was one of them. This was the first time that I found you could go fishing while feeling blue. I didn't forgive myself for speaking so to the only mother I would ever have, but in the small zigzag stream that traversed a bird-filled swamp at the edge of town I seemed to dissolve into a larger reality in which acts of meanness could be isolated, examined, then joined to plans for not repeating them. It's possible that my association of church and fishing, though admittedly unoriginal, began there and that on Sundays I still felt upon awakening the need to be fishing. I don't think I ever imagined when crossing the cemetery with my fishing rod that I would one day find my mother and father there.

I walked to my house, discarded my paint clothes and the stupid hat, picked up my rod, and went back to fish that small creek burbling through a woodlot that, entangled in an absentee estate, had for generations avoided being turned into tract houses. It was almost as if I were addressing my late parents: "Look, I'm still doing this." With my rod, a pillbox of flies, and shoes I didn't mind soaking, I loved the deceit of this little waterway, presenting itself along the sidewalk as a trickle, no more than runoff, then expanding to something you could jump across but carrying enough spring water to undercut its own banks. Only a single pool formed, turning slowly in the roots of old spruce trees, before the stream resumed its deception by emerging from the woodlot alongside a grocery store parking lot, on its way out of town.

I backed into the brush beside the pool and pulled line from the reel, holding the small gray fly between thumb and forefinger. I stood motionless as a heron and watched the dark surface of the pool. It moved, quite slowly, as part of the stream. Perhaps it was an hour before the first mayflies popped on the surface and drifted away. There were never many, but in the end a trout appeared to dine, making small drifting rings on the surface—at first opportunistically, then when the flies became more numerous, the fish fed in a regular rhythm. I cast and caught it, and held the beautiful trout with the delight I once felt holding my plastic bag of fish to the lights speeding past the Greyhound. I let it go. Then in sloshing shoes, I headed for my parents' graves but never quite arrived there: a woman was arranging flowers at the graves of Cody and Clarice, and I stopped to watch her.

18

MY MOTHER DID NOT CARE TO HEAR war stories. She thought they were bad luck, and I suppose they were. For all my father had been through, she was really the tougher individual and she had the backing of her Big Ally. She thought that God worked in mysterious ways and if He said the War was Over, the War was Over. She saw impiety in ongoing talk about the War. After she died, my father began to have a few fellow soldiers over for drinks or meals. There was a substantial stream of them through his VFW membership, only recently revived, and as I heard the stories of their experiences and tried to relate them to the humble civilians retailing them, I experienced a profound suspicion of appearances. When mild Johnny Markovitch who worked for the rural electric company described how, when taking prisoners to the rear, an officer's command to "hurry back" meant execute the prisoners, I could never again see Johnny—who had been so kind to me when I was a little boy—in the same way. Albert Cassidy served under Theodore Roosevelt III in North Africa and described him as just a fellow infantryman, dirty, unshaven, and reliable. Out went my views of Hudson River aristocrats. The most peculiar was Arthur Boyle, who had gleefully watched the massacre of Germans at Falaise Gap. He later joined my father's unit at St.-Lô and was with him on a day of deep snow when the first German King Tiger—the dreaded Königstiger—burst from the woodlands. With all the pine trees falling before this monster, Arthur Boyle lost his mind and, again according to my father, never got it back. My father, sharing my genetic predisposition to detachment, had been transfixed until the seventy-ton behemoth wheeled forward under the roar of its gasoline engines, locked down, and began firing the 88. His fascination lasted until long after the war, when he drove to the Patton museum at Fort Knox to view a captured King Tiger on display there, surrounded on a hot day by schoolchildren in short pants. After explaining his past, he was allowed to sit at the controls. He enjoyed telling me it was built by Porsche. Arthur Boyle blew up when my father told him of his adventure with the Königstiger and ruined a nice barbecue. This proved to be the occasion for my mother's outlawing war stories; she had been dragged along on the Fort Knox trip and then had to endure Arthur going nuts in her house on what she described with accusatory inflection as "a perfectly lovely summer day." Fortunately Arthur and Johnny Markovitch had enough interest in sports, especially baseball, to successfully circumvent the war in my mother's presence and continue to visit.

Arthur was the custodian in a grade school in Helena, and he'd had that job since coming home. He had never married and was an anxious person, institutionalized more than once at Warm Springs State Mental Hospital, where he got, in his words, "a much-needed rest." My mother got a few nice rests there too. For my part, listening to too many veterans' stories was liable in peacetime to give a boy the feeling of worthlessness.

We had just had supper in the backyard in the shade of the old burr oak. My father was helping my mother clear the dishes, and that left me alone with Arthur Boyle, who was looking at me fixedly. From household hearsay I knew that "poor Arthur" was crazy, but at this moment he looked as if he had something urgent on his mind. He kept rebuttoning the shiny suit coat that stretched across his narrow chest and sliding his pale plastic eyeglasses back up his nose. His meager hair was combed over a high round dome, and he was nervously vigilant about stragglers. He leaned close to me and said, "Someday you'll see through your father and his happy stories about over there. He was a deserter. Did he ever tell you that?"

From the back door, my father heard him and said, "Not yet, Arthur. I will in time." And helping Arthur to the door with a firm grip on the back of his suit coat, he added, "It's an interesting tale, Arthur. When he's older he'll enjoy it."

After Arthur Boyle was helped into the night, I heard him wail, "But where will I go?"

· · ·

I went to see Niles Throckmorton at his office on Calender Street, right around the corner from the post office. A broad flight of steps led to the porch of what had once been, in the 1920s, a manorial home but which now served as home and office to Niles, the first floor given over to the latter. I had no sooner caught the eye of his receptionist than I heard Niles explode in his office behind her desk. She waved me in with the faintest possible rolling of her eyes before an indifferent return to papers in front of her. Niles was behind his desk, rooting through a cardboard box and throwing handfuls of excelsior onto the floor. "I just don't believe these bastards," he said, addressing the box. "I ordered a wheel of very expensive Canadian cheddar and they forgot to put it in the box. Instead, they send a CD explaining all the things you can do with the cheese. What a country." He held up the CD. "Give this to Maida and have her put it on her computer. Have her tell me if there's anything on it I need to see. And have her get online and track the cheese."

Maida wrapped one hand around her forehead as she received the CD and said, "I heard." I went back to the room.

"Close the door," said Niles, and I did. "You'll be pleased I got you reduced to negligent manslaughter." I started to open my mouth. "Oh, not too interested? No death penalty for manslaughter. Most people in your position would see that as a good thing."

He made up a small plate of cold cuts from the mini-fridge alongside his desk. They were welcome, as I had not had a substantial meal all day. We went through most of it before our discussion even began. Finally, Niles looked squarely at me, holding my gaze for a long moment. I was anxious to know what might come. Slowly and deliberately, his hand drifted my way, stopping over the nearly empty plate between us; his forefinger opened and pointed to a piece of ham rolled around a black olive. He said, "You gonna eat that?" I shook my head. I guess that was it.

Presently he wiped his lips and began: "I don't think these charges are likely to be reduced below where they're at, i.e., negligent manslaughter, and if you abandoned yourself to jubilation over this news I'd be the first to understand." I remained impassive. He stared at me, awaiting an answer. I didn't want to let him down.

"Niles, remember, I'm pleading 'no contest.' "

"I see. Well, in that case you, sir, are an idiot."

"I'm sorry to hear it."

"Some jurors will see that as a guilty plea. In any case, nolo contendere has the same standing as a guilty plea for sentencing purposes."

"But it's not a guilty plea," I said. "The jury will decide if I am guilty."

"The jury will note that you are not putting up a fight."

I said, "This is my fight, Niles."

Throckmorton stood up from his desk, eyes gleaming, and told me he was still famished, adding, "But I won't be able to eat until you're gone."

I was reluctantly fond of Niles and admiring of his intemperate love of life. He ate too much, lived with more than one woman at a time, cynically asserting that one or the other was his housekeeper. At one time, he had smoked a lot of marijuana, and not too covertly, so it was more than local legend that illegal smoke poured almost continuously from his office. He would take on any case at all—murders, divorces, business malfeasance. His best-known case was his pro bono defense of a family of Assiniboine Indians who had lived for more than a century over the last resting place of a dinosaur which a well-funded group of archaeologists wished to excavate. By encouraging the family to hang tough, he was able to milk a wide array of society dinosaur buffs and sufficiently enrich the family that they could depart for Phoenix in their new motorhome. Niles knew the law with rare erudition, and the many judges who despised him knew him to be their unwelcome transportation to appeals court, where they were likely to end up with egg on their faces.

Their faculties notwithstanding, my reasons for pleading no contest were, I knew, well outside his ability to understand them; therefore I spared him the explanations, especially since I was still devising them. With all my regrets, I saw this as an opportunity for equitable review: I would accept the consequences. Niles said that even though I had tied one hand behind his back and we would probably draw a judge who hated him, he would, per usual, fight like a junkyard dog. I said, "Thank you."

When I explained all this to Jocelyn, she said I just didn't want to be a doctor anymore. My mouth fell open. "What do you think I want to be?" I demanded. I had, as requested, put on a clean shirt and taken her someplace nice—to wit, the Grand Hotel in Big Timber, where remarkably good wine and cigars could be had by anyone knowing enough to ask for them.

She said, "A house painter."

"A *house painter*. I needed to find something to do. I'm not going to twiddle my thumbs."

"As you wish."

"So let's just get the waitress over here and order something."

"I'm for that." Jocelyn said, pretending sudden interest in the other diners. I needed to start over.

"I've spoiled things, haven't I?"

Jocelyn smiled and said, "You may have a bit of work to do."

I could see that I was attracting some attention. I caught a few eyes, forcing them to get back to their food. Possibly some jurors there: we'd see. I didn't think they could be disqualified for seeing me eating. It would be otherwise if I brandished a bottle or displayed my privates, but just dining, I didn't think so. And why did I think there would be jurors, anyway?

Whatever problems we might have had were gone by the second bottle of nice red wine, a Medoc I'd never heard of but which the waiter assured me was from the Commune de Pauillac and had appeared in Napoleon's 1855 Classification. Jocelyn wanted to know what that was all about, and I told her in the form of song that I mistakenly thought only she could hear:

> *I got a nickel, you gotta dime,*
> *Let's get together and buy some wine!*
> *Drinkin' wine spodee-odee,*
> *Drinkin' wine.*
> *Drinkin' wine spo-dee-odee*
> *Drinkin' wine!*

She said, "You've had enough. Shall we?" She waved for the bill, which I paid with my head down, and we went out the door into the cold air with a nearly full white moon lighting up the mountains to the north. When we shortcut through the alley to my parked car, Jocelyn detained me, and leaning against the old brick wall of the hotel, we kissed for a long time. I slid my hands down her lower back, feeling the heat from her face against mine. She began panting and said, "Let's go to your house. I want you to see me."

We were hardly through the door before Jocelyn undressed. I

wouldn't say that I was taken aback, but this was no striptease: she just wanted to show me something. She was lean and fit and well made, but it was hardly erotic. She seemed proud of herself in a guileless way. "Where's the bedroom?" she asked. I pointed, without saying anything. "We go there," she said.

Jocelyn's ardor proceeded from one extreme inspiration to another. I couldn't imagine what dark place needed such fulfillment. I was hoping I'd held up my end, but I honestly wasn't sure. When she sat up on the bed, I asked, "Who exactly is Womack?"

Jocelyn arose and dressed. She said, "I thought you knew better than that," and left. I looked at the doorway as though she was still in it.

I slept for a few more hours, got up, ate breakfast, and went to the paint store for rollers. When I got to the Haineses' house, formerly amiable Mrs. Haines was waiting for me. Her husband, agog with worry, watched from behind the screen door.

"You scoundrel," she began. "Are you ever going to finish painting my house? You've been scraping and showing up when you feel like it and leaving the ladder leaning against the front. The neighbors think we can't afford to pay and a half-painted house is going to ruin their property values—" I looked over at the husband, probably for support. "Don't look at him. He can't help you. I'm in charge here!" She gazed at my hat and seemed to be spelling out the words, "Don't be slippin' in yo pimpin'."

So my hope of correcting the poor impression I had left with Jocelyn—and doing it that day—went up in smoke. I slaved away until sundown, when evening shadows crossed the surface upon which I was rolling Chantilly Pearl enamel—never saw either of the Haineses—and headed straight to the pharmacy for aspirin. I could barely move.

I was in something of a bad mood. Bad moods for me usually consisted in being unable to grasp the meaning not of life necessarily—that was hopeless, as witness the thousands of years of philosophical mishmash—but simply of the way people lived. Happily, this terrible impulse only surfaced occasionally. Today, with a bottle of aspirin in hand, I strolled the neighborhoods that usually cheered me, and arrived at the sort of overview I hoped would soon go up in smoke, even as I conceived it.

Staying in one place long enough, you saw the rise and fall of domestic arrangements and the physical appurtenances that accompanied them. At a certain hormonal stage, tempered by moderate practical knowledge, the couples formed and began to construct the cheese ball. The cheese ball consisted of a building known as the home, the transportation equipment, the sustenance gear including heating and cooking facilities, the investments and liquidity that kept the cheese ball from rolling backwards and ruining its owners; then, in most cases, the eventual collapse of the agreement that had generated the cheese ball in the first place and the subsequent deliquescence of the cheese ball itself into its component parts, to be reconstituted in the generation of new cheese balls by less-fortunate couples or, in some cases, the complete vanishing of the cheese ball entirely.

Only at the end of this rumination did I recognize that I myself had no cheese ball and, moreover, that I had always wanted one. Perhaps I was needy. Needy was bad. I knew needy was bad, but I embraced needy. Needy was human. My principle in life so far had been to avoid dying with a grievance on my lips; maybe that was not enough. Maybe I needed to change. I had two more days' work painting the house for that poor old man and his asshole of a wife; after that I was hanging up my roller.

When I first saw the judge, Daniel Bowles Lauderdale, I thought I recognized him, if dimly. For a moment I wondered if he was a relative of some sort, or a friend of my parents. I was able neither to rescue his face from memory nor get it out of my mind. Until I heard his voice: this was the Billings lawyer of my school days who had declined to pay me for painting his cabin in Harlowton! He still had the perm but it had gone gray. I supposed the secretary he'd been squeezing in the cabin had been replaced with a fresher one. I don't think Throckmorton had gauged the potential bellicosity of Judge Lauderdale. When he, Throckmorton, opened up the matter of Tessa's previous brushes with the law, Lauderdale exploded. "That's enough. Have you no sense of decency, sir, at long last? Have you left no sense of decency?" And we went to recess. Throckmorton slumped briefly in his seat and said, "That's the only piece of rhetoric the old turd ever learned. Nevertheless, I think I got us off on the wrong track, which I shall undo: crow is best eaten when it is still warm."

Once we were before Lauderdale again, the judge said to Niles, "Attorney Throckmorton, I too survived law school at Missoula. I too endured life among woebegone professors and hippie degenerates. But that does not make us soul mates."

"Of course, Judge, of course you're right."

"I'm going to wind this up until I can speak to and/or depose some of Dr. Pickett's colleagues. Otherwise, I am obliged to listen to you, Attorney Throckmorton, and you are unreliable."

As we sat in Niles's Audi, ruing the day, his phone rang and he answered it. After he listened for a moment, he told the caller the police were taping the call. Then without further comment, he hung up and said, "Disgruntled husband. Idle threat. Stock item in the trade."

When I was a boy, I made a few trips with my mother to Arkansas. My father stayed behind. Our trips to Arkansas were mostly taken up with Pentecostal doings which included my maternal grandparents and involved the usual strumming, staggering, falling out, and most alarming, "holy laughter." To me, that was Arkansas; imagine my surprise when an Arkansan became president of the United States. A fellow medical student, a reasonable young woman with whom I fornicated purely as a relief from our studies, theorized that my experience in Arkansas surely left me with religious longing, a theory I tested by attending several churches, starting with the Catholic church, which astonished me by its morbidity. When I told the pleasant young priest that I thought I'd try some of the others, he said that I was wasting my time and that those churches were "spin-offs." I tried them anyway and was briefly tempted by an Episcopalian congregation whose pastor was a lesbian in a tuxedo. I thought the discourse was at a higher level, featuring such concepts as "ecumenical" and "ecclesiastical," but in the end it seemed bloodless. It was too bad that I found the Pentecostal church absurd, because that's really where my heart lay. As insincere as my occasional episodes of falling out and jerking on the floor may have been, the approval I got as a child who had been touched by the Holy Ghost was transforming, even if my father, learning of it, called me a bullshit artist.

I remembered a conversation I had with Alan Hirsch about our work. He remarked that there was a fine line between a rut and a groove in a way that suggested we were in a rut, and that professional life necessitated recognizing that you were in a rut; but most pointedly I recalled feeling that this didn't ring a bell at all and that I badly needed to get out of my very satisfying groove and broaden my life with travel, romance, etc., because I liked my work too much. Now that work was somewhat withheld, this was a painful thought.

I wished this recollection had waited, because little old Mrs. Haines was closely supervising my work as I prepared to scrape and mask around the window frames. "I'm just not going to put up with careless work," she said. I hung on the ladder with a gallon can dangling from my other paw trying to find a place for my scraper, my sanding blocks, and my masking tape. I didn't really need the paint yet; it had been a mistake carrying it up here imagining I had a place for it, but I was reluctant to let Mrs. Haines see me reverse course and return to the ground. I should have suffered that loss of face, because in attempting to rest the bucket on the shelf at the top of the ladder, I lost control of it and it fell to the ground, followed by my tools, making a big, terrible splash of Spicy Chrysanthemum exterior paint and setting off the most god-awful caterwauling from Mrs. Haines, as well as the barking of Mr. Haines, who asked, "Do you know what you're doing?" That was the first I'd ever heard from him.

"I'll replace this myself," I cried out to the old bat.

"What about the grass you've killed?" the vicious old whore inquired. I told her that it would recover in no time. "Why did we ever decide to trust you to paint our home?" she wailed.

"Yes, why?" the husband inquired from behind the screen.

"I quit," I said. This brought them to their senses. The hubby emerged.

"But what will we do?" she asked, eyes wide with fear of the current half-finished project. The spineless hubby suggested that we let quieter heads prevail, which brought out the obsequious side of the devious banshee, who allowed she thought I was doing the best I could. I told her she could bet her ass on that one. The old couple tried laughing at my careless vulgarity. I aimed the bristles of the brush, still miraculously in my hand, at the bargain-hunting couple and said that I would proceed to finish the job if I could do so without supervision and that I would do the best job I was capable of in accordance with our original work agreement. "Now let's see a couple of smiles."

What actually happened was that I finished the job in what I thought to be an adequate fashion. I did not stop by for my paycheck or even reimbursement for the paint, on the grounds that these dim bulbs had suffered enough in my pursuit of folly and sublimated frustration. I accepted that my nostalgia for plain folk was challenged by the experience and acknowledged that by any ordinary standards I was flailing—yes, flailing and making a fool of myself.

Because of her faith, my mother faced mortality with something approaching glee. At the end, she had so many things wrong with her that I, her physician, and other doctors ended up lumping them under some lupus-like autoimmune disorder that produced terrific suffering including joint pain and widespread rashes. Then the adult-onset asthma and bacterial infections in her lungs started her down the road to the end. I had called in Blake Cohen, an internist who died several years ago, and Blake did everything in his power to help my mother; he was at her bedside more often than I. My mother accepted her suffering as little more than the clarion call of approaching Rapture. Making the rounds of other sick, even terminal, people, I had to consider the great emotional protection my mother's faith had provided her. In my then scientific turn of mind I wondered whether biology and evolution hadn't produced this endorphin engine. However, I was tempted to exempt my mother from my scientific worldview. In fact, I did exempt her. That is, I concluded that her physical discomfort was cured by death though she died contradictions intact, with her last breath calling solicitous Blake Cohen a kike. I regarded her corpse as a troublesome object she was well rid off. The most important aspects of my mother seemed to have gone on, flitting about with all those waves and signals I held between my hands. Her voice, that semiliterate Arkansas twang, was clear as a bell.

I tried to understand why the fiasco of house painting triggered such a painful state of mind. It felt very much like loneliness, but I didn't think it was, and I was nearly bent over with an aching heart that manifested itself in all sorts of ways, loss of appetite for one and a conversational style that turned casual encounters into occasions for gruesome discomfort and stampedes of fleeing acquaintances. I locked all my doors, drew the shades, selected the room closest to the center of the house, sheltered by the most walls, and abandoned myself to a kind of objectless grief. This proceeded on a futon in a storage room. It was far easier to acquire a futon than to get rid of one, and this one had languished in an unused room for a long time. A leak only recently repaired had soaked it, and the damp seeped into my clothes, discomfort overcoming my grief. This turned out to be an excellent thing, since grieving over apparently nothing was disorienting me and suggested that in terms of my mental health I was a pickle short of a jar and had better get a grip before my large problems became even larger. I did have one commonsense thought, which was that I just wanted to go back to work. I stood on the futon and said "work" out loud, bestriding the waterlogged pad with a defiant air. I was imagining myself useful again.

I actually caught family members of Ernest Leeteg, b. 1928, d. 1989, moving the flowers I had planted at my parents' graves to that of Mr. Leeteg. I made sure they saw me arrive before I went over to stand wordlessly before them, two women old enough to be the sisters of the deceased, rural in appearance and handy with their trowels. One looked ready to argue but the other, sharply elbowing her in the side, directed the restoration of my flowers into the uncovered holes the pair had left behind. I did not say a word.

I was not much for prayer, though as admitted, I did sometimes give it a try, but my reason for regularly visiting the graves of my mother and father was to think about them. I felt that so long as I did this, they continued to exist in some way and of course I still loved them. So many people did likewise that it must have been instinctive. Contrary to appearances or the sort of representation such activity might get in books or movies, we did not stand before the final resting places of our parents eaten up with lugubrious and undifferentiated piety. What we did was try to figure out who they were and what they were doing together. I doubted anyone was deterred by realizing we'd never get to the bottom of it, that their lives and our inquiries would travel on parallel courses until no one remained to pursue the matter. But all this flower tending at the cemetery seemed to help a lot of people with their sadness, as though death was a jeweled bower through which you skipped on your way to glory.

The woman I found at the graves of Cody and Clarice turned out to be Cody's mother. I thought I'd breeze by with a few absorbing glances, wiggling my fishing rod absently, but just as I passed, she said firmly, "Hey." A pair of picnic chairs faced the headstones. "Have a seat." I looked again at the direction in which I had been arbitrarily traveling, as though I had other business than passing this way. But I sat down and learned that the woman, who looked to be about my own age, was named Deanne. She seemed slightly mature for the clever T-shirt she wore: "Make Awkward Sexual Advances, Not War." Or the open-toed shoes and the tiny stone in her nostril.

Staring at the words "Cody" and "Clarice" cut in stone as I sat with Deanne felt like entrapment, not helped by Deanne's saying, "I know you."

"Do you? Maybe you've seen me come to look after my folks' graves."

"I've seen you when you come over here for a look." Deanne was quite tall, as tall as me, and had becoming gray streaks in her thick dark hair. She might have been fifty. She wore some kind of insulated jacket over a black turtleneck shirt and Carhartt work pants with a loop for a hammer above her right thigh. She lit a cigarette and left it hanging from her mouth as she talked. "Naw, there's more to it. You were at Cody's funeral. You're the doctor?"

"I'm afraid so."

"You were there."

"I was."

She took away the cigarette. "I don't want details."

"Of course not."

"My only child. My boy. I don't know what the matter with him was. Do you?"

"I wish I knew." I promised myself to give no hint of what a vicious little bastard Cody was. "There's nothing stranger than our own children."

"Do you have kids?"

"No."

"Then why did you say that?"

"Well, I—"

"That's a doctor's job, isn't it? To have some half-assed comment on every aspect of life."

Since it was she who was suffering, I simply agreed. "That does seem to end up being part of our job. I'm not surprised you've seen right through it."

"I wish I hadn't. I wouldn't mind being comforted. Even if it's phony. I've got a great big hole right in the middle of me. Smoke?"

"No. Thanks."

"I didn't mean to show bad manners." She gestured weakly toward her son's headstone with the cigarette. "Deal like this doesn't help your manners. To have good manners, you have to give a shit, right?"

"Right."

"Well, sometimes I do. Depends. Obviously I didn't do the greatest job in the world with Cody, but I didn't mean for it to be like that. I loved him with all my heart. He didn't know who his dad was, that didn't help. I wasn't a whore, I was single. It's not the same thing. But them other kids, their moms, it might have been they was jealous." She ground the cigarette out in the dirt and ran her finger around the inside of the turtleneck.

"Crazy."

"I mean, I know who was starting it. I went to PTA and read their attitudes. Once I figured it out, I went after the husbands, and believe me they was ready. I only did it for the boy. I was on a mission. Those moms, they brought it on themselves. Which I should of never did. Everything got worse for Cody. I guess the facts show he had it in for women. Wise commentary, please."

"I think you've already said it."

"I ain't said shit. Why don't you fill in the blanks? You're the doctor. Where's the bullshit when you need it?"

I could have skipped the bullshit, also known as wise counsel, and told her how I urged her son on. I could have said, "Good riddance," but I didn't have the guts. Furthermore, this conversation had acquired a squeamish intimacy. But I was at the scene, and she knew that: couldn't change it. I did try asking her where she worked. She said, "I don't."

"Oh."

"I'm a homemaker." With this, she began to laugh, loudly and at length. "I married one of the husbands. The ex lives alone. My husband thinks it's a good deal. He writes 'thank you' on every alimony check."

It began to dawn on me that it was possible Deanne could handle the truth. If I told her the truth, maybe I could change my plea to not guilty, yet I was unsure that I could do it. When she found out my part in her son's death, I would face her at last: I would be shriven. I would begin to pay for my sins.

I tried the idea four days later. I had a meeting with Throckmorton scheduled for late afternoon, and I was milling around doing errands, paying bills, walking to the post office. I spent an hour reading magazines while a chip was removed from the windshield of my increasingly unreliable Oldsmobile 88. Jays and pigeons were getting all the bird food I put out, so I bought a special feeder for thistle seed that would serve the smaller birds, the finches, titmice, white- and rufous-crowned sparrows, wrens, and nuthatches that had been run off by the bruisers who sprayed sunflower shells around my lawn. I installed a bracket intended for hanging plants above deer level but in sight of my bedroom, hung the feeder, went over to Boyer Street and knocked on Deanne's door. Her husband answered, and I was surprised to see that it was the owner of the grain elevator, Jerry Perkins, who I knew slightly but cordially. "Jerry," I said, making no secret of my surprise. He smiled and drew the door back invitingly.

"Come in, come in," he said. "Deanne said she'd seen you."

I was in the hallway, the door closed behind me, before I learned Deanne was out. Jerry was a warm and forceful guy and before I could arrange to come back, he had me out on his enclosed back porch drinking coffee and admiring his own arrangements for feeding birds and his heated birdbath for winter. "That sucks them in more than the feed 'long about January." Jerry was such a big, powerful brute, bulging in his blue dashboard overalls, that his enthusiasm for birds seemed remarkable. His widow's peak of close-cropped red hair and his big hands made everything he said emphatic.

"What a coincidence," I said. "I've just bought a hundred pounds of Nijer seed. It's in the backseat of my car."

"They'll go right through it. That's about all the company you have, isn't it?"

"Pretty quiet."

"Think you'll get off?"

"I don't know."

"I assume you're innocent."

I laughed mirthlessly. "I'm waiting to find out."

"You're waiting to find out?"

"I mean, they'll let me know, I guess."

"I'm not sure I'm following this," said Jerry.

"I mean it's anybody's guess how these things turn out."

"What I'm trying to say," said Jerry, "is I hope you know the facts here, because they're going to bang you around in court and you need to be ready." I had the sense Jerry was lecturing me.

"I'm ready."

"Well, good." He got up and opened the glass louvers to let more air in. "Just be careful. There's always bad shit waiting to get a guy. Deanne said she seen you," he said again. I wondered if he meant to emphasize it particularly.

"That's right, I—"

"I don't suppose she'll ever get over that punk."

I thought for a minute, then said, "It's tough."

"He wasn't but eight or nine when me and Deanne got together. He was a mean little punk then. I swear before God I did my best to knock it out of him."

I was stumped but struggled to reply. "Not much luck?"

"I made him work at the elevator when he wasn't at school. Had him load grain, cake, salt, whatever, in trucks. He could work like two men, I'll give him that. He was just a little kid, but he worked like a Georgia mule. I don't know what he wanted. I couldn't stand the sight of him. Had to go. Can I get you something?"

"I'm fine, thanks. What do you mean he had to go? I thought he was a hard worker."

"I told you: I couldn't stand the sight of him. How did we get on this?"

"I'm not sure."

"You seen Deanne at the boneyard. That was it. I knew you discovered the situation there with Clarice. What a mess. And she was a good kid. One of them kids gets beat up by every man she meets. You could just feel it around her. Spend an hour with Clarice and you'd want to boot her in the ass and never know why. It was something about her."

I saw Clarice a lot and never felt any such thing, but I thought not to mention it. It was clear by now that my connection to the deaths was provoking Jerry to fill me in on the background, though I was growing less inclined to hear it, something he didn't notice.

"What about a beer?"

"No."

"Suit yourself. The deal is, I give up a lot for Deanne. I was married to a Callagy from up the Shields. They had ten sections of grass and a thousand acres under sprinklers. It was a money deal and I walked away from it because Deanne was good-looking and a ton of fun, but Cody come with the package. My ex had a good income at the courthouse and even though she weighed over two hundred she carried it well. Carried that suet like a champ. Everyone agreed she carried it well. Since Deanne married me she hadn't done shit-all, but she's exciting and keeps a great house and, hey, I love her to death, but the Cody years was an inch short of a deal breaker. I'd be lying if I told you I was sorry he's gone. It's too damn bad he took Clarice with him, but if it hadn't been him it would've been someone else. She was that kind."

This was making me sick. I was able to suppress an outburst because I knew I had business with Deanne. What business was that? I only knew it was connected to my own survival.

"I don't want you to think I have any regrets about the ex, whatever that Callagy deal is. She was too serious. She was serious as lip cancer. A guy needs to have some fun every now and then. Which leads him to whatever bar where all the man-eaters live. And believe you me, I'm not bitter. I just wish Deanne would quit smoking and writing 'thank you' on my alimony checks. No need to be rubbing it in."

19

WE YOUNGER DOCTORS had been substantially democratized by comparison with our older colleagues. The senior doctors seemed to bask in their original status as small-town aristocrats, content in their golf, cocktails, and domestic architecture, their thin but emblematic connoisseurship, and their eccentricities. Dr. Gallagher—now gone—wore his kilt to dinner parties, GP Boland Mercer exercised his wolfhound by tying bacon to the end of its tail, and dermatologist Joe Mariani tried year after year to interest the town in building a bocce court. When I first arrived, nearly all of them were former smokers who had greeted the surgeon general's warning about tobacco use with unified astonishment.

We of the next generation have been all over the map and at one point indistinguishable from the rising tide of hippies. We prided ourselves on unexpected remarks and enthusiasms. At the first dinner party including most of us, I especially recall Jinx holding up an empty highball glass and declaring, "One more of these and somebody's going to put out." We occasionally partook of controlled medications by way of inducing artificial elation and when work prevented sleep, we might well have turned to pills for stimulation too. Generally, this was dispensed on an as-needed basis, but before Alan Hirsch took up cycling with such passion the pharmaceuticals rather got away from him and soon he had a child in Miles City. This produced if not pain for Alan, at best inconvenience, but he met his obligations and when the child grew up and led Miles City to the Class A football play-offs, Alan made no secret of being the father. He even showed some conviction about his own work by expressing his wish that Jared ("I didn't name him, for Christ's sakes") go to medical school, while Jared taught his father how to ride a horse.

Our lessons in the ways in which one generation succeedeth another were exceptionally diagrammatic.

I wasn't sure what I had done to annoy Jocelyn, but whatever it was she seemed to have forgotten it. She was preoccupied with selling her father's ranch. I took her around to the Realtors' offices trying to get a sense of its value. It was too small to provide a living for a family and it had no recreational potential short of stargazing such as might have made it a vacation property. The land booms of the Rockies were in a down cycle; it was too far from the airport; the house was in disrepair. In the general national gloom, fewer people were investing in faraway follies in the West; it was enough to keep the roof on back in Westchester. When the last Realtor that Jocelyn approached suggested a test drill for coal bed methane, she decided to lease the grazing to a neighbor. We talked about bulldozing a landing strip for her airplane but decided against keeping fuel or building a small hangar. Facilities at White Sulphur and Harlowton were adequate. As it turned out, Womack was not a boyfriend, or no longer one, but an airplane mechanic. Hence his annoyance. I still didn't understand why she needed her own mechanic, unless it was one per airplane. But then, I didn't understand airplanes and flying. I didn't even like going up a ladder to paint. Womack got a room in Martinsdale over a retired schoolteacher's house, and we rarely saw him. I don't know whether they were just talking about the flying facilities elsewhere for my benefit, at any rate Womack soon rented some equipment and bulldozed an airfield a quarter mile west of the old homestead.

Jocelyn said that since the place was going to be uninhabited and she didn't want the expense of insurance, she thought she ought to get rid of the house. I suggested she insure it for a year to be certain, since this was where she had grown up, after all, the scene of her childhood. Maybe that was the point. On her instructions, Womack burned it to the ground, dug a hole with a backhoe, pushed all the wire, pipe, and ashes into it, and covered it up. I expected something valedictory from Jocelyn, but all she offered was "Womack can do anything he sets his mind to." Pictures of the blaze made the paper with commentary about the loss of pioneer structures including a cavalry bunkhouse from the days of the Indian Wars. "Another reason not to join the cavalry," said Jocelyn. It was a real inferno and left a very strong impression on people. I heard from Throckmorton, the all-knowing, that the Meagher County sheriff was so offended he tried to make an issue of it but Womack's permits were entirely in order and none of the accelerants were illegal. Word had it, however, that the encounter left a bit of bad blood between the two.

"How do you know these people?" Throckmorton asked me. I was in his office for a much-avoided consultation. I told him it was a long story. I didn't have the will to describe the plane crash, and I particularly didn't want Throckmorton's opinion on these matters. Throckmorton was in one of his comedic moods, despite the fact that my future hung in the balance, the present reason for my being there. "I'm giving up the law," he said, "to become a forensic barber. 'What your 'do says about you.' Forget DNA, dental records. Look at the coif. You'll know." His secretary rang into his office, and Throckmorton said there was water on the receiver. "Are you pissing in the other end?" Then after a long silence, "Stop blubbering!" He put the phone down. "Jesus H. Christ. Has no one a sense of humor anymore? I'll be right back." He went out to comfort his secretary. When he returned, he said, "She's in love with me. She says I have no respect. There's no object. What ever happened to grammar? I have no respect? For what? She didn't say. Perhaps it's for the best. I have no respect for her, something she has yet to learn. An excellent secretary, lucky to have her. I just wish she had a little respect for me."

I had known Throckmorton for a long time, since the seventh grade, when he was often in trouble and I was ever on the margins because we had moved quite often; my parents had so little standing in town that the children were only too happy to reproduce these dismal social patterns from kindergarten on. My mother wanted to teach me at home, using the Bible, but my father, strengthened by new friendships at the VFW, put his foot down. I saw now that it was the beginning of our joining a community, and gratitude to the VFW aroused my fascination with my father's service in WWII. I badly wanted to belong to something, and my father may have felt the same way: as I have so often said, our house was full of old soldiers. On the other hand, my mother's passions produced little or no society for us. Those zealots were too focused on their journey for the sort of convivial pleasures enjoyed by my father's friends and their wives. While my mother complained about the bad language of the former or the recklessness of their wives, she had a surprising capacity for fun, especially if it involved music and dancing. She could dance all night long. I remembered the strange feeling I got when I noticed the electricity she generated at some of our backyard parties, despite—or because of—her fixation on God. I remembered my father's assertive forefinger in the chest of one of his contemporaries who had let my mother's allure embolden him in the form of an impulsive kiss.

I was rescued from my life on the margins not just by our burgeoning VFW social normalcy but by the friendship of Throckmorton, the only boy in our class who, though popular, seemed sufficiently immune to peer pressure to anoint me a friend. He was a striking olive-skinned, round-faced boy with a jet-black Mohawk who loved the outdoors and feeling up girls, a pastime I learned from him once I'd achieved a minimal social aptitude. It still surprised me that the girls' permission to feel them up so readily represented the general opinion of the whole class. Throckmorton and I were entirely focused on breasts, of which we were connoisseurs, commenting on their apparently limitless attributes. This was my first real vocabulary challenge.

Throckmorton and I spent our free time out of doors, in the sagebrush hills north of town with our small falcon, Speed—a kestrel we had taken from its nest, raised, and taught to hunt grasshoppers and mice. Speed rode the handlebars. We fished in the small snowmelt streams we could reach by bicycle. At a cabin far from town, we often observed a border collie on a chain, unsheltered in all weathers. We stole this dog too and named him Pal, lied to our parents about where we found him. Pal lived out his life, alternating between our houses. Throckmorton's parents said my parents overfed Pal, and my parents said that Throckmorton's parents spoiled Pal by never asking him to do anything. Pal's training consisted of "sit" and "shake."

Throckmorton played football. He was a gritty defensive lineman, the position most suitable for his thick frame, and always had a bloody nose or mouth, which he held aloft as he jogged to the sidelines for treatment. Throckmorton claimed that football enabled one to see more breasts than any other sport. That seemed to be the case, though I counted on baseball's superior elegance to serve this end in the long run. Throckmorton thought this was a trifling idea and asserted that women were drawn to violence.

One day when we were hunting grasshoppers in a big alfalfa field, Speed flew away for good. "Ungrateful bird," said Throckmorton, but his eyes were filled with tears. Mine too. We were about to start high school. Afterwards, Throckmorton and I saw less of each other, though we were still good friends. He dated one cheerleader after another; and as he was now a big aggressive brute and I knew his vividly carnal imagination, I rather felt sorry for these girls he described as "squealing like pigs."

"Jury selection will be a breeze. I've been down the list, bunch of good folk from the tax rolls. I'll let Numb Nuts fuck around with the jury pool, toss in a few peremptory challenges to make it look like he's in charge, and then I'll nip in and winnow those who've got it in for doctors. You're well liked. An admired practitioner. Eccentricities forgiven. Giving freaks a pass is the oldest tradition in Montana. And you, my friend, are a blue-ribbon, bull-goose freak."

"Don't get complacent, pardner, I'd like to go back to work." I wish he hadn't brought up my trade. I missed it tremendously. Numerous fresh faces walking into my office with their problems, too beautiful, too stirring for words. My mother's rearing suddenly surfaced as I asked God to let me work.

"I'll go through them very carefully. The judge has already indicated that the jurors need not be death-qualified. So there's little for you to sweat beyond the Big House."

I didn't like this, joke or not. I feared confinement more than mortality. It was curious that I didn't seem to fear it more than indelible guiltiness, which felt more like a recurrent cancer in remission. But I could be guilty and still work, whereas I couldn't work in the Big House.

"Why in God's name don't you smoke cigars?" He held up a handful. "Mexican maduro number 3 ring. So darn good."

"I've tried them."

"You haven't tried them enough. I wish you'd get off this austerity stuff. You're missing out altogether unless you're angling for canonization. You're not taking your own pills, are you?"

"Don't be silly."

"I need something to sleep."

"We'll talk about it."

"It's got to knock me on my ass. No pussyfooting around. Brandy and cigars before bedtime, it takes a Class Three narcotic or you're counting sheep. Plus, I have worries. I'm not austere. I spend money, I travel, I have a mistress."

"What say you hold off on the foreseeable heart attack until my trial is over?"

"Plus, something to perk up the love machine?"

"Tons of stuff out there. It all works so long as you feel pretty with a beet-red face."

"Would you mind if we got off this for a moment and focused on your trial?"

This was classic Throckmorton, one of the most doubt-free people I had ever known. I wished it had rubbed off on me.

The Stands family moved to town my sophomore year when Mr. Stands was transferred by the railroad from Forsyth. They were Crow, real name Stands Ahead, and their daughter, their only child, Debbie, my girlfriend all through high school, raised my prestige—though not with everybody, as there was a residue of prejudice toward Indians and a few thugs began calling me "Chief"—since Debbie was the best-looking girl in school. The family was probably what inclined me to intern at the Indian Health Service, but more important, Debbie taught me how to study. I spent three years believing that our destinies would forever be intertwined; the very chastity of our relationship, excepting only limited familiarity with her breasts, seemed to elevate our love to a mythic plane. Then I went to college in the Midwest, where my gruesome immaturity returned like a virus dormant in my spine, and Debbie married a class-mate at Missoula. I still heard from her at Christmas. The family picture on her card, husband and two children, gave me a pang. Her father, Austin Stands Ahead as he latterly styled himself, was my patient until dying of congestive heart failure. He kept me up on Debbie, and I con-cealed my pain with a congratulatory smile as he detailed her accom-plishments: she was a state legislator. I met Debbie once at a high school reunion and with a trembling face. Thereafter, I avoided such things.

Years later, I thought to relent, but even if Debbie had grown big, fat, and old I was afraid it wouldn't matter.

I seemed to be a bachelor. For years I wondered whenever the phone rang late at night if it might be Debbie. It never was. I realized now that it never would be. There were quite a few things like that.

"Did that fellow ever bring you an airplane?"

"Womack. Yes, a while back actually."

"To start crop dusting again?"

"This is a different kind of plane. Takes off and lands on small runways. And it can carry quite a load."

"To do what?"

"Oh, there's always a call for a plane like that."

"Mining equipment, I suppose."

"Sure."

"So, where is Womack now?"

"He got a room."

"Where did he get a room?"

"One of those little towns. Over near Rapelje, I think, somewhere in the Golden Triangle."

"And he looks after the plane?"

"What is this, Twenty Questions?"

So, later, Jinx came over, after doing her grocery shopping, and brought me a few treats, including a pint of Cherry Garcia, a little wedge of artisanal cheddar, and a bottle of Pouilly-Fumé, which I offered to drink with her, but she wouldn't consider it as she meant to spend her evening reviewing cases. But we did have a cocktail, despite my being briefly low-spirited and envious that she would be working. I hadn't had a drink in a week, and just one was enough to produce a wave of warmth generally, but especially toward my friend Jinx. Therefore I regaled her with an overly detailed account of my infatuation with Jocelyn, including hints of its erotic aura. It was a masterpiece of thoughtlessness, but Jinx bore it with her usual grace and composure, questioning me attentively about something I cared about, and only because I cared about it. I glimpsed that people at work, like Jinx, must look across a great divide at people like me, atwitter over their love lives, or even people like Jocelyn, trying to think what their airplane is good for. That was hardly an account of the facts, but Jinx's world could not be called dull just for its steadiness. Adding to the picture, I years ago met Jinx's parents: what a surprise, a retired car salesman with a highly visible gold tooth married to an aging but still painted party girl. Though it took thirty years, they finally drank themselves to death in the St. Louis apartment building where Jinx had grown up and launched herself into a real life of real work. I specifically recall the days she took off from the clinic, one year apart, to bury her mother and father and how downcast she was to lose two people who seemed spectacularly negligible to anyone who had ever met them. They had named her after Jinx Falkenburg, whom I could not recall. Jinx remarked ruefully that she was a "sweater girl."

Ever since Throckmorton and I had our little kestrel, Speed, I've been interested in birds. Every bird I learned, if it was a migratory bird, I soon forgot. Didn't we meet last year? I kept a life list, but its utility as a mnemonic device was quite limited. The spring warblers moved faster than my ability to memorize them, and frankly the sparrows were a nightmare. Anyone interested in birds and living near the Great Plains had to face the sparrow problem, which was that they all looked very similar: rufous, white-crowned, Baird's, Henslow's, house sparrows, grasshopper sparrows—all a blur, the bastards. So I switched to raptors, a bit of a copout, as they were more easily differentiated. Priapic male birders all liked raptors because they seemed flatteringly emblematic. Many of the hawk lovers I knew were big-bellied fellows with facial hair and a passion for cocktails. As yet, I didn't fit this profile. My father, who never claimed bird expertise, remembered every bird he ever saw, even when he was overseas. He liked talking about them, too, but my mother would cut him off with, "Seen one, you've seen them all." He assumed a conspiratorial air when he pointed into the willows and said, "Carolina warbler." When he rode a tank into Germany, the storks on roofs were the thing that struck him most. He thought that a stork sitting on its eggs and watching an army roll by showed what nature thought about mankind.

With my new leisure following upon my indictment and my failure as a house painter, I had time to walk the woody creek bottoms where I observed the short-winged woodland hawks, Cooper's and sharp-shinned, speeding through the trees with uncanny nimbleness. I had several times watched prairie falcons diving into blackbirds when I walked around the uplands, and the chaos they made seemed to briefly fill the sky. These jaunts were hardly adventurous, as I never went more than a few minutes from town, but it was greatly reassuring to find wildlife so close to humanity. In fact, I could still make out the old water tower through the trees where I first came upon the goshawk, a northern goshawk, to be precise. Since I came upon her unawares and she was going about her goshawk business under my eye, it made a tremendous impression on me: almost blue-black on her back with a creamy and precisely barred breast. She was swiveling her head from side to side, broadcasting her oddly relentless screams. Over time, I would see her often, hunting, soaring, sleeping. And she saw me often enough that she no longer fled at my sight, moving me by her acceptance.

I also went birding with Jinx, a genuine expert. She had a beautiful pair of Leitz binoculars whose protective covering she had nearly worn away. My optics were el cheapos from Wal-Mart but good enough for my skill level. I was hardly able to keep up with Jinx, whose bird cognition was Olympian and betrayed my slow-witted tagalong efforts to identify those blurry sparrows which she saw as separate races with little in common beyond their genus. I accepted my inferior status as a birder just to be with her.

However, I knew a lot about my goshawk, had watched her fly, run down songbirds, pluck voles, and dine. I had narrowed the field of vision to the point at which I actually knew what I was talking about. So I invited Jinx to join me, knowing she would have to rise above my recent pariah status to accept. Frankly, she was a bit wary on the phone, but the bird interested her and we made a first-light foray into the creek bottom east of town.

I couldn't find my goshawk.

"Where's the bird?" Jinx demanded after we had wallowed along the low-water perimeter of the stream, scanning the treetops.

"She's always here in the morning."

"Are you sure about this?"

"That she's always here?"

"No, that there's actually a bird."

"Why would there be no bird?"

"I thought you might want to talk privately."

"Oh, no, no, no. There's a bird. I've watched her every day. Very beautiful. Very queenly. I thought she was the bird for you."

We fanned out and moved as quietly as we could in the brush. Bohemian waxwings had gathered in a wild crabapple tree, and some jacksnipe probed around the muddy creek. I was pleased to hear the sounds of children at the grade school a short distance away.

"Come here," called Jinx. I had to look carefully to see her about twenty yards away in her nearly camouflaged clothes. I started that way. "I've got her." When I reached Jinx, she was holding the goshawk by the corners of her wings. She had been shot.

Jinx said, "You're just bad luck." I felt, and must have looked, quite crestfallen because she put her arm around my waist and said she was sorry about my hawk.

We went to breakfast at a café by the switching yard, thinking we'd beat the morning crowd, but we didn't and had to wait for a table. The ambient noise, a miasma of voices and silverware, was substantial. Desperate-looking waitresses navigated the crowd with plates aloft. I got a few stares but had been getting used to that. Quite soon, four ranchers rose and walked past us to the cash register picking their teeth, and we took their table. They wore the big Stetsons they would replace with billed caps as soon as they got home. Three of the ranchers faced the cashier, but one had turned to look at me. "A splendid bird like that," said Jinx. "Someone just couldn't stand the pressure. I'm glad I don't know who it was. It might be someone I delivered and I'd just hate myself for missing my chance." I compulsively did the math: Jinx was a bit over forty, with enough years of practice in the community to have delivered someone now armed.

When she was indignant, her eyes flashed; she had beautiful eyes. Even when we had both grown old I was fascinated by them. She once said, "My eyes and my ass are my long suits. I'm no sweater girl and without emphatic breasts life in the U.S. can seem quite proscribed." That had been at one of our wine-soaked dinners at my house at which I grew so alarmed at Jinx's intimations and proximity. I'm not sure why.

She might have been too smart for me at that stage of my life. Now that I was somewhat shriven by circumstances and Jinx had begun to accept me as an unadulterated friend—someone to go birding with or share a ride to racquetball—I saw more in her. My mistakes seemed to accumulate like channel markers behind a boat. But at least I had a friend; I was sure of that.

Jocelyn came into town a couple of times a week, and we usually slept together after I'd taken her to dinner or helped her stock an odd array of supplies: hose clamps, fuel bladder, energy bars, distilled water, anti-icing spray, electrician's tape, multipurpose tools. I wasn't much interested in what these things were for, and my casual inquiries were waved away wearily. I had always been wary of sex as something which imposed a not always welcome bonding; it reminded me of those old movies in which a storm strands a group in a bus station or some likewise unpleasant place and they all slip through layers of unearned intimacy, like it or not. I actually fell in love with my aunt, who shooed me away after getting what she wanted. But this was different. I had not bonded with Jocelyn. I was not at all sure I liked her. And while I realized it was irrational to make the connection, the more I saw Jocelyn, the more trouble I had with the 88. At first it wouldn't start, because power was only intermittently getting from the ignition to the solenoid. I had to change a headlight, which was unreasonably difficult as there was no room to get a hand or tools in there. Once I had it running, it smoked too much and I drove through town followed by a white cloud. Otherwise, it went along okay until the following Saturday, when having made love to Jocelyn again, I began getting alarming noises from the water pump and idler pulley, which, combined with the smoking exhaust and unreliable starting, made me think my car was about three fucks from the wrecking yard. I didn't actually believe this; it was just a feeling, an association. If we could have made love just once without my car going haywire I believe that feeling would have gone away. It was disquieting. I had gotten used to the non-working dome light, the malfunctioning passenger-side window, and the water trapped in the trunk lid, but the correlation of these new failures to my sex life was unusually troubling. My car had run beautifully for five days when I ran into Jocelyn behind the IGA store and we had a bit of a grope. Jocelyn went on her way and I went on mine, but for the first time in over a hundred thousand miles there was a screeching knock in the steering column which was never resolved, while the heater blew only cold air. I realize that this was some sort of automotive route to erectile dysfunction, and I enjoyed all the attendant irony, but what else was I to conclude?

At some point I said to the old man, "Tell me, Pop, what made you desert?" We had just brought a load of well-weathered cow manure from Gladys's ranch for him to spread around the raised beds of his cherished vegetable garden. I couldn't have gotten a bigger rise if I had shot a big-game arrow through his thorax. He stiffened, lowered the handles of the wheelbarrow, and turned to me very slowly.

Everyone must look back over their lives and consider what the big mistakes were. This surely was one of mine. If this spell of forced leisure had a mission, it seemed to be this review as to how I got to this place. It was dawning on me that only while working did I focus on what was under my nose.

My father made me see how demoralizing hedge warfare was, a lethal enterprise on a sort of chessboard, where the terrifying art of ambush became a cerebral exercise. My father's longing for his native plains became more emphatic as woodlands became death traps. Months of digging in had given him a fear of daylight and transformed him into something of a homebody once he had a choice. Night had been a friend, and the terror of German flares had altered his diurnal habits stateside; my mother told me it was a long time before walking around in broad daylight gave him much pleasure. He had befriended a Mormon officer from Idaho early on and stood near him on a sunny afternoon when the officer's map board flashing in the sun gave him away to a German sniper; a distant crack and his new friend fell at his feet. A bout with scabies had made him, once home, a fervent bather: even when we were on the road cleaning rugs, wherever we stopped he sought out the water source, the tubs and showers. My father was not a particularly reflective man, but watching prisoners transported to the rear perplexed him; late in the war young Wehrmacht grenadiers were packed in trucks like the ones used to haul cattle, though in this case far more crowded than would be considered acceptable for livestock. The only signs of the penned humanity were the streams of urine and vomit seeping from between the planks on the sides of the lorries. In circumstances where he had been advised to "eat every chance you get and piss every chance you get" this dismal image never left him. The ethnicity of the truck's contents faded in the mind of a man who had once thought of killing the enemy as life's greatest pleasure. A word or two from comrades might have had a similar effect, for in every unit there were thoughtful individuals who doubted that war made any sense in the first place. He was given profound pause as he watched a captured German medical team ordered to treat Allied wounded: his description of their care and efficiency might have had something to do with my early enthusiasm for medicine, as it was the first war story I ever heard from him but it was about making people well.

He disclosed a substantial litany of experiences that inclined toward dismantling a human mind: the silence of incoming mortars, the endless hover of flares, the scream of rockets, the otherworldly burp of the Schmeisser machine pistols. And of course, the 88s. Because of my impertinent question, I heard this, if not for the first time, in greater detail than ever before. My father's gaze remained level, his eyes fixed on mine as he answered my question.

My father loved horses all his life, and toward the end of the war, when the enemy could be located by the sound of their horses, he realized the end was in sight. The Germans were running out of everything, including fuel and transportation machinery, so farm horses were being commandeered to move their guns. The Allies were pouring a firestorm upon them, and increasingly the POWs were walleyed lunatics indifferent to what their captors had in mind for them.

As they approached Aachen and Germany itself, my father's unit captured a group of German soldiers: frightened children in rags. Taken to the rear, one of the boys pulled out an antiquated pistol and shot the sergeant. The escort threw the boy up onto a roll of barbed wire and machine-gunned him. That night my father deserted. The Luger he carried to Paris he had found on a fully dressed skeleton under a tree in the Hürtgen Forest.

"Had enough?" he asked me. I said that I had.

. . .

I rarely heard about the war after that, until right at the end of my father's life. I remember visiting him after my mother had died and I was his sole medical care, though he needed little assistance and was remarkably independent. VFW friends of his vintage were starting to fade away, mostly grateful for having lived so long. But when I visited him that day he was agitated. Radio personality Rush Limbaugh was being interviewed on television and my father was certain that it was Hermann Göring. "I thought he committed suicide at Nuremberg!" he cried. After this, my poor father began to assume he had been lied to about nearly all other things and that he could never be sure which ones they were. I can't say his last days were good ones, for he increasingly suffered from an abstract sense of betrayal until the day that he greeted my arrival with a wry look of miserable resignation: he had begun to suspect me as well. But even as dementia swept over him, he was able to putter around in his garden and refill the hummingbird feeder. Here, shovel in hand, seated on the railroad ties that supported the earthen beds, he died. I buried him beside my mother on a beautiful June day, cottonwood seeds filling the air and new perennials popping up from some of the earliest graves. Several old soldiers attended and a veteran of the Iraq War played taps on the bugle. Seeing the headstones paired at last, I was unable to conclude that I knew these two people very well, or understood them. I would quite painfully miss them, but only as people I once knew. Religion had surrounded my mother with an impenetrable reality, and war had done something quite similar to my father. I had the sense that I had been alone since birth.

20

I WAS DRIVING EAST on the interstate in my cherished 88, skating over black ice at about seventy miles an hour. The days were getting short and I was headed to Big Timber, another dinner with Jocelyn at the Grand Hotel. I didn't want to go that fast, but if you went slower, the big trucks would nearly mow you down and suspend you blind in a cloud of snow, ice chips, and diesel fumes. Radio reception was shitty to say the least, or else supplied fascist newscasts from the Nashville stations broadcasting overproduced studio music for brain-dead hillbillies. Looking down the unequal beams of my headlights, I saw that the windshield wipers wiped only in selected places, requiring me to raise and lower my head to find a clear view. Wildlife T-boned by unyielding traffic was pitched up on the roadside with twisted heads and limbs, strewn intestines. That we accepted gut piles along the motorway as a gift of the automobile struck me then as a grisly novelty. In other words, I hated the highway. I must have been in a dissociative state because even the word "automobile" seemed strange. I said it aloud. "Automobile, automobile, automobile!" It didn't help. I had the feeling I wasn't entirely sure what an automobile was.

The 88 was ruby red and the interior a red Naugahyde with white piping. The upholstery held the cold of night well into the day, even while the heater irradiated my shins. Still, I trusted it; and that is why, just past the Mission Creek exit, I was slow to respond when the driveshaft just fell out of it and the universal joint tried to beat through the floor under my feet. I thought the 88 could keep going. It could not.

I had no way to notify Jocelyn, or to call a wrecker. It was too cold to walk and the nearest sign of life, a minuscule light suspended in remote

darkness, was too far. I had no choice but to wait for a highway patrol-
man to stumble onto me, which happened in about an hour. The patrol-
man called for assistance and a wrecker arrived an hour and a half after
that. Wild lights of vehicles streamed by me all that time, flying on snow
and ice. I could easily imagine being killed or mangled. I tried the philosophical exercise of imagining the world without me. It was easy. It was
a little too easy.

I believed I could pass the time by embracing radio music. I hunted
the dial until I found some rhythm and blues, where a phrase like "all
night long" or "yes, it's me" could last half a song. I didn't usually listen
to lyrics, but these tunes were really wrapped around the words and it
was a pleasant exercise to listen and think. I was surprised to hear how
many of the country crooners admitted sneaking out on their marriages.
It came up so often that despite the disclaimers and professions of suffering a kind of exultation was implied. An equal number sought to
"put a ring on your finger." The cycling between hoped-for togetherness
and feverish cheating was disconcerting. Even stranger, the glamorous
barflies of the lyrics described the liquor of their choice as being wine if
the song was about marrying or cheating on your spouse. If beer was the
beverage, it signaled a rowdy call to arms for "country" values. There
was a surprising number of quite threatening songs of patriotism, often
with a semi-thudding march tempo, a gathering of violent warnings.
Lots of biography on the part of the singer about other famous singers
he knew or admired. Our deteriorated modern world was often
deplored, from heaven, by "Hank." God took a wider view, but Hank
had a streak of sarcasm and disappointment over how sorry things had
gotten. Another decried those who preferred sandals to "manly foot-
wear." I turned the radio off: I was sick of these people, all prison-
bound, where they would be challenged to avoid sodomy by monsters
from the inner city. It was easy to think like this when the driveshaft fell
out of your car at seventy per.

The tow truck was driven by a nice young man named Lane who was
happy to have the work. He had big work-hardened hands and wore
green zip-up coveralls with a sky blue bandanna tied around his neck.
His billed cap said ICE DOGS and displayed a flying hockey puck trailed
by stars, and all around the edges of the cap his thick blond hair stuck

out. He winched the 88 up with a cable drum, chocked the wheels, boomed it down with chains, and invited me into the cab. As we drove east, I enjoyed the elevation and the wide beam of lights that declared our progress and right-of-way a long distance ahead. The big meshing noise of the diesel seemed authoritative and reminded me of my father's descriptions of the sound of Panzer tanks.

Lane said, "Let's have some music for the occasion" and punched a button on the tape deck. A booming song emerged, "I'm in love with my car," with extraordinary words—"When I'm holdin' your wheel, all I hear is your gear"—all sung against screaming arena rock guitars and keyboards and end-of-the-world percussion. At last it was over and Lane turned it off.

"You like Queen?"

"Sure . . ."

"I've got news: that wasn't Freddie Mercury."

"Oh. Who was it?"

"That was the drummer, Roger Taylor. Freddie was backup and backup only on this one. But bottom line, great album. Triple platinum, to be exact. You like glam rock?"

I didn't know what glam rock was, but I was so averse to having Lane explain it to me that I told him I liked it very much. That seemed to satisfy him and he sank into a steady concentration on the road ahead.

We dropped my car in the parking lot of a repair shop. A cold wind blew. I paid Lane and walked to the Grand, where I got a room and tried to figure out how to get hold of Jocelyn. Nothing worked; it sounded as if she just had her cell phone turned off. I crawled into bed in a vague state of worry and managed to go to sleep. In the morning I went downstairs to check out. Womack and Jocelyn were sitting in the lobby reading the *Big Timber Pioneer*. I said, "My car broke down."

She said, "Whatever."

I chirped, "Good morning, Jocelyn!"

"Right."

Without looking up from the paper, Womack said, "You needed to get rid of that piece of shit a long time ago. Don't look to me like being a doctor is doing you no good."

I stood in front of the hotel, furious, as I watched the two of them drive off. I think that describes it. I knew I was offended and belittled by my own jealousy. I disliked caring about Jocelyn so much, but there it was: her swagger, skills, and independence were so attractive. Our love-making was something of a clash, but it was powerful and showered sparks. She regarded the missionary position as an ironic exercise and threatened me if I closed my eyes. I felt vacuumed by orgasms and rarely regained full consciousness before finding myself admiring her naked body through the bathroom door as she concentrated on brushing her hair. She was very unconscious of her body until she needed it to make something happen; when she thought there was a chance we'd make love again, she would stand next to me as I lay on the bed, and brush her teeth in a mischievous way, blowing bubbles in the toothpaste. Then with a laugh she would whirl away, giving me time to think and knowing I'd be ready as soon as she had rinsed. She was never wrong. And if she thought that by luring me into this erotic cellar she could addict me to her with no other effort at being thoughtful, she was right. It was not good for my self-respect.

I resolved to discuss it with Jinx. The Olds was out of the shop and the hands of reluctant mechanics, who urged me to haul it to the wrecking yard. The weather had abated and I was heading for the Corral Motel in Harlowton, plying the heaving road across the northern half of Sweet Grass County, not a cloud in the sky. I was no longer a sitting duck in my house—though I felt the tug of possibly missed walk-ins, and the day-and-night worry over Jinx's plan to move away. And that was just about how specific a plan it was: away, a yawning destination to say the least. I wanted to forbid it. Was this friendship?

The desk clerk—or I guess he was the owner—just said "five," leaving me to work out that it was room 5. I left the Olds parked by the office and walked around the front of the building in a rising disorientation that made my feet on the gravel sound like someone was following me. And yet the smell of pavement and sagebrush, the cloudless sky and great distances visible all around, were almost pleasant intimations that I was in a story and it was my story.

I knocked on the door of room 5, which produced a scurrying noise from beyond. Finally, the door opened: Womack. He didn't open it very far but we were face-to-face. As though he had never seen me before, he said, "What can I do for you?"

I held his gaze and said, "Jocelyn, may I speak to you, please?"

Womack said, "Who?"

I said, directly over the barely exposed left shoulder of Womack, "Jocelyn, may I speak to you?"

Womack said, "Pardner, I think you must have the wrong room. Go back and ask the desk clerk to get you a way safer room number. That's today's tip." I was prey to sufficient self-doubt that I had a moment of thinking that I actually had the wrong room and this was not Womack. Somehow an idea penetrated my nausea: "5" was the only room number I was going to need.

Throckmorton said, "My God, are you okay? You look okay. Jesus Christ, I hope you're okay. I don't know if you realize this, Mr. I. B. Pickett, but everyone hates you."

"No doubt. Where've you been?" I asked wanly. We were at the threshold of his office and his secretary was staring at me with the same gaze she would have bestowed upon Lazarus. I preceded Throckmorton just to get away from it. We flopped in our respective overstuffed leather chairs, Throckmorton scooting his around the side of his desk to better see me.

"Tahiti."

"Seriously?"

"Always wanted to go. It was full of surprises. The first thing I saw when I got off the plane was a billboard for Colonel Sanders chicken. Those Tahitian pricks tried to clean me out, but I'm home now, I'm okay."

"I thought I'd see how we're doing."

"Well, it looks like it's still going to be Judge Lauderdale. I made the mistake once of citing the jurist Benjamin Cardoza, which inspired Lauderdale, once he had me in chambers, to caution me against confusing things by 'citing some obscure wop.' "

"How's he going to feel about me?"

"Hard to say. We hope for 'valuable citizen.' But he might suspect immorality in your relationship with the deceased."

"Tessa."

"For our purposes, 'the deceased.' "

"Whatever he'd want to call it, it was a long time ago."

"For the Lauderdales of this world, immorality never dies. First, we try for a dismissal. You had an enemy on the hospital board, old moneybags—"

"Wilmot."

"Whatever. I want to see if we can't neutralize him. He is connected through common stupidity to a number of state legislators. So it might not be easy."

I abruptly knew that it was not certain I would be absolved, and that it was possible I could no longer do the work at which I was most useful. Previously, I had dreaded loss of freedom. Now I was uninterested in freedom. I wanted to be useful and I wanted it more than anything—or almost anything, because I was also raring to be with Jocelyn.

I think it must have been late, at least eleven. I was still awake, in fact, not even sleepy. The neighbors were fighting and I helplessly listened in. "I don't care what it smells like! I care what it looks like!" I hadn't seen Jocelyn in several days and I was worried. While I felt she cared for me as much as ever, I did consider she had become somewhat perfunctory in our lovemaking, as would be appropriate for a preoccupied person, is what I believe I thought at the time. Or something. Whatever misgivings I might have had were canceled by a kind of gratitude—yes, somewhat stupid gratitude, but all of my thoughts were of Jocelyn, her grace and particular self-propulsion, which in my enforced idleness I possibly overvalued. So what, I loved her. And even so what if she didn't love me. Of what final good was love if valued only when reciprocated? As I ran this rhetorical question around my thick skull, I recognized for the first time that Jocelyn did not love me. However obvious it was, I found this a disquieting discovery. Nevertheless, I figured I could go on loving her anyway, and her willingness to make love with me could be a stand-in for actual love until I could make her love me. But how? What if I learned to fly an airplane? There was something about all this that was arousing memories of a long submerged state of mind, that period of my college days when I slipped off to Florida with my host's wife. That world of eroticism, subterfuge, guilt, and fear set against meaningless vistas of sea and tropical vegetation had produced a sort of disorientation that I felt for the first time in a very long while. Happily, my mind shifted effortlessly to Jocelyn and her marvelous limbs. But it wouldn't stay there. I should have jacked off, slept, and gone to breakfast, but I wasn't that smart. I was in that moronic oblivion that makes the world go round. To make things worse, my neighbors were still fighting and I could hear them all the way across the street. The man with the bass voice shouted, "There's cat hair on my ChapStick!" And shortly after that, "For Christ's sake, hold the snow peas!" And back came the woman's tiny, shrill voice: "I won't let you spoil one more Christmas!" This was just too troubling because we were nowhere near Christmas. I had to get out of there.

What I meant to do was drive over to Jinx's house and get her out of bed, but by the time I got to her door she was up. "I heard that awful car of yours." Of course, there were a lot of awful cars and it was interesting that she was so attuned to mine that she got up before I could get to her door. She motioned me in.

Jinx was in a bathrobe and barefoot. I noticed what pretty feet she had and was touched that she liked them well enough to paint her toenails, then had the ridiculously inappropriate thought that if I painted my toenails Jocelyn would never speak to me again. Jinx had tied her hair at the top of her head, and it made her face, which always revealed such a play of moods, seem even more expressive.

I sat at the table while she made a pot of tea with the electric kettle. "You couldn't sleep?"

"I didn't try. It wouldn't have worked if I had. Did I wake you?"

"Uh-huh. You don't want anything in this, do you?"

"No." I only wanted to talk about myself. Once we sat across the small round table and smiled at each other over our tea, we were comfortable again. I felt at ease in pouring out my passion for the fair Jocelyn. I threw in various ironies including the uncertainty of Jocelyn's feelings. I hinted at her lovemaking and described her great skills as a pilot. Jinx listened, smiling quietly, occasionally sipping her tea. At length, tears ran down her cheeks and I felt a wave of gratitude that our friendship was so strong she exulted in my happiness. Jinx had her own sort of beauty, which her tears brought out from where it resided in a deep nature. I admired Jinx and in my excited state could easily picture someone—someone I couldn't quite imagine—falling in love her, in a different way than I loved Jocelyn but love is love is love.

Right?

. . .

I did see Throckmorton once that week. I stopped at the desk of his receptionist, Maida, who had a cake in front of her. She sat there, arms crossed, glowering at me. "He in?" I asked but got no reply. Then Niles emerged and said without emphasis, "It's her birthday. She's not speaking. Are you, Maida?" No reply. "See?"

He led me in and I slumped in the special chair that by forcing the client into a degraded slouch allowed Niles to lay down the conditions by which he would stream billable hours into the client's mailbox.

Niles's face crumpled in a look of worry and pain. I didn't like the anxiety it produced in me. He laid his hand across his stomach and stared at me without a word. My anxiety rose in the eternity that transpired before he spoke. He said, "Ribeyes and bourbon don't mix."

"Right . . . ?"

"Gotta slip off and pinch a loaf. It's killing me. Keep talking—" He abruptly crossed his office, entered the bathroom, and closed the door. "Go ahead, I can hear you from here!"

"Jesus, Niles!" A fart and a booming laugh were the only reply. "You want me to come back?"

"Oh, hell no. You're here, let's get some work done. Plus, I've got news. I went to see Wilmot and the board. What a mausoleum! I think Wilmot has been behind this all along. He's got a sympathetic audience with a few of the doctors who are not operating on the facts of the case but on a visceral loathing of you and your calamitous lifestyle. Excepting of course Jinx Mayhall, who thinks you're cuter than a speckled pup." I didn't reply but went on looking at the bathroom door as though it were doing the talking. "One thing I bore in mind is that the way you get on hospital boards is by demonstrating a capacity to create and maintain a substantial bank account. This is where I trained my jeweler's eye for persuasion. Pretending sympathy for these deviant swindlers, I commiserated over the loss of value to the clinic once this malpractice case hit the papers. I suggested that in such a scenario if turkeys were going for ten cents a pound they wouldn't be able to buy a raffle ticket on a jaybird's ass. No, I didn't really say that, but I hinted as much. Thus I began to pave a trail leading to fabulously ignorant and corrupt Judge Lauderdale's chambers, where a pagan reverence for lucre also obtains. Hey, you don't have to hang around here, Berl, that's all I've got for today. And no sense sharing the details of my current physical discomfort. But if you need help interpreting the legal niceties with which I've showered you, let me say this about that: the news is good."

"All right, well, I'll wait to hear."

"Sorry about this. I may have to turn to the Lamaze method."

Odd how you adapt to things: I waved good-bye to the door, walked through the reception area where Maida stared past the birthday cake into the middle distance, out into the street, the sunshine, and the welcome faces of a few pedestrians, picturing freedom with Jocelyn. It wasn't until the next day that I learned that Niles had been having a heart attack. A remarkable number of hard-driving Type A men die on the toilet. It's almost traditional. Some seem to see it coming, as witness Elvis Presley clutching his Bible. Niles didn't die, but he was never the same again, and I no longer had a lawyer. But while he was in the hospital, he insisted on having me as his physician, so by this peculiarity, I was employed.

I'm reluctant to admit this level of self-absorption, but standing next to Niles's bed I was giddy to be back to work, almost hysterical. Alan Hirsch, an actual cardiologist, had briefed me about Niles's condition, somewhat stablized with the current onboard levels of Coumadin. He grimaced when I told him all the vitamin K things he would need to limit or avoid—beef and alcohol being particularly painful subjects.

"Broccoli."

"I hate broccoli."

"Spinach."

"Hate that too.

"Parsley."

"I throw it on the floor. If I avoid all of those, can I have the booze and beef back?"

"In moderation. This is warfarin. It's like rat poison."

"Why do doctors hate lawyers?"

"It's one of nature's laws. Now, if you have any sort of unusual bleeding, I want to know about it. I mean like when you're flossing your teeth. Niles, I want you take this seriously so you can avoid surgery."

"Berl, let me tell you how seriously I'm taking this: I'm retiring. And not just to avoid seeing Maida's face or hearing her baleful screeches when a bit of work is required of her. The record shows that I took my job seriously but I never took myself seriously. That's why I am not a judge like that ignoramus Lauderdale. A lawyer wishing to become a federal judge like slime king Lauderdale does not turn his own home into a notorious fornicatorium. I'm going to get off this rat poison if it's the last thing I do. I'm going fishing. You and me, we started out as fishing boys, but we strayed. I'm going back. I may have sex occasionally, but I assure you it will be with a girl who if she moves at all moves very little."

I acted as a go-between for Alan, whose patient Niles really was. It preserved the relationship Niles insisted on having with me and allowed him to conceal his terror of death with the familiar jocularities that had always marked our relationship. He would have felt emotionally naked with anyone else, a state Niles could hardly face. I never gave Niles bad medical advice, I gave him Alan Hirsch advice, which was meticulous, cutting-edge cardiological guidance, guidance which Niles declined to follow. The last time I ever saw him was the middle of the day; he was in his pajamas, mildly drunk; he held up a large can to my view, said, "With this I can glue anything." He was dead in less than three months, enduring his last myocardial infarction at over eighty miles per hour in the big Audi, Gladys Knight on the sound system and a bottle of champagne on the passenger seat. The woman he must have been on his way to see never, as they say in the papers, came forward. Alan did not take this as a failure on his part, offering the opinion that Niles died not of heart disease but of priapism. Parenthetically, when I next saw Judge Lauderdale he seemed quite saddened by the death of Niles Throckmorton. "We always had such fun," said Judge Lauderdale. "He'd say terrible things about me to my face and I'd try to do the same back. But I was never in Niles's league. He was very creative. I bet he's making them sweat up there."

Lauderdale did not mention my case. Was it possible he'd forgotten that I was on his docket? Was he too polite? Did he think I was innocent? Did he not care? Did he think a nice guy like me was guilty as hell and it was all just too bad? It hardly mattered: Niles had handed me on to a smart young guy just out of Northwestern Law who "blew away the Montana Bar exam" and who Niles thought was his brand-new best friend. But the young lawyer, Donald Sanchez, looked at my situation and dryly remarked, "Throckmorton must have enjoyed your company," adding, "Oh, well, this is where you should have been headed in the first place. I hope he didn't charge you."

I was about to send Counselor Sanchez on his way. "There wasn't time for him to charge me. He died. And he was my friend. And he sent me to you with his highest recommendation."

"I'm sorry, but if he was a friend he should have told you more about his relationship with the victim."

I was stunned. "Was there one?" I asked.

"Two night owls in a small town? You need to get your head in the game."

Sanchez prepared for the dismissal hearing with a fistful of affidavits, the gist of which was that my colleagues found me gifted but erratic, someone who, despite the quality of his work, created an atmosphere of possible malpractice. Sanchez said that Wilmot had gotten to every one of them except Alan Hirsch and Jinx Mayhall.

I spent a very long evening in my basement going through old papers and documents until I found what I was looking for, a large, yellowing envelope that I carried on my visit to Judge Lauderdale, who saw me in his office with a look of skeptical surprise. I sat down after handing him the envelope. Judge Lauderdale put on a pair of glasses and emptied the contents of the envelope onto his desk. "What is this?" he said after a short time. "A bunch of receipts for paint and supplies?"

"Yes."

"For what?"

"For painting your cabin in Harlowton."

Judge Lauderdale removed his glasses and placed them on the desk in front of him. "Was that you?"

"Mm-hmm."

"My God." He laughed. "You were just a green kid. Now look at you!"

"Time flies."

"I have to admit, you didn't do much of a job. Lots of overruns."

"You never paid me."

"Like I said, it wasn't like Leonardo da Vinci."

"Your secretary thought it was a big improvement."

"Oh?"

Whatever change I may have induced in Judge Lauderdale was unclear to me until Sanchez called me in with his helplessly imperious manner. I didn't know whether he had learned this at Northwestern or it was just his nature, but his no-nonsense style took some getting used to. His first words were, "Sit down." His office had none of the upholstered quality of my late friend Niles Throckmorton's ordered lair. In fact, it appeared that the vertical stacks of paper on the floor and against the wall were ongoing cases or some sort of filing system. I'd have bet that he scared the daylights out of blustering Judge Lauderdale.

He said, glancing at his watch with a look of suppressed fury, "Let me give you the boiled-down finding on the frivolity to which you have been subjected, which at this point, we hope, is little more than toxic residue. Judge Lauderdale is now apprised of the following: misleading representation by previous counsel resulting from said counsel's undisclosed relationship with the deceased, Tessa Larionov. Complicity of clinic staff with the intentions of board chairman Wilmot, placing one and all in the line of culpability for a defamation of character suit. Putting the crosshairs on their wallets, I found the good doctors' views softening abruptly. This won't go away—and should you feel vindictive and wish to get rich, call me. Credit to you for softening up Lauderdale in your unauthorized private meeting. Not interested in the details. Long story short, all momentum from your adversaries has dissipated. I have nothing more for you. I've got to be in Helena in two hours. Should you wish to stay here and collect your thoughts, the coffee machine is in the john. Pull the door shut when you leave, it locks itself and I have a key. Congratulations, you're innocent."

I didn't think so. Sanchez threw all his papers into a satchel and, running his fingers through his thick black Mexican hair, turned and went on his way.

I had to do something about my real crime. My so-called innocence had no more than isolated the problem. I arranged to meet Cody's mother, Deanne. I am not exaggerating when I say that I suffered over this one. When I finally went to see her, I thought, Here goes nothing, just more whistling in the dark. I was well aware that I might not have the nerve to tell her how I had encouraged Cody on his way, but I had to do this or I would never be free. And was that it? Freedom? The cemetery was the safest place to meet, as she believed that we would start rumors if we were seen together. "People will think we're getting it on." This inappropriate tone made me understand with a sinking feeling how little she suspected what I really had in mind. Nor could she know how much I was my mother's son in the quest for forgiveness and the desire to be shriven.

Where the walkways separated, a pleasant bower of green ash encircled three wrought-iron benches, virtual hemorrhoid machines in any season but summer. Here I awaited Deanne, pronounced "Dee Anne," who arrived on time, rather dressed up and wearing the emphatic eyeliner I had always associated with availability. But the long, hard years shone through the makeup and gave me the sense that I was speaking to two people, one just behind the other.

"How old would Cody be?" I asked. I thought to go to my subject straightaway. She gave me an inquiring look.

"I don't know."

"I'm not quite sure why I asked."

"I'm not either. Can we sit over there?"

"Oh sure, of course, I didn't even see it." A plank bench put us a little more face-to-face than I wished. We sat down. I looked at my shoelaces and Deanne looked at the treetops. I knew she would soon say something and she did.

"Before I married Jerry I was running around pretty hard. I had a bad reputation and, who can say, I probably deserved it. When it hit bottom I got to be pretty good friends with your old flame Tessa—"

"—well, she wasn't exactly—"

"—a very special person, a very spiritual person."

I listened closely. I felt panic: I didn't come here to talk about Tessa. I hardly thought of Tessa as a spiritual individual, whatever in God's name that was, though it was a concept much in currency, with little sign of going away. I knew from experience that "spirituality" was producing some ghastly scenes around the dinner tables of North America, and here it was, in the air again.

She went on. "Tessa told me she had done everything in her power to have your baby, but it was just not to be."

"No, no. Oh, no."

"So there was very strong feeling from that end."

"Yes, yes, of course."

"And maybe, who knows, from your end too."

"Well—"

"Well what?"

"Well, I was pretty young."

"Are you trying to wriggle out of this?"

"Not at all!"

"What I'm leading up to is, is there anything to all this stuff I'm hearing? Isn't that why you asked me to come here?"

"I'm not sure what you've been hearing, Deanne."

"That you did away with Tessa on your operating table."

"They're looking into that."

"For Christ's sake, don't you have an opinion?"

"I do but—yes, I do."

"Want to share it?" she asked. Clearly she could make no sense of me at all.

"No, Deanne, I do not," I said but thought, Maybe afterwards.

"Well, I have no clue why you wanted to talk to me, then. I thought you knew Tessa and I were friends. I thought you might come clean. In fact, I told somebody, 'I'll bet that quack is gonna spill the beans to the only friend Tessa had in this town.' "

"I'm sorry to disappoint you."

"You got a light?"

She had a cigarette in her mouth. I slapped my pockets futilely. She was plainly agitated; looking right and left, she said, "If you come on to me I'm going to scream my lungs out." I'd seen two men strolling down the diagonal toward the First World War monument and I ran them down, two startled older men, and got a match for Deanne. She bent over my cupped hands to light the cigarette but kept wary eyes on me.

"Look, Deanne, Clarice was my patient. I took care of her after a lot of bad beatings—" She blew the smoke off to one side, then seemed to look where it went. "I could have just treated her, left it at that, but it kept on and I got involved."

"What d'you mean, you got involved?"

"I got caught up in what I thought was heading for tragedy."

"Oh."

"So, there at the end I was in that house, and she was, well, she was—I couldn't really do anything for her."

"I know the story."

"I'm afraid you don't, Deanne."

"What did you say?"

"I said, I'm afraid you don't know the story. Not all of it. Not about Cody."

"I wonder if I need to hear any more of your story," she said levelly. "I live with a man who said 'good riddance' when my son died. I don't have a knack for a lot more of this."

I was afraid she'd jump up and leave, but I had to finish. "Just one more thing, Deanne. You see, Cody wasn't really going to do away with himself."

It was time for me to take a stand. I just wasn't sure I could.

"Oh?"

"No, I really don't think so."

"So what happened?" I was, in a way, frightened by the quiet way she asked because I knew it was the end of the line. "Are you going to tell me something?"

"He was there with, uh, with the gun, and I could see that the whole thing had dawned on him—"

That was true. Cody had been in a rage for a long time and now it was gone and he couldn't get it back. He was alone, kind of weightless. There was in his face a bleak sort of amazement. He was mine and I knew it. I was his god. In the long years I'd had to think about it, that was what I had come up with: that I was the cold unblinking god of Cody.

"I felt very strongly that I knew what had to happen and that Cody didn't and that Cody was waiting to hear it from me."

"And what?"

I made myself look straight in her eyes. "I told him to kill himself."

"You did."

"I thought that was right."

"And so he did."

"Yes."

She froze for a moment, then screamed and tried to put the cigarette out in my eye. I felt her claw down both sides of my face as she cried and screamed at once. She was not very strong, and I was able to get my arms around her and subdue her until she gasped that she would stop, she would calm down, and she would stop. I released her carefully. Her makeup was smeared crazily across her face, and in her expression I beheld such forlornness, such despair, that I felt as vacant as Cody had looked when he saw what he had done.

"Okay," she said, "okay. Let me just get a grip here—" She pulled back on the bench and took a heavy breath. Then she fished underneath for her purse, which she put in her lap. "Let me just pull myself together here—" She started to get something from her purse, then covered her face and sobbed, the tears running out between her fingers. I could only think what a terrible price I was exacting for my own cheap absolution. She uncovered her eyes and said, "Okay, okay," and got a Kleenex from the purse and dabbed and wiped her face carefully. She folded the Kleenex and tucked it back into the purse, pulling it open to look inside.

I didn't realize what she was doing until she had stabbed me. I moaned and fell off the bench grasping the knife handle at my chest with both hands. Deanne stood over me and said she hoped I didn't make it. I honestly didn't know how much time I might have; whatever it might have been, I used it to tell her that I was innocent. She said that I had picked a bad time to lie, and walked away.

There must not have been time for my diagnostic skills to offer perspective on my plight except to say that a very comprehensive debility was creeping over me almost as if a heavy rug were being pulled onto my body from several directions at once, everything going soft or limp with weight, except the astonishing rigidity of the knife. I recall thinking that this generalized enfeeblement and draining of life must be death with the peculiarity of the mind imagining even to the last minute that it was somehow exempt from this process. That was either adaptive protection to avert suffering and struggle or the very fragile thing that supported convictions about the imperishability of the spirit. I had always thought religious assertions as to the latter were a form of hysteria, but for the moment I was prepared to keep an open mind. I had often observed in my work, especially in those days in the ER, that there is an unreliable floor to American life and if you find yourself going through it, life is quite dangerous. What I hadn't learned was that it could apply to me.

But in that immortal phrase, I lived "to tell the tale." A man on a bicycle came by (I was not entirely conscious) and found me squirting blood onto the walkway, and called for help. I had such a riveting view of my savior, whom I've never seen, that the picture stays with me still: one foot extended to hold himself up on the bicycle, he flips open his cell phone and looks at the sky as he calls for help; there is a pause, after which he cranes around urgently looking for ways to describe our location. He is a Good Samaritan, etc. I have no idea who he is. He has not chosen to "come forward either." We would be together forever, my phantom and I.

I learned later on that Alan had been called in to Emergency for some arterial repair and that quite a lot of blood replacement had been necessary as a result of, I guess, near-fatal hemorrhaging and hypovolemic shock. I later saw Alan's vital signs documentation and was moved by its obsessive notations. I had benefited from spontaneous closure of a small breach of the left ventricle, and was surprised by the irrational if faint horror occasioned by a description of one's own injuries. I was relieved to learn there was negligible fluid retention in the pericardium, wherein pumping volume might have been reduced to the point of my returning to my life with a greatly impaired brain. There was a relatively small transfer of kinetic energy in a stab wound, as compared to say, a gunshot wound. So any emergency treatment provider was spared from having to worry too much about collateral injury. In other words, I was grateful that Deanne hadn't shot me. Sweet!

I had a small incision in my chest, not far from the wound, and Alan later explained, "The way you presented, dude, I had to look around."

By the first evening, lying in my hospital bed, I was not much worse than sore. I was even visitable. Instead of watching the television hanging from the wall above and to one side of the utilitarian sink, I looked out the door as doctors and nurses came and went. I watched them for nearly an hour before I began to cry. I cried hard but without making a sound. It wasn't because of what had happened to me. It was because I wanted to go to work. I asked God to let me go back to work. I don't think I had experienced such anguish before.

About then, Jinx arrived and closed my door. She stood there and looked at me for a long time. I was too miserable to speak or to dry my face, and my body shook with suppressed sobs. Jinx locked the door, got in bed beside me, and held me in her arms. I recall a moment of incomprehension, and then gratitude for the heat of her body. After her embrace had stilled my various shudderings, quite long after, Jinx got out of bed, fussed a bit with my covers, unlocked the door, and left. The next day she dropped off some bird books with the floor nurse, who delivered them. They only rekindled my astonishment.

Several of the staff stopped in to see me, and the aversion I had expected was nowhere in evidence. They were even friendly. Haack, Hirsch, Wong, even McAllister paid their respects. Bets were really off when you got stabbed. I was strangely fascinated by the telephone beside my bed, which seemed to be beckoning me to communicate, a challenge I was not entirely up to, not because of my injury but because of my all-consuming bafflement. I thought almost continuously of Jocelyn and wondered if she knew what had befallen me. I had no reasonable explanation of the facts and was using my reduced energy to make up some sort of harmless story. I fought the drag of time by picturing her and imagining how she felt; I was plunged into mild despair when I reimagined sex with Jocelyn or tried to get my mind around her peculiarly abstract ferocity. These were lavish erotic fancies which kept me from turning on the television.

Alan thoughtfully held off the cops until I was feeling better and was less affected by the various medications, which had produced not just pain relief but a two-day erection, a various maypole around which visions of Jocelyn's private parts danced. But then Officer Weiland, Terry Weiland, came to see me in order to file a more complete police report than the one produced when I was admitted and not conscious. Terry was in early middle age, a compact, purposeful man in the local cowboy style, very mannerly, very direct. He said, "Feeling any better?"

"Yes, I am, thank you."

"Dr. Hirsch said he'll have you out of here soon."

I took this wrong at first, and then understood he meant only that I would soon be released. I had feared it meant I couldn't work here.

"Was this a personal disagreement?"

"Not at all. You mean the guy who stabbed me?"

"Yes."

"I don't know who he was. He might have mistaken me for someone else. Unless I was robbed. I don't know that we've checked that, have we? Where's my wallet?"

"We're struggling with this and just hoping you might have learned something that would help. Isn't this your wallet?"

"Yes, oh good."

"Was there time—I mean, did you get much of a look at him?"

"Absolutely."

"And he just stepped up and assaulted you?"

"He seemed to recognize me. He told me to stay away from her, that she was his and his alone. He must have confused me with someone else."

"The old triangle."

"Except there was no triangle." I was trying to keep this straight. I could no longer imagine why I took this tack. I suppose I was improvising and it got away from me. I began to labor mentally over a description of the assailant, which I knew I'd have to provide. I was a little bit panicked. I didn't really wake up until I was required to supply "Caucasian" to Officer Weiland, who had drawn a pair of reading glasses from his shirt pocket and was balancing a clipboard on his knee.

"Age?"

"I'm guessing late thirties." I did notice that I was beginning to picture the assailant. I had no answers for scars, tattoos, etc., but I was able to describe the assailant in sufficient detail to satisfy Officer Weiland: dark brown hair combed straight back, a lean and narrow face with prominent teeth, ice blue eyes; he was wearing straight-cut black jeans, work boots, a snap-button western shirt with a barbed-wire motif, and a baseball hat advertising an Oklahoma fuel company.

At the end of our interview, Office Weiland told me to make a "victim personal statement" describing the impact of the crime upon me. "These are used by the judge to help him decide on an appropriate sentence."

I said, "I learned what anyone in that situation would learn—that life can end at any time and that whatever it is you want to do with your life you should do right away. I feel that things early in your life that were unresolved can suddenly crop up later on and try to do away with you."

"What do you mean by that?"

"I'm not sure."

"Well, I'll just write it down. Maybe it will mean something to the judge."

I don't know what possessed me to describe Womack so exactly. Honestly, it was unintentional. By nightfall, he was featured in a composite sketch in our newspaper and, I suppose, a few thousand people were poring over it. I saw the paper myself and was startled to see what a fine job the sketch artist had done.

Deanne was carrying the paper when she visited me, my first real visitor. She was also carrying the same purse! I stared at it and asked if she was here to finish the job. If she tried again, I'd have to accept it. Her eyes filled with tears as she shook her head and pitched forward, her face against the side of my bed. I was turbulent with emotions, as I had been interrupted in the midst of a rich fantasy of Jocelyn. But this astonishing development was pushing even Jocelyn from my mind. For the moment, I had lost interest in everything. I was also overwhelmed by the sensation that I didn't know what I would do next. Unexpectedly, I pitied Deanne and was on the verge of bursting into tears all over again. She said, "I'm worthless, aren't I?"

"Not in the least."

"Don't be nice. I'm nobody." She looked miserable, and I was aghast at what I had just done. As though parsing some term or concept for the local philological society, I tried to persuade Deanne that it was I who was worthless, not she, but I really didn't get anywhere. Worthless seemed to apply as a general condition in Deanne's life, and she was determined to hang on to it.

I had another wave of terror as she retrieved a Kleenex from her purse, this time to blow her nose, and having done so, she raised the newspaper as evidence and asked why I had protected her. I had to give this long thought before telling her that I believed that she was entitled to her action. "Oh, no!" she cried. I had known Deanne only as a worthily combative force, and I was desperate to absolve myself of having reduced her to this abject state. I had to believe that I was free of cruelty. Without that, in the words of Deanne, I would be Nobody. I would be Worthless.

So I poured myself into confessing my sins against her all over again. She had only one child and I'd seen to his demise. I left so little doubt that without my interference Cody might have lived that I half expected she would again try to kill me, but she seemed to absorb the long, slow death of Clarice. I really relived those scenes, and suffered them all over again. Never mind the knife, I was finally at her mercy, but she said, "I understand." She didn't say it quickly—she weighed my fate in her eyes for several long moments—but she said it. She said it with such gravity that I must have glimpsed what she was giving up.

21

HAD I LEARNED ANYTHING? I'd learned that I was remarkably unformed for a man of my age and experience. It wasn't until I lay in a hospital bed fingering a near fatal wound that I gave any thought to mortality. Then I knew that the spiritual component of my self, while small, was inextinguishable. My mother had instilled in me a longing but populated it with figures I found unbelievable: the omnipotent old man with the white beard, the sad boy with the crown of thorns, the virgin mom, the board of directors called the saints. I never succeeded in differentiating them from the equally compelling characters in my collection of comic books. I confused God with Space Man, whose battles with the robot monster that controlled outer space formed my first cosmology; meanwhile my compassion for Christ caused me to submerge him into Naza the Stone Age Warrior, who returns to kick Herod's ass and work mayhem on the Philistines.

Another thing occasioned by my close call was a vivid remembrance of childhood friends. I'd built the tree house with Chong Wells. His real name was Don Wells, but his admiration for Cheech and Chong supplied a nickname which followed him all the way to the Persian Gulf, from where he did not return. Dave "Second Hand" Smoke moved to Miles City, where he had a backhoe business. When I get out of here, I thought, I should give Second Hand a call. Childhood friends call me "Hook" for Captain Hook, which was a reference to my love of fishing.

What was left of my rudimentary religiosity? Only my question: What was far-fetched about the continued existence of the human spirit? Why was mankind in all places and all ages convinced of it? Fingering my knife wound, I went on believing that the real me could shoot out of this tiny hole in the event of a shutdown.

But most emotions attending the long hours of daydreaming were occupied with thoughts of Jocelyn, some remarkably impure, but most idealistically pastel and conceived as operatic scenes of reunion and promise. In the encounters I pictured it was only remarkable that the players were not winged. This might have been a reference to Jocelyn's flying, but I didn't think so. I pictured her in the cockpit with the headset pulled down over her International Harvester cap, and as I dragged her from the fuel spill at the crash site, then at the hospital in White Sulphur when I was a still-employed caregiver offering diplomatic advice in the bailiwick of another physician. In short, I could hardly wait to get my hands on her.

This grueling need so pervaded my imagination that it encouraged me to think about a long-term relationship with Jocelyn; and here I hit a wall because her air of independence betrayed a smidgeon of aversion directed either at me or, more likely, at any form of predictability. Too, I found her lack of sentimentality over the burning of the old homestead and her generally harsh remarks about home and family to be a tad extreme. Her strictly genital approach to sex could, I dimly supposed, grow thin without a larger view, but I could always supply that—thought I foolishly. As was so often the case, romance was well to the rear of the united front of thighs, breasts, etc. The little twang in her voice had me shivering with ecstasy. My most elevated thoughts were of the clean lines of her cheekbones, her smooth, round forehead, her full and insolent lips. At the moment, I could not picture her nose. Fidgeting under the sheets, I worked away at recalling the nose, then finally left it that she had one, and that was that.

She must not have known I was in the hospital.

Alan Hirsch came in to see me with his athlete's bounce and sat, one leg on the floor, on the edge of my bed. "I think it's time you blew this pop stand, Irving."

"I do too." I couldn't mention that I had nowhere in particular to go, or that seeing him and other physicians speeding past my doorway had given me an insurmountable heartache compared to the longing for Jocelyn.

"You look blue."

"I am blue."

"Nothing to do with your injury, I hope?"

"I want to work."

"You want to work? Are you crazy?"

Alan was just trying to cheer me up. He liked to work, I knew that. His needy athleticism had led him down the path of extreme sports, but he was always on the job, always good, and the huge Kodachromes of his rock climbing and of his son on the Miles City football team which adorned his office walls seemed to reassure his cardio patients. He gave me a protracted, considered look and then tapped me with his clipboard. "You'll get through this. You have my word. I personally don't think this ever needed to happen, but Wilmot used all his grease to get the law involved."

"He hates me, but he is my patient."

So I went home, and I felt fine; but my first thought at entering my house was, "What am I doing here?" There were reentry issues, which I met by housekeeping and replenishing food supplies. A nap helped. I found a baseball game on the radio. Still under a legal cloud, I concentrated on the everyday. I ran the vaccuum. Then for several days I was just lost.

I'd been rattling around there for a day and a half, only occasionally staring at the telephone, when Jocelyn burst in. She filled up the room with her anger. She said, an inch from my face, "They've arrested Womack!"

"They . . . who?"

"Womack! You described him perfectly, thank you very much, down to his pants, his hair, and his boots. You get down there and tell them Womack didn't stab you."

"But this is just entirely a—"

"Stop talking and get down there."

I was just beginning to feel indignant when Jocelyn's face softened. "I'll be here waiting," she said. I gave her my best doofus smile.

Here was addiction. I didn't seem to care that my soul was shrinking to some meager artifact: I scuttled down to the police station to liberate Womack, I was too late, though. Lieutenant Crosby took me into his office to show me the results of Womack's background check, which included a raft of unpleasantries that cried out for resolution. Before affirming his innocence of my stabbing I was obliged to view Womack glowering at me from behind bars and declining to return my wink. Back in Crosby's office, I said, "That's not him. A lot like him. But not him. The guy that stabbed me is still at large." Crosby nodded wearily.

"Be that as it may," he said with exaggerated slowness, "I'm going to extradite Mr. Womack to Texas. He's got a lot of problems in Texas." Crosby searched in the desk. He produced a long, thin object and held it aloft. I stared at it. "You like beef jerky? I made this myself. Be my guest."

I walked out into the street, stunned and carrying my treat. What on earth was Jocelyn doing with this bird? I quickly figured it out: Womack may have had some issues with the law, here and there, but his skill as an aircraft mechanic was indispensable to a pilot doing high-risk work. I admired Jocelyn for keeping such a worrisome yet useful man at arm's length. Such nuanced and practical talent for management was something I could do no more than admire from afar.

I'm just saying all this.

I went back to my house, and the waiting Jocelyn, on speeding legs that seemed to have a life of their own. I thought it best to manage the information and confine my remarks to a plain statement of vindicating Womack of any responsibility for my injury. I myself would be like O. J. Simpson looking for the real killer. I understood that news of Womack heading south on a rail might reveal itself as glee on my part: my good thing, my love, would go up in smoke.

I tugged Jocelyn down the hall to my bedroom. We undressed quickly and without teasing delays. I noticed for the first time that she had had her breasts enhanced; they were lovely in their gravity-defying shapeliness. I was repressing unwelcome mirth based, I suppose, on some combination of relief and adoration, but also on an old memory of Alan Hirsch dancing around his office, a silicone implant in each hand, doing a terrible rendition of Dean Martin singing, "Mammaries are made of this," to a kind of muted Latin shuffle. I had to push that one well to the rear. I came from an era when breasts just happened, were not built to suit.

I returned to the matter at hand, which I hoped to prolong, having already pictured a virtual afternoon of foreplay. But Jocelyn seemed to be in a rush—I suppose "eager" might be a better word and throughout my leisurely fondling seemed bent on pulling me atop of her and getting it over with. By forcing her to slow down, I thought I was being provocative, but she expelled air through slightly parted lips in a way unmistakable for anything but impatience. It seemed advisable to get down to business. Jocelyn performed her part with exemplary animation, crying out as I came but falling still abruptly thereafter and staring at the lamp. We lay beside each other without speaking in the dim light of the room. My mind wandered briefly and then I remembered the nose. I remembered that I couldn't picture Jocelyn's nose. I turned my head until her profile came into view, and experienced a shock: her nose appeared to be almost, well, less a nose than a . . . snout. I jumped up and lifted the blinds. Jocelyn had raised herself on her elbows to watch my sudden activity. I came back to bed, where I snuggled up to her warm body and reexamined the nose, which was, in this light, quite normal after all. In my not easily understood relief, I told Jocelyn that I loved her. Without turning her head in my direction, she said, "Puh-leeze." I was shocked. I waited, hoping there was time for one more erection. I was down to that.

Like I said, I'm only reporting this.

The ancient truism that a stiff prick has no conscience is misleading. It would be better to say that a stiff prick arouses unreasonable hope. Or, as the late Throckmorton once said, "No erection should be allowed to go unattended." Many a fine man has been led by one into a morass of emotional entanglement, unfulfillable dreams, and unworthy or inglorious fates like bankruptcy. In today's political climate no one would have the nerve to say that a moist vagina has no conscience, but the case can be made; and in fact a good many candid and enlightened women are prepared to acknowledge as much. It's not just my hat that's off to them.

The fact of the matter, the matter of Jocelyn, is that I simply could not be rebuffed. I found her every attempt to lower my expectations just one more thing to find either A. ravishing or B. adorable. That's love and I freely declared it in the face of "puh-leeze." Jocelyn was always honest.

Jocelyn was not at her father's old place and neither was her airplane. I really didn't know where to start. Meanwhile, Jinx was driving me crazy by arbitrarily booking patients for me to see right in my own disordered house, ones she claimed were not exactly pediatric. I saw them in the front room, which I'd turned into something of an office. These were routine cases, but I was at least back to looking at people, worrying about them and writing a few scripts. I have to admit that I would have been pretty happy if I hadn't been stewing about Jocelyn and daydreaming about combining our skills in flying and medicine for some sort of wilderness thing or other. Alpine sort of backdrop, lonely rivers, etc.

But then she called me on the telephone. "Is this you, Berl?" I said it was. "Berl, you got my ass in a world of hurt."

I was somewhat startled by her tone, not exactly creamy with longing. She was snapping at me. I said, "Oh?"

"When you turned Womack in. I know you went down there and talked to those people."

"I didn't turn Womack in. Womack got picked up."

"Thanks to your description of the attacker. You're a damn fly in the ointment."

Now I headed for shakier ground. "I was stabbed, understand? I did the best I could to describe the assailant." I was still wondering what in my consciousness had caused me to describe Womack to a T. Squeamishly clinging to my imaginary attacker wasn't fortifying the tone of conviction I needed at this moment. "Where are you, anyway?"

"I'm back at my dad's place with the plane."

"I know that, but you—"

"Room in Harlo. At the Corral. You could come see me. I mean, the choice is yours. They've got Womack locked up in Texas all over again. Mission accomplished, sport."

Outrageous really, but all I could come up with was, "Well, yes." Good God. Was this the gruesome tug of my childhood and youth? To what else did I owe my lack of character in the face of such a quandary? I wasn't working enough; I was not being useful. When hard at work I knew what to do about such things. Maybe that was why Jinx was putting me back to work. She seemed to know what I needed. I was grateful that she couldn't hear my obsequious "Well, yes." And really I knew better, but Jocelyn was my vision and my craving; when she spoke to me I watched her lips with rapture and didn't hear a word. Without her before me—that is, with her on the telephone—I had a chance to take in a certain hardness in her demeanor, but I passed it up. I had only one thing in mind and that thing was laying a cold trail for me, one foot in front of the other. Did anyone ever rise above it?

We met at the Corral Motel in Harlowton and went straight to bed. It was most unsatisfactory. I had so long anticipated this moment that I made something of a fetish of foreplay, and it was clear that Jocelyn got nothing out of it. She said—joking, I assume—"Stick it in. Pull it out. Repeat. Keep it simple." I found it nearly impossible to rise above this "joke," but stupefied by adoration, I managed to carry on despite Jocelyn's finding everything I did funny. I'm quite aware of how abject I must have seemed, but one look at Jocelyn would clear that up for anyone. She was such a gorgeous woman, and the fact that she administered her beauty with coolness and perhaps calculation didn't seem to detract from it. I don't think anyone has quite understood the merciless power of women at their apogee. We are reduced to worship—and I do mean reduced. I wasn't sure brains and character added much at all. Look at Jinx: smart, good, pretty—she just didn't work it like Jocelyn did. Jinx was a goddess and Jocelyn was a tart—but where did knowing that get me?

"You've never been in my plane, have you?"

"No, no, I haven't. Maybe some—"

"Let's go now. Let's crank that baby up. Get dressed."

I did and watched her do the same. As I observed her flesh disappear into her panties, then her jeans, then her bra, then the bright checkered cowboy shirt I particularly liked, and finally the yellow North Face Windbreaker, I had a fleeting sense of seeing these ravishing objects of my attention for the last time.

In the end, the gooberish demeanor of the supplicant, whether it was someone working me for prescription pills or me trailing Jocelyn to the airplane, was remarkably consistent. Even when angry and demanding, the goober was still an addict. That's all an addict was, a goober. The long road to terminating exposure to the abused substance was littered with heartbreak. It was part of the training. Oddest of all, it greatly improved the survivors once you acknowledged the many who didn't make it.

Jocelyn was at the controls, and I sat beside her, cautioned to avoid contact with the parallel set of controls in front of me. The back of the plane was filled with all sorts of things, groceries mostly, but also a big-game rifle and a short-barreled shotgun. I didn't know she hunted. We both wore headsets and I quickly grew infatuated with the sound of Jocelyn's voice, slightly distorted as though heard from a faraway place we could both go where our voices would have a slight electronic buzz and all would be renewed. Jocelyn sang into her microphone, "Off we go into the wild blue yonder!" and I felt her excitement at flying even as we rumbled down the rough airfield at her father's old ranch. I watched her hand with its bright red nail polish on the stick, and it seemed to bespeak her remarkable mix of glamour and ability.

At the end of the field, she pivoted the aircraft, and we looked through the windshield, straight back to where we had just come from. I noticed a strip of surveyor's tape tied to a tall pole set in the ground. It fluttered in our direction as Jocelyn increased speed, inciting the roar of the engine, the propeller a pale blur in front of us. We'd moved forward slowly at first but accelerated rapidly toward the end of the field. The shuddering of the fuselage abruptly stopped and we were airborne, gaining altitude and sailing toward the line of foothills before us.

"Having fun?"

"Yes! Where are we going?"

Jocelyn turned to me and laughed. I couldn't see much of her behind the microphone and her aviator's sunglasses, but she was distinctly laughing, and it seemed more than a little emphatic with the distortion through my headset. She said, "We sure are, honey. We're going someplace."

I gazed at the landscape passing beneath us and it seemed to bear an expansive sense of time and of the imperishability of the earth. I had a glimpse of myself as a particularly pathetic exemplar of our race and its fragile gyrations. Never comfortable with this long view, I was grateful when it passed. Only animals really knew how to live.

Airplanes had come to seem quite different machines after the catastrophe in New York. They were overnight turned into projectiles; even if, as now, we used them for something else, they went on being projectiles. I let my gaze drift to Jocelyn's skillful hands on the controls and could feel the relationship between her floating hands and the movement of the aircraft. Her eyes interrupted their almost robotic scan of the horizon only to flick temporarily to the instruments. The sun coming through the canopy made me sleepy, as did gazing at the wavering shapes that appeared in the blur of the propeller. The inside of the plane smelled entirely of its new upholstery. It was surprising to compare our considerable airspeed to the slowness of the passing landforms below: they came and went as though operating in a different timescape from the one in which the airplane flew. We had stopped talking.

We began to descend after meeting what looked like a wall of mountains; a shadow in one of them slowly opened to reveal a pass into which Jocelyn, still descending, guided the plane. I looked anxiously from side to side as the blue sky in the opening above us seemed to be narrowing. Jocelyn lifted one hand to point through the windshield at a mountain goat grazing at eye level. We were in a canyon that turned slowly to the west between many-hued granite walls and grassy ledges. Below, some trees were scattered on either side of a sparkling creek which, with its regular flashes of white water, must have had a considerable gradient. Teal scattered up from back channels of the creek so far below. The walls on either side confirmed that the only possible direction for the plane to fly was straight forward. I couldn't picture climbing back out. I was uncomfortable.

We were nearly on the floor of the canyon. There was no possible place to set down, and my attempts to exchange some kind of glance with Jocelyn failed. When I asked her what was going on and got no answer, I could see that she little wished to have her concentration broken. Then the canyon curved quite rapidly to the west, narrowing all the while, and, more quickly than I could quite absorb, a flat meadow rose up before us and we were on the ground, tail wheel down and the windshield elevating as the plane changed its angle and stopped. Jocelyn increased the throttle slightly before slowing the propeller to a pause. The quiet was startling. She swept her headset off with one hand, shook out her hair, then turned to me and said, "Happy?"

"Can we get out of here?"

"We'll find out!" She laughed. "Isn't it beautiful?" She pushed open her door, and the cockpit filled with balsamic air and the fragrance of wildflowers. I looked around as best as I could beyond the bright wings of the plane. This was some sort of box canyon, and on either side of the meadow in which the plane sat, aspens grew straight up, protected from winter winds. Here and there water ran down the walls of the canyon, catching the light. I imagined the place quickly filling with shadows later in the day, and this thought came with some apprehension because despite the great natural beauty, my main interest was in getting out, which looked to be something of a feat. It was reassuring to climb from the plane and feel solid ground once more.

But Jocelyn's cheer was infectious. "Come on," she said. "I've got to show you something." So I followed along. The only bearing I had was Jocelyn herself, and she moved confidently along the meadow at her persistently lively clip, the same gait she used when walking around her airplane or coming into town and into my room, the same heedless forward motion. With one hand, she gathered up her long hair and twisted it into a knot on top of her head. She tied the Windbreaker around her waist by its sleeves and hopped on one foot as she retied the shoelace on the other. There were many hawks in this canyon, small, rapid short-winged hawks that cried out to one another as they crisscrossed overhead. "You'd never get out of here on foot," said Jocelyn. It was true, but I couldn't think why she'd say it. When I asked her where we were going in such a hurry, she only smiled. It seemed to me that we were heading toward a small grove of old cottonwoods at a place where the granite wall receded in a kind of shelter. It could have been an Indian place or a shepherd's place: I observed some smoke blackening its stone from this distance. When we reached it, I saw that it was indeed habitable—there was a rough lean-to shack apparently thrown together from fallen trees and limbs, enclosed nonetheless with a canvas fly secured against a small opening in front. "You don't think we're staying here tonight—"

She said, "We'll see," and held the canvas back for me to enter.

The sudden new light into the interior must have been dazzling because it was a moment or two before Womack put the gun down. Or he may simply have been confused, for he was clearly in very bad shape.

Jocelyn said, "I've brought the doctor."

"I didn't know who it was."

"Who could it have been?" Jocelyn said, I thought rather sharply, and then to me, "See what you can do. I need Womack." She bent to sweep a little spot on the floor and sat down. Womack was covered by the sort of light blanket that might have been from the airplane's supplies.

He said, his tone a slight wail, "My leg is broke." His speech was impaired by a lip swollen with infection.

"How do you know?"

"I know, I just know."

Jocelyn said, "He doesn't know. He's not a doctor, you're a doctor."

I would have to examine Womack. I have examined an infinite number of people old and young, fat and thin, with little other than appropriate objectivity, but I had a strange aversion to examining Womack. His darting and conspicuously dishonest eyes and the fleshy face that seemed at odds with his remarkably skinny body gave me the creeps. I uncovered him and found that he was quite naked under the blanket. Jocelyn burst into laughter and Womack looked over at her, lips pulled back over his crooked teeth in imploring misery. She covered her mouth in a mock attempt to conceal her mirth, then left to get some things from the plane, which turned out to consist of a very nice collection of medical supplies.

"Where did these come from?"

"The nice old doctor in White Sulphur."

I couldn't understand that at all, but treating Womack seemed to loom before me. I did quickly think I could see the problem—a swelling and discoloration over the upper tibia quite obviously emanating from within. Just the same, I diligently palpated my way up the dirty leg, well aware of the rising terror in Womack as I approached the injury. "I'm going to have to touch this," I told him, "but I will be very careful." The rest was entirely straightforward despite my inability to X-ray him. Womack had an avulsion fracture; a tendon had detached from part of the bone, though from the looks of things, I didn't believe surgical reattachment would be necessary. I didn't ask how the injury had occurred; I was confident that it had to do with Womack's criminal departure from Texas. If I had known how to read the engine hours in Jocelyn's airplane, I might have learned that she had gotten him out of there. I pulled the blanket back over Womack's disturbingly gaunt frame, wondering at my own aversion, and explained the injury to him. I was already reflecting upon Jocelyn's radiant frostiness in assuming that Womack's whereabouts were safe with me. Finding this offensive was an early symptom of the possible gradual return of my mental health.

This gave rise to a rather distant explanation of what Womack should do to return to good health. First, though, I cast the leg, using the supplies in the duffel bag brought by Jocelyn. She helped as we applied plaster to the gauze and wound it over the stockinet thoughtfully included, Womack whimpering the entire time. Of course his pain was real. At one point, and with an air of annoyance, Jocelyn presented him with a syringe and an impressive array of injectable painkillers, which seemed to feed his hungry eyes with an attractive future. I thought Dr.

Aldridge in White Sulphur had shown extraordinary trust in Jocelyn's correct use of these things. I myself wondered what he thought they were for. Maybe Jocelyn could bring a cooler when she brought food, which I thought would be necessary. She said she already had a lot of food in the plane on the assumption Womack would be staying for a spell. I was enacting my physician persona with remarkable alacrity as I prescribed the range-of-motion exercises needed to avoid joint stiffness and atrophy of the unaffected muscles. I even stretched out on the ground and demonstrated the isometrics that would aid his recovery. I was weirdly excited to be practicing medicine. "Contract the muscle without moving the joint, hold the tension, and release it, again without moving the joint. Let pain and not too much pain be your guide." I was able to apply myself to this demonstration on the dirt floor because I could foresee that Jocelyn would find ways to get me to treat Womack and I wasn't going to be through with this duty until he got well. I honestly didn't know if it was my enthusiasm for justice or my suspicion of Womack as a rival for Jocelyn's affections, as if that word actually applied to her. However, I rose above all that to concentrate my attention on Womack's physical well-being. I had a lot of responsibility in seeing that the fracture was not disturbed. If there were contradictions here, I couldn't see them.

I asked Jocelyn, "Will I be coming here on a regular basis?"

"It looks like you should."

But it never came up.

I asked Womack, "Does that suit you?"

"Gonna have to."

"I never really asked—did you do this in leaving Texas?"

"Uh-huh, pretty much of a train wreck."

I said, "You'll get through this, and I don't anticipate any complications. It's going to hurt for a while. I won't lie to you. Jocelyn has brought you something for it."

"Yeah, good. We had some street stuff in the plane, but I'd rather have the real deal." I didn't ask about that. Nor did I take issue, much as I might have wanted to, when Womack suggested that keeping my mouth shut was an excellent beauty hint.

As we returned to the plane, I saw that Jocelyn was worried, and I sought to reassure her. I hadn't seen her worried before, so I lavished attention on this new aspect of my darling. I could hardly wait to see the exhibition of skill it would require to get us airborne again. I had found that every small detail of her being that I could mix with her heedless carnality increased the cocktail's potency. I suppose I could have seen through the whole thing if I had wanted to. But I didn't want to. Got it?

We took a different route out of the canyon and it served my purposes very well. Instead of tracking the canyon from its source in the foothills, which must have helped orient Jocelyn to Womack's hiding place, we climbed as rapidly as Jocelyn could manage, a very steep diagonal along the canyon wall until we topped out in uplands that were familiar to me. We might have been overtaken by dark had we gone out the way we'd come. The departure required Jocelyn's concentration to the point that beads of perspiration stood out on her face almost as they did during our lovemaking. Pressed into my seat by the angle of ascent and fastened there by my harness, I gazed at Jocelyn and the clouds racing past the windshield, my state one of remarkably foolish transport because this was, as I sensed and she explained, all quite dangerous.

I knew exactly where we were. I could see the ridge of mountains to the southeast where we'd once hunted sheep, my dad and I; and to the north, grasslands managed by the latest husband of Cody's mother. To the west were the four old grain elevators. We were less than twenty miles from town over some of Dr. Olsson's favorite hunting places, and most specifically over the country I had followed when I appropriated his dog, Pie. As the yard lights came on in the dusk, I was able to count them back to the place where I had recovered her. All of these things conspired to suggest an atmosphere of divine guidance. The lights on our wingtips popped on in the growing dark.

Jocelyn said, "Womack's got enemies just like everybody else, but they didn't have to do that to his leg." Because the headset obscured her face and the microphone distorted her voice, I couldn't tell if she was joking. It was as if I had heard a radio broadcast from nowhere.

22

I HAD ALWAYS ENVIED THOSE who held a steady course in life—were raised conventionally, set their sights on a goal lasting a lifetime, found a partner to raise a second wave for when they and the partner had gone on to meet . . . God. Yes, God! For they had a well-carpentered cosmology that aligned them with time, for all time, including the big kahuna, Eternity. I remembered thinking when I lost Tessa that she was just as dead as King Tut. Death was remarkable in that it did not admit of degrees. What you saw was what you got. Hasta la vista.

I labored under the barrage of malarkey that was the messages I got from what is currently known as the family of origin—the chronically unhappy God of my mother, the sly cynicism of my father, which seemed common among his veteran friends, the goat-like bucking of my aunt, which made the world of procreation something of a barnyard. I sometimes wondered why we kept fixing up these bodies that came to us; I could only conclude that they wished to live and we wished to avoid suffering. But the natural world restored my hope by its capacity for renewal. Renewal alone should have been my religion.

When I hunted and came upon the old homesteads that had failed, I thought briefly of the people who had moved on, but more pointedly of the myriad things nature was doing to reclaim these scenes of disturbance—the grass, the hawthorns, the chokecherries, the sagebrush that took thriving homes and made them into tumuli. Not so bad. A litter of coyotes in the old parlor. Of course they sang.

I had learned much of this love of nature from Dr. Olsson and what I had believed to be the great sustenance he drew from the natural world. But because of the way Olsson wound up, I was somewhat on my own with the earth. Olsson had a dog or two after the great Pie died of old age, none quite as good as she. He was without a dog for a year—big mistake—when Lawyer Hanson left for China, his new life, and his new bride.

To my astonishment, this opened a long-sealed door between Shirley Hanson, my old squeeze, and Dr. Olsson, who had been in love with Shirley his entire life. He moved back to Ohio and married her. He spent the rest of his life as a henpecked homebody but surprised Shirley on his death by leaving part of his worldly goods to an animal shelter in honor of Pie, or "Eskimo Pie," as it appears on the plaque, and the remainder to a society for the protection of shorebirds, provoking Shirley to famously cry out, "I should have been a pelican!" Shirley moved to a rest home where, I have reason to assume, she survived. When I went to Olsson's funeral, my first visit to the town since my college days, there was the formidable Shirley, a little old lady who cut her eyes at me once before sitting through the ceremony as though neither I nor anyone else existed.

The apartments across the street from my house were more animated than ever, and the life within them was entirely nocturnal. I knew there were couples living there, as well as the sort of single people you would associate with night noise. I lay awake that night thinking about my mailman and the thread into my own past which he seemed to represent. But because I was awake later than was normal for me, I began to hear fragments of excited commentary from the open windows across the way, and they disoriented me entirely. "You call that a hat?" Someone, a man, was clearly disapproving of this article and he wished the hat to be replaced by another hat or no hat at all.

The next voice I heard, and it may have been an hour later, was a rich and expressive contralto. "I don't care how it smells!" I got the feeling she was starting an argument, but it didn't go anywhere. Then suddenly from the voice that had complained about the smell, "Hold the snow peas!" So I guessed the first outcry was about food. Anyway, I managed to drift off.

I confronted the idea that I might have time on my hands and was pulling together my fishing tackle, my prized fly rod, the fly box given to me by Dr. Olsson long ago and made, as he said, of "airplane metal" or aluminum. I had begun to speculate as to which creek might have which bugs—a rumination that got me to imagine the loop of line suspending the imitation insect slowly descending toward the speckled beauty feeding below. I was really getting in the mood when the phone rang and one Thad Pelletier, unknown to me, wished to bring in his eight-year-old boy, who had stepped on a broken bottle. Another Jinx referral, and with no warning I was startled, but agreed. I then ran around like a madman to make sure I had everything I needed—that is, I seemed propelled by joy. In a very short time, father and son were at my door, and I admitted them to the former parlor of this old house. I already loved this pair, but now meant to get to know them. I had hastily pushed a few items of furniture into the parlor, chairs for both Pelletiers. Thad Pelletier came in the front door cautiously leading his son, who even with a small towel duct-taped around his foot was managing to hobble. The father was quite young, in his twenties, I thought, a city maintenance man, and his son, Cory, seemed frightened, not of his injury but of me. I rubbed my hands together as though we were about to have a wonderful time and asked them to sit. The father, wearing heavy work boots that seemed to embarrass him as he drew them back under his chair, apologized for calling me at home, and I joked that that was the only place to get me these days. I turned to Cory, who was making himself as small as possible in his chair, a pink-cheeked boy whose sandy hair stuck out in every direction. I could see blood seeping through the towel. "Cory, what happened here?"

"I stepped on some glass."

"Did it hurt?"

"Yes, sir."

"Were you scared?"

"Yes, sir, when I saw the blood."

"Did it bleed a long time?"

"I was home," said Thad. "I don't think it was too long."

"Cory, may I look at it?" I asked and Cory nodded rapidly.

I lifted Cory's foot into my lap; it was trembling. He had a deep cut in the ball behind his big toe, the length of which I was slowly converting into millimeters as I calculated the anesthetic, which I decided would be topical. Cleaning the wound was quite straightforward, as there seemed to be no foreign material in it. Cory several times involuntarily pulled the foot away from me, which I continued to treat as a joke until he could see it was funny and laughed through helpless tears. Next I applied a mixture of tetracaine, adrenaline, and cocaine—TAC—great stuff for kids as it doesn't scare them quite like other anesthetic approaches, but we had to wait for it to work. With Thad I discussed the removal of trees compromised by pine bark beetles in the city park, and flag football with Cory, who was a wide receiver. Once I determined sufficient numbness had set in, I had Cory rest his foot on his father's thigh—I didn't have the appropriate table in my parlor—so that I could close up the wound. My emergency room days made me quite expert at this sort of thing and I gripped the suture needle with a needle driver—actually an ordinary hemostat I was using for this purpose in the face of short supplies—and began quickly stitching, making certain the needle penetrated below the base of the wound before rotating it out, reaching through to pull up the loops and tying the square knot. I was frankly a bit mesmerized at how reliably this skill was embedded in my muscle memory and I seemed to watch from afar as the elegant stitches marched to the end of the wound. When I looked up I could see that Thad was close to fainting, his face pale. I said to Cory, "Dude, we're done. Let's put something over this and you can head out." And before the smile had faded from his face, I had the tetanus booster in his arm and they were free to go. Thad wanted to pay me and my explanation that I was going fishing anyway seemed not to satisfy him. So I accepted twenty bucks and saw the two on their way. I then sat down, fingers laced behind my head, and gave in to thoughts of office furniture. Holding the twenty-dollar bill up to view, I smiled.

Less pleasantly, my thoughts turned to Womack and his broken leg—that is, to the leg first and then to Womack, who was undoubtedly suffering in his brush shelter. I supposed that Jocelyn had been in to visit him, bring him things, and that soon I would hear from her. But I hoped I would also hear from her in some context other than the health and well-being of Womack, who, despite his somewhat stark affect, I had some trouble picturing in other than the select occasions we had shared. I tried to imagine an ordinary Womack day and failed. If I had turned on reruns of the *Grand Ole Opry* and there was Womack in a spangled cowboy suit I wouldn't have been surprised. He had a little Porter Waggoner to his rubber-lipped but skinny I-see-right-through-you gaze. And cruel eyes that stood out, unflinching predator eyes. It was mostly what you saw. It abruptly occurred to me that he was certainly not an airplane mechanic. I was a little slow in reaching this conclusion, even though Lieutenant Crosby had let me glimpse the rap sheet. Someone more alert than I at that moment would have had a hard time connecting its details to his purported profession.

I had not seen Jocelyn in a while, though she was so often in my thoughts that encountering her corporeal self might have been beside the point. Her absence was acutely on my mind for the most irrational of reasons: it was daylight savings, time to adjust my clock. I went through my customary confusion over the spring-forward-fall-back business, something I could never quite understand—which gave rise to a reflection, based first on the non-sighting of Jocelyn, on the tyranny of time, feeling it as a sort of bully pushing me down a corridor where family members, acquaintances, and companions were regularly picked off into rooms along the way, never to be seen again. At the moment I could not think of a single instance in which time was my friend. My temporary inability to sort out the spring-forward-fall-back business seemed to emphasize that the rules were made elsewhere.

Furthermore, my infatuation, which had formerly produced a nice demarcation between Jocelyn and her circumstances, including the persistence of Womack, had begun to sag. Something so unexpectedly disturbing had come along that I seemed to have lost focus, if losing focus on an obsession is technically possible.

Jinx and I went on one of our nature walks, well, more than that because we had made a foray of several miles into the hills before we took our surroundings seriously: Jinx was on a mission. I didn't bring my field glasses and so we shared her nice old Leitz binoculars. It was one of the first genuine spring days; some of the earliest wildflowers, the ground-hugging phlox and violets that seemed to creep right in behind the receding snow, were already appearing in the sagebrush openings amid the bunchgrass and needle grass stands. We were high above the Yellowstone River, and in its broad valley the new warmth had raised a sun-shot fog. I had suppressed an impulse to ask Jinx where we were going simply because it was more interesting to tag along and guess.

By following a game trail in a small grove of junipers, we found ourselves on an elevated wooded point that looked out on a small valley between the ridges. I was increasingly cautioned to be quiet, to walk softly, to slow down—and finally to sit in a horseshoe of stacked stones, which I recognized as a hunting blind built by Indians. This gave us a protected view of the small valley and would have been an ideal place for its builders to launch an arrow at animals grazing toward them. We sat here for a long time; at first I thought I was supposed to stay silent, and after a while I was disinclined to talk at all. I wondered if this was meant to be some exercise in meditation, but whatever it was, I seemed quite happy to sit next to Jinx on a sunny spring day and to, in effect, enjoy her breathing. I even had a brief erotic impulse flit past like some bird, which caused me to smile. Jinx was quite resolute in scanning with her binoculars, and I found myself waiting for the steady sweep to come to a stop. When finally it did, she put a hand on my knee and handed me the glasses. She whispered, "Look right above the rock outcrop."

At first I could not find the outcrop at all and even once I did, it was another moment before I saw the wolf. I went through the same experience shared by everyone else who sees a wolf: surprise that a wolf doesn't look like anything else on earth.

She seemed to stare right at us from across the grass and sage, then elevated her nose in the beginning of a long and luxurious stretch, after which she looked carefully around the basin, then disappeared behind the rock, to emerge moments later carrying a pup by the scruff of its neck. She carried it a good distance and deposited it amid the sagebrush. Then she went back for another, squirming and dangling in her teeth, and placed it in a new place. After six were hidden here and there, she rested on the rock, lying on her belly with forelegs dangling. Jinx let me have the binoculars more than my share of the time: this was not her first visit to the wolves. We spent the entire morning in the old Indian blind watching as the wolf went from one hidden baby to another, nursing each. It was almost high noon before the wind came up behind us and the wolf knew of our presence. In an instant, she simply was no longer there. She seemed to evaporate.

On our way back to the trailhead where we had left Jinx's car, she no more than responded to my various questions. I found her indifferent even to my excitement at what we had seen. At her car, she mentioned that she was leaving town to practice elsewhere. She rather tossed that off, but I didn't take it well. She was the only real friend I had. She had hinted at it before, but now it seemed like a plan. Where would I go?

I made several trips to Jocelyn's old homeplace and found nothing. The airplane was gone and in fact the runway looked unused. Because word had gotten out that I was available for basic medical services—and was cheap!—I found myself with several patients a day who simply showed up. I had no one to manage appointments, and no inclination to turn anyone away if I could treat them without special equipment. Several who needed other kinds of help I hustled over to the clinic, recommending whichever of my old colleagues best fit the case. Therefore, it was nightfall before I could turn my thoughts first to Jocelyn and my seemingly abiding love of her, and then to Jinx, whose move threatened to leave me friendless. It was not easy to see why these two appeared in my imagination roughly at the same time. Jinx and I were not lovers; our compatibility had gotten in the way. How weird was that? The very sight of Jinx filled me with delight, and our forays in the outdoors were perfect little idylls. I thought she was pretty, even physically attractive, for crying out loud. But we were friends! We loved each other, in some way. And we found in the earth, the land of our beautiful West, what others had found in religion or some world elsewhere. The land and its wildlife were our miracles, and our gratitude did not extend to prying questions about how these came to be: they were enough. And we both liked patching people up! There was some connection between being useful and loving the place where we lived that made a nice circle for us. Why, then, were the forces driving me toward Jocelyn so irresistible?

As would be, I was seeing an old gent, Carl Tate, for his rheumatoid arthritis, which had been caught too late because of Carl's stoicism, with the result that cartilage damage and bone erosion could no longer be averted by some anti-rheumatoid strategies, though I was still following them to lesser effect while averting pain with the usual stuff—when Wilmot appeared, and said with some mystification, "Still seeing patients?" And I had Ellen Coopersmith waiting for me in the parlor. I was determined to finish what I was doing.

I asked him to wait. I finished with Carl shortly and he sort of bowed out with a wordless glance at Wilmot, stuffing a few bills in the blue glass flower vase Jinx had given me, into which I had failed to put flowers, letting it now serve as repository for my fees, such as they were. When Jinx saw what I was doing with it, she said, "Oh, boy," since she went on performing the ministrations of a bookkeeper despite the claims of her own busy practice.

I was not looking forward to seeing Wilmot, or to doubtless polished explanations for my situation, to which I had no doubt he had contributed generously. I was not sure why, but I sensed that he thought I wasn't playing the game as it should be played, that the puzzle pieces of the hierarchy were not well served if doctors went around being undignified. Perhaps he had learned of my brief service at the hot dog stand, or my indiscretions with nurses and others—all commonplace among bachelors in such a setting. My association with Tessa, during her happier days, was not viewed positively, and the latest event seemed to spread the stain. There was an awful time when Tessa was living in a homeless shelter and telling tall tales in which I sometimes figured unfavorably. She had long been displeased with me and even wrote letters to the editor about certain persons who had "grown too big for their britches," widely viewed as a reference to me.

I think Wilmot had expected me to stop what I was doing, but I had to see Ellen Coopersmith, age fifty-one, who believed she had pneumonia, though she did not. She had bought an old rock house near her job teaching school in the country, and on a very cold morning discovered there was no water in the kitchen sink, so she went to the downstairs bathroom for water to make coffee. The next day the water in the bathroom was gone too, and she had to go to the second floor for water to make coffee. The following day, also cold, there was no water on the second floor and teaching school without coffee had seemed an impossibility. But Ellen forbore this inconvenience, and the weather abruptly warmed up that night, as it does in this country, letting Ellen know why she'd had no water for her coffee: every pipe in the house had burst and in the thaw Ellen was now showered in falling ice water while each room in the house flooded. Still, she did not have pneumonia, she had a cold; and I showered her with samples and placebos while declining payment, though she stuffed something in the vase anyway. Then I turned to

Wilmot, who had elevated his chin a degree or two with every delay, and smiled coolly to Ellen Coopersmith as I saw her to the door.

"Not missing a beat?" asked Wilmot. I was jubilant just from having seen a couple of patients.

"Pecking along as best I can."

"But you look quite pleased."

"It's a living," I said.

"Well, good then. I say, in fact, 'Marvellous.' "

I was sorry I had to hear that. "So, Raymond, what's up?"

"A courtesy call, really, just a courtesy call. We are working on the status of your situation, which is many-layered."

"Like a cake?"

"Well, sure. Could be. I did want you to understand that it wasn't only the staff and board that are the voices being heard. There is always an unseen presence in the room whenever we go through a bad patch like this, and that presence is the community."

"I'm anxious to know about that," I said sincerely, even though I knew that "the community" was a bogus concept generally invoked in the service of self-righteousness.

"Oh, rest assured, they'll be heard. Would you like to be kept in the loop?"

"Not really."

"Oh?"

"Just tell me how it turns out."

Wilmot was already backing to the door, having assumed a look of bafflement. "I will. I promise." I thought about Wilmot's style of communication: speaking to you in supposedly transparent earnestness while his face grimaced faintly as though from acid reflux. It was a form of snobbery that looked like it could be cured with Pepto-Bismol.

"Adrienne sends her best regards. She was always very fond of you."

"It's good you're still in touch."

"Adrienne really landed on her feet. I still feel challenged. She married a guy retired from some boutique bank in New York. He needed something besides issuing letters of credit to occupy his time. So he bought a sawmill and a forest. He's almost ninety, no prenup. I'd love to have her back. Always wanted a forest."

He was backing out the door as he glanced around the room, looking for medical equipment, I suppose. I meant to get a catalog, but as there were still a few home doctors I thought I could just as well wait for one to die. I realized I was drifting toward this obsolete category, but it seemed to fit. Maybe I had resigned myself to being a square peg in a round hole and welcomed a setting where I could spend less time on explanations.

Perhaps I had gotten ahead of myself, though, because no one called for my services the rest of that day, and by the end of it the little respite I'd enjoyed from obsessing over Jocelyn was gone and I was frantic. I was so uncomfortable that I had to act. I fired up the 88, relieved not just to be doing something about my torment but to find that the car was willing to start, as was not always the case when it had been parked for more than a day. When the Oldsmobile had not been used, the steady press of sunlight on its plastic upholstery produced the smell of obsolescence reminiscent of my pleasant rides with Throckmorton in his giant Audi with its radar and satellite uplinks, the silent highway rushing under its hood. Perhaps in imagining a time when I might stop pushing this old boat down the road, I foresaw days of great change. Nice!

I left town on Highway 12 and soon passed Two Dot, where I once had a patient, a superstitious old lady who described suicides in the distant past and several local ghosts, including a girl on Alkali Creek guzzling blood from a bottle, a cowboy ghost with a hole in his chest, and a woman on fire holding a jug of gasoline. After Mrs. Tierney told me of these things, she always looked me dead in the eye and said, "I'm of sound mind." And I'd say something like, "Of course you are, but if you don't measure your glucose regularly and write it down I'm not going to be able to help you." These phantoms seemed to haunt the benign but lonely landscape as I drove.

Perhaps I was starting to calm down, because as I passed the Hutterite colony at Martinsdale I thought fondly of the beautiful vegetables they brought to our farm markets. When I reached Checkerboard, I spotted the bar among a number of trailers. The sign just said BAR. If it had said EXCELSIOR TAVERN or something I wouldn't have stopped. I was alone with the bartender under a low ceiling covered with dollar bills.

Not much light in there. A jukebox. I drank a shell of draft without a word from the bartender and left. The phone booth outside with its bifold door ajar and phone hanging at the end of its metallic cord seemed to taunt my increasingly forlorn state of mind. I hurried on to White Sulphur Springs, reviewing how I had enhanced the concept of "bar" into some kind of cow-town Brigadoon with fiddle music, two-steppers, and irrepressible ranch hands throwing their hats in the air.

At the medical facility in White Sulphur Springs, I identified myself at the desk and went straight to the office of the physician who had treated Jocelyn, Dr. Aldridge. He did not seem pleased to see me, but I launched a wave of cordiality his way. "I understand that you and Miss Boyce have gotten very close." He just stared at me.

He said, "Yes, we have. I don't think that needs to get out, do you?"

"Not because of me, Doctor!" I said.

"How did you find out?"

"I guess she had to share it with someone. Feelings are running pretty strong. She realizes it's not a simple situation."

Holding his head in his hands, Dr. Aldridge stared down at the papers on his desk. "I just don't know what to do."

"It's not often that true love opens its arms to us, Doctor. What do you have to lose? Jocelyn is a beautiful young woman and she has such marvelous skills." This last brought Aldridge's head up; perhaps he smelled a rat. What skills? I let him marinate this bit of psychic mildew for just a moment before I eased the silly bastard down. "It's as if she and the airplane were one."

Relief spread across Aldridge's face: I knew a fellow nincompoop when I saw one.

"But how I wish she wouldn't fly! Remember, it was I who first treated her after that accident."

"I do remember. And I have to confess, I was jealous of the gaze that greeted you whenever you entered her room. Well, there's medicine and there's life. We know that, don't we, Doctor? Isn't that the burden we share on behalf of humanity?" I surprised myself at the level of poison and spite infusing my remarks. And shame. I suppose I got a bit of relief watching another sucker head out on the sleigh ride, but it was cold comfort against the nausea and cross-purposes and lovelorn anger that were making me squirm. To add to my shame, I was well aware of the dramatization involved as I pictured myself crawling up into a culvert like a wounded coyote.

I didn't really know what Jocelyn and Womack had in mind, for themselves or the airplane, but I was beginning to think that Jocelyn had foreseen the heat that seemed to follow Womack. It might be that she thought she could do better on her own.

Still, I sat in my old 88 chewing the top of the steering wheel, which I grasped in both hands, squirting salty tears. Fearing that in this sunny parking lot I might soon be making noises the average pedestrian would have trouble understanding, I turned on the radio, one of Paul Harvey's last broadcasts, and was pleased to drift off into his cheerful anecdotes of a more wholesome world.

But I had not lost focus. I drove back the way I had come and turned off once more toward Jocelyn's old ranch. A lot of effort had gone into making it something of an airfield, and I was sure it would be used again. As soon as I crossed the cattle guard, I saw a vehicle and felt a helpless surge of excitement, "helpless" because I was determined not to give in to any sort of happiness at seeing Jocelyn until I found out what her game was. I was sure she had an excellent explanation for the various anomalies I was uncovering, but I wanted to hear it from her. I don't think I doubted that we would soon enjoy our accustomed affection again.

It was not Jocelyn. Two very old men in short-brimmed Stetsons stood by a battered green sedan with Jordan plates, watching me come up the road. I stopped and introduced myself. The stocky man with bushy white eyebrows was Harley Collingwood, a retired roundup cook. Next to him, somehow bravely erect despite touching frailty and leaning on a diamond willow cane, was Con Boyce, Jocelyn's father. I was nearly certain she'd said he was dead, so I questioned him. He was in a state of acute dismay because someone had burned down his house. Collingwood barked, "Maybe you just forgot, Con. Maybe you can't remember."

"Where are you living, Mr. Boyce?"

"She put me in a home."

"He didn't want to go," explained Collingwood. "She just got herself appointed and that was that."

Boyce looked around and said, almost to himself, "I liked it here. I wanted to wind up here. She didn't give me a choice."

"He thinks there was a house here," said Collingwood.

"I know damn well my house was here," said Boyce with surprising authority. The three of us walked over to the house site. It was easy to see where the backhoe and bulldozer had covered the location. Boyce pointed at the disturbed ground and looked significantly at Collingwood, then at me. "You a friend of hers?"

"Yes. Yes, I am."

"You see Jocelyn, tell her I found out about this."

"Sure will."

"Next time you pick your friends be more careful."

By the way Boyce returned to the old green car, I could see he was the leader of this expedition. Collingwood glanced back at me with a shrug, twirling a forefinger alongside his temple. At the car door, Con Boyce was abruptly less sure of himself. He said he had a rug made when his old horse Rags died. As he looked toward the disturbed ground, he said it was in the house.

23

I GOT UP EARLY after a broken sleep. The people across the street were arguing again, and the husband's by-now-familiar voice carried all the way to my bedroom: "I can't eat any more of these fuckin' macaroons!" I went downstairs and made myself a bowl of cereal and a cup of coffee, taking both out to my porch, where I sat on the glider and watched the street. An old farrier, Charlie Noon, bent from half a century underneath horses, set out each morning, driving past my porch in his old Dodge truck, forge lashed in the bed, tools and kegs of iron shoes rattling like a circus wagon, heading to his customers with the inevitability of the seasons. There must have been something amiss with his defroster, because he always went by wiping the inside of the windshield with a huge rag, which he waved in my direction if I happened to be on the porch. I had the whole house to myself now, and this allowed me to sit out there in front of the living room window in a state of contentment. That living room now stored books, a canoe, a bicycle, and a female manikin wearing a rubber Ronald Reagan mask and hip boots—some forgotten gag. Charlie was often accompanied by Teresa Borski, a retired stewardess from the coffee-tea-or-me era, who held the horses while Charlie shod them. Teresa had a handsome Missouri Foxtrotter, a tall chestnut with the noble head of a Civil War officer's horse, which Charlie kept well shod with special shoes to emphasize his elegant gaits. I'd seen Teresa ride him right through town, single-footing in a straight line across town and out the other side.

Parnell Swift is the gloomiest man in town and such an obsessive walker that he brings his gloom to every neighborhood. He's completely bald, and his frowning visage results in a series of pleats that stop only at the crown of his head. He wears a Pendleton shirt at all times and packers' boots with undershot heels. Parnell was once a fastidious, in fact hard-nosed, livestock inspector who impounded the horse of a young soldier who, killed in Vietnam, never returned to claim it. Community outrage and the intimate politics of Montana assured that Parnell's days of public service were over. He collected coins at two car washes for their owners and I don't know what else.

Since I had no patients until the afternoon—and with Jinx fooling around with my appointments I didn't know who or what they would be—I was carrying a plastic sack of plant food out to the cemetery. I could have driven, but the sun was out, the wind had died, and so many people were walking around, I didn't want to miss anything. On days like this, I always daydreamed about running for mayor so that I could look after my constituents like an adoring father. Love was in the air. Prolonged bad weather aroused distaste for one's fellows, but life had taught me that the quality of light could enlarge the heart. Wasn't that the Gospel of Thomas? That we came from the light? The cosmology of the Plains Indians? All the same.

Roy Sherwood, dressed like an old western movie star, sauntered along and said, "What a day!" He owned a curio shop and was the son of a world champion bronc rider and one of the founders of the Turtles, the first professional rodeo association. Roy was a gay man in a town where they were still called "fairies." I could never associate big, hearty Roy Sherwood with the word "fairy" but there it was: old geezers at the coffee shop, "Here comes that fairy Roy Sherwood." I just couldn't get a handle on it, but Roy embraced it and turned up at New Year's Eve parties with sparkling wings and a silver wand, a star at its end. I will say, people appreciated his sense of humor. Roy got censured by the state's Better Business Bureau for making his own "artifacts" and ended up dropping the price on his arrowheads to the point that they were no longer worth the trouble.

Taking in the ordinariness of my town was a kind of anesthetic for the pain I held in abeyance. I took a moment to watch Jay Houston carry a case of Riesling down into his father's old bomb shelter, and I remembered making out there with Debbie in tenth grade when Jay's dad had rented the house out to the priest at St. Michael's. Debbie's house was next door and we would slip through the hedge and climb down into the shelter for endless kissing. Since kissing was all it ever amounted to, moving our heads around was the only way we could express our rising passion, and we always ended up with sore necks.

It seemed the perfect reminiscence to offset my anguish over Jocelyn and my fatuous identification with her father as though we were brothers in abuse. I thought about changing places with him, letting him walk around my hometown trailing my regrets while I retreated to the rest home and a full platter of resignation. The whole thing was becoming such a long story it baffled me that I hoped to tell it all to Jinx. I really didn't know anyone else who might understand it. Nor did it seem the best expression of friendship. I did think that if I cared about Jinx I'd want her to hear everything; otherwise, what use would I be to her? My story was nearly all I had.

It began badly. I walked the few blocks to Jinx's house, knowing that she would be making herself lunch there between appointments. It was a short drive from the clinic, and I was waiting inside as I heard her pull up, the distinctive motor sound of her old Jaguar. She usually rode her bike. She didn't seem surprised to see me and asked if I would like half of her egg salad sandwich. I declined. I had her kettle boiling and made myself a cup of tea, which I placed before me on her dining room table. The dismay and humiliation of my relations with Jocelyn burned inside me, and I anticipated thoughtful words and relief from my pain once Jinx grasped my situation. Jinx seemed to recognize that something was up, because as she sat down with her sandwich and glass of juice, she neither said anything nor took her eyes off me. I thought I'd go ahead and get started but was surprised by my vehemence once I did.

As I bawled out my forlorn and embittered hopelessness, Jinx listened attentively—I'm really embarrassed by this; I honestly don't know what inspired me to put it down—and it might have been this quiet attention that encouraged me to lavish my story with details. I told her about Jocelyn's airplane accident and recovery at the clinic in White Sulphur Springs, and the growth of my infatuation. I described how I missed all the signs of Jocelyn's exploitative nature and how my adoration kept me from ordinary self-protection. With lugubrious thoroughness, I depicted the heartache and love blindness that led me to overlook such quirks as her burning down her own home and lying about the death of her father. Worse, the recitation had the effect of reawakening Jocelyn's malign romantic appeal. I may have even smiled as I recounted the passionate adventures with decorative hints as to the erotic attraction. Nevertheless, nothing in the world could have prepared me for Jinx's response. She told me to go fuck myself. The cat was out of the bag.

"Jinx, what could you possibly mean?"

"I mean, why on earth would you think I'd want to hear about you and your castrating harpie?"

"Have you even met her?" On recollection, this question would appear to be at the heart of my inanity.

"Good God, why would I want to do that? So I could kneecap her?"

"Oh, Jinx."

"She must have seemed so cuddly in her little airplane."

"Jinx, please stop."

"And this Womack, he sounds like a real treat. You've got a little Womack in you, too, don't you, Cuddles. Can all three of you get into the tiny airplane? But let little Jocelyn do the driving or you might crash!" At this, she burst into tears. I attempted to sit quietly holding my teacup, but Jinx's sobbing didn't seem to be abating. I got up from my chair and went around to her side of the table. For some reason, my eyes fell on the untouched egg salad sandwich. I put my arms around Jinx's shoulders and asked her what the problem was. Her answer startled me. She said, "I don't know why you don't love me." In the face of these words, my towering self-absorption stood in a kind of glare, but I didn't hate myself. I was just tired of myself. I seemed to be an unbearable weight. I seemed quite useless. Somehow, I continued to fan a glimmer of self-worth, possibly in vain.

I thought if I could re-imagine all the forces that had acted upon me in my life—my parents, my nympho aunt, Dr. Olsson and my professors, the lawyers, colleagues, neighbors, Jocelyn, even my patients, my most unreasonable dreams, my love of the earth, roadside hard-ons, experimental churchgoing, and work—I would finally find myself by implication. I had left Jinx off this list because to comprehend her I would have to step out of the shadows of all those things telling me who and what I was and try to emerge as an actual human being. This seemed not unlike twisting in the wind, and it came with a kind of dread. Jinx set out in my direction quite alone; why couldn't I have had her courage?

She abruptly pulled herself together, wiped her eyes with a napkin, got to her feet, and walked out the door. I went to the window, where I saw her mount her bicycle and ride up Custer Street; she may not have been entirely composed because the two pedestrians she passed stopped and turned to watch her. I hurried out onto the sidewalk to better see her progress, which was steadily to the north and, I supposed, out of town. I ran home and got my lucky 88, but at first I couldn't find the keys, neither under the seat nor in the ashtray. I went wild. The macaroon-averse neighbor waved from his window and I gave him the finger. I found the keys, after a ripping search, under the porch glider and ran to my car, where I saw the neighbor advancing from his stoop in battle mode; but I was already behind the wheel and on my way to Custer Street and northward progress out of town.

I went out through an informal trailer park, past the packing plant, across the river and into undulant sagebrush hills. I pressed on because she would have had to come back the same way she left, and after a long rise that seemed to end at blue sky and cumulus clouds, I saw her, a speck in the distance. I flattened the accelerator, and the 88 responded with its signature twisting lurch. In less than a mile I overtook her, but by a glance over her shoulder I could tell she did not intend to stop. I blew the horn and immediately understood that the honking seemed to express everything that was the matter with me.

I passed Jinx very slowly, but she never looked in my direction and it was clear a roadblock was my only hope. I pulled ahead twenty yards, swung the 88 across her path, and got out. She rolled to a stop before me and climbed off her bicycle, holding it upright by one handlebar. She asked me if this was necessary. She swept her hair off her face with one hand, letting go of the bicycle with the other. It clattered to the ground. I went to her and put my arms around her. I meant to comfort her, but something else was going on.

Business, if that's what you want to call it, was picking up. I would have to get some help. I probably needed a nurse, but I didn't want to move out of my house and I wasn't sure where I could put her. The battling couple across the way continued to disturb my sleep. I must have been able to stand it because I didn't think of moving and I was getting more of my former patients, the ones who felt that I had over the years acquired some valuable familiarity with their problems. Patients for whom depression was a component of their condition were loyal to me out of embarrassed reluctance to add to their anxieties by explaining them to someone new. The twins Olan and Darwin Ickes, farmers in their seventies with the biggest hands I had ever seen, fit this description: they had been raised to put their lives into "the place" and had only gradually realized that their grueling existence had resulted in a grudge against both life and "the place." In short, they were depressed. I knew they wouldn't see a counselor, so the counselor, a very effective practitioner named Joyce Erikson, and I visited the twins from time to time on "the place" and I think she might have helped them some. Olan and Darwin continued to see me.

A rancher from over near Shawmut, Kurt Merrill, was willing to talk to Joyce and try some medication as well. He was in bad shape. His only son, Terry, had committed suicide over a girl who was not his wife, and since they had always been close, Kurt could not believe that Terry had not communicated with him. Kurt had trained his grief into an obsession with cell phone records and was certain the phone company had lost a final message from Terry. I was very worried about Kurt and so was hugely relieved when he consented to be put into better hands.

I really didn't know why anyone would want my advice on such things unless they were so needy as to want the inside scoop from a fellow nut. I wasn't being modest: people in some circumstances will only trust a misfit, and that is where my long life in this town had its uses. My shabby past and the reputation of my family for shiftlessness were assets of which I could finally be proud. My former nurse Scarlett summed it up when she said, "If an idiot like you can be a doctor, anybody can be a doctor." Even an insult had its uses. Scarlett had left nursing to write a novel and despite her contempt for me, she once asked me to read it. I vividly remember a line introducing the heroine: "Using her ball gown to prop up the toilet seat, Annette turned her thoughts to the evening." Scarlett never had much in her pretty head. It was only a matter of time before she ran for office.

Well, Jocelyn turned up. By that time, I had some office furniture and she walked in as I was examining the loudmouth from across the street for strep throat. I had just told him that by irritating his throat in shouting matches with his wife he had made it susceptible to bacteria and viruses; there was some truth to this, but the fact was that I had subjective interest in the diagnosis in my hope to get the couple to quiet down. This was the first time I had seen Chaz close up, and I was somewhat surprised to find him such a meager individual—bespectacled, male pattern baldness, a tiny paunch, girlish little hands. His shyness was in contrast to a baritone which he had some difficulty keeping at a low volume. I could see right away that Chaz lived through his voice, that it had a life of its own, even delivering all sorts of messages that might not have been entirely authorized by Chaz. As he sat on my examining table, I had great difficulty imagining this meek fellow bellowing about "the fucking macaroons" or diabolical snow peas. Quite formally, I instructed Jocelyn to have a seat in the waiting room, once the downstairs bedroom where we had fornicated. She looked at me in disbelief, gave a little laugh, and did as I suggested. Then, just to be safe, I cultured Chaz's throat while he intoned around the swab, "Great tits." Chaz had a screw loose, but I treated him as I would have any other patient, glad to have the work. Eventually his wife became an occasional patient; she must have been thirty years older than Chaz and twice his size. She bore an authoritarian air, even with me, and having already scoured various medical manuals for some self-diagnosis, she was ready for argument.

To be safe, I locked the front door the minute Chaz was on his way and went into the parlor to see Jocelyn, who was just then running all ten fingers through her thick, streaky hair to retie it with an elastic. Unwillingly, I took note of the beauty of her hands and her shapely forearms. An image of Jinx wobbling up the county road on her bicycle caused a sharp pain in my forehead. Jocelyn hiked up on the library table, sat with hands clasped before her and said, "What's up, Doc?"

"You tell me."

"Thought I'd stop by and say thanks. I'm fixing to head on down the line."

"Sounds like a song."

"It is to me. Before I breeze out of your life I wanted to clear up a few things that might have bothered you. Womack and I did some stuff with the airplane some people might say we shouldn't have. I don't know who those people might be, since the country is run by criminals: read the paper. I just wanted to fly, but when you're between jobs flying gets expensive. We both got pretty involved with the product at that time and so judgment-wise, things could have been better. I'm afraid I let him take me down some roads that were probably a mistake." She spilled this all out in a somewhat prepared manner; I shouldn't have absorbed it quite so easily.

"Like Mexico?"

"Sure, some roads in Mexico. For what Womack had in mind, Mexico is always where it's at." She was just tossing these replies at me. "Airplanes make all these little old countries run together. From the air, you just can't tell one from another."

"What was the point of coming here?" I liked to think this question suggested my suspicions, but I was flattering myself.

"Well, I had the homeplace and Womack was pretty fascinated with Canada. Canada is one big pharmacy and I guess he saw some opportunity there."

"There were so many warning signs," I said. "I wonder what made me fall for you like I did." The nincompoop within thought that casting doubt on her story would bring her to heel. She laughed heartily, and I felt myself going down that slope all over again.

"You really need to look into that," she said. "You've got a long way to go!" In retrospect, this was her one burst of candor. Even as I felt myself illuminated I was aware of her crazy allure—I think it had to do with a certain feral, almost sovereign amorality disguised as freedom. Jocelyn was also a brilliant liar. I ought to record the best one, whose inner mechanism was not unlocked for a few years. The preliminary deception—after me!—of Dr. Aldridge in White Sulphur Springs, which fell short of his actually leaving his wife, began and ended with his providing a morphine drip pump and enough ingredients to keep Womack comfortable for quite a while. She didn't tell me this, Dr. Adridge did after I paid one more awkward visit to his clinic. Jocelyn told me that Womack had held so many incriminating things over her head that she was obliged to go along with him if she wanted to keep flying. After I caused him to be arrested, she was threatened with exposure all over again. To keep him from talking she had no choice but to help him escape, or jump bail anyway. I pressed her about the broken leg, which I thought was the result of his escape, but it was only the work of someone to whom Womack owed money. I got a neurotic pleasure going through all this because in my deplorably gaga way I was still buying it. Therefore, she went on feeding me the following: her conscience unexpectedly struck and as much as she loved her freedom, it was time to accept the consequences of her life and actions. She flew Womack back to Texas, persuading him that there he would be safer and it would be easier to get him the medical care he needed; she couldn't fly me back and forth into the hills because in the end suspicion would fall on all of us. When she got to Texas, she turned Womack in, and either he didn't know it was she who had fingered him or he too finally accepted his fate, because he never betrayed her. She visited him in jail, she said, and he was remarkably transformed, as though having found a kind of peace he'd never had. The jailer had gotten him a guitar and he was writing songs, even some Christian ones.

All bullshit. I imagined looking back on myself sitting there with a dorky smile on my face, buying the whole thing. Maybe I was being too hard on myself, because when she suggested we make love as a sort of farewell, I declined. She wore a blue tube top which she pulled down to show me her stripper's breasts. I concealed the abrupt knot in my stomach and said, "Lovely, thanks, maybe another time." This occasioned, for the last time, a superb laugh and she told me I was finally getting somewhere. All I did was ask her what she was going to do next. She said, "I think I'll try California. Everyone else has." She did seem too confident that her old friend Womack would keep his mouth shut. I should have pursued that. It pleased me to think I smelled a rat and saw through her, but probably I didn't. That's why we got to tell our stories later.

That season long ago in medical school when I drank and ate so much was instructive in many ways. Watching my body take off on its own was probably the most remarkable experience of those years. The way it commandeered my hands and mouth to get its way was very much like being on a runaway horse. I remembered following the fortunes of Haystack Calhoun, greatly disturbed by his death from diabetes as though even a farm boy who could carry his cows around the pasture or toss hay bales into a high loft could be brought down by the indifference of his own body. Other phenomena had accompanied my new morphology: I several times proposed matrimony to astonished women as though, as a husband, I would be slender. I kept an article about an eight-hundred-pound woman who had to be removed from her Florida apartment: the medical technicians charged with this task reported that they had sought special advice from SeaWorld.

I eventually emerged from this spell of your-body-is-not-your-friend and returned to my schoolwork with new sobriety. A summer job in teeming New York had something to do with the change, as the stark individuality of humans that I had known growing up was swept under the infinite crowd of the great city, and humanity came to seem a substance like air or water. I had to claw my way back to my original vision in which each person was surrounded by space. I knew somewhat abstractly that even New Yorkers had to have space around them; I just didn't believe it.

I tried explaining all this to Jinx on one of our hikes in the rolling hills north of the Musselshell River where we had found a line of cairns marking an old Indian trail that led us through some wonderfully expansive vistas. I don't know how Jinx found all these things—buffalo jumps and old wolfers' campsites—but she did, and I expanded my sense of the earth thanks to her vigilant eye. She found a ruby-crowned kinglet's nest in the bushes next to my front door—something I had failed to notice—and reproached me by noting that they had nested here for years.

Jinx said, "You got all this from your mother."

"What d'you mean, 'I got all this from my mother'?"

"The separation of body and spirit. As though we can be attacked by our bodies while the spirit saddles up for the next world. We are our bodies. That's it."

"Are you trying to tell me that the human spirit, which we have believed in for tens of thousands of years, doesn't exist?"

"It's a coping tool in response to grief."

"Jinx, you hold a square foot of air between your hands, and in that piece of air are radio waves, GPS and television signals, microwaves, light waves, sound waves. And the human spirit can't exist because you can't see it?"

"You guessed 'er, Chester."

"I and my millions of forebears, many of whom predate formal religion of any kind, just don't believe that."

"Momma's boy."

If a difference of opinion could be called pleasant, this was it. We walked for miles, and in a way I thought my point was made by simply following this old human trail toward the distant hills beyond which were more distant hills. We rested under the cottonwoods, and I nearly fell asleep as Jinx read to me from one of the battered paperbacks she carried in her day pack. " 'Take a look at the neutrality of this globe that carries us through space like a lifeboat heading for shore.'—Are you listening, Toots?"

"Yes," I said, "of course."

" 'Today a virtuous couple sleeps on the same ground that once held a sinning couple.' " Long pause. She stared at me. " 'Tomorrow a churchman may sleep there, then a murderer, then a blacksmith, then a poet.' And here, my dear, is what I want you to listen to carefully: 'They will all bless that corner of the earth that gave them a few illusions.' "

My life seemed to sweep in a better direction. I didn't quite know why at first, because I had enough work that there was little time to spin myself into a hole of self-deception. And Jinx was on a mission to replace all those invisible things in the square foot of air between my hands that I insisted contained the human spirit with the earth itself; she led me on day trips up creeks, over the hills, and across the prairie. I don't really know if it was in this same spirit that she took my Oldsmobile 88 to the wrecking yard and had it reduced to scrap metal. If so, I'm still absorbing it. One trip to the Teton River to watch fledgling prairie falcons required us to take sleeping bags, and I suppose it must be clear what happened and what sort of flood ensued after this particular dam was breached. I'm surprised Jinx didn't have octuplets.

I don't believe that I am particular prey to superstition, but Jinx left me a note the other day about some plan she proposed to hike into a little ghost town that existed on a ranch whose owners' grandchildren were her patients. A grave there belonged to an old mountain man. There was a hanging tree, an old saloon, and a few crumbled houses. Well, of course, this was an interesting idea, but what startled me was that Jinx's handwriting resembled my mother's to such a remarkable degree. My residual superstition kicked in and I more or less panicked. Numerology, black cats, hats on the bed, walking under ladders don't mean anything to me, but I was alarmed by coincidences.

I ransacked my desk at home until I found one of my mother's crackpot letters from my college years warning me to not lay up treasures but to prepare for the Judgment Day. Then, I still entertained the idea that my medical degree would be the Midas touch, and I recalled the guffaws this letter had occasioned. It would be a long time before I unwound the fact that when my mother died I lost all interest in both God and money; they must have been connected in my mind. I just didn't know how.

I found a graphologist who invited me to fax my mother's letter and Jinx's note for analysis. I pretended to be curious to know whether the handwriting was by the same person. I got a rather snotty reply and a fifty-dollar charge on my credit card. My mother's writing was described as flamboyant and not the work of someone given to details, while Jinx's was that of a person with "broad perspectives" and "firm judgment." My mother's handwriting was that of someone who would "have great difficulty meeting schedules" despite trying to micromanage anyone in her vicinity. The graphologist could hardly have known that with God on their side, micromanagers could really make it happen. I was pleased though by the graphologist's last question, as to whether or not I was trying to fool him by suggesting that these were the same person.

I don't know how much longer Jocelyn's outlaw aura hung over my mind; I suppose it never went away entirely, but its last real flare-up came in the year Jinx and I had moved out to our house on the river, a sunny spot hung with bird feeders and tucked into a grove of aspens with a view to the south and three big bends of the river. The bench below the house was enclosed by a jackleg fence and there our saddle horses grazed. Jinx was reading the Sunday paper while I watched a thunderstorm forming over the Absaroka Range. Perhaps after forty years in medicine I was trying to decide whether I wanted to be a doctor. I was close to retirement, and I hoped to work it out before then: such was my accustomed style. In a startled voice, Jinx read from the paper: hunters had found in some sort of collapsed brush pile the remains of a man with his leg in a cast. Since no one had come forward with a missing-person report that fit the situation, authorities suggested it would remain a mystery. Like everything else.

A NOTE ABOUT THE AUTHOR

Thomas McGuane lives in Sweet Grass County, Montana. He is the author of nine novels, three works of nonfiction, and two collections of stories.

A NOTE ON THE TYPE

This book was set in Bulmer, a typeface based on William Martin's popular English letterforms that were designed for William Bulmer of the Shakespeare Press around 1790.

Composed by Creative Graphics,
Allentown, Pennsylvania
Printed and bound by Berryville Graphics,
Berryville, Virginia
Designed by Wesley Gott